BILLIONAIRE BOOGEYMEN

A NOVEL BY
TODD PARKER

SANDCASTLE PRESS

For Dana, Ivy & Toby,
You are the air I breathe.

1

NIGHT IN BOSTON

THE SHOWS WERE LONG OVER, and Boston's theater district was still. The only signs of life came from Dominic's Lounge, the late-night base camp for everyone who worked in the theaters, nightclubs, and restaurants nearby. Ties were taken off, hair was let down, and all the other polite pretenses put on for customers and bosses were cast aside as they drank away the shift's annoyances. The bartender knew almost every patron by name or face and served beer and cocktails long after the legal cutoff time.

"More coffee, hon?" he asked Cheryl, the prostitute sitting at the end of the bar.

"No, thanks." She fidgeted with her seashell bracelet. Her fingers turned the cream-colored shells around its string as she watched people enjoy themselves. She focused on a young couple slow dancing by the jukebox. They laughed together as they swayed to the music, their bliss on full display.

Why not? she thought. *They don't have to go back out there and suck off creeps.*

Her mouth filled with the phantom taste of latex. She was surprised. It had been years since she'd felt this kind of revulsion.

Being clean for a month brought back all kinds of emotions, even hope. *Maybe I can get out.*

The thought was terrifying. The last time she had it, she was young and beautiful. A lifetime ago. She was still attractive from a distance or in the glow of the neon beer signs, but up close, the hard lines of her face showed all too well.

Cheryl realized she needed to get back on the street. She didn't want to risk the chance of Trey cruising by and catching her inside. He'd been in a shitty mood all day. Another coffee wasn't worth him getting in her face and squeezing her arms black and blue.

An hour later, she walked down Stuart Street. The night was silent. Few windows remained lit in the buildings she passed, and the only sound was the low buzz of the electrical wires above.

Whenever headlights interrupted the quiet night, she turned to look at the drivers, hoping they would pull over but partly relieved when they passed.

She stopped walking, leaned against a low brick wall, and felt its cold surface through the thin fabric of her skirt. A light mist in the air felt good on her face. She leaned her head back and closed her eyes, breathing in deeply as her fingers again played with her seashell bracelet. She'd had the bracelet for years, a gift from her friend Heather, another working girl.

Whatever happened to Heather? She tried to remember the last time she saw her, but a pair of headlights broke her from her thoughts.

A black SUV pulled up just ahead of her, and she approached the passenger window.

"How much for a blow job?" the large man behind the wheel asked.

"Fifty." She answered without a smile.

"Sold."

She got in the car, but as soon as the door shut, she saw something in his eyes wasn't right. "You're a cop, aren't—?"

Before she could finish, a syringe stung her neck.

"No!" she yelled and fumbled for the door handle. It felt rubbery in her hand. Her arm suddenly weighed a thousand pounds, and the windshield started to spin.

Wait... Wait...
Her head rolled back, and she was out.
The SUV drove into the night.

Cheryl opened her eyes. It felt like a wet towel was wrapped around her brain. As her vision slowly cleared, hazy greens and browns turned into bushes and shrubs. Above her was a ceiling with multiple rows of track lighting.

Where am I?

Nearby were large rocks that formed an entrance to a cave. Even with her eyes still blurry, she could tell they were fake.

She looked to her left and saw something bizarre. There was a glass wall separating her from what appeared to be a dozen or so people. They wore tuxedos and gowns, held glasses of wine, and watched her through the glass with interest.

Cheryl got dizzy when she stood and realized she was in her underwear. She took a few awkward steps toward the glass wall.

"Hey," she said, "I need help. Please. I was abducted."

No one answered.

She placed her hands on the glass and looked at the faces watching her. Most of them were gray-haired, older men. The women were all much younger, and each one was more beautiful than the last.

"How do I get out of here?"

The group stared as if she were part of a show and ignored her pleadings. Heavy fear crept in and took root.

Why aren't you helping me?

Cheryl cried and leaned her forehead against the cool glass. She saw part of the floor was covered with what looked like dried blood, and a chill ran down her spine. She hurried toward the cave, trying to escape, but stopped in her tracks when a loud growl echoed from within. Her heart sank to her stomach. She scanned her surroundings. There was nowhere to go. She ran back to the glass.

"Please," she screamed. "Let me out!"

She pounded on the glass until she saw the people focus on something behind her. She turned to see what it was.

Cheryl let out a low, guttural moan, the sound of raw panic as she stared at the dark shape emerging from the cave. She didn't know what it was. Her first thought was a bear standing upright, but the shape was all wrong. The thing towered over her... a huge, humanoid creature covered in thick, matted hair. The eyes were bloodshot, yellow, and filled with rage. It lunged at her, and its snarling teeth were all she saw in the instant before she was knocked completely off her feet.

An explosion of pain shot through her shoulder as she crashed to the floor. She struggled to stand and realized her right arm was gone. Blood poured out of the ragged wound where it once was. She trembled so uncontrollably she felt her teeth clicking together. The shock combined with nausea as she saw her dismembered arm between the teeth of the thing. As the creature chewed the flesh from the bones of her stolen arm, she saw her seashell bracelet bouncing on the wrist and vomited. Several of the women who watched through the glass turned away, but others remained transfixed as they sipped their wine.

Cheryl crawled away and begged God for help. Quick memories of going to church as a kid flashed through her. The wooden pews, the stained glass windows.

The thing savagely dragged her closer and flipped her onto her back. Its massive claws clutched her thigh and chest, and it sank its teeth into her stomach. She screamed and leaned her head as far back as she could, frantic for help, but saw only uncaring, upside-down faces.

An elderly, silver-haired man met her gaze. Cheryl's body jerked from side to side as the beast shook its head. The pain was excruciating, worse than anything she'd ever experienced. But as she felt herself go numb, a feeling of euphoria flowed into her. A strange sensation of calm even as the creature's teeth ripped out one of her lungs. The numbness in her head got so thick it shut out all sound.

It was time. This is it. It's okay.

As her vision grew dim, she remembered a gazelle being eaten by a lion on the nature show she watched with her grandmother as a kid. Back when her innocent eyes saw only a fresh, friendly, happy world.

"I feel bad for the gazelle, Grandma."

"Well, sweetie, the lion has to eat too, doesn't she?"

"But… the poor gazelle…"

"It's the circle of life."

In her last few seconds, Cheryl remembered the feeling of complete safety of that long-lost haven, sitting on the shag carpet beside her grandmother's green recliner, eating crackers with jelly on them as Grandma worked her needlepoint.

Her dead face stared up at the silver-haired man through the blood-streaked glass. He watched her frozen expression lift and drop as she was devoured. The deep wrinkles around his eyes narrowed as he looked on.

2

THE SILVER-HAIRED MAN

HAMILTON TOWNE FELT HIMSELF FALL, and his hands flailed as his eyes burst open. He gasped for air and looked in every direction until he realized he was safe in his chair on the bedroom balcony.

Towne, eighty-year-old billionaire and longtime resident on the *Forbes* list, put effort into standing and shuffled to the railing. He looked out over the grounds of his home, the largest mansion in Newton, Massachusetts. The driveway alone was a quarter mile to the house, weaving through dozens of tall, underlit pines on each side.

"Damn it."

It had been months since that night, and the whore's face still filled his mind. He couldn't figure out why. It wasn't the first time he'd witnessed such a scene, and it had never bothered him before.

Why now? Could it be a side effect of the medication?

Maybe knowing his own days were numbered was causing him to consider the mortality of others. He drew in a deep breath. Again, the image of her lifeless face jolted him.

Towne finally understood.

It's fear. Fear of being helpless.

He knew what his doctors had in store for him. They'd told

him how unpleasant it would all be. The thought of lying in a hospital bed at their mercy... He knew that, despite their attempts at concern, they'd all share a small measure of joy at being in control over someone as powerful as him.

Bastards.

His blood pressure rose as he imagined how weak he would appear. He didn't want to allow them that kind of dominance.

Even if the chemo works, how long will it last?

Towne picked up his glass of warm bourbon and walked inside to his bathroom. His numerous medications were neatly arranged on the counter, placed in small color-coordinated plastic boxes by a revolving staff of nurses that visited each day.

Towne hated the boxes, hated the pills, hated all of it. He emptied a handful of Xanax into his palm and looked at them. All he saw was himself lying in that hospital bed, thin as a skeleton with tubes stuck in him, shitting into a bedpan, and the look on the face of the nurse who'd have to replace it.

He cupped all the pills into his mouth, washed them down with the bourbon, and made his way to bed.

Drifting through the realm of semiconsciousness, he grumbled as he tossed and turned. For several months now, he'd considered sharing what he knew... if not for any other reason than to wipe the smirk off the face of James Winthrop. Winthrop had originated the club and never let anyone forget it. The smug prick had gotten much too full of himself, but Towne always did a good job of hiding his true feelings. Winthrop had no idea of his disdain and liked him a great deal.

The more he considered it through the thick haze of the Xanax, the more he approved of the idea. He got out of bed and half stumbled into his study, a showplace of mahogany and bookcases that resembled the murder scene in a hundred movie mysteries.

The old man dropped into the leather chair at his desk,

which was uncluttered except for a short stack of opened letters. He sorted through them and pulled the one he wanted. He leaned forward with the letter beneath the glow of the lamp and read it again.

Dear Mr. Towne,

My name's Kirby Cronin, and I'm a paranormal enthusiast. I have a website at www.CryptoKirby.com, and I would love the chance to interview you regarding your Bigfoot sighting back in the 1970s. When you first reported it, you were adamant about what you saw. You disputed that it could have been a bear or some more believable explanation. Over the past two decades, however, you seem to have changed your tune and gone along with other more skeptical explanations.

Being a Sasquatch witness myself, I'd really like to hear your reasons for changing your story. Did you remember some other details?

I know what an important man you are and imagine your schedule must be crazy, but I also reside in Massachusetts and would be thrilled to be able to come to you at whatever time would be convenient. If you would rather speak by phone, I'd be grateful for that as well.

Thank you so much for your time,

Kirby Cronin

Towne glanced at the website listed on the letter and typed it into his computer. Graphics of Sasquatches, UFOs, and other paranormal imagery came on-screen. Kirby's photo on the About page showed him holding a plaster cast of a Bigfoot print. Towne scrolled through the site, watched videos, and read Kirby's theories.

Towne picked up his phone.

3

KIRBY CRONIN

ALTHOUGH IN HIS MID TWENTIES, Kirby still lived at home and had no plans to move out. His dad had died when Kirby was in high school, and leaving his mother was out of the question.

He and his mom, Debra, enjoyed meals together and watched Netflix a few nights a week, but Kirby spent most of his time in the basement. Every wall was covered with posters and photos of Sasquatch, aliens, or some other paranormal activity. The wall above his desk was filled with newspaper and magazine articles featuring headlines such as WEREWOLF CAPTURED, and CORPSE HAS ALIEN DNA.

His desk had an editing bay beside shelves crammed with various cameras and video equipment.

The middle of the room was set up in a traditional TV interview format. Video cameras were on tripods, each one aimed at the two chairs facing each other. A pair of LED light panels on stands illuminated both interviewer and subject.

Kirby was dressed in jeans and a vintage *Close Encounters* T-shirt, laser focused on the task at hand. He sat with a notebook in his lap and several more pages of notes leaned against his chest. He wasn't crazy about being on camera, but he hadn't yet found someone with the ability to ask decent follow-up questions.

The camera shooting him was unmanned. He'd been doing this long enough to know how to stay in frame. The other camera, stationed behind Kirby to film his subject, was manned by his best friend, Spence.

Spence shared most of Kirby's beliefs and loved taking part in the interviews. He squinted through his thick glasses and adjusted the focus on the camera aimed at Kirby's current subject, a man in his late fifties who'd contacted him about a Sasquatch sighting. The man wore old stonewashed jeans and a matching stonewashed jean jacket over a black golf shirt. A single turquoise earring hung beside his long gray hair.

"How far away from you was this thing you saw?" Kirby asked, his expression serious.

Jean Jacket squinted upward as if trying to remember somehow hurt his eyes. "About twenty feet," he answered. "It was easily eight feet tall with straggly brown hair all over it."

"Did it see you?"

"Absolutely it did," Jean Jacket replied. "It stared right at me."

Spence slowly zoomed in on the man's face.

"How long did it stand there?"

"Well, I don't know exactly. It was so surreal. It could have been twenty seconds or twenty minutes. I was kind of in shock."

"I bet," Kirby said. "What happened next?"

"As soon as I was able to think again, I took out my phone and got a few pictures."

"You didn't mention that when we spoke."

"Guess I forgot to tell you that part. Sorry. I printed them up though."

"Let's check them out."

Jean Jacket bent down and picked up a manila folder, then removed three photos and proudly handed them to Kirby.

Kirby's heartbeat sped up as he realized this might be the day he would hold proof of Sasquatch in his hands. Spence lifted his eyes from his monitor to get a better look at the photos.

"Great shots, aren't they?" Jean Jacket asked. "I think these are the best photos of Bigfoot ever taken."

The instant Kirby saw the photos, he physically deflated, the excitement on his face replaced by anger.

"Cut," Kirby uttered with disgust as he stood up.

Spence stepped forward. "What's wrong?"

Kirby answered while glaring at Jean Jacket. "These are fake."

"What?" Jean Jacket stammered.

"You obviously just photoshopped a Sasquatch into these shots."

Jean Jacket's face grew stern. "That's not true."

"Oh please," Kirby said. "This is the Sasquatch from those jerky commercials."

"Those are real. I swear."

Kirby removed the lapel microphones from him and his subject. "Whatever."

Jean Jacket scooped up his photos. "This is bullshit."

He stormed out the basement door and slammed it behind him.

Kirby shut off the light panels and dropped onto the nearby sofa. "Damn. I should've known."

"You screwed up," Spence said.

"I didn't see those photos until just now."

Kirby and Spence had been hanging out since high school. They not only shared the same interests but both made a living as videographers.

"No. Just because the shots were fake doesn't mean you shouldn't interview him." Spence continued. "People would be just as interested to see you debunk someone as they would be in your showing possible proof. It makes you look more credible about everything."

Kirby felt the sting of regret and squeezed his eyes shut. "Damn it. You're right."

"I'm gonna head home and get some sleep. I've got an early shoot tomorrow." Spence grabbed his phone and keys.

"What are you shooting?"

"Dentist testimonials. Exciting stuff," Spence said sarcastically. "Oh, can I borrow your gimbal? I may do a walk-through of the office."

"Yeah, sure," Kirby replied. "Long as I get it back by next week though. I've got a bar mitzvah to shoot."

Spence laughed. "Man… are we living the dream or what?"

<hr />

After Spence left, Kirby broke down his equipment. He looked at one of the glossy photos that Jean Jacket had left behind and shook his head with disgust.

"Dumbass," Kirby mumbled to himself.

He dropped the pic in the wastebasket beside his desk and sat down, his eyes turning to a framed photo of him with his father. Kirby picked it up and wiped a smudge off the glass with his T-shirt. He missed him. Badly. He was a great guy and a hands-on dad. When Kirby's classmates knocked him for being lousy at sports, his dad always made him feel like a king.

Kirby's infatuation with the cryptozoological stemmed from an event that had taken place with his dad years earlier. They were on a camping trip to the White Mountains in New Hampshire, something they did every summer since he was a small boy. Debra hated bugs, so those weekends were guys only, and Kirby loved every minute of them.

The trip when Kirby was ten was the time he remembered best. He helped his dad set up the tent a few yards from the river. After a disappointing day of fishing, father and son were sitting in their fold-up chairs by the fire, heating up hot dogs Debra had packed for them.

Kirby recalled every detail. The smell of the pine trees mixed with the burning hickory. The bubbling sound of the river. The way the fire's orange glow on his dad's face contrasted with the cobalt twilight sky.

Then it happened. His dad had been telling him a story when something caught his attention. His eyes shifted and took on an expression Kirby didn't recall ever seeing on his dad's face. He turned to see what it was.

On the other side of the river, roughly ten yards away, something stood by the water's edge.

"Don't move," his dad whispered.

The thing was about eight feet tall, covered in thick, matted hair. Its arms were unnaturally long. They hung past its knees. Its face was similar to a gorilla's with a slightly more humanoid nose.

It appeared to be watching them. The creature knelt and reached into the water with both hands, cupping its long, dark-skinned fingers together to scoop up water just as a man would do. When it was done drinking, it stood up and looked even taller than before.

For several minutes time was frozen. Kirby and his father watched the thing watch them, all three locked in mutual fascination. There was no fear or concern of danger, only of the inevitable moment when the magical occasion would end.

A coyote cry broke the silence. The creature took a last glance at them and walked into the trees.

"Bye," Kirby whispered.

His dad put his arm around him. "Kirbo... We just saw something most people never get to experience."

"What was it?" Kirby asked. "Was that a monster?"

"No."

His dad told him everything he had ever heard about the legend of Sasquatch. He told him about the alleged sightings, the 1970s Bigfoot movies, everything. Kirby hung on every word. His dad always spoke to him naturally anyway—never added in the nuances and accentuations that most adults put into their conversations with kids.

Five years later, his father died of a heart attack. It left a hole in Kirby's being that would never be filled. He thought of his dad often, but that camping trip, those moments of wonder by the fire, remained his single most vivid, emotional memory of him.

"It's just the two of us against the world now." Debra often said.

She became a bit too protective in the next few years. Kirby understood why and did his best to be patient with her. He was only human though, and the times he did snap at her, he never stayed angry for long.

For her part, Debra did her best to not smother him. The one thing she regularly got on his case about was his obsessions. A few times, she tried to steer his interest toward something more normal. Sports, a musical instrument, but it was no use, and she soon gave up.

The only other thing he was passionate about was video production. He took an A/V elective sophomore year and fell in love with it. Not just filming but editing as well. Eager to support his new hobby and secretly hoping it would take the place of his paranormal obsession, Debra bought him his first video camera. When she handed him the CanonXA25, Kirby hugged her tighter than ever and couldn't stop smiling. The camera became a part of him, and he took it everywhere.

His dad had always told him to figure out what he loved doing most. If he could find a way to make money at it, he'd never have to work a day in his life.

He found his dad's advice to be true. Since starting his own small production company, he filmed and edited everything from low-budget commercials to weddings and other private events. For the most part, he enjoyed it. It also gave him enough time to work on his own projects.

His main passion was his website. He filmed interviews with people who claimed to have seen any strange phenomena. Over the years he posted firsthand accounts on his website and YouTube channel.

There were thousands of sites like Kirby's across the net, but of those, only a handful featured content that could be taken seriously. From the start, that was something Kirby was determined to do. He had no interest in filling his site with interviews of nuts with phony stories.

That was the main reason normal people got mocked for mentioning any kind of sighting. They got lumped in with every redneck who said an alien stuck a probe up his ass, or the idiot hunters who claimed Bigfoot stole the tires off their pickups and raped their girlfriends. Those people drove Kirby crazy. Reading their accounts made his eye twitch.

He wanted to use his site to showcase the best possible witnesses giving the best possible testimony. In fact, it was his pursuit and research of "respectable" people with sightings that had put him on his current investigative path. He was enough of a realist to understand that nothing brings respect as money does, so he focused on researching rich people with claims of paranormal experiences.

———•———

To his surprise, there were quite a few of them. Some famous, some not. He was fascinated by the accounts he found from millionaires and billionaires on old talk shows, in print interviews, and quick conversations caught on camera. It led him to what he considered a major discovery. Something he felt was more than a coincidence.

A year earlier, Kirby noticed several wealthy men who previously claimed they saw a UFO, a Sasquatch, a ghost, a sea monster—all eventually recanted their stories. They somehow decided they were wrong. It was strange. What struck him was that before they changed their stories, they spoke of their sightings with passion and intensity. Later, just cold recantations.

Kirby posted a few samples of the behavior on his site.

CryptoKirby.com Post #55

THE BILLIONAIRE & THE UFO

"Absolutely no question about it. Sure as I'm standing here, it was a UFO."
Jonathan Stubbs Electronics Tycoon, 1979.

While on a ski trip in Vermont, Stubbs claimed an alien craft circled above him on the slopes. Here's his original story:

"My friend Pete and I were night skiing. It was brutally cold out and snowing, so we had the slopes to ourselves. We were the only ones stupid enough to be out there. Pete and I were racing to the bottom, but I took a tumble. I wasn't hurt or anything, but I needed to adjust my boot. Pete sped by me, mocking me as he went around the bend. After I fixed my boot, I noticed a red light on top of the tree line. As I looked at it, it started to move. My first thought was that it was a helicopter, and I remember thinking how crazy the pilot was to be out on a night like that. I figured it was an emergency; maybe someone was lost or something. But I looked up, and it wasn't a helicopter. I didn't know what it was. It looked like a round piece of iron glowing red-hot. The falling snow was making me blink, but I couldn't take my eyes off it. It circled me, and the red light coming from it moved around the slope like a spotlight. Suddenly the red beam turned off and it zipped away, traveling roughly ten miles in the span of a second. There was never any sound at all. Nothing."

Mr. Stubbs told this story many times from 1979 until 1990. After that, he had a new answer when asked about the story.

Reporter: "Mr. Stubbs, there's a well-known story about you seeing a UFO in Vermont in 1979. Have you ever seen another one?"

Stubbs: "Well, (laughs) that was a big misunderstanding. I found out later it was just a military helicopter."

Reporter: "But sir, you were quoted as…"

Stubbs: "I must have had a few too many ciders beforehand. Next question."

CryptoKirby.com Post #56

THE BILLIONAIRE & THE GHOST

In 1980, before Bob Lyons became one of the richest real estate developers in America, he was just a struggling businessman. In Los Angeles for a meeting, he stayed in a single room at the Roosevelt Hotel in Hollywood. Lyons was wide-awake, watching an old

Dean Martin Western on TV, when suddenly there was a knock at his door. He looked through the peephole and found no one there. He opened the door, and the long hallway was empty.

From an interview Bob Lyons gave in 1985:

"I thought it strange but passed it off as my mind playing tricks on me. But when I turned back, there was a man in my room, standing by the bed. I was shocked and yelled, 'What are you doing here?'

"The man said nothing. He just stood there, staring at me with a blank, expressionless face. He was a fiftysomething, wearing a dark suit. I yelled at him to get out of the room, and he didn't react. He didn't say anything, but started walking toward me. I didn't know if he was heading toward me or the door, so I raised my fists to defend myself. He came right at me, and he—I know this sounds bizarre—he walked right through me."

Reporter: "Do you mean he shoved by you?"

Bob Lyons: "No. He literally went through me. His body somehow passed through me. It was the strangest sensation I've ever experienced."

Reporter: "When you say *sensation,* what do...?"

Bob Lyons: "It felt like an ice-cold wind blew through me... as if for a few seconds I was standing naked in a blizzard."

Reporter: "That's... That sounds..."

Bob Lyons: "It sounds crazy. I know. It got even crazier. Because when I turned around, he was gone. Just gone. I suddenly felt very nauseated, and I ran to the bathroom to throw up. When I got to the sink, I saw that... my reflection in the mirror wasn't me. I was in shock. The reflection reacted to my movements, but it was the man instead of me. I could feel myself getting dizzy, and just then all the lights went out. When they came back on, it was me again. I checked out of that hotel immediately."

In 2002, a paranormal investigator asked him about the story. Here's his reply:

Bob Lyons: "That's ridiculous. I never said any such thing. Just another case of a hack reporter trying to make a name for himself."

TWO BIGFOOTS & A BILLIONAIRE

In 1971, businessman Hamilton Towne claimed two eight-foot-tall, hairy, bipedal creatures walked alongside the river he was canoeing down while on vacation in the Pacific Northwest. From that date until 1980, he retold the same story about how the strange creatures kept pace with his canoe and watched him with humanlike expressions.

Here are his own words, taken from a 1973 interview in *American Outdoorsman:*

"They walked like humans, were built like humans, but were much larger and covered in fur. They were not bears. They were not moose or deer. Their heads didn't have snouts or horns. I could see them as perfectly as I see you. I don't know what they were. Their faces were flat and apelike. The oddest part was that I never once felt threatened by them. They just walked along with me; although their terrain was rocky and uneven, they kept pace with me for several minutes. It was something I'll never forget."

However, when Hamilton Towne was asked about the story in 1986, he had a much different take on the experience.

Interviewer: "I'd like to ask you about something from many years ago… your Bigfoot sighting. Can you tell me about that?"

Hamilton Towne: "Well… (*laughs*) That got blown out of proportion. It was just a couple of large brown bears and a little too much whiskey."

———•———

Kirby's big question was, *Why?* Why did all these people change their stories? They didn't refute them until after they made their money.

He had a theory, and it was a whopper. He believed that they were telling the truth in the first place, but once they became billionaires, the answers to all the world's questions and mysteries became accessible.

"You think it's an Illuminati thing?" Spence once asked him.

"Yeah," Kirby answered, "I do. I think when you make that kind of money, all the doors open up for you."

Spence smiled. "And who exactly is opening these doors?"

"That I don't know."

"For what purpose? Why keep these things secret?"

Kirby wished he had a better answer. "I don't know."

The more he researched, the more he believed it. Kirby was clever, and although it wasn't easy, he tracked down various ways to reach out to some of those billionaires. He got the addresses of their lawyers, tracked down the email addresses of their personal assistants, even managed to find some of their home addresses. He sent out letters introducing himself and requested interviews.

It had been three months since the last letter went out. Not a single response. Despite not having any interviews, he promoted the theory on his site anyway and was happy to see many positive comments.

It was almost midnight. Kirby was awake in bed, still pissed at himself for stopping the interview with Jean Jacket. He imagined all the things he should've said to the phony. He was jolted out of self-disgust when his cell rang from a blocked number.

"Hello?"

"Hello. Is this Kirby Cronin?"

"Yes."

"My name is Hamilton Towne. I received your letter."

Kirby leaped out of bed and fumbled for a pen in full frantic mode. "Mr. Towne! I — Thank you for calling!"

There was silence on the other end. Kirby's heart dropped.

"Mr. Towne? Are you still there? Mr. Towne?"

A few deafening seconds of silence went by, followed by a single sentence delivered in Hamilton Towne's deep voice.

"You're right about all of it."

"Sir?" Kirby stammered, "How —"

"Everything you suspect is exactly correct."

Kirby's thoughts formed tornadoes in his brain. He had so much he wanted to ask. His heart pounded. Towne's next sentence would be one that Kirby would play over and over in his head.

"I would take you if I could, but you're going to have to find it on your own."

Anxiety filled Kirby's brain. *What the…? Think. Think!*

"Good night," Towne said.

"No. Wait! Please, Mr. Towne! Take me where?"

The call ended. Kirby stared at the phone.

"Holy shit."

His fingers trembled as he wrote down every word Towne said. His whole body tingled with electricity. All of his investigating, all those years chasing down leads and rumors, and the truth just reached out to him directly to tell him he was on the right path.

Kirby couldn't sit. He couldn't stand. He paced like a lunatic.

With his hands shaking, he grabbed his phone and called Spence. "Dude! You're not gonna believe this!"

———•———

Hamilton Towne's call to Kirby repeated through the headphones of a man sitting in front of a large computer screen. The room was dimly lit, with most of the light coming from all the other screens that lined the walls.

The smart screens featured worldwide digital maps. Each of them monitored red dots and highlighted specific areas of interest. Dozens of other men in headphones watched their own monitors at individual workstations. They were each dressed in casual clothing, but they all shared a military-style haircut beneath their headphones.

As the voice of Hamilton Towne played back, digital audio levels on the computer screen rose and fell with his words. The man removed his headphones and picked up a special phone.

4

JAMES WINTHROP

VERONICA'S FLAWLESS BODY BECAME SILHOUETTED as she walked past the floor-to-ceiling window high above the twinkling Las Vegas skyline. She took an open bottle of Cristal from a gold ice bucket and ran a hand through her wild mane of hair. Joelle, the other twenty-year-old model, sat on the floor with her back against the sofa. Like Joelle, Veronica wore nothing but a black thong and dark eyeliner. Veronica returned and nestled her face into the gray-haired chest of the penthouse's owner.

James Winthrop kissed the top of her perfumed head. He ran his manicured fingers down the small of her back while his other hand fumbled with the TV remote. His eyes narrowed, trying to make out the words on the screen's guide.

"Joelle, honey?" he said, his voice deep and smooth.

The blonde turned up to him with a slow smile that would cause most men to stutter. "Yeah, babe?"

"Be a doll and get my glasses from the bedroom, would you?"

"Sure thing." Joelle bounced from the floor effortlessly, causing Winthrop to shake his head in wonder.

"Don't take those knees for granted." Winthrop was in decent shape for his seventy-two years. He took care of himself, exercised, and kept a full-time chef on staff to ensure his healthy meals remained delicious. Whatever it took to continue enjoying the life he had. Despite being a billionaire since his twenties, Winthrop still appreciated his good fortune. He took immense pride and pleasure in being a member of what the liberal media painted as the greedy one percent. He couldn't care less. He knew he and his friends held all the power. They knew the way the world really worked. They knew its secrets.

Joelle returned with his glasses.

"Thanks, dear."

"I'm going to make myself a cocktail," Joelle said. "Want one?"

"No, thank you," he answered as he clicked the remote, now able to channel surf successfully.

The satellite phone on the coffee table rang. Winthrop looked at his watch as Veronica handed it to him.

"Yes?"

"Hi, sir. It's Travers."

"What is it?" Winthrop asked.

"You were right about your friend. It seems we have a breach."

Winthrop's eyes narrowed as he exhaled. "That's too bad. When?"

"Just now."

"To whom did he speak?"

Travers took a few seconds before he answered. "No one important."

"I see." Winthrop looked at the colorful strip below. "Thank you."

It didn't take a genius to see it coming. Ol' Hammy had cancer. When Richardson got sick a few years back, the same thing happened.

He truly liked Hamilton Towne. Still, betrayal was betrayal. The secrets could not be spilled.

Towne must go.

He turned back to see his gorgeous playthings drinking and laughing, a sight he never tired of. Their names and faces changed through the years, but the beauty and promise of pleasure stayed fresh.

Winthrop pressed a button on his phone.

Just outside the penthouse door, a mountainous bodyguard in a dark suit touched his ear radio. "Yes, Mr. W?"

"I've got an urge to play blackjack," Winthrop said.

"I'll make sure your table is ready, sir."

Winthrop hung up and turned to the girls, who were looking back at him with hopeful eyes. "Would you like to join me downstairs?"

Joelle and Veronica jumped up and let out happy squeals.

"Good," Winthrop said. "Go get a few outfits so I can tell you what to wear."

They turned to the master bedroom, where a dozen new outfits from a shopping spree earlier in the day were spread over the bed. Winthrop watched the way their bodies moved as they walked away. Their skin was impossibly tight and smooth, softer than the finest silk.

"Wait," he said.

The ladies turned back and watched him pick up the phone again.

"Ready to go, sir?" the bodyguard's voice asked through the line.

"No," he answered. "I'm going to need about thirty minutes."

He hung up and looked at Veronica and Joelle.

The girls started back toward him slowly, teasingly. They knew what he wanted and were happy to oblige. They dropped to their knees in front of him with devilish smiles. Winthrop pondered what tiny percentage of them truly cared for him... if any at all.

He leaned his head back, closed his eyes, and decided it didn't matter.

5

MASON SPECTOR

Hamilton Towne awoke earlier than usual. He sat up on the side of the bed for a moment before resigning himself to the arduous task of going into the bathroom.

Ah, the good old days... when he could not only piss strong and easy but stand up doing it. The things he once took for granted.

He saw his empty bourbon glass and remembered what he'd done the night before. A sense of panic crept in, adding to the dull cloud from the pills. His thoughts paralyzed him until his bursting bladder begged for release. The old man stood, his joints aching as he made his way into the bathroom.

While Towne listened to the sound of his urine trickling out, he tried to figure out a way to undo the damage he'd done. It wouldn't be easy. Unknown to him, such plans had already been set in motion.

A man silently entered the bedroom. He'd managed to avoid a handful of gardeners, housekeepers, and other daytime staff to get to this point. Clad in casual street clothes, Mason Spector stopped just beside the bathroom door. A former Navy SEAL, he had the discipline and patience to watch for the precise second to strike.

As he waited, he took out a unique EpiPen. It was smaller

than the standard injectors used for allergic reactions. Mason heard the toilet flush and the sink turn on.

The second Towne crossed the threshold into the bedroom, Spector forced him facedown onto the bed. The old man struggled, but Mason was six-four and solid muscle. He yanked Towne's pajamas down and injected the EpiPen into his ass cheek.

Almost immediately, Towne's face contorted. Sharp pain shot up his arm, and the weight of a building crushed down on his chest. Between grunts of agony, he tried to speak, but the words were inaudible through the wheezing that accompanied them. His panicked, wide eyes stared into Mason's calm, cold ones.

The men knew one other well. In fact, they'd enjoyed each other's company for over a decade. Yet Mason showed no sympathy. He pointed a finger an inch from Towne's face, as you would to a dog that peed on the carpet.

"This is your fault," Mason whispered. "You know it is."

Towne's white-knuckled fingers stopped squeezing his chest, his pupils locked in place, and he was gone.

With Towne being in his eighties, odds were there would be no need for an autopsy, but Mason was a perfectionist. He knew what to do to hide an injection mark. He arranged Towne's body onto his back. Within a few hours, all the blood and fluids in the body would pool up at the lowest point, being Towne's buttocks. The skin would turn a dark purple, making the tiny injection point completely impossible to find.

6

VIC MITCHUM

D ETECTIVE VIC MITCHUM STORMED THROUGH the homicide division of the Boston Police Department, his face red with anger and disgust. He burst into the office of his superior, Captain Rona Guidley.

"Are you kidding me?" Vic barked. "Was this your idea?"

Guidley showed no emotion as she slowly put down her mug and wiped a coffee streak from the top. She turned to the uniformed cop sitting across from her. "John. Excuse me. Would you mind if we finished this later?"

"Not at all, Captain."

Once the door closed, Guidley shot forward in her chair. "Who the fuck do you think you are?"

"Oh, and it would be okay if we dressed up someone you love like a hooker and used her for bait?" Vic scowled.

Guidley liked Vic. He was a brilliant detective with an impressive record of closed cases. She also knew he was a hothead. She'd figured he was going to take the news of his fiancée's undercover assignment badly, but not this badly.

"Calm the hell down," she said. "First off, it wasn't my decision. Vice Squad asked me for Kelsey's help. I figured a little undercover work would help her down the line, so I told them it was fine with me, but they'd have to ask her."

Vic stepped forward. "And nobody thought to ask me?"

"Why would anyone ask you?"

"Because she's my fiancée."

"Jesus Christ, Vic. You're a fucking dinosaur."

"You're telling me that—"

Guidley cut him off. "I'm not telling you shit. She can take care of herself, and if I were you, I'd seriously rethink my whole attitude. If I know Kelsey, she'll kick your old ass out if you try any of that macho shit with her."

Vic considered. "When is this happening?"

"Tomorrow night. Don't worry. She'll be in good hands."

"*If* she does it," Vic replied as he turned to leave.

"Hey," Guidley said, "you ever talk to me like that in front of anybody again, I swear you'll be working a school crosswalk in a neon vest. Got it?"

"Sorry about that," Vic mumbled.

As Vic made his way back through the station, he called his fiancée.

———•———

"Hi, honey." Kelsey smiled into her phone as her partner drove their patrol car through the North End.

"Hey, babe," Vic replied. "So… what's new?" he asked with pretend curiosity.

Kelsey grimaced. "Damn. Who told you?"

"Doesn't matter," Vic answered. "Why didn't you tell me?"

"I was going to talk to you about it tonight at dinner."

"Uh-huh," Vic said. "I'll meet you at the Dockside at seven."

Kelsey frowned. It was the first time in years they'd hung up without an *I love you*.

———•———

Vic hung up as he arrived at his desk. His area was centered in the middle of a dozen workstations filled with other detectives, uniforms, and civilians. The large room had a constant background noise of chatter and movement, and the stuffy air carried many scents, but predominantly it was a mix of cheap deodorant and sweat.

The desk beside Vic's belonged to his partner, Tony Petrillo. Tony had a heavy frame and a face capable of the warmest of smiles and the most menacing of stares. Vic dropped into his seat and looked at him, as well as the younger guy with him. The kid looked familiar, but Vic couldn't place him.

"Who's this?"

"Kirby Cronin. He's a friend of your kid brother."

"Hi," Kirby said.

Vic sized him up and tried to guess why he was there. "Hey. How do you know Dave?"

"I'm a videographer. I filmed his anniversary party last year."

"Ah. That's where I saw you." Vic nodded.

"Dave and I hit it off and stayed in touch. You know, Instagram and stuff. He mentioned you were a cop."

Vic was everything that Guidley accused him of. He was only forty-eight but had the mindset of a much older man. The mere mention of Instagram put a bad taste in his mouth. He detested almost everything about the current generation, from their dependence on devices, their disgusting displays of entitlement, and their lazy work ethic.

Millennials, he thought. *Yech.*

It was through these eyes that Vic met Kirby Cronin.

"So… what can we do for you?"

———·———

Kirby's instincts were sharp, and every fiber of his being screamed at him to hold back certain details of his theory.

"You saw that Hamilton Towne died yesterday?" Kirby asked.

Vic nodded. "The billionaire in Newton. Yeah. Heart attack."

"A billionaire at eighty? I'd take that deal." Tony laughed.

Kirby shook his head. "I'm pretty sure he was murdered."

Vic leaned back with a condescending smirk. "Why do you think that?"

Easy… Easy… Kirby shifted in his seat. "The day before, I

got a phone call from him. We talked a bit, and he was going to call me again."

"Wait," Vic said. "You knew him?"

Kirby took a deep breath. "I didn't really know him. I knew who he was, but I didn't actually ever talk to him until just the day before he died."

"If you didn't know him, why would he call you?" Tony asked.

"I'd sent him a letter. He was getting back to me."

"What made you think it was really Hamilton Towne who called you? Are you sure it was him?" Vic asked.

"I'm sure, yeah. I'm a YouTuber, and…"

As soon as the words *I'm a YouTuber* came out, Kirby could see Vic's disdain. The cop exhaled a breath of disgust, undoubtedly putting Kirby into the same big, fat, useless category as the Kardashians.

"…film interviews and do stories about people with different experiences," Kirby finished.

If he came right out and said he was an amateur paranormal investigator, these two tough Boston cops would laugh in his face. So he did his best to put a more respectable spin on everything he said without lying.

"I've done several videos about Hamilton Towne and other billionaires like him. I studied all the existing footage of him that was out there, from old talk shows and interviews. I know his voice, and it was definitely him."

Vic watched his face intently as Tony spoke up.

"Okay. Let's say it was really him who called you. What does that have to do with murder? The doctors said it was a heart attack with no sign of foul play."

Kirby shook his head. "It's too convenient. What are the odds that he'd have a heart attack right after calling me?"

Vic's face contorted as if he smelled raw sewage. "Wait. Are you suggesting he was killed *because* he talked to you?"

"I think so. Yeah."

"Just what did he tell you that would have been worth killing him for?" Tony asked.

Kirby stared back at him. Then at Vic. "He... told me that one of my theories was right."

Vic gave Tony an amused look before turning back to Kirby. "And what theory is that?"

Kirby's lips scrunched into the corner of his mouth. He looked around the room, a room with an atmosphere based completely in hard reality. It made his ideas sound even nuttier, but he had to continue.

Here goes...

He took a breath and spoke slowly. "I'd noticed, and done a few videos on the fact, that several rich, powerful men, at one point in their lives, in most cases before they made their money, all shared similar beliefs about... certain topics, and would discuss them freely. But soon after getting rich, they changed their feelings about those beliefs."

Vic wasn't sure where the kid was going.

"What certain topics do you mean?" Tony asked.

Don't do it, Kirby thought.

Kirby waited a few seconds, then spoke. "I'm sure you know that dozens of prostitutes and homeless people have vanished from downtown this year alone? I've researched it, and I realized that it's been happening in cycles."

Both detectives looked shocked, and Kirby knew he'd hit pay dirt.

"How do you know that? Vic asked.

"It happens in fours."

Suspicion floated across Vic's face, then disappeared just as quickly.

"What does that have to do with Hamilton Towne?" Tony asked.

Kirby leaned forward and continued, "I've also noticed that every cycle, after the fourth person is taken, something even stranger happens. The richest people in the country all come to town for some reason, all at the same time."

Vic glanced at Tony and raised an eyebrow. "I'm not sure if that's accurate."

"It is. Check it out," Kirby replied.

"Okay. Let's say that's true. How does that connect to Hamilton Towne?" Tony asked.

"Yeah," Vic added, "And what are these certain topics you're talking about?"

"That doesn't matter," Kirby replied.

"Spill it, kid," Vic said. "What did all these billionaires once believe and then not believe?"

Tony looked at him. "We have other things we need to do, bud."

Kirby looked up at the ceiling as if an easier way to say it was written there for him. "Okay. Paranormal things."

"Sorry, what?" Vic asked.

Tony laughed and spun his chair back to his desk. "Of course."

Vic smirked. "You're saying that a bunch of billionaires will come to town to somehow abduct hookers and homeless people to give to ghosts or aliens?"

"No," Kirby answered. "Not like that."

Vic and Tony laughed again.

Tony took it further. "No, that's not what he means. He means the billionaires come to town, turn into aliens themselves, and then take the hookers back to their home planet."

"Kid... that's the best thing I've heard all week." Vic shook his head.

Kirby tried to explain. "No. I'm not sure exactly what's going on. I don't know what the connection to the missing people is, just that there is a connection. I'm just saying that..."

It was no use. The detectives had deemed him nuts, as he'd known they would.

7

KELSEY MOSS

K ELSEY WAS DIFFERENT FROM EVERY other female officer Vic had met over the years. First off, she wasn't some third-generation cop doing it because her dad and brothers did. She'd been a business major focusing on marketing when a chance conversation with a cop changed her plans.

In her freshman year at Northeastern, Kelsey's roommate and best friend Lisa was a victim of date rape. Watching how the policeman did his best to calm her while getting the information he needed impressed Kelsey. She'd complimented him on that, which prompted him to discuss how much he enjoyed helping people when they needed it most. It wasn't always the easiest job, but most times it was extremely gratifying. Something about the passion in his voice convinced her she was meant to hear these things.

When she considered a career that could make a difference in many lives, it made her marketing plans sound selfish in comparison. Kelsey took a few days after that to officially decide, but her mind was made up. She was going to become a police officer.

In the meantime, she and Lisa started taking jujitsu lessons. At first she didn't take it too seriously. It was more about keeping Lisa busy, helping her get over her trauma, a sort of therapy. Kelsey was surprised to discover she not only enjoyed it, she loved it. Not just the new circle of friends but learning and mastering the techniques instilled in her a physical confidence she found empowering. The adrenaline rush of besting someone on the mat became addictive. She continued training long after Lisa grew bored with it, and it became a cornerstone in her life, something that would always be a part of her.

Kelsey was different from all the other women Vic had met as well. She spoke with an honesty that was a breath of fresh air compared to the other women he'd been involved with. There was simply no bullshit. If she liked something, she was quick to point it out. If not, she said so.

She was a uniformed patrol officer for five years, and in that time, she'd never dated a cop. Kelsey decided early on no good could come from that. It was hard enough being a female officer without all the unneeded drama and gossip that would bring. She worked too hard to get where she was, and she wasn't going to risk becoming a whispered punch line.

Not that her fellow cops never tried. She shot them all down, usually in a manner befitting the way they asked. The ones who approached her politely and privately, she let down easy, explaining her rule. The obnoxious ones who crudely propositioned her in front of others, she emasculated with a smile as onlookers laughed.

Even after it was understood by all that she would never say yes, it became a running joke to hit on her just to hear her hilarious rejections.

Then she met Detective Vic Mitchum.

It was at the scene of a carjacking gone bad. When Vic arrived, Kelsey was taking a statement from a witness. The victim was an obese man, lying dead on the pavement, his Bruins jersey covered with blood.

As Vic approached, one of the other first responders made a bad joke about the dead man's weight.

Vic heard and immediately wheeled toward him. "Hey, asshole. This is someone's son. Grow the fuck up."

Kelsey saw the exchange and was impressed. It was refreshing to see a man of intelligence and sensitivity after all the caveman behavior that usually surrounded her. Despite her own rules, she was attracted to him. She watched Vic study the scene and lingered close to him, thinking about the right thing to say to break the ice. But any attraction she felt dissipated immediately when he turned to her, eyed her up and down, and referred to her as Officer Barbie.

She didn't respond, but the next time they met, at a holiday party, she busted his balls about it.

"I said that? What a jerk. I'm sorry." He smiled. "What *should* I call you?"

She sipped her wine. "Kelsey."

"Kelsey," he said. "Vic."

There was a definite connection even though Vic was fifteen years her senior. He did his best to take in the features of her face without being obvious.

"Where are you from?" he asked.

Kelsey ignored the question. She narrowed her eyes as if studying his face.

"How old are you?" she asked in the most demeaning tone possible.

He smiled. Her serious expression broke with a laugh.

As they laughed together, the moment became forever embedded in their minds... the other's smiling face, the scent of the fresh Christmas pine, Nat King Cole's smooth voice, even the silver tinsel hung above the large bay window of falling snow in the blue night.

It was a life-changing moment, and they both knew it.

Vic was divorced and used to the idea that another marriage was not in his future. He doubted he'd have any kind of relationship with a woman that didn't immediately end with his zipper going up, and that was fine with him.

Although this one, with her funny sarcasm and eyes he

could fall into... she was a game changer. It started slowly. Coffee here and there. Lunch on the weekend.

They became inseparable. When he looked into her eyes, he had serious difficulty turning away. They drew him into a place he didn't want to leave, as if everything else stopped while he was there.

A big part of their connection was humor. While many other than his partner felt Vic had no sense of humor whatsoever, nothing was further from the truth. He and Kelsey laughed all the time. Being with her always made him feel instantly calm, physically lighter, and watching her laugh gave him true euphoria. The way her eyes sparkled filled him with the most overwhelming feeling of happiness he'd ever had.

With Kelsey, he finally understood what the term *soul mate* meant.

She felt it all as much as he did. The two of them belonged to each other and believed everything that happened in their lives up until they met had happened for the sole reason of bringing them together.

———•———

Most cops went to the Clover Pub when they were done for the night. When Vic and Kelsey wanted to be alone, they headed over to Robert's Dockside. Bobby was an old pal of Vic's, and no matter how busy the place was, they always got a table. Located on the wharf downtown, the restaurant featured spectacular views of the waterfront.

Vic preferred it at night. There was something about the way the reflections of the city lights danced on the water that spoke to him. The scent of seafood and butter-soaked bread crumbs filled the air, and every so often, a foghorn added a note to whatever song the jazz pianist was playing in the corner. Quite simply, he loved everything about the place— the maritime decor, the vintage sea-lantern wall sconces, everything. Not that he'd ever mention those details out loud.

Growing up in Boston in the 1970s had taught Vic that

discussing decor or wall sconces was an invitation for ridicule. The men in Vic's neighborhood were all tough guys who laughed through bad times and blizzards and feared nothing other than a losing sports season. In the circles Vic came of age in, complimenting light fixtures would be the equivalent of saying he wanted to become a ballet dancer. Homophobia was instilled into Boston boys as soon as they could walk. Vic still remembered how his dad teased him mercilessly for playing with *Star Wars* action figures.

"Why are you playing with dolls? Are you a fag?"

Although that ignorance had been drilled into him, Vic grew to understand how stupid that way of thinking was and developed a sense of pride in knowing he was smarter than people, both his own age and adults, who subscribed to those dumb beliefs.

Despite that, small scars of childhood insecurity remained deep down. But whenever something triggered them to the surface, they brought not fear but headshakes and smiles. Youthful nostalgia was powerful enough to paint a warm glow on everything... even ignorance.

———•———

"Who's working the van?" Vic asked Kelsey as he gave her a few of his scallops.

"Gum," she answered, referring to Detective Wrigley.

"Gum?" Vic asked. "That guy's an idiot."

"No, he's not."

"What about Eddie?"

"He's on paternity leave."

Vic looked out at the ocean. "I don't know," Vic said. "I'm not crazy about having Gum working point."

"It'll be fine," Kelsey said. "You'll see."

Vic shook his head slightly. "If you're doing this, I have to be in the van."

Kelsey was bringing her fork to her mouth but froze in place before it got there. "No way. If you do that, I lose all credibility. It'll look like I need my boyfriend to protect me."

"Boyfriend?" Vic put his hand on hers and turned the ring

on her finger slightly to straighten it. "Kel. Come on. Either I'm in the van too, or you can't do this at all."

As soon as the sentence left his lips, he knew he'd chosen the wrong words, but he was too stubborn to take them back.

Kelsey folded her arms and her shoulders tensed up. "I beg your pardon?"

"It's too dangerous," Vic said, doubling down. Surely she knew his main concern was her safety. It was out of love, not dominance. He thought he saw realization in her eyes for a few seconds and pushed his case even further. "The more I think about it, the more I think you're not doing this."

The words didn't come out stern or commanding, but in a softer, almost pleading tone. It didn't matter.

Kelsey's eyes narrowed. "You're joking, right?"

"No. I'm sorry," Vic replied. "You're not doing it."

Vic could tell by the look on her face that this was not going well.

"Is that what you think our marriage would be like? You telling me what I can or can't do?" She glared at him the same way she did at men who stood smirking behind badly bruised women on domestic-abuse calls.

"Kel. Come on. Stop it."

"Maybe you should throw in an 'I won't allow it,'" she said as she scanned the room to look at anything but Vic.

"Oh, grow up. Don't try to—"

Shit. Where had that come from? The quickest way to piss Kelsey off was to tell her to grow up. Sure enough, she slammed her fork on the table hard enough to knock over his wineglass, then grabbed her purse and stormed out, not even looking at him.

———·———

Vic shook his head in frustration. Why couldn't she see he was only worried about something happening to her? He was right, she just needed to see it. His thoughts about Kelsey were suddenly pushed aside by the realization the entire dining room was staring. He was used to being the center of attention at crime scenes, with annoying press and idiot bystanders watching him, but a situation like this, especially at the Dockside, made his skin crawl.

He turned to the nosy couple at the next table. He didn't say a word, just aimed his gaze at them, wearing the dark expression he used when trying to get a suspect to talk. The couple got the message and immediately stared at their plates.

Slowly the sounds of moving utensils and light conversation returned. He considered going after her.

No. Let her cool off.

He took a bite and replayed the conversation in his head.

8

NEW BLOOD

S ILICON VALLEY SOFTWARE CEO TOM Ackerman stood in awe of the custom paint job on his new Boeing 787 Dreamliner gleaming against the early-evening sky.

"Fantastic," Tom said to Boeing's representative. "It's beautiful."

"Completely our pleasure, Mr. Ackerman. Wait until you see the interior."

As Tom mounted the steps, he felt like he was stepping into a dream. This had always been his secret aspiration. The idea of being able to fly whenever and wherever you want, on your own schedule, with whomever you chose to invite along, was the ultimate freedom.

He'd never truly believed the day would come to pass. But then, he never believed a website he created would become a household word either. It was an insane thought. With thirty billion tucked away, one hundred and fifty million didn't seem so outlandish.

The jet had cost much more than that, of course, by the time he was done customizing the interior and keeping a few pilots on call twenty-four seven. He didn't care. To Tom, it also served to feed his malnourished ego.

Despite international success, he had a deep sense of insecurity that no amount of money would heal. Not professionally or business-wise. Tom knew exactly what his standing was in that sense. He was now a major player, and his face was popping up on TV and magazine covers with regularity.

It was when Tom looked at himself on those covers, or in the mirror, that his insecurity kicked in. In early childhood, Tom learned he was ugly. Beginning in kindergarten, his classmates pointed and laughed at him.

Tom's full adult height was five foot five. His facial features were odd, his eyes a little too far apart, and one of them was noticeably lower than the other. The first time he was called Quasimodo was in sixth grade. He started losing his hair very early, and by the time he was twenty-three, the remaining hair on his head formed a strange pattern that served as a type of partner in crime, and rival, with Tom's eye deformity. Both competed in his head for the first-place insecurity trophy.

His scars ran deep. This big, shiny new toy of his was just his latest attempt to convince himself he was better than his appearance. He wasn't just Quasimodo.

As he entered the plane's doorway, he took in all the completed changes and additions he'd requested.

Tom made his way toward the back of the plane. He crossed through the dining room, several guest cabins, the home theater, until reaching his bedroom suite. He dropped onto the bed and stretched out. He breathed it all in and thought of how far he had come since first fantasizing about this, enjoying a rare bit of self-congratulation. It lasted several seconds until his old demons bullied their way to the front of his mind and kicked out the positive thoughts.

Quasimodo did pretty good, he thought.

A cell phone rang on the nightstand, but it wasn't his ringtone.

"Hello?" Tom answered.

"Hi, Mr. Ackerman. I was hoping I could take a moment or two of your time."

"Uh, I'm sorry. Who is this?"

"My name is James Winthrop, and I'm sitting in the car beside your new plane. Congratulations, by the way. It's a thing of beauty."

Tom walked to the nearest window. Indeed, parked beside the plane was a long black SUV.

"I assure you, Mr. Ackerman. You'll be very interested in this."

———•———

As Tom walked down the plane's steps, his security detail waited at the bottom. The two men were enormous with shoulders as wide as refrigerators.

"How's it look, Mr. A?" one of them asked.

"It's better than I hoped."

When Tom was several steps from the bottom, he paused and motioned for the bodyguard to come closer so he could talk privately without the huge man having to bend down.

"How long has that car been here?" Tom whispered.

"About ten minutes. Want us to get rid of them?"

Tom looked at the SUV as he spoke. "No. But the guy inside wants to talk to me, and I don't know who he is."

The bodyguard turned to the car, then to his partner. "Go see who's inside."

Tom watched his second bodyguard walk to the car. As he did, the driver and two equally large men in suits got out of the car to greet him. He offered his hand to Tom's man.

They spoke briefly, and the driver opened the back door so Tom's guard could look inside.

He rejoined Tom and his partner. "There's an older gentleman inside named James Winthrop. His guys told me they'll stay outside the car with the driver while you two talk. I think he wants to discuss doing business with you."

The first guard spoke up. "You want to talk to him or just leave?"

"I'll talk to him. I'm curious," Tom said.

He walked to the car with his guards and peeked inside to

see a white-haired man, presumably James Winthrop, smile back at him.

He looks harmless enough, Tom thought.

"Please," Winthrop said, motioning for him to get in.

Cautiously, Tom slid into the back seat and the door was closed.

"I'm so glad to meet you," he said, offering his hand. "James Winthrop."

"Tom Ackerman."

"That is a beautiful aircraft you have there."

"Thanks."

"Whiskey?" Winthrop offered, pointing to a small bar with sparkling glasses.

Tom shook his head.

"I must say I'm extremely jealous of you. No matter how much I try to brainwash myself into believing I'm a self-made man, I know I inherited most of it. And you are actually the real deal."

Tom smiled and shrugged off the compliment.

"What did your father do for a living?" Winthrop asked.

Tom had a feeling the cagey old man already knew, but he answered anyway. "He sold insurance."

"Amazing," Winthrop replied. "How old are you?"

"I just turned twenty-eight."

"Fuck me," Winthrop said. "Twenty-eight!"

"I was very lucky. I happened upon something at the right time, at the right place, at the—"

"Oh, nonsense." Winthrop grinned. "Save the modesty for when you're talking to the poor or the press. You're among friends here."

Tom laughed. He liked the guy. "What did you want to talk about, sir?"

"Before I get to that, let me ask you a few questions. Bear with an old man."

Tom smiled.

Winthrop took a sip of his whiskey. As his sleeve pulled

back, Tom noticed the Rolex he sported was unique from any other he'd ever seen.

"Do you have any religious beliefs?" Winthrop asked.

"No. Not really," he answered. "I was born Jewish, but my parents weren't very observant."

Where the hell is this going? Tom asked himself. *Who is this guy, and what does he want?*

"I don't want to be rude, but I have plans tonight and..."

"What if I told you that the answers to many of life's mysteries could be available to you?"

Tom was taken back. The question came across both serious and yet half-hearted at the same time. The older man smirked and raised an eyebrow. Tom felt like he was being pranked.

"You mean like who really shot Kennedy?" Tom chuckled.

Winthrop took another sip of whiskey, then swirled his glass to make the ice cubes click before looking Tom directly in the eye. "Yes."

Tom's smile dropped. *He's serious.*

A long moment passed as Tom's mind raced.

Winthrop sat back and said nothing. The older man simply watched Tom's eyes bounce between belief and doubt. "I have a more important question for you."

Tom was spellbound. "I can't wait."

"Do you believe in UFOs?" Winthrop asked point-blank.

The question took Tom off guard. His pulse quickened. "Well, I, I'm not sure."

"I think you are."

How the hell could he know? It's impossible.

———•———

When Tom was a junior in high school, he went on a school retreat with sixty other students. A handful of teachers went along as well, one of them being Mr. Feldberg, the history teacher. Tom got the feeling Mr. Feldberg was a geek at heart too, and often he and Tom had fun conversations on a wide range of topics.

Unfortunately, he wasn't in Mr. Feldberg's group on this

trip. He got stuck with Mr. Daniels, whose attention was spent mostly on the pretty underage girls. The idea of being under his protection among a bunch of jocks who made a regular habit of torturing him put him on edge. Tom had to share a cabin with Ronnie and Sal, assholes who never missed a chance to put him in a headlock or throw a fake punch at him.

"Hey, Quasimodo," Ronnie said. "If I was you, I wouldn't fall asleep." Then he laughed along with Sal as the two Neanderthals high-fived.

Shit. May as well not sleep at all, Tom thought.

They taunted him about it constantly as they walked the trail with the group and took part in team-building exercises that lasted all day until lights-out.

"Nighty night, Q!" They laughed.

Tom was exhausted but didn't dare fall asleep. He listened to them rate the girls and play cards for what seemed like hours until they finally nodded off. Only then did he allow his heavy lids to close.

———·———

Huh...? He thought as he woke up.

Tom was still in bed, but the bed was moving, bouncing all over the place.

What the hell?

His immediate thought was an earthquake. He quickly ran through emergency tips and remembered to get under a doorframe. As he tried to rise, he discovered something was holding him down. He was stuck in place in the darkness, like a fly in a web. His heart pounded as panic set in.

He heard laughing, somehow underneath him.

What is under my bed?

His eyes adjusted to the dark, and he saw the night sky come into focus above tall pine trees stretching upward. He realized the cabin was gone. Increasing terror jolted him awake fully, and he grasped what was happening. Ronnie and Sal had duct-taped him to his mattress and were now carrying him over their heads into the woods.

He tried to speak, but his mouth was covered as well.

Fuck! he thought. *I am so sick of this shit!*

He tried to shake himself loose, but it was no use.

"Hey!" Ronnie said. "Don't bounce around, or we might drop your nerdy ass!"

Sal just laughed, an annoying high-pitched laugh that would make him the butt of endless jokes at his telemarketing job years down the line.

When they found a spot Ronnie deemed appropriate, they placed Tom on the ground by the lake and then removed the tape from his mouth.

"Guys, please! Let me go!"

The begging only elicited more laughter.

"Watch out for bears!" Ronnie said as he and Sal walked away.

"Hey!" Tom yelled. "HEY!"

The two morons laughed as they faded into the darkness of the woods.

"You guys! This is dangerous! There might really be bears out here! GUYS! GUYS!"

Even as he panicked, he felt like an impostor for using the word *guys*. It was too familiar. It implied that he considered himself one of them when he knew, in an unspoken agreement with them, he was so much of an outsider as to be from a different species.

Their laughter faded in the distance. Tom was alone, unless you counted the thousands of living creatures that filled the woods around him, which was the thought that frightened him the most. When he stopped struggling to catch his breath, he laid his head back and saw millions of stars.

Something else caught his eye. It was down by the horizon, where the ocean of stars sank into the dark ripples of the lake. There was no moon, but something was illuminating the water. A greenish blur that seemed to grow larger by the second.

Tom realized it wasn't growing in size; it was getting closer. As it did, he saw quick flashes of light pop from it.

What is it? If it was a helicopter, I'd be able to hear it. It doesn't look like a plane either. UFO?

Even a teenage mind can be molded by society into becoming cynical toward such things, and his was no exception. He quickly tried to debunk the idea. Now that the thing was a hundred yards away and getting closer, there was no room for false skepticism.

Suddenly, the constant sound of crickets stopped short. So did the tree frogs and whatever else was responsible for the forest orchestra that had been playing. It happened so abruptly that for a few seconds Tom thought he'd gone deaf.

Hovering thirty feet above the lake was a craft unlike any he'd ever seen. There were no wings. It was not round but had curves. The surface looked like smooth, beveled glass. Various colored lines ran throughout the translucent shell of the craft. In other areas, there were what could only be described as windows. They were the same texture as the body but had lights glowing from within. It was those lights that were reflecting on the surface of the lake.

There was no denying it now. Tom was looking at an actual alien spaceship. Time itself slowed down to him as he stared, spellbound.

A glow on the bottom of the craft grew wider, and a bright beam of light shot down onto the water. Tom craned his neck to look. The water in the beam's circumference went from pitch-black to so bright that it looked like daytime.

A hum came from the craft, and immediately following it, the beam of light. Within a fraction of a second, its radius grew, stretching out and over everything from the horizon to the tops of the pine trees that circled the lake, then promptly disappeared.

The instant it finished, the entire craft moved silently through the air until it hovered directly above Tom.

"Oh man."

Tom was already afraid, but now he felt all the pores in his face open and push out sweat. The hum started again.

A thin beam shot out from the bottom of the craft, this time placing a small circle of light on Tom's duct-taped legs.

He craned his head up to be able to see his illuminated legs. *Oh. My. God.*

His legs were completely transparent within the circle of light. He could see his blood coursing through his veins, his fat tissue, his muscles twitching, his femur bone shivering.

The hum grew louder. Tom had no idea what would happen next.

Is it going to take my legs? Is it going to kill me?

"No!" he screamed. "Please NOOOOOOOOO..."

The beam shut off, along with the hum. Tom's legs were back to normal. The opening at the bottom of the craft closed, and it slowly floated back out over the lake again. Tom watched the craft slowly ascend to the star-filled sky.

It didn't shoot away or zip across the sky as he'd seen in movies. It just simply ascended higher and higher until it disappeared into the stars, like a released balloon at a backyard birthday party. The forest came alive again.

Teenage Tom Ackerman, bound and left in the dark woods by bullies, looked up into that vast, starry sky... and smiled.

———•———

Twenty-eight-year-old Tom looked at James Winthrop with a mix of curiosity and confusion.

"I know you once saw something you can't explain," Winthrop said.

"How do you know about that?" Tom asked.

Winthrop sat back in his seat. "I apologize. I could arguably say I know everything there is to know about you. Before I offer an invitation, I have to make sure. My associates have spoken with hundreds of people about you. You've met and passed every guideline. I'd like to offer you something. Something that few people in the world can claim to possess... the truth."

Tom cracked a smile. "So that *is* what's going on. A sales pitch."

"Fair enough," Winthrop replied. "I'm inviting you to join a club. The most exclusive club in the world. We meet several times a year. Our members include billionaires like yourself and world leaders."

"I'm not really into golfing."

Winthrop grinned. "It's not that kind of club. This club's main activity is learning and sharing the answers to all the world's secrets."

Tom listened as Winthrop's words took on an air of excitement, like a master storyteller weaving a tale.

"Only the most elite are members. If you join us, you will see many things that will alter your sense of reality." Winthrop smiled. The wrinkles around his eyes deepened.

"That sounds pretty intense," Tom replied. "And what's the cost to join this club?"

"We can discuss that after you see it."

Tom was intrigued. "What if, after attending, I turn you down?"

A warm smile crossed Winthrop's face. "Then you simply don't join. I would only ask that you never mention anything you see or hear… and would kindly ask you to sign an NDA to that effect, with an exorbitant penalty, of course. The things you'll experience have been hidden from the world at large for many years and must be kept secret. That said, I have no concern at all that you would decline once you've attended."

Tom looked out the tinted window at his plane. Everything Winthrop said carried such confidence.

"You don't have to take my word for it." Winthrop took out his phone and initiated a FaceTime call.

After a couple of rings, the face of movie mogul Bryan Blackstone came on-screen. Blackstone was the epitome of Hollywood royalty, having directed or produced more than a dozen blockbusters over the past forty years. Four of them held positions among the top-ten-grossing films of all time. His face was as globally familiar as the stars of his films.

"Hello, James," Blackstone said happily.

"Wait. What?" Tom gasped.

While he'd enjoyed rubbing elbows with celebrities since

becoming wealthy, Bryan Blackstone was another matter altogether. Since childhood, Tom had spent more time with the characters in Blackstone's films than he had with actual friends. The name *Blackstone* to Tom brought with it magic and the brighter aspects of his childhood nostalgia. Now here he was, on a FaceTime call with the man. Winthrop summoned Tom to get closer so that he could include him on the screen.

"Bryan, I'm sitting here with Tom Ackerman, the young man who started LittleBirdy."

"I love that app," Blackstone said.

"I don't believe this. Mr. Blackstone. I've been a megafan of yours my entire life."

"That's kind of you to say. Please call me Bryan."

Tom shuffled in his seat, unable to stop moving. His hands nervously fiddled.

Winthrop said, "Bryan, I'm trying to convince this young man to consider joining our little club."

"Absolutely you should join," Blackstone said. "Tom, you'll enjoy it more than I could ever explain. I've been a member for over fifteen years, and I couldn't imagine my life without it."

"Wow." Tom grinned.

Winthrop smiled. "Okay, Bryan. Thanks for taking the time."

"Don't be silly," Blackstone replied. "Happy to help get some new blood."

"You'll be there this weekend, yes?" Winthrop asked.

"Absolutely. I can't make the dinner on Friday because we're doing a last-minute reshoot, but I'll definitely be there for Saturday night."

"In doing my due diligence, I discovered that Tom is a huge *Ten Day Wait* fan," Winthrop said.

"The greatest movie of all time," Tom added excitedly.

"Well, I wouldn't go that far. Tell you what, Tom… Saturday night, you and I will sit down with some drinks and I'll tell you all the crazy stuff that happened on that one."

"Are you kidding me?" Tom burst out. "I would love that!"

"Done!" Blackstone said. "James, I need to catch up with you as well."

Winthrop replied, "I look forward to it. See you Saturday."

"See you then. Great meeting you, Tom," Blackstone said.

"You too!"

Winthrop ended the call and turned to Tom with a smile.

Tom leaned forward. "Saturday night where?"

Winthrop laughed.

9

FOLLOWING THE MONEY

I *WOULD TAKE YOU IF I could, but you're going to have to find it on your own.*" Kirby's fingers flew over his keyboard. He'd been up since six a.m., digging through everything he'd accumulated over the past year.

He knew he was right about all this. It was the only thing that made sense. He'd researched everything he could find about what each billionaire did while they were in town the last few times they visited. He discovered that while they took part in individual activities, various dinners and meetings, they also always appeared all together at one event.

From the *Boston Herald* two years earlier:

AUCTION ATTRACTS WORLD'S RICHEST

The Sotheby's Auction over the weekend drew some of the world's wealthiest, including real estate giant James Winthrop and Japanese manufacturer Keiji Fujiyama. The items included an original Claude Monet oil painting, which sold for $85 million; a Samuel Colt revolver once used by Billy the Kid for $23 million; and the highlight of the auction, a recently discovered sword owned by Julius Caesar brought in a staggering $135 million.

Each article mentioned the fact that at least once during each trip, all the billionaires were at the same place at the same time.

Another from the *Boston Globe* the year before:

SHOW ME THE MONEY!

Not one, not two, but a dozen billionaires attended the gala opening of the brand-new Boston Fine Arts Museum on Boylston Street. Its star-studded grand opening Friday had an invite-only guest list that included Beantown's richest residents and the uberwealthy from around the globe. The current exhibit focused on the lesser-known works by the masters of French impressionism. The world's upper crust enjoyed champagne and seafood hors d'oeuvres as they took in the paintings, pastels, charcoal sketches, and other collected works by Monet, Van Gogh, Cassatt, and many others. Several of the visiting billionaires were also seen coming and going from the Tremont, long considered one of the country's most elite private clubs.

Kirby discovered that on every trip, these men stayed at the Tremont Club. Apparently it was one of the dozens of ultra-high-end private clubs around the world. These clubs charged hundreds of thousands to join.

The Tremont, however, differed from the rest. It wasn't listed anywhere. Whoever ran it didn't appear to do any promotion at all. Although all maintained a strong sense of privacy, Kirby could still find mentions of them in various top ten private clubs articles or other Lifestyles of the Rich & Famous type stories. The Tremont only existed when mentioned with these visiting billionaires. There were no articles about it, no marketing to be found.

If there really was a secret society keeping the world's secrets, the Tremont would be the kind of place they would go. Kirby leaned back from his screen.

Is this the place Towne was talking about? Do they have actual evidence?

The idea that there was definitive proof of cryptid creatures being kept secret by billionaires had long been an obsession. Now that Towne might have pointed him to a location, he decided to take a closer look.

He knew he'd never get inside, but maybe he could learn something from poking around outside. The truth was, he just had to see it, to get close to it.

Kirby gathered his equipment and put together a gear bag with everything he might need. He grabbed his trusty Canon 5D Mark III and stuck a 400mm lens into the bag with it. He picked up his drone, made sure it was charged, and placed it into the bag as well, along with backup batteries. Excitement filled him as he headed out. For the first time in years, he felt he was on to something.

10

BAIT & SWITCH

KELSEY STEPPED OUT OF THE bedroom, wearing a short miniskirt, thigh-high boots, and more makeup than she'd ever worn before. She wasn't sure how Vic would react to the outfit. Part of her hoped it would alter the mood and trigger an apology from him.

He broke the silence, but his eyes stayed on the TV screen and the air remained thick. "Who's picking you up?"

"Bailey."

"What time are you going until?"

"Two a.m."

Minutes passed with no further talk. Her phone buzzed with a text message, and she replied with a voice text.

"Okay. Out in a minute."

She looked back at Vic, his face still staring at the TV screen. *Come on, you stubborn asshole. Apologize.*

"See you later."

"Okay." His voice was flat and he didn't look at her.

She closed the door behind her.

An hour later, Kelsey walked along Stuart Street and tried not to trip in the four-inch-heel boots she thought would've been

Vic's favorite part of her getup. She'd even predicted that he'd joke about her keeping them.

Sure called that one wrong.

Many of the missing prostitutes were last seen in this area. Detective Bailey watched her from an unmarked car. At the other end of the street, Detective Wrigley and another cop, Duff, were inside a van, ready for anything. It was past midnight on a Tuesday, and everything was slowing down. The bars were still open, but the restaurants were locking up. It had rained earlier in the day, and the street was still wet. Streetlights, neon signs, and headlights reflected on the slick pavement.

Kelsey looked down at her ring finger. She hated to see it bare, but an engagement ring didn't go with the rest of the getup. She half expected to see a stripe of lighter skin, but she and Vic hadn't spent enough time outside lately. Wrigley's voice came through her ear radio.

"There's a hooker coming your way. Remember, if she gets territorial, just walk away."

Kelsey saw the prostitute approaching. She was too heavy for the spandex miniskirt she wore. Her eyes focused on Kelsey, and she didn't look friendly.

"Hey," she said.

"What's up?" Kelsey replied.

She looked Kelsey up and down and smiled. "Nighty night, Officer," the hooker said and walked on by.

What? How the hell can she tell? Kelsey thought.

The cops heard the exchange over their radios.

"Son of a bitch," Wrigley said.

Kelsey looked over her outfit, curious what might have given her away.

"How'd she know?" Kelsey whispered to her radio audience.

"I know what it is," Duff said.

"Well?" Wrigley asked, "How?"

"With all due respect, Kelsey," Duff said, "you're too hot to be a street hooker."

Wrigley chimed in. "Oh jeez."

Kelsey turned toward the van.

"It's true," Duff continued. "A high-end Vegas call girl, maybe. But not a—"

"Okay. I get it," Kelsey said.

———•———

By two a.m., her feet were killing her. She'd circled her route over and over and gotten in and out of several undercover cars to maintain the act.

"Okay, guys," she said. "I'm wiped."

"Yeah. Let's pack it in," Wrigley said into his radio, "Bailey, pick her up and take her back to the station."

"Will do," Bailey replied.

The thought of kicking off the heels filled Kelsey with silent glee.

Thank God, she thought as she took a few steps to the curb. The corner of Warrenton and Stuart was so quiet now... barely any cars passed by at all.

Truth be told, Kelsey was more than ready to get out of there. There was something creepy in the air downtown at this time of night that the streetlights didn't erase. As she waited for Bailey, she heard something in the alley behind her. She turned and heard it again... a weak voice coming from the darkness.

"Help me." The voice was childlike and pitiful.

"Hello?" Kelsey said.

Wrigley's voice answered through her ear radio. "Yeah, Kelsey?"

"No, not you...," she replied. "There's someone hurt. One sec."

She entered the alley, but it was too dark to see where the voice had come from. The light from the nearest streetlight faded across the bricks of the alley wall with each step. She winced at the stench of urine.

"Please... help me," the voice whimpered.

Kelsey used her phone as a flashlight and tried to make out shapes ahead of her. As she squinted, a large hand covered her mouth and she felt a bee sting on her neck. Without thinking, her martial arts training kicked in. She peeled off the hand, twisted her attacker's wrist, and jerked his arm back, forcing him to bend over so she could get behind him. Kelsey shoved his face against the brick wall of the alley. He was big, maybe six-three.

"Gum!" she yelled into her ear radio. "Get in here! Now!"

Wrigley, Duff, and Bailey scrambled to get to her. Wrigley threw the van into drive, but as he peeled out of the parking spot, a bus came to a stop and blocked them in. He slammed on the brakes and the van heaved forward on its shocks, causing Duff to crash to the floor.

"Damn it!" Wrigley yelled.

He pushed his door open and ran toward the alley with Duff following behind.

Her attacker pushed off the wall, knocking Kelsey backward over some boxes and trash. She got to her feet, but as she turned to defend herself, the alley itself started to twist and turn in a crazy way that didn't make any sense. She also felt her lips go numb and the sensation of a hundred tiny little needles poking her face.

Kelsey looked down. The floor of the alley suddenly started to spin beneath her feet as if she were on a merry-go-round. She took a couple of steps to try to keep up with it, but everything went black.

The man threw her over his shoulder and disappeared into the darkness of the alley.

Less than thirty seconds later, Bailey's car screeched to a stop by the alley, followed immediately by Wrigley on foot. The detectives ran into the alley with guns drawn.

"Kelsey!" Wrigley yelled. "Where are you?"

Bailey's flashlight caught something. Kelsey's purse was lying on the ground, just a few feet away from her ear radio.

"Gum!" Bailey said as he pointed his beam at the items.

"Fuck!" Wrigley yelled. His heart dropped, and a numbing

cloud filled his head as he pulled out his radio. "This is Wrigley at Warrenton and Stuart! I need backup units immediately! Possible officer abduction!"

Bailey took off farther into the alley, dodging trash and discarded junk. Wrigley was frantic. They'd planned and taken every precaution for a vehicle arrest, not for something this bold.

Wrigley turned to Duff. "Did you see any cars pulling away? Anything?"

"Nothing."

Wrigley ran into the alley after Bailey. It emptied on Warrenton Street, where a small theater was letting out its late show. Audience members filled the street out front. There were a few hundred of them talking, smoking, and waiting for the valet. Wrigley shoved through them as he tried to look over and past them. There was no sign of Kelsey. Bailey came running back to Wrigley and shook his head, his face pale.

———·———

Twenty minutes later, Vic's car screeched to a halt at the scene. The transmission banged as he threw it into park before he stopped. There were now cops and flashing red and blue lights everywhere. He cut through them, his heart thundering in his chest. He was consumed with more anger than fear, and it was all over his face. People got out of his way as he stormed toward Wrigley's full unit, who were arguing and yelling at each other.

The instant they saw him approach, the shouting stopped. Wrigley stepped out from behind the others.

"Vic," he said, "I... I... We're going to..." He stopped talking when he saw the rage in Vic's eyes.

Vic broke into a full run at him.

"Vic! Please! Wait!" Wrigley stammered.

Despite everyone trying to stop him, Vic tackled him and landed multiple blows to his face. Bedlam erupted. It took five of them to restrain him. He screamed and struggled until his fury finally broke. He was trapped in a tornado of two emotions he rarely felt—utter panic and complete helplessness. His entire world was blasted into disarray.

11

NIGHTMARE TO NIGHTMARE

KELSEY DREAMED SHE WAS LAUGHING with Vic. Their friends were there too. It was a birthday party or some other kind of joyful occasion. Drinks were raised, the atmosphere pure fun. There was no actual talk. It was like the happiest moment of the night had dissolved into a slow-motion movie.

Suddenly Kelsey's smile faded. Something was wrong. She turned to look at Vic to see if he noticed the mood change as well, but it was no longer Vic beside her. It was a dead man with a decomposed face and a bullet hole in the center of his forehead. His name was Harvey Wilcox, the first murder victim Kelsey had ever seen up close.

This wasn't the first time she'd dreamed of Harvey Wilcox. He'd popped up a dozen times over the years, turning dreams into nightmares. Kelsey sometimes went years without a Harvey nightmare, but in times of high stress, he always showed up.

She was a rookie when she'd first encountered the real Harvey Wilcox. She was working the scene of his murder, keeping civilians out of the way and assisting the detectives. He was a shut-in and his body hadn't been discovered for several months. The landlord found him on his apartment floor in a dried puddle of blood that almost perfectly circled his head.

A detective called Kelsey over to the body. Up until that point, she'd only gotten a view of his feet between the many people working the scene in the room. The face was horrifying. It was frozen in the last awful expression he'd worn when he was killed, one of pure fear. The eyes were wide open but looked more like crumpled grapes with pupils painted on than actual eyes. The skin was gray and dry, unnaturally wrinkled as it lay over the protruding cheekbones underneath.

The detective asked Kelsey to get the landlord. Halfway through her stride, she looked down at Harvey's face again. Her gaze happened to fall directly in line with Harvey's death stare. As his horrific face glared at her, a camera flash went off, causing the illusion that Harvey's face was moving.

Kelsey tripped and fell on top of the body, producing loud crunches as Harvey's rib cage snapped beneath her. She felt all eyes on her and her head went numb. Her stomach turned and she felt vomit rising.

Oh God, no.

They all stared. Most judged. A few groaned. It was the worst moment of her career.

Ever since, when something was bothering her, Harvey Wilcox visited her dreams. He lumbered after her with his decayed hands outstretched like the Frankenstein monster. With nowhere to run, she would feel Harvey's ice-cold fingers grab her until she screamed herself awake, as she did now.

Her eyes began to work, but everything was still hazy. A ceiling with fluorescent lights came into focus: Bluish-gray walls, bluish-gray floor. Yet there was something familiar... the smell. The room smelled like the floor and stairs of her grammar school when she came back after summer break and everything was freshly painted. Kelsey hadn't smelled that aroma in twenty years, yet it all came back to her in a nanosecond.

She found herself lying on a mattress on a cement slab. Her back ached as she pushed herself up onto her elbow. Her head felt like it did coming out of surgery after her appendectomy.

Oooh. Damn.

She lay back down.

"Take it slow," a voice said.

Kelsey looked to her right where two women sat on mattresses against a wall. As her vision came more into focus, she could see the voice belonged to a woman, most likely around twenty but maybe younger. Her eyes were bloodshot, and she looked exhausted.

The second woman, like the first, also looked like she'd been through hell. She sat against the wall with her chin on her knees, her hands wrapped around her shins.

Kelsey tried to process everything. She saw the girls were in their underwear and realized she was as well.

Where am I? How did I get here?

Her mind started to piece it all back together. The sting operation. The van. She still couldn't remember how she got here though. She was in the alley, fighting that guy, then... nothing.

"You don't look like no ho," the first girl said.

"I'm not," Kelsey said. "Do you know how you got here?"

"I got grabbed by some psycho like in the movies," the woman said. "I got into a car. Then everything went black."

"Do you know how long you've been here?" Kelsey asked.

The girl stood up and stretched. "About three or four days, I think."

"I'm Kelsey."

"Annika," the girl replied. "That's Gia."

Kelsey turned to the other girl. "Hey."

Without moving anything but her hand, Gia waved but stayed silent.

"She don't talk much," Annika said.

Kelsey scoped out the room. It was a typical cell: four cement walls, about fifteen square feet. There was a stainless steel toilet and sink combo in one corner next to a bolted-down trash can. The room had no windows except for a small two-way mirror on a steel door. The door also had a sliding slot, presumably for meals.

"Has someone been bringing you food?" Kelsey asked.

Annika walked over to the door as she answered. "Yeah. But not the guy I got into the car with."

So there's at least two. "Has he said anything to you?"

"No," Annika said. "Nothing. He just puts the food down and leaves."

"Have you heard or seen anyone else?"

"No," Annika answered. "You ask questions like a cop."

"I am a cop," Kelsey said.

"For real?"

"Yep."

Annika kept talking, but her words faded into background noise as Kelsey turned back to the door and tried to figure out her next move.

12

DIGGING

K IRBY SAT ON A BENCH in the Common across the street
from the Tremont. As his fingers worked the controls, his
drone hovered high over the Tremont's roof. He kept it at least
two hundred feet above the building so no one would hear the
loud hum of the drone's rotors.

Kirby knew it was safer this way. The drone shot in full 4K
resolution, so even from farther up, he'd be able to zoom in on
the footage later and have crisp results. He turned his toggle,
and the drone zipped over to the building beside it, the
Harvard Trucking Company. He adjusted the gimbal, aimed
the camera down at the roof, and recorded from various
angles.

There was something mysterious about the building itself.
Kirby knew in his bones he was on the right track.

Vic didn't sleep for over twenty-four hours. His every moment
was spent trying to find anything that could lead to Kelsey. He
pored over the details of the other missing person cases. He read
and reread the witness statements and went back to the location
multiple times, hoping to see something he'd missed.

For the first few hours after she disappeared, he felt the
urge to yell that he'd been proven right. Each time the urge

rose, it was immediately followed by waves of self-loathing and transformed into unbearable regret. It clung to him like dead weight around his chest. The memory of how cold he'd acted the last time he saw her played on a loop in his mind.

"See you later."

"Okay."

He and Tony watched footage from all the security cameras in the area. Vic studied every frame over and over until his eyes blurred.

When trying to convince Vic to get some rest proved useless, Tony put some Valium into his soda. Even as it took effect, Tony still had to argue with him as he pulled him out of his chair and onto the couch in the break room.

The pills only kept him down for a few hours, and then he was back at his desk.

His mind bounced between reality and imagination. One part objectively began to process the facts and concluded the woman he loved was gone forever. It began to consider harsh possibilities, like the thoughts of having a funeral service and how he could go on without ever seeing her face again. It was like a part of his brain was trying to move forward, to guide him out of the pain.

The other part exploded forward with dreadful thoughts... What were her last moments like? Had she already had them? How horrific was it? Was she hoping and praying he would burst in to save her at the last moment? Was she screaming his name?

Everyone in the station grieved with him. They also knew him well enough to know the best thing they could do was give him space.

———•———

Vic went home for the first time since she disappeared. The only light in the bedroom came from the hall, but Vic could still see enough of his reflection in the mirror to know Tony was right. He needed rest if he was going to keep a clear head.

He'd been going nonstop since she was taken, working every possible angle. His eyes were glassy and bloodshot, and he smelled like a locker room. Vic plopped down on the edge of the bed, exhausted but still unable to shut off his mind. He took off one of his shoes and fell so deeply into his thoughts and fears that twenty minutes passed before he took off the other one.

On the dresser was a framed photo of him with Kelsey.

Kel.

It was a perfect shot of a perfect day. A friend who was a professional photographer took it at a backyard barbeque. He remembered Kelsey's reaction the first time she saw the photo.

"I love how he made the background blurry like that. He's good. Maybe he can shoot the wedding!"

Vic's stomach turned. Tears filled his eyes until the room took on the look of a watery funhouse mirror. He screamed her name so loud the neighbors heard him.

13

A STRAW TO GRASP

WHEN TONY PICKED HIM UP the next morning, Vic looked like he'd barely slept, but at least he smelled better.

"You showered? Thank Christ."

"Fuck off."

He wanted to go straight to work, but Tony insisted he get some food in him. At a diner on the way to the station, they ate mostly in silence until Vic finally spoke up.

"It's killing me I don't know what else to do." He looked at Tony, feeling utterly pitiful. "What are we missing?" he asked, more to himself than to Tony.

Something on the TV mounted above the counter caught his attention.

"...and if you wanted to catch a glimpse of the recently discovered Egyptian pharaoh and many of his priceless belongings, you're out of luck. The exhibit will be held at the Tremont, the elite private club downtown, and it's strictly members only. Planned attendees include some of the country's wealthiest, such as Douglas Radcliffe, Tom Ackerman, and media mogul Bryan Blackstone. Weather-wise..."

Vic's mind flashed back to Kirby's prediction that after the next prostitute abductions, the richest people in the country would all come to Boston for some kind of event. He jumped out of his seat and ran closer to the TV.

Tony wasn't making the connection. He walked to Vic.

"What?" Tony asked.

"That kid," Vic said. "The thing the kid said about the billionaires flying in."

Tony turned toward the TV, but the anchor had moved on to the next story.

For the first time in days, Vic entertained a small amount of hope.

"That kid who came in with the crazy theory about Hamilton Towne? Do you have his name anywhere?"

"No. He knew your brother though."

"That's right."

"But you're not actually considering what that nutbag said, are you?" Tony asked.

"He said some crazy shit, yeah. But he also said the rich fucks would come to town after the fourth abduction. Kelsey would be the fourth." Vic nodded.

"Shit."

Vic threw some cash down, pulled out his phone, and bolted for the door. Tony grabbed the last sausage from his plate and chased after him.

———·———

Kirby's mom was clearly concerned about two plainclothes cops asking to see her son. To calm her down and save time, Vic said they needed to hire a videographer for a party.

As she showed them to the door that led to the basement, Vic took in all the hanging family photos on the walls. They ranged from five-by-sevens to eight-by-tens in various unmatched frames.

He noticed the dad was only in the older photos. The more recent photos featured Kirby and his mom without him.

Not divorce. The dad's in too many of them. Nope. Kirby's dad's dead.

He made a mental note to be a little kinder to the kid. When they reached the bottom of the stairs, Vic's eyes were immediately drawn to Kirby's wall. Hundreds of photos and artist renderings of Bigfoot, aliens, and every other possible creature you could imagine.

Oh jeez.

His heart sank as almost two decades of untrustworthy witnesses flooded his mind. Over the years, he'd gotten to the point where he'd dump an informant at the hint of a red flag suggesting lies or exaggeration. Now he found himself needing help from someone whose credibility was beyond laughable. He knew if it were anyone other than Kelsey he was trying to find, he'd walk out before hitting the bottom step.

Even without the headphones on, Kirby most likely wouldn't have heard the two men enter. He was deep in the zone, focusing on his computer. Vic tapped him on the shoulder.

"Shit!" Kirby yelled. He took off his headphones, more than a little self-conscious. "Jesus."

His embarrassment quickly turned to curiosity.

"What's going on?"

"Listen… I need your help. It's important," Vic said.

Kirby shot him a look. "My help? Why? You need a few laughs?"

"Yeah, well… Sorry," Vic replied. "Something you said might be true."

"You don't say."

"Look, kid. Don't be a dick," Tony replied.

"Just answer a few questions for me, okay?"

"Fine," Kirby said. "Have a seat."

Kirby pointed to the sofa and wheeled his chair around to face them.

———•———

Tony wouldn't say it, but he feared Vic was letting his emotions affect his judgment. For the time being, and with the lack of anything else to go on, he gave him the benefit of the doubt. A little hope would be good for him.

"You here because of the billionaires coming in for the pharaoh thing?" Kirby asked.

"Yeah," Vic answered.

"Another person was taken?"

"As a matter of fact, yes," Vic said.

"I knew it. Was she a hooker?"

"She was dressed like a hooker, yeah. I need you to tell me everything you know about this."

"Dressed like a hooker? She wasn't a hooker?"

Vic stood up and ran his hand over his forehead and through his hair. "Actually, she was an undercover cop posing as a hooker."

"Shit," Kirby said. "She a friend of yours?"

"She's my fiancée."

Kirby sat up. Now it all made sense. His heart immediately went out to Vic as he imagined what horrific thoughts must be filling the detective's head.

"Oh my god. I'm sorry."

Vic saw the sincerity in his eyes and took a few steps closer. As he did, he also saw the many photos on the wall of Bigfoot, UFOs, and other silly things and immediately shut them out of his head before they could trigger any doubt and destroy his hope.

"I need to know how you knew those billionaires would be coming in. Tell me everything."

———•———

After Kirby explained what had brought him to his conclusions, he wrapped it up with the call from Hamilton Towne.

"The thing is, Towne had terminal cancer and may have been on some heavy-duty drugs when he called you," Vic pointed out.

"No way!" Kirby shook his head.

"Take it easy," Vic said. "Just tell me what else you have."

"Well, for one thing, every one of the billionaires who once talked about having a paranormal experience is a member of a private club downtown. The Tremont."

Vic didn't say anything, but Kirby could tell that didn't mean much to him.

"Towne told me there was a place he wished he could take me. I think that's the place. I did some digging. The guy who owns it is a billionaire named James Winthrop."

"We know that. Winthrop is a big donor to the police."

"Did you know that he also owns the building right next to the Tremont but under another name?"

"Which one?" Tony asked.

"The Harvard Trucking Company."

Vic sat forward, deflating a bit. "It's not uncommon for guys that wealthy to have properties under different companies."

"Maybe. But explain this… Years ago, it underwent a major renovation, and every contractor and all the workmen had to sign nondisclosure agreements."

"That's standard," Tony said.

"Yes, but after it was completed, six of the contractors died in freak accidents."

"How do you know that?" Vic asked.

"It's all online. I can show you." Kirby opened photos on his computer. "Look… Car accidents, accidental electrocutions, twenty-year-old healthy guys having heart attacks. It's way too strange."

Vic and Tony shared a glance.

"And check this out," Kirby said, pointing to his screen. "The trucking company is basically a hangar three stories high. It's not a skyscraper or anything. Why does it have six industrial-size A/C units on the roof? Holiday Inns don't have that many."

Vic's eyes narrowed as he studied the images.

"What does that have to do with anything?" Tony asked Kirby.

Kirby looked at them, unsure if he should answer. "If I tell you, you're probably going to just shit on me again."

"Try us," Vic said.

"Promise me you'll let me finish before you start laughing."

"Fine."

Kirby started pacing. "I think they've built something underground. A big space where they keep proof of paranormal stuff they keep secret from the rest of the world.

Like a..." Kirby read their expressions again before finishing the last part of his sentence. "...a secret museum."

Both Vic and Tony stared at him, expressionless.

Tony put his face in his hands.

Vic didn't laugh but seemed to focus harder on Kirby. "Kid," he said, "you've pointed out some strange things, but..."

"Wait. Just look." Kirby sat back down at his computer and opened up different photos. "Look at the walls around the trucking building. There's razor wire going around the whole building. Why would they need that?"

"Where did you get these photos?" Vic asked.

"I took them with my drone."

Vic looked over the photos of trucks coming and going out of the back entrance to the building.

"Wait a second," Tony said with a smile, clearly trying to be the voice of reason. "A bunch of A/C units doesn't mean there's some secret underground facility. This is one of the busiest parts of the city. You're talking about excavation and construction. How could anyone install something like that without anyone noticing?"

Kirby smiled. His face took on a cocky expression, like a poker player holding a royal flush. "The big renovation I mentioned took place from 1991 to 1993."

Tony didn't make the connection at first and looked at Vic.

"Jesus," Vic said. "During the Big Dig."

The words *Big Dig* still caused many Bostonians to have heart palpitations. It had been a massive construction project downtown that rerouted the central artery of Interstate 93 through the heart of the city. It was plagued with mistakes, failures, and corruption. The poor design and execution became a traffic nightmare that lasted years, cost billions of dollars, and also caused the city to become a national joke.

"They would have blended right in," Vic said under his breath.

"Wait a minute. You're talking about Tremont Street,"

Tony said. "That city block is dense with back-to-back buildings and structures. I'm not an engineer, but I understand basic physics. If there was a huge underground area like what you're describing, it wouldn't be able to support all those tons on top of it. The street would collapse."

It was a good point. It hung in the air until Vic's eyes widened.

"That's true," Vic said, "but the Common starts thirty feet from the Tremont's front door, just across the street. That's fifty acres of park with no structures on it."

Tony sat down on the sofa beneath an oversized poster of the famous shot of Bigfoot from the Patterson-Gimlin film. "I, uh…"

Vic looked at Kirby. "Kid, can you give us a minute?"

"Sure." He headed upstairs.

As soon as the basement door closed behind him, Tony stood up. "Look, I don't want to sound like a prick. You know I want to chase down every possible lead too, but this is crazy. I hope—"

Vic cut him off and spoke in a much lower voice. "No, no, no. Take the nutty stuff out of what he's saying. Clearly there's no secret monster museum club or whatever the hell he thinks it is underneath Boston Common."

Tony breathed a sigh of relief. "Oh. Thank Christ. I thought you'd lost it."

Vic went on. "But the kid has convinced me that *something* is going on here. It's just not what *he* thinks it is."

"What are you thinking?" Tony asked.

Vic considered the possibilities, each one growing more likely to him by the second. "Maybe some kind of high-end sex trafficking thing. A secret, rich man's S & M club. Something like that I can buy."

Tony nodded. "Could be, yeah. So, what do you wanna do?"

"I want to swing by there and check it out."

Kirby was coming back downstairs. "You have to take me with you."

"Sorry, kid. Can't do that," Vic said, waving a hand in front of him.

Kirby scowled. "Why not? I'm the one who told you about it."

Vic's mind was already working out reasons to give for entering the Tremont, and his jaw tightened as his thought process was interrupted by Kirby's pleadings. He motioned to Tony that it was time to get out of there.

"I appreciate your help, but we can't put you in danger like that," Vic said as he headed for the stairs.

"What if I sign something? Take away your responsibility if something happens to me?"

"Doesn't work that way," Tony said.

"I've seen movies. I know you guys do ride-alongs and stuff."

"Those are movies. This is real." Vic frowned.

"No. This is bullshit," Kirby said, following them to the basement door.

"Easy, kid."

"At least can you let me know what you find?"

Tony stopped and turned back to him. "Yeah. If we find a monster museum in the basement, we'll definitely let you know."

14

CAGED AND ANGRY

KELSEY SAT ON THE EDGE of her mattress. There was no clock, no way at all to judge time. It could be noon or midnight. She watched Gia and Annika sleep. Annika was on her stomach, and Kelsey marveled at the way her bubble butt rose high above her lower back.

An ass you could bounce nickels off. That's what Morris at Dispatch would say, although she'd never understood the expression.

She asked Vic about it one lazy morning as they lay across each other on the couch with iced coffee and the Sunday edition of the *Boston Globe*.

"It's just a joke." Vic glanced at her.

"Bullshit," she replied. "You're all morons."

He laughed. "It's harmless. It doesn't mean we have any less sensitivity to the plight of women."

"The plight of women?" she repeated back with a raised eyebrow.

"Yeah," he answered. "You know, the smaller brain and lack of reason." He smiled mischievously and took a sip of his coffee.

She used her toe to tip his cup high enough to spill a bit. They laughed and put the newspaper aside. With the morning sun forming a cinematic beam in the room, they made love. Life was perfect.

The memory put a lump in her chest. Suddenly she was overcome with worry for him. She knew he'd be blaming himself for this. Even though he tried to stop her, he'd still be pissed at himself for not insisting. He was most likely going crazy trying to find her.

He probably hasn't eaten or slept.

Kelsey scanned the room for the thousandth time, taking in the cold, blue-gray walls and fluorescent lighting.

She thought about scenes from TV shows and movies when abductees recognized certain sounds while in captivity. Trains, foghorns, things that would help lead to their rescue. The prisoner would manage to get to a phone for just a few seconds and call the hero, but before the bad guy cuts off the call, the cops or whoever would hear just enough to give them some kind of clue.

"Wait! Play that back! Is that a foghorn? She's somewhere by the docks!"

She could hear nothing. It was maddening. Neither she, Gia, nor Annika ever heard anything. No noises, no conversations, nothing. The man who delivered the food never spoke. She'd tried talking to him, dropping down, trying to see him through the food slot. She never saw his face but did her best to memorize his hands, the left one wearing a white gold wedding ring.

She prepared herself for anything. With three of them in the room, when whatever was going to happen did go down, most likely it would be more than one man she'd have to fight. She tried to envision how they'd enter the room—probably with weapons of some kind. No idea what, but it made sense they'd be armed somehow. Picturing how they'd approach, she tried to develop a step-by-step plan for the best way to attack them.

15

THE TREMONT

V IC AND TONY WALKED WITH Guidley toward her office.
"Why not?" Vic asked through a mask of anger.

"DA said there's not enough to justify searching the Tremont," Guidley said.

"That's ridiculous," Vic scoffed.

"I know," Guidley replied. "Marsha said she tried three different judges. Not one of them will sign a warrant."

"Those pricks. They don't want to blow any donations," Tony said.

"We don't have time for this shit. How about I go to one of the judges myself? Let them tell me to my face there's nothing there," Vic suggested.

Guidley stopped walking. "No. Don't do that," she said. "Let me try Judge Freeman. I'll go to him directly."

"Thanks," Vic said.

———•———

Vic read everything he could find on the Tremont building. As old as it was, there were plenty of online articles about it. Yellowed newspaper photos from the turn of the century showed how the structure stood unchanged while the buildings around it transformed over the decades.

Click after click, he took it all in, although none of the information he found told the whole story.

The eight-story building was built in 1883. Located on Tremont Street about halfway between the Park Street Church and Boylston Street. The exterior brick-and-stone structure remains the same as it was over 130 years ago.

It was originally named the Tremont Inn, and it was the intention of its owners, Paul T. Hitchborn and his business partner, Robert Boatwright, that the stylish building they'd invested all their family money into would become the first and only choice for the country's elite visiting Boston.

The hotel was an immediate success. Within a few years, the Tremont Inn became a mecca for both the visiting wealthy and the upper crust of Boston. The restaurant off the lobby, called the Tavern, was the hottest spot in town.

From its official opening in 1884 until 1918, Hitchborn and Boatwright enjoyed a successful partnership. In 1918, Boatwright was killed in a horse-riding accident in New Hampshire. His children opted to sell their shares of the hotel back to Hitchborn.

He remained the sole owner until his death in 1929, at which point ownership was bequeathed to his wife and upon her death in 1940, to their only child, a son named Harris. Harris Hitchborn had pretty much been running the day-to-day operations since graduating from Harvard Business School.

Harris was a ladies' man and never married or had children. After running the hotel in the black for over thirty years, he decided to retire in 1962. Serious offers came in from all over the country. The one thing that concerned Harris was that he sold to a Bostonian. He didn't want an outsider to take it over. His entire life, Harris had been a strong supporter of his hometown. He loved Boston. He loved its history, its beauty, and its people.

The only local to express interest was Bryce Winthrop. He and Harris had met several times at social functions but were more acquaintances than friends. To the public, Winthrop made his fortune in finance. In truth, most of his wealth came from bootlegging during Prohibition. Unlike others who did the same thing, Bryce Winthrop was more adept at keeping his criminal associations discreet. He headed several charitable foundations, donated large sums to his community, and projected the very picture of the Proper Bostonian.

Harris agreed to sell the Tremont Inn to Winthrop. However, just one day before the paperwork was to be signed, he learned of Winthrop's seedier connections. Not wanting to sully the reputation of his family's legacy, he changed his mind and met with Winthrop to tell him the deal was off.

Harris Hitchborn walked out of Winthrop's office but never arrived home. He was never seen or heard from again. His body was never found. Winthrop took ownership of the Tremont Inn days later with forged documents several witnesses claimed to have watched Hitchborn sign.

After some renovations, the Tremont Inn reopened as simply the Tremont in October 1963. In the years following, Winthrop became a successful hotel mogul, opening luxury hotels throughout New England. When his only son, James, turned twenty-one in 1965, Winthrop gave the boy the Tremont as a birthday present.

James Winthrop was, by all accounts, a brilliant young man. He'd graduated from Harvard, had been crew captain on the rowing team, and came across to one and all as a highly charismatic figure. He was fascinated by history and especially enthralled by its secrets, the stories and mysteries not found in the average history books.

He started his own secret organization at Harvard called the Cobblestone Club. The club was dedicated to discovering the deepest secrets about anyone and anything. Under Winthrop's leadership, the members came to enjoy the sense of being omniscient. It was highly satisfying for them to possess secret knowledge the masses didn't and never would. For Winthrop, it was intoxicating. He would go on to spend the rest of his life trying to learn the truth behind the myths… to solve mankind's mysteries, to share and keep the answers with his friends.

Upon his father's death in 1980, James Winthrop inherited just under a billion dollars. He closed the Tremont to the public and turned it into a private club. Membership started at one million dollars with annual dues of a hundred thousand. It didn't really matter to the people who joined. This was the elite of the elite, a group of the wealthiest and most powerful. They fancied themselves the most exclusive club on earth, not just above common society but above its rules and laws as well. For the rest of the century and into the next, the Tremont served as home base for the clandestine Cobblestone Club. Several times a year, James Winthrop and his friends met at the Tremont to share discoveries, evidence, and artifacts.

In an ironic twist, the exact day the Tremont closed to the public, lobstermen off Gloucester's coast hauled up an oil drum with holes drilled into it. Inside were the remains of an adult male. The only identification was a pair of cuff links inscribed with the initials H.H.

It was as if the closing of the once majestic Tremont Inn had caused Harris Hitchborn to rise from the grave.

Vic stared across his desk at Tony as he spoke with Guidley on the phone. "Okay. Yeah," he said through a clenched jaw and slammed his cell down. "Shit."

Tony shook his head. "I thought she was tight with that judge?"

"I guess not tight enough." Vic stood up fast, sending his chair rolling back. He felt the urgency to do something, anything, to try to find Kelsey. There was a chance she was inside the Tremont, and his frustration was about to boil over. "Look, I won't be offended if you stay here."

"You're going over there?" Tony asked.

"Yeah. Screw it. She might be in there, and I'm not going to lose the chance to find her in time because of some chickenshit judge."

"I'll drive," Tony said as he got up.

"Hey, I don't..."

"Whatever. Let's go."

16

UNWELCOME VISITORS

T REMONT STREET WAS BUSY THIS time of day. Tourists were everywhere, filling the sidewalks and strolling through the Common. The sun put a bright glare on the golden dome atop the statehouse, and the smell of a street vendor's fried onions and sausages filled the air.

They pulled into the entrance of the Tremont. The same cobblestones guests had stepped onto when exiting horse-pulled carriages now served as a valet station. There was quite a bit of activity as workmen carried large pieces of Egyptian decor into the building.

Vic and Tony approached and were almost knocked over by several workers rushing past, followed by a party planner loudly lecturing the men about their professionalism.

Before the detectives got to the door, a hulking security guard intercepted them. "Can I help you?"

Vic flashed his badge. "Just got a few questions."

"Okay. Shoot."

"Inside," Tony said.

"I'm sorry. That isn't…"

Vic stepped closer to the guard. "No time for this. Take us inside."

"Do you have a warrant?"

"I don't. But we're going in."

"Don't fuck with us," Tony said, flashing his trademark stare.

Vic and Tony stepped past him, and he immediately got on his radio.

Walking into the lobby was like entering another time. Lush carpets, highly polished oak-paneled walls, warm lighting from chandeliers. Behind the front desk hung a beautiful cityscape on a custom-sized canvas the same length as the counter. The painting was a commission by Claude Monet and had never been published, seen, or documented anywhere else. Like many other things within these walls, the painting didn't exist to the rest of the world, its beauty reserved for its members.

"How can I help you?" came a pleasant voice.

They turned to see a dapper blond man in his late forties. He wore an expensive cream-colored suit and projected an attitude of sincere warmth as he offered his hand.

"Michael Barclay. I'm the operating manager. What can I do for you?"

"I'm Lieutenant Mitchum with the Boston Police. This is Lieutenant Petrillo."

"How exciting!" Barclay said with glee.

Vic took out his phone. On-screen was a photo of Kelsey. "Have you seen her?"

Barclay looked closer. "Gorgeous... but no. I'm sorry."

"I understand you're having a big event soon," Vic asked.

"Yes," Barclay answered, "The pharaoh exhibit on Saturday."

"And you'll be hosting a bunch of wealthy guests."

Barclay smirked with pride. "Well, all of the club's members are extremely wealthy."

Vic looked around the room as he spoke. "How many floors do you have?"

"Eight."

"What's upstairs?"

"Residences," Barclay replied. "The members have year-round apartments."

"How many?" Tony asked.

"There are twelve residences and ten guest rooms."

Vic asked, "Are people living upstairs right now?"

"No," Barclay replied. "Even the residences are only used a few times a year. Right now everything's empty until Friday."

"Would it be possible to see what they look like while they're empty?" Vic asked.

"I'm not sure about that," Barclay answered. "I'd have to get permission."

"We'll wait," Vic replied.

"Sure. Please excuse me a moment." Barclay took out his phone as he walked away.

———•———

James Winthrop stood in a private art gallery, admiring a painting, a Gustave Caillebotte streetscape.

The only other person in the room was an impeccably dressed curator who pointed to one of the figures within the painting. "Caillebotte often inserted his family members into his work. This man strolling is his brother, René."

Winthrop listened but kept his eyes on the painting. "No," he replied. "That's incorrect."

The curator said nothing. Winthrop figured he wouldn't dare disagree with him for fear of offending him and losing the sale. To his surprise and delight, the curator not only spoke up, but he did so with a hint of condescension.

"Please forgive me, Mr. Winthrop... but it was told to me by several associates from the Louvre that it is indeed René Caillebotte in the painting."

"Whoever told you that was mistaken." Winthrop stepped closer to the painting. "Do you see what is in the man's hand?"

"I believe it to be a valise," the curator replied as he leaned closer to the canvas.

"A bit wide to be a valise, is it not?"

"Perhaps. But a valise nonetheless."

"Its odd boxlike shape and distinct straps match perfectly with vintage camera cases of the day. Caillebotte's other brother, Martial, was a photographer. Which would suggest the man in the painting is him and not René." Winthrop briefly enjoyed watching the curator squirm, then let him off the hook. "What are they asking?"

The curator answered while staring at the painting as if it had betrayed him somehow. "Thirty-two million."

Winthrop's phone buzzed and he glanced at the screen. "Forgive me," he said to the curator.

"Of course." The curator stepped away.

Winthrop took the call from Barclay and strolled to the next painting. "I see."

He wasn't shocked. He'd been informed the police had expressed interest in the Tremont. Winthrop considered canceling the upcoming weekend festivities, but his ego quickly vetoed the idea. He'd put in too much work and waited far too long to show off his latest acquisition to postpone because of some peon cops.

"Let them in. Yes. Do whatever they ask."

———•———

In the Tremont lobby, Barclay returned with a smile. "We're all set. Where would you like to start?"

Vic was shocked but didn't hesitate. "How about the top floor and work our way down?"

Barclay escorted them to the elevator, pointing out areas and items of decor of interest. Using a master key card, Barclay showed them the interiors of every room. It took almost an hour to get back to the lobby.

They saw nothing suspicious. Part of Vic had hoped Barclay would refuse them entry to one of the rooms so he could believe Kelsey was being held inside, but he showed them everything they asked to see.

When they first got into the elevator, Vic took notice of the buttons. It appeared there was nothing below the lobby.

"Strange the building doesn't have a basement," Vic said.

"I always thought so as well." Barclay nodded.

In the lobby, Vic took him aside from the party planner and workers. "One sec," he said in a lower tone. "I need to ask you one more thing."

Barclay also lowered his voice. "Of course. What would you like to know?"

Vic looked him directly in the eye. "I'm sure you provide these members with all kinds of perks and pleasures?"

Barclay wasn't fazed. "Absolutely. We see to it they always have anything they might require."

"Would that include women?"

"Oh," Barclay replied, "I, uh, am not sure how to…"

"I need to know."

Barclay stepped closer and whispered. "Some members do require… special services."

"How do you supply these services?" Vic asked.

Barclay looked nervous for the first time.

"I give you my word. No one will ever know you said anything," Vic said.

As Barclay spoke, his eyes darted from Vic to others out of earshot. "We use a company called Elite & Discreet."

"Do the members ever bring back or have someone pick up street prostitutes for them?" Tony asked.

"Are you kidding?" Barclay laughed quietly. "These are the richest people in the world. The escorts they're used to average ten thousand dollars a night."

"I see. Thank you."

"Lieutenant, if it gets out that I…"

Vic waved him off. "It won't. Thank you for being so cooperative."

"Absolutely my pleasure. Have a good day."

Barclay walked back to his office, and as Vic watched him, he knew the guy was clean. *If anything is going on here, he doesn't know about it.*

As they walked out, a security camera followed them.

"Let's check out the building next door," Vic said.

The front entrance of the Harvard Trucking Company was locked. From all appearances, it looked like the business was still in operation, just closed for the day. They walked to the back, where they found another set of doors. This set was huge, big enough for oversized trucks to drive through, also locked.

There was an abundance of security cameras placed throughout, many more than were necessary for a trucking company. The tall walls around the building were lined with razor wire.

"Is this a truck depot or bin Laden's compound?" Tony asked.

"Yeah. A little extreme," Vic replied.

As they looked around, Vic convinced himself it was worth further investigation even as he feared he might be giving himself false hope. In any case, they couldn't find a way in, even illegally.

"Very strange," Tony said.

"Yeah."

Both their phones buzzed with a text message from Guidley.

"My office NOW!" their screens read.

"What's that about?" Tony asked.

"No idea."

A horrific thought flashed into him.

They found Kel's body.

He called Guidley back several times, but it kept going to voice mail.

His mind raced through all the murder victims he'd seen over the years and where they were found. In dumpsters, alleys, abandoned buildings. His heart sped up, and his fingers began to shake.

No. Stop it. If they found her, she would have immediately called. Unless she wanted to give the ME time to clean her up as much as possible before I see her. She may not be in one piece. NO. Dear God, please no…

Uh-uh. No way. It's probably something that has nothing to do with her.

They found her body but not her head, and I have to identify her. How would I do that? That birthmark she hates beside her belly button.

Shut up.

"VIC!" Tony yelled.

"What?" Vic jumped.

"I'm talking to you, and you're just staring at me."

"Sorry."

"If it had anything to do with Kel, Cap would've called you right away, not texted."

"I know."

They sped back to the station despite every possible obstacle putting itself in front of them.

———•———

When they finally burst into Guidley's office, they were breathing as if they'd just run a marathon. She saw the sweat coming through their shirts.

"Oh shit," she said. "I'm sorry. This has nothing to do with Kelsey."

Vic bent over with his hands on his knees.

"Thank God," Tony said, catching his breath.

Guidley had them sit down and took her own seat behind her desk.

"Then, why the urgency?" Vic asked.

"I'll get to that. But listen… you know there's still a good chance we can find her alive."

Even as she said the words, both she and Vic were painfully aware that they'd all said them before to loved ones for which a happy outcome never came.

"Yeah," Vic replied.

"Remember," Guidley continued, "the stats don't support it, but the stats don't consider that none of the other missing women have been trained police officers. Kel's a smart, tough cop. How long has she been doing jujitsu? At the July Fourth fireworks last year, I saw her take down a three-hundred-pound asshole like he was made of paper."

"I remember that," Tony said.

"It's only been a few days. I believe, I truly believe, she's still alive and just waiting for the perfect time to make her move." Guidley stared into Vic's eyes, clearly not going to turn away first.

Her words triggered several memories. Often, when Kelsey got back from jujitsu class, she'd be excited to show him the latest maneuver she'd learned while he made condescending jokes. But always, within a few lightning-fast moves, he found himself flat on his back with her shin against his throat. He'd never forget the look on her face in those moments... her pride, her confidence, her laugh, as she helped him to his feet.

She's right. Once they get close enough to her, she'll beat the shit out of them.

"Thanks, Captain," Vic said.

Guidley didn't answer. She just nodded.

"So why the text?" Tony asked.

Guidley picked up her laptop and turned it around so they could read an email she had open. "Thought you could explain this to me."

Captain Guidley,

Please be advised that I, along with the undersigned law firm, represent the Tremont Club, hereafter called "the club."

I have become aware two detectives from the Boston PD came to the club today to inquire about ongoing matters at the club.

Although these officers did not have a search warrant, our manager, Michael Barclay, was happy to have them inside and cooperate in any way possible.

As I am sure you are aware, the club has among its members some of Boston's most prominent citizens, who have collectively donated near $50M to *improvements in the city and contributed heavily to both the mayor and the governor of Massachusetts.*

Our members are very concerned about their privacy, and as I am sure you are aware, the club is a private, members-only club that prides itself on its exclusivity and extreme discretion.

While I do not believe any apology is required, I am certain that no other law enforcement will visit our premises without a search warrant.

In that event, I would expect a courtesy call from you or a superior notifying us you intend to visit our highly esteemed and reputable establishment.

In the future, if you have any questions about the club, its members, or our activities, please do not hesitate to contact me directly as I am instructing you not to disturb the individual members of our club, its management, or employees.

Please govern your actions accordingly.

Sincerely,

E. John Arnett
Arnett & Richardson
Attorneys at Law

Vic finished reading and slumped back.

Guidley looked at Vic and Tony, and in the calmest tone possible, asked, "What the fuck?"

Vic felt like a doctor had told him he was pregnant.

"That's nuts," Tony said. "We left there less than twenty minutes ago."

"What were you guys thinking?"

"We aren't going to get a warrant, and we only have until Saturday," Vic said.

"Why's that?" Guidley asked.

"That's the night they're using the whole pharaoh thing as the reason for getting together."

"I checked out some of the private flights, and almost all of these assholes leave the next day," Tony said.

"Whatever is going on," Vic said, "it's happening Saturday night. I just know it. I can feel it."

"And you think it's taking place underneath the building?" Guidley asked with more than a touch of doubt.

"I thought that was a little crazy at first too," Tony said, "but now there's enough to convince me there *is* something down there. Some kind of facility."

Guidley locked eyes with Tony for several silent seconds, then did the same with Vic as she considered everything. She got up from her desk, walked to her window, and looked out at the city. Vic and Tony watched her quietly, preparing themselves to be disappointed. They genuinely liked and respected Guidley, but they knew when it came to ruffling the feathers of the town's rich and powerful, she was usually overly cautious.

She turned back to them and broke the heavy silence. "Okay. That gives us two days," Guidley said, "I'll get a warrant for you to see what's down there."

Both men felt a wave of relief.

"Thanks, Captain." Vic said.

17

GIA & ANNIKA

K ELSEY LISTENED AS ANNIKA AND Gia explained how they'd ended up working the streets. Gia was twenty-five and had been raised with strong Christian values by loving parents.

Despite developing early and getting a lot of attention from boys, she stayed a virgin until her senior year of high school. Although it went against everything she was taught, she discovered she enjoyed sex. Junior year at Wellesley College, after seeing how much money her roommate was making as an escort, she tried it out. She liked it. The men were older, smart, and treated her well.

Her parents found out and completely disowned her. Her father stopped paying for college and she was almost forced to drop out. One of her clients offered to pay her tuition, under certain conditions. Feeling she had no choice, Gia accepted his offer. He introduced her to heroin, and within the year, she left school and became a full-time plaything not just for her sugar daddy but for his friends as well.

The pleasure she felt from the heroin filled the wound left by her parents. When her benefactor replaced her with a fresh new girl, she was discarded like trash. With no money and having alienated all her friends, she had no other way to survive than to start stripping and hooking. Whatever she had to do to get her fix, she did.

———•———

Annika's was a story Kelsey had heard before, but that didn't make it any less heartbreaking. It had all the same sad plot points… little money, an uncaring mother, a father who continually molested her. She didn't know how to tell her mother what was happening, so she resorted to other ways to get her mom's attention. She began taking drugs and cutting her arms. When her mother still failed to notice, Annika looked elsewhere for someone who would care.

She and two other girls left home to live with a guy who appeared to be the father figure she'd been searching for. When her friends realized he was actually a pimp recruiting new girls to work the street, they left. They tried to convince Annika to leave as well, but she had already bought into his web of lies and illusions. She turned her first trick on her seventeenth birthday.

Kelsey thought about how fortunate she'd been. Her parents had always been loving and supportive. They rarely even raised their voices to her unless she was physically fighting with her brother and sister.

Something clicked in her mind.

She looked at Gia and Annika as she processed an idea. Her eyes scanned the dull room. She turned to the heavy steel door and then to the concrete floor, as if she were watching an invisible performance.

Maybe. It's worth a try.

———•———

Kelsey huddled with them and whispered, "When we hear him coming with the next meal, we start fighting. I'll get on the ground and one of you get on top of me like you're strangling me. Maybe he'll come inside to break it up. They want us alive, right? When he comes in, we attack."

Gia shook her head. "I don't know."

"I'm trained in martial arts. I can teach you some moves so you both can help."

"That sounds silly." Annika adjusted her body on the mattress and shook her head. Her long braided extensions swayed lightly.

"We can do this. We *have* to do this." Kelsey clenched her fists.

"I just mean, we've been in here for days and no one has hurt us or anything." Gia shrugged.

Kelsey was baffled. "What does that mean? They're going to."

"No, I know," Gia said, "but what if this speeds them up?"

Kelsey took a breath and altered her tone. "Okay. I get it. You two have been through a lot of shit, and I'm sorry. But this is a whole different story. Sooner or later, some asshole, or assholes, are going to come through that door, and rape is just the beginning. Odds are when they're done, they're going to kill us. God only knows what kind of sick fucks we're dealing with here. We have to do whatever we can to fight back. It's our only chance."

Annika scanned the room and focused in on Kelsey. Kelsey saw the moment Annika realized she was right.

"Okay," Annika agreed, "fuck these muthafuckas."

Gia nodded. "Yeah. Let's do it."

"Good. Come on, get up," Kelsey said.

"What? Now?" Gia asked.

"Yeah. We don't know how long we have. They could be at the door in ten minutes. There's no time to waste."

———•———

Kelsey taught them some basic moves and techniques, demonstrating several ways to render an attacker helpless. A few times while guiding their arms, she felt quick glimpses of being in class, teaching younger students, before the stark reality returned.

This is it, she thought as she imagined what her opponent might look like.

This is the day. This won't be a smiling classmate. If this goes badly, if I can't beat him, then… there won't be any tapping out. No friendly words of support as he helps me up.

No laughs over lattes at Starbucks after class.

If I don't win… I'll never see Vic again. How will Vic handle —
NO!

Don't think like that. I'm going to beat and choke out whoever walks through that door. That's all there is to it.

18

FRIDAY MORNING

AROUND NOON, VIC AND TONY learned Guidley was placed on a two-week unpaid suspension. The two detectives walked into the Clover Pub and gave nods to the bartender. A few other employees wiped down tables and mopped up, although all the lemon-scented cleaner in New England couldn't erase the sour stench of stale beer.

Guidley sat alone.

"What the fuck?" Vic asked Guidley as he and Tony slid into her booth.

"It's bullshit." Guidley stared at her beer.

"We know that," Tony said. "What happened?"

"The chief said IA is investigating me."

"For what?" Tony asked.

"That's all I got."

"They can't do that without a specific charge," Vic said. "What did your union rep say?"

"It doesn't matter. This came down less than an hour after I requested the warrant. It's a warning to back off." Guidley took a swig of her beer.

Vic's mind raced as he glanced at all the framed vintage posters announcing turn-of-the-century boxing matches hanging beside the booth. Every one of them was yellowed and faded, adding to the burnt-umber tone of the room.

"What now?" Tony asked.

"We've got to stay under the radar as we figure out a way to get down there before tomorrow night," Vic said.

Tony sat back against the dark leather booth. "Any idea who they're putting in your place?"

———·———

Deputy Captain Bob Sweeney was made acting captain while Guidley was on suspension. Sweeney was a loudmouth with a history of dick moves. Few cops were fans of his, and it appeared clear to all of them that the man was well aware of their opinions and didn't give a shit.

His appearance matched his personality. While most modern men have taken to shaving their heads when they start to see more scalp than hair, Sweeney was determined to fight to the very last follicle. He was left with thin patches of salt-and-pepper hair on each side of his head above his ears and a ridiculous comb-over of long strands connecting them. Also differing from other men his age, he had no visible laugh lines.

The most noticeable thing about him, and the main ingredient in every imitation performed behind his back, was the ever-present sound of phlegm in his voice. Every few seconds he cleared his throat by snorting deeply and swallowing.

Sweeney summoned them before even unpacking his essentials. Despite knowing his promotion was more than likely only temporary, Sweeney insisted on moving into Guidley's office.

The whole meeting was odd. No small talk at all. Not even a mention of concern about Kelsey. Even the new janitor, whose name he didn't know, had offered Vic awkward words of sympathy and support.

Instead, Sweeney brought up a case they'd already closed. "What's going on with Thornton?"

Vic and Tony exchanged a look.

"We handed that over already," Vic replied. "We found the gun a mile from his condo and his prints were all over it. Ballistics matched. DA didn't bring up testifying yet."

Sweeney looked as if he were watching a student trying to bullshit their way through an answer. "Did you get a confession?"

"No," Tony replied, "but the DA said he didn't need it."

Sweeney shook his head. "I want it."

"You think I'm going to stop looking for my fiancée to get an unnecessary confession for a finished case?" Vic blurted.

"I expect you to do your job. There's a whole task force working on tracking down Officer Moss."

"And they have nothing."

Sweeney sat down. "Also, what's this stuff about the Tremont Club you've been doing?"

Ah. There it is, Vic thought.

"It's nothing." Vic pasted on a smile. "We were just following up a lead. Dead end."

Sweeney studied their faces. "So, you're done with it?"

"Yeah," Tony replied. "Nothing there."

"Okay," Sweeney said. "But listen to me closely, just in case. If anything changes, you come to me directly before going a step further."

"You mean if something new —" Vic started.

Sweeney cut him off. "I mean you are not to go anywhere near that place for any reason. I don't care what you think you might have."

Vic felt his blood pressure rise as Sweeney exposed himself as a pawn of whoever framed Guidley.

"Can we ask why?" Vic asked in an accusatory tone.

"Because I said so," Sweeney yelled.

"No problem," Tony said, stepping forward with two quick slaps on Vic's shoulder.

"Good," Sweeney said, clearly more relaxed. "Now go get that confession from Thornton."

Vic and Tony walked back to their desks.

"He may as well have told us he was bought off," Tony said.

The thought of Kelsey suffering suddenly hit Vic like a gut punch, and he took a quick turn into the men's room. Tony followed.

"I know she's down there somewhere."

Tony's reply came out in a softer tone, one he usually reserved for the parents or loved ones of a murder victim. "We'll find a way in."

19

CHASING ELEVATORS

THEY BOTH HIT WALLS, ALTHOUGH every obstacle only demonstrated someone had taken extreme steps to keep any details about the building secret. The architectural firm who designed it was long gone. All paperwork, permits, and plans having to do with the many renovations were either lost or destroyed over the years.

Each search turned up more questions than answers. The Harvard Trucking Company building was built more recently, but the architect who designed the building was also killed in a mysterious car accident.

The A/C system was installed by a Swiss company sold to a larger company that went out of business not long after the buyout. Vic was able to track down a couple of former Swiss employees. Still, between the language difference and their strange legal obligations to not discuss past projects, he learned nothing of importance.

Vic looked over the drone photos of the roof of the Harvard Trucking Company Kirby had given him. He turned his attention to an oversized structure he couldn't identify. It looked similar to an elevator machine room but much bigger.

He dug up everything he could about the country's top elevator companies and compared images of their roof units' styles and designs to the ones on the Tremont. Once he narrowed his search to three companies using a similar design, he contacted each one to find who did the installation.

The company who installed the elevator units wasn't one of the major companies. In fact, it seemed on paper that the company, Crimson Elevator, had only been in business for a few months before the job and went out of business almost immediately after. The elevator system in the Tremont building was their only project.

No. I don't think so, he thought.

He dug further until he found out the most successful elevator designer of the three companies was Jacob Neary, who worked for a company called Cambridge Whitley. Neary was widely regarded as the best in the business.

Vic contacted Cambridge Whitley and found a friendly human resources employee more than happy to brag about Neary's history with the company. Oddly, Jacob Neary had taken a three-month leave of absence during the same time the Tremont underwent a major renovation.

Vic felt a rush of excitement upon learning Neary was alive and living in Rockport, Massachusetts, where he owned an art gallery.

He picked up his phone.

———————

"Hello?" a male voice answered.

Vic leaned forward. "Hi. Mr. Neary?"

"This is he."

"Hi. Are you the same Jacob Neary who worked for Cambridge Whitley Elevators?"

A few seconds of silence.

"Yes, but that was a long time ago."

"Yes, I know. If you could give me just a moment, I'm trying to find some information about a company called Crimson Elevators."

More silence.

"Do you know anything about that company, sir?"

"No. I'm sorry. And I'm really in the middle of something right now."

"I see. But if you could…"

"I'm sorry. I have to go."

Vic felt the best he had in days despite being hung up on. *Gotcha.*

———•———

It took thirty minutes for Vic and Tony to get to the small coastal town of Rockport, even using the lights and siren to cut through the traffic along the way. The Neary Gallery was halfway up Bearskin Neck, a walking road that led from the town square to a long row of breakers that stretched into Rockport Harbor. The road was surrounded on three sides by the Atlantic Ocean and lined with art galleries, gift shops, and seafood restaurants.

In front of their galleries, artists worked on paintings as passersby stopped to watch. That's exactly what Jacob Neary was doing as the detectives joined the small crowd of onlookers who watched him add brushstrokes of cerulean blue to his latest seascape. He was a slender man with receding light sandy hair that accentuated his dark tan.

Vic watched him, impressed not just by his obvious ability but also how he was able to keep his focus on the painting while answering questions and conversing with the people around him.

"How long does each painting take you?" a heavy midwestern woman in a new, much too tight Harvard T-shirt asked.

Neary answered with a second paintbrush in his mouth. Not like a cigarette, but sideways. "It depends," Neary said. "Sometimes a few hours, sometimes a few weeks."

He cleaned the excess paint off the brush in his hand with several quick swipes on his left forearm, which already bore a multitude of the other colors from the canvas.

Vic stepped forward. "Painting the ocean must be a lot more relaxing than designing elevators."

Neary's brush stopped cold. He turned to Vic, who stepped closer.

"Got a minute?"

He put down his brushes and stood up, almost knocking over the small table that held his paint box. "Okay. Just give me a second to wash my hands."

With that, Neary went into his gallery.

Vic signaled Tony to go around the back of the small building while he followed Neary inside. As he expected, it was empty and the back door wide open. He walked out to where Tony had Neary's face pinned to the shingles on the back of the gallery. The artist was shaking and sweating.

"Look, I never said a word," he stammered.

"We're not here to hurt you," Vic said, "I just need a few answers."

Tony released him, and the artist sagged upon seeing Vic's badge.

There was a picnic table behind the gallery, and Tony motioned for Neary to sit. Sounds of shuffling came from within the gallery.

"Honey," a male voice called out, "you left your wet canvas outside agai…"

Vic and Tony turned to see Neary's partner come out holding two coffees.

"Oh. I'm sorry," he said.

Vic locked eyes with the man and raised an open hand to the seat beside Neary. "Please. Sit."

20

SPILLING SECRETS

N EARY LISTENED TO THE DETECTIVES explain why they were there and what they wanted, which was to know exactly what was going on in the basement of the Tremont and how they could get down there.

He took it all in as he gazed at the ocean. Several fishing boats were anchored nearby. The bright colors of their hulls reflected in the water beneath them. A few feet away, a seagull stood on a large stone and squawked for scraps. The faint smell of fried clams mixed with the salty air.

"I honestly don't know what goes on down there, and I don't want to," the artist said.

"How did you come to be involved in it?" Vic asked.

"I was the lead designer for Cambridge Whitley Elevators," he started. "One of the owners told me we were going to take on a private project, but for legal purposes we were starting a second company under a new name."

"Crimson," Tony said.

"Yes, but Crimson never did another project. Only this one."

Vic asked, "When you install an elevator system, is the rest of the structure already complete?"

"In most cases, yes."

"So you've seen the basement?" Vic asked.

Neary looked at his partner, who gave him the slightest possible shake of his head with concern in his eyes.

Vic saw it as well. He slammed his hand down onto the chipped wood of the table.

"Listen," Vic said. "I understand you're nervous. But if everything we suspect is true, several people are going to prison for a long time. Whoever you're afraid of will not be able to hurt you."

Neary's partner spoke up. "Umm. Before we say anything further, do you have a warrant?" His words came out in the same tone as if he were asking a teenage fast-food employee if he could speak to his manager.

Vic and Tony turned to him simultaneously.

"What's your name?" Tony asked.

"Charles."

"Charles. If you speak again, I'm going to bang your head off this fuckin' table," Tony said.

Charles's face lost all color.

"Please," Neary said, "nothing will ever happen to these people. They are beyond the law. They're beyond everything."

Vic and Tony shared a look.

"Now tell me, how big is the basement?" Vic asked.

"It's not a basement," Neary said, "When you say *basement,* it sounds like you're talking about file cabinets and storage units."

Tony said, "Then what is it?"

Neary looked at his anxious partner, who was still silently trying to tell him to stay quiet.

"It's a facility of some kind. I don't know what for. And it's not just beneath the Tremont. It's underneath the building next door and beneath most of the Common as well."

"Most of the Common?" Vic asked.

"It extends under the Common for about forty acres," Neary said.

"Forty acres," Vic said, barely audible.

"How many football fields is that?" Tony asked.

"About thirty," Vic answered, turning his gaze to the ocean. "You don't know what's going on down there. But you've seen the construction. What do you think it's being used for? Are there rooms? Is it all open space?"

"There are open spaces, but it's got rooms too. Some larger than others."

"How can we get down there? How many elevators are there?" Vic asked.

Neary dropped his forehead into his palm and closed his eyes, and Vic realized it was hard on the man. From his research, he'd discovered a lot of Neary's coworkers had suffered mysterious "accidents."

"There are a total of six elevators that go down to the facility. There are four inside the Tremont. They go to the upper floors and down to the underground area."

Vic shook his head. "No, that's not right," Vic said. "We saw the inside of the elevator in the Tremont. There weren't any buttons for anything under the lobby."

"Yes, there are. You just can't see them," Neary said. "Above the normal buttons, there's a round brass logo for Crimson Elevators. Behind it is a thumb scanner."

Tony's brow scrunched and his neck stretched up. "No shit?" Tony asked, "like in a movie?"

"Yes."

"What about the elevator next door in the trucking company?" Vic asked.

"That's a freight elevator. The biggest one I ever designed. They used it for the large equipment and materials."

"Do you need a thumbprint for that one?" Vic asked.

"I don't know. I didn't handle that aspect of it."

"Who did?" Tony asked.

"A man named Luis Fallon. But he died."

"How?" Vic asked.

"He fell in front of a train at the State Street Station."

Vic and Tony exchanged a look.

"Fell?" Tony asked.

"That's what the Herald said."

A loud boat horn broke the silence, causing Neary and Charles to jump. Neary used his forearm to wipe the sweat from his face.

"You said six elevators," Vic asked. "Where's the other one?"

"To the right of the Tremont, down the block, is a six-story apartment building with a coffeehouse on the first floor," Neary replied.

Tony looked at him. "You're talking about the Uncommon Grounds?"

"That doesn't make sense," Vic said. "It's too public."

"Yes, exactly," Neary said. "It's got people coming and going all day. No one would notice someone going in the elevator and not coming out. We installed two elevators inside. Both can go up to the floors above. Lots of people use it. But only one of them goes down to the secret level. Not visibly shown of course. If someone uses the thumb scanner to go down to the basement, the indicators outside the elevators on every floor give a false floor."

"Which elevator goes down?" Tony asked.

"The one on the right."

Vic leaned back, causing the picnic bench to let out a small crack. "Why would they need a third elevator system down the street in a public building?"

"It doesn't matter if it's in a public building," Neary answered. "It's a hide-in-plain-sight strategy. You see, when you get on the elevator, the people that see you get on don't know what floor you're going to. Once the thumb scanner is used, the system overrides any other button that may be pushed on other floors until the car returns to street level. If someone else gets on with someone trying to get to the lower level, the person just has to wait until they get off before pressing the scanner."

"But why have it down the street, so far from the Tremont?" Vic asked.

"I only have a guess." Neary paused a few seconds before

he continued. "The coffeehouse elevator probably serves as a sort of employee entrance. So the members at the Tremont don't have to look at the lower-class workers or let them in through the front door."

Vic and Tony exchanged another glance. That sounded correct.

Neary continued. "It's actually pretty clever..."

In midsentence, half of Neary's face exploded. Blood, skull, and brain sprayed onto Tony. There was no loud gunshot, no sound except for the actual bursting open of Neary's head. It sounded like a watermelon hitting the pavement from high up.

There were a few seconds of shock before Vic and Tony instinctually hit the ground and pulled their guns, looking for where the shot had come from. Charles screamed, and Vic pulled him to the ground beside him.

"Get down!"

Vic scanned around, but with all the boats, and the backs of the galleries, stores and restaurants, there were too many places a sniper could hide.

Charles was still screaming and crying as Vic pointed him to the back door of the gallery.

"Go inside! Stay low!"

He didn't stay low enough. A penny-sized bullet hole opened Charles's forehead, and the back of his head spurted blood and brain. Vic hit the ground fast.

Tony yelled, "Go! I'm right behind you!"

Vic crawled for the door. Another shot ripped through the top plank of the table, sending pieces of wood splintering back.

"Fuck!" Tony said.

Several more shots popped against the back of the gallery as they made it inside.

———•———

On a boat in the harbor, Mason Spector watched through the scope on his rifle as the two detectives fled. The last few shots he fired were just for fun. If he'd wanted to kill them, he easily could have, but his orders were only to take out Neary and his partner.

He put the rifle down and stepped to the wheel. After brutally ending two lives, he closed his eyes to savor the cool ocean breeze on his face as the salty air mixed with the fresh scent of gunpowder.

They burst out the front door of the gallery, their adrenaline pumping as they cut through tourists.

"Jesus Christ," Tony said, his eyes scanning all around them as they moved.

Vic did the same, although he sensed the threat was over.

None of the tourists and other passersby had any idea what had transpired seconds earlier behind the gallery. For the detectives, it was surreal to be in heart-pounding danger one second and among happy people laughing with ice cream cones dripping onto their knuckles the next.

Vic bent over and put his hands on his knees as his breathing slowed.

Tony continued to scan the area surrounding them. "You okay?"

Vic let out a heavy breath and straightened up. "Yeah. You?"

Tony nodded. "That was intense."

Vic gazed at Neary's unfinished painting on its easel. The bottom area was blank white canvas, never to be completed. "With two bodies, Sweeney has to get us a warrant."

"Fuck," Tony said. "We gotta call it in though. We can't just take off."

"I know."

As Tony took out his phone, Vic looked at his watch.
Damn it. More time. I need more time.

21

THE FIGHT OF HER LIFE

T HE OVERWEIGHT MAN REMOVED A few hot dogs from the microwave and placed them into rolls. As he put the empty hot dog wrapper in the trash, he got some of the bag's juice on his wrist. Instead of grabbing a nearby napkin, he simply wiped his hand on his navy-blue chinos, causing the key chain on his belt to jingle.

He added several ketchup and mustard packets to the paper plate and carried it out of the small kitchen-like break room. The door clicked shut behind him as he made his way through a wide, dimly lit corridor. It reminded him of the wide backstage hallways he'd seen in rock videos that the bands would use to get to the stage. Except here there were no other people to be seen. No roadies, hangers-on, or groupies lingering about. It was empty. Dark, empty, and ominous. The only sounds were his black sneakers on the concrete floor and his keys clinking together.

His name was Lance, and he'd been delivering these meals for several years now. It wasn't his favorite part of the job, but it wasn't the worst either. He'd much rather drop off a plate of food than clean blood off windows. Even sweeping and mopping was a joy compared to some of his other tasks, but he couldn't beat the paycheck.

Lance's eyes narrowed as he heard something break the

silence. It was loud, female voices yelling up ahead. It wasn't the sound that concerned him — he always heard the women screaming as he approached the holding room. That was normal. The women would always yell when he came around. They'd beg to be let free, scream for mercy. It was the part he hated the most. This time it was different. They were making a racket before he was anywhere near the door.

When he did arrive at the door, he looked into the thin, one-way window and saw why. The women were fighting. One of them had the other on the ground and was strangling her.

He banged on the window. "Hey! Stop! Stop it!"

They ignored him.

He banged on the door and bent down to yell through the food slot. "Stop! Stop it!"

They kept on fighting, still ignoring him.

He quickly got on his radio. "Cobb! We got a problem in the holding room! Get down here!"

Kelsey heard him through the open food slot.

That's right, asshole. Come on in, she thought, *any second now, the door will open. Once I feel them close enough, I'm going to spring like a bear trap.*

———•———

Cobb, the man who *would* be getting close enough, was a former Marine. He'd joined Winthrop as a freelance employee, and as soon as the billionaire recognized his invaluable combination of badassery and moral flexibility, he became a full-timer. He performed a range of duties for the club and specialized in making problems go away.

He walked up to Lance outside the holding room, irked by being summoned by a glorified janitor.

"What?" he growled.

"They're killing each other," Lance said. "I think the one on the floor might be dead."

Cobb looked through the window. "Damn it," he said. "Unlock it."

Lance opened the door and stepped aside so Cobb could rush in. He ripped Annika off Kelsey and threw her aside.

"Get back," he ordered.

Kelsey froze as she heard him getting close. His knee cracked when he bent down to feel her for a pulse. She felt two fingers touch her neck.

———·———

Now, Kelsey ordered herself.

She grabbed Cobb's wrist, twisted it, pulled him forward, and wrapped her legs around his waist. She flipped him over and attempted a chokehold, but he blocked her and landed a punch into her side that knocked the wind out of her.

Lance had no idea what to do. Action and crisis were nowhere near his wheelhouse. He considered trying to help Cobb, but Annika and Gia were on him before he could decide. They didn't use any of the moves Kelsey taught them. Instead, in the heat of the moment, they just attacked with wild punches and kicks.

"You like that, motherfucka?" Annika yelled down at Lance as she repeatedly kicked his ribs and stomach.

Cobb pushed Kelsey back against the cinder block wall. She blocked his incoming punch and got enough of a grip on his arm to twist it back and spin him around again. He tried to reverse it but only succeeded in falling to the hard floor, entwined with Kelsey.

As she struggled against him beneath the fluorescent lights, Annika and Gia continued their attack on Lance, who put up no fight at all. He did his best to protect his face as they punched away at him.

Kelsey managed to get her calves around Cobb's neck and had his arm pulled back as well. He struggled first to free himself, and when he failed, he tried desperately to breathe. Kelsey put everything she had into her grip and let out loud groans as she squeezed against his throat. After what seemed like forever, Cobb stopped moving.

Kelsey held the position a few extra seconds to make sure

he was out. She stood up, breathing heavily, her heart racing. She pulled Annika and Gia off Lance, who was frozen in a ball and holding his bloody nose. He was no threat.

"Okay, okay. You did good," she told them.

She turned to the door, which had shut during the scuffle.

Kelsey looked down at Lance. "What's the code to open the door?"

Lance looked at the blood on his fingers. The only sound blurting out of him was a moan of pain. She kicked him in the ribs.

"Hey! Asshole," she yelled. "The code!"

"Six six, eight three, six five," Lance said.

Kelsey punched in the code. There was a click, and she pulled it open.

She turned to Annika and Gia. "Come on."

Annika gave Lance one last kick. "Punk-ass bitch!" she shouted at him.

———•———

Kelsey led Gia and Annika out of the room and through the long corridor. It reminded her of a service hallway inside a mall, but darker. She noticed something else. Something familiar. A distinct smell.

What is that? Horses? Elephants?

Down the hall, they saw a door similar to the one they'd been held behind. It also had a food slot and a window on it. Kelsey looked through the one-way glass. It was another holding room with a straggly man asleep on a mattress. Her mind raced.

Where the hell are we? What is going on?

Annika and Gia looked inside as Kelsey tried punching in the code she just used. It didn't work.

"They abducting men too?" Gia asked.

Kelsey banged on the door, but the man didn't move.

"We gotta go," Annika said.

Kelsey knew she was right. They moved on down the corridor.

There were different types of doors on the left side of the hallway. Large, oversized, steel doors, each with a circular dead bolt locking system like something in a submarine. Beside each one was another, smaller door. Kelsey's mind raced.

Why so many doors? Which one leads outside?

She went for the smaller one. It had a simple dead bolt, but the bolt itself was as thick and long as the end of a baseball bat. She grabbed the sidebar of the dead bolt and instantly let go of it when she felt how cold it was. It was like touching the handle of a walk-in freezer. She grabbed it again and struggled with it.

"Guys. Help me," she asked.

With three of them pulling, the door cracked open and a rush of cold air blew through them. They experienced a second of pleasantness at the sensation of the chilly air hitting their faces.

Cold air. This could be the right way.

The sensation was instantly replaced with disgust as a rotten, rank odor filled the air.

"Ugh. That's nasty," Gia whispered.

"Maybe it leads out by the dumpsters or a trash area," Kelsey reasoned.

"I don't give a shit about no smell as long as it gets us the fuck out," Annika said.

22

KELSEY AND HARVEY MEET AGAIN

K ELSEY HELD HER NOSE AS they approached the end of the narrow hall. The rancid smell was the worst odor she could remember since Harvey Wilcox's apartment. It was the same reek of putrid decay. Her eyes began to adjust to the dark. She turned the corner at the end of the passageway and saw grass below her. There were a few trees not too far away.

"We made it!" Annika said.

"Are we outside?" Gia asked.

Kelsey saw what looked like open countryside at night with a tree line leading back at least a mile.

"Yeah. But I don't...," Kelsey replied.

She stopped in her tracks. Harvey Wilcox, the first decomposed corpse she'd ever seen, the murder victim who still appeared in her nightmares, walked toward her out of the dark.

It can't be! It's impossible! she thought as he lumbered closer.

Her heart pounded so hard she thought it might burst. Even in her shocked state, she pushed Annika and Gia behind her.

"Shit!" Annika said.

"Is that real? It can't be real!" Gia added.

Of course it wasn't Harvey Wilcox. But he looked like he had the same level of decomposition Harvey had all those years ago. The crumpled-grape eyes, the wrinkled skin over the accentuated cheekbones, it might as well have been him. The only thing missing was the gunshot wound in the center of the forehead.

"Hey!" Kelsey yelled. "Back up! I'm a cop!"

She tried to figure out why there'd be a guy dressed up like a zombie walking around.

"I said back the fuck up!" she yelled.

He reached for her.

His hands, Kelsey thought. *The bones of the fingers poke out of the skin.*

"I'm not telling you aga—"

Kelsey didn't have time to finish her warning before she was within his reach. She grabbed his wrist, bent it back, and pulled the arm up to spin him around. Normally the bending of the wrist would inflict enough pain to cause the attacker to turn in whatever direction she steered him in.

This time it was like the man had no feeling. The rest of his body didn't react at all. She could feel the arm dislocate from its shoulder, and the sensation caused her to let go. The arm just fell limp and swung by its side as the other arm kept reaching.

He's so drugged he doesn't feel pain, Kelsey thought.

She cocked her arm back and drove a punch into his face. The force of the blow knocked his head back so hard she was sure both Annika and Gia heard his neck snap with a crunch. His head fell back all the way until it bounced against his back and swung there like a sock with rocks in it.

"What the fuck!" Annika yelled.

Kelsey tried to understand what was happening. It didn't make sense. The guy was still stumbling toward her, even with his head dangling behind him. He looked like the headless horseman. She stood frozen until he grabbed her shoulder, then opened her palms and gave him a hard push to the chest that knocked him off his feet. He went down with his dangling face behind him, hitting the ground first with his body on top of it.

"What the fuck?" Annika asked.

Gia and Annika stared, mystified, as he struggled helplessly on his back.

How can this guy still be moving? Why is he wearing zombie makeup? What the hell is going on?

They watched as he managed to get onto his side. When he did, his head rolled with each movement. It was the most unnatural thing any of them had ever seen. It held them spellbound until a sound nearby stole their attention.

Kelsey doubted her own eyes.

They must have drugged us. That's the only explanation.

She looked at her arms, but it was too dark to see any kind of needle prick. Kelsey felt herself twitch as her brain struggled to figure out what was real and what wasn't.

"What was that?" Gia asked.

Kelsey turned to her in complete confusion. Her eyes were narrow and blinking, her mouth half open as if she tasted something disgusting.

Is Annika real? Maybe all this has been a hallucination? I may not even be here. I could be in some…

"Let's just get outta here," Annika yelled.

Either way, you gotta move, Kelsey thought.

"Yeah. Stay close together."

As they moved forward, their eyes adjusted enough to make out more of the area. It was surreal. The ground looked like they were outdoors. It was uneven and covered in dirt and grass, but there was a ceiling above them with sophisticated lights. They were in a large room about half the size of a basketball court. Kelsey realized the tree-lined countryside was actually painted onto the wall. Between them and the wall were a dozen or so headstones and bushes.

A cemetery?

In the corner of the room was a stone mausoleum. It was gothic with a wrought iron gate around it. The gate's door was off its hinges and lay crooked against the entrance. A mechanical black crow stood on one of the tree branches, squawking.

What is going on? This whole place looks like the graveyard set from the "Thriller" video.

"Just keep moving," she said to Annika and Gia.

They headed away from the cemetery and into the dark. Annika was farthest ahead and walked straight into something before falling backward.

"Jesus Christ!" she yelled.

Kelsey reached out and felt a wall in front of them. Right after, a light came on ahead of them.

Shit, she thought. Either the one she knocked out recovered faster than expected or it was other bad guys searching for them. The light was too far ahead of them to illuminate the area they were in, but the odd glare made Kelsey realize the wall Annika had walked into was made of glass.

What is this?

She jumped when Annika grabbed her arm.

"Jesus!"

"Look!" Annika pointed at several figures coming through the gates by the mausoleum. They were just dark figures in this light, but they moved and shambled as the first guy had. Their feet shuffled and their arms dangled by their sides lifelessly.

"Quick, we have to go back and find another way."

"Where did we come in?" Gia asked.

They fumbled their way back but had trouble finding where they entered.

Once they did, Kelsey pushed Annika ahead of her. "Go. Go."

Kelsey saw more of them than she'd first thought, and they were much closer than she cared for. Annika and Gia felt their way back into and through the narrow passageway until they got to the small door. Their hands ran all over the surface in search of a knob or handle.

"Shit! Where's the fucking doorknob?" Annika panicked.

Kelsey realized it was only meant to open from the other side.

Okay. Think. Come on. Come on.

The sounds of the dark figures stumbling behind them got louder. Annika banged on the door.

"Let us out! Hey!" she screamed.

Kelsey tried running her fingers along the line of the door and pushing, but it was no use. Even in the dark, she could see the figures enter the narrow passageway. They were almost climbing over each other to get to them, causing several in front to fall. Their bodies hit the floor, almost doll-like as others tripped on them.

The closer they got, the more visible their faces became. Kelsey saw each one was also wearing zombie makeup. They were all different levels of decomposition. The makeup had a more realistic look to it than anything she'd seen on TV or in movies. These guys looked like actual corpses. She'd seen bodies in various levels of decay, both firsthand as well as in photos, and had always thought when compared to movie corpses, the real ones looked somehow fake.

Whoever did the makeup on these guys knew what real corpses looked like.

But why?

"Those are real motherfucking zombies," Annika said as if hearing Kelsey's thoughts.

That couldn't be true, but Kelsey had no other explanation.

The herd surged forward and the closest ones fell to the floor. The ones behind them fumbled on top and over them as they squeezed themselves closer.

"Get back!" Gia yelled.

They were just a few feet away now. The ones that had fallen were crawling on their stomachs with others on top of them.

The space between them and the zombies was almost gone. Annika's and Gia's shoulders bounced against each other as their backs pressed against the wall. Their screaming filled the tight space, echoing louder and louder to a crescendo.

One of the zombies fell so close its head hit Annika's foot. It grabbed her ankle and tried to pull it to its mouth as Annika screamed and kicked. Kelsey kicked at it too, bringing the balls of her bare feet down as hard as she could. It felt like stomping on the carved face of a Halloween pumpkin.

The door behind them swung open, and light flooded in. Cobb grabbed Annika's arm and pulled her out of the space as if she were a heavy trash bag. She crashed to the floor at the feet of Mason Spector, who stood over her with a cattle prod. Cobb quickly pulled Kelsey and Gia out the same way, slammed the door, and slid the dead bolt shut.

Mason raised the prod as Kelsey got to her feet.

"What is this place?" she asked.

"Don't worry about it," Mason replied.

Kelsey helped Annika up.

"Fuck you! Y'all sick muthafuckas," Annika said.

"Come on, ladies. Let's go." Mason waved the cattle prod.

"Not yet," Cobb grunted.

He grabbed Kelsey by the throat and pushed her against the wall, pinning her with his forearm. "You think you're a real tough bitch, huh?"

She rammed her knee at his balls, but he expected it and dodged easily.

"Oh, you'll never get the drop on me again," he said as he squeezed her neck.

Kelsey wanted to tell him to fuck off, to spit in his face, but she couldn't breathe.

Cobb spoke to Mason without taking his eyes off her. "Where'd you find this one?"

"By Back Bay."

"She doesn't have the face of a hooker," Cobb said.

"That one does." Mason laughed, nodding toward Annika.

"Fuck you, you piece of shit," Annika said.

Cobb leaned his face so close to Kelsey his nose poked into her cheek. She could smell his breath. "Listen, bitch. We're gonna take you back to your room, and you're gonna stay there like a good little girl. You got that?"

Kelsey grunted. "Fuck you."

Her mind ran in circles. She considered several moves to escape his grasp.

If I can get my arm over his…

"I'm sorry," Cobb said as he put even more pressure on her neck. "What was that?"

She was so frustrated she wanted to cry, but the instinct to defy him and piss him off was much stronger, so she let out as much of a laugh as she could manage. As she hoped, it infuriated him.

"Let go of her, motherfucker!" Annika yelled and started to move toward him.

"Ah-ah," Mason said. "Don't be stupid." He turned to Cobb. "Come on. I've got other shit to do."

Seeing Kelsey laugh in his face, refusing to acknowledge his power over her, clearly enraged Cobb. He pushed his arm against her neck with everything he had.

"Stop it before you kill her. We don't have time to get another one," Mason said.

The words made their way through Cobb's anger, and he released her. She fell to the floor in a combination of wheezes and coughs. Annika and Gia rushed down to her.

"Come on," Mason said. "This way."

For the first time, Kelsey feared she might not get out of this alive.

23

TICK TOCK

VIC POUNDED HIS FIST ON Sweeney's desk so hard the plastic Red Sox mug holding his pens fell over.

"Why the hell not?" Vic yelled. "How can you say no?" Every vein in Vic's neck threatened to pop. His face was deep red, and his jaw muscles tensed.

Sweeney sat back in his chair and took a breath. "I understand you're feeling a lot of stress right now," Sweeney said. "I think it's clouding your judgment."

"What are you talking about?" Vic said. "They got shot right in front of us."

"I've still got brain on my jacket," Tony chimed in.

"I don't dispute that," Sweeney replied. "I just don't see what a hate crime in Rockport has to do with Kelsey's case."

Both Vic and Tony's faces went blank.

"A hate crime? Is that a joke?" Vic said.

"The chief at Rockport told me there have been threats against the LGBTQ community for weeks."

Vic paced the room as Sweeney continued.

"It makes more sense than thinking it's somehow connected to the Tremont because the building next door has a good air-conditioning system. Secret thumb scanners in elevators? Are you nuts?"

Vic was exhausted and his nerves were spent. Time was running out—he had no choice but to follow his instincts head-on. He turned to Sweeney, and after several seconds of glaring at the man, he just came out and said it. "Who told you to shut us down?"

Tony looked at Vic.

"Excuse me?" Sweeney asked as if Vic were insane.

"Just shut up." Vic moved toward him with his eyes never breaking away.

"Hey!" Sweeney yelled as he stood up. "Screw you! I'm your commanding…"

"I said shut the fuck up!" Vic yelled.

Vic got to the desk and made his way around it. With each step, his anger intensified and any thought of restraint faded. Sweeney must have seen the look in his eyes because he took a subconscious half step back.

"Kelsey is somewhere in the basement of that building. I know it. All the evidence points to it. We have more than enough for a warrant, and you won't sign off. Why? *Why?*"

Vic's angry yell on the last word made Sweeney flinch.

Sweeney looked through the open blinds at the dozens of other cops working in the outer office, then wiped the growing sweat off his forehead and turned back to Vic. "Listen. I'm gonna cut you some slack because of what you're going through, but you're way out of line to suggest—"

Vic smacked his hand on the desk. "You're gonna tell me, and you're gonna tell me now."

Tony appeared concerned. He took a few steps toward his partner, to Sweeney's obvious relief.

"Yeah," he said, "talk to your partner before he ruins his career."

The cocky expression on Sweeney's face faded when Tony walked right past Vic, locked the office door, and proceeded to close the blinds so the people in the outer office couldn't see in.

Sweeney's face lost all color. "You've both lost it." He walked backward from Vic as he continued raising his voice. "I want you out of—"

Vic slugged him with an uppercut that sent him back over his desk. The computer and stacks of paperwork fell to the floor. Sweeney lay on the floor, stunned. He raised a hand to protect his face as Vic got on top of him and grabbed him by the throat.

"Listen, you piece of shit. I don't know who's pulling your strings, but you're going to get me a warrant to go down there with enough uniforms to search the entire place. Understand?"

Sweeney's eyes bulged as Vic squeezed his throat. He looked like he was about to black out but managed a pathetic nod. Vic released him and stood as Sweeney went into a coughing fit. There was a knock.

"Everything all right in there?" someone asked through the closed door.

Tony cracked it a few inches. "All good," he said to the uniform.

When Sweeney got his breath back, he sat up against the bookcase behind the desk. "It's not my fault," he said. "I had no choice."

"I don't give a fuck," Vic said.

Sweeney picked up the phone. Before he called, he looked at them. "Just listen. All this is gonna do is…"

"Get that warrant, or I swear to Christ your jaw will be wired for six weeks." Vic glared murderously.

Sweeney made the call. "Judge Tompkins? It's Acting Captain Sweeney. Sorry to bother you."

———·———

Vic and Tony sped through the suburb of Swampscott to get to the judge's house with the warrant to sign. Once they had it in hand, they'd get everyone together and do a briefing. They'd probably be able to get to the Tremont by nine. Vic planned on requesting a dozen uniforms to back him and Tony up, with SWAT on standby.

"Do you think we have to notify Human Trafficking before we go in?" Tony asked.

"Damn," Vic said. "We're supposed to. But I don't want to wait for them."

Once they turned onto the judge's street, an unmarked car with flashing blue lights, along with several squad cars, cut them off. Two detectives, Chang and Morales, got out and approached as Vic and Tony also got out. Chang was built like a champion weightlifter with arms like propane tanks. Morales and all the uniforms behind him looked like stick figures in comparison.

"What's this?" Vic asked.

Chang looked upset. "I'm sorry Vic. I mean, with everything else you've got going on, Sweeney ordered us to bring you in."

"That motherfucker," Tony said.

Vic shook his head in disgust as the blue lights flickered across his face.

"He said you guys assaulted him," Morales added.

"What's really going on?" Chang asked. He and Vic had known each for more than a decade and had complete trust in one another.

"Whoever took Kelsey has powerful friends trying to shut us down. They set up Guidley because she knew it too. Sweeney's in their pocket."

"No shit? How sure are you about all this?" Chang asked.

"Ninety-five percent," Vic replied.

Chang looked at Morales to make sure he was on the same page.

"Sweeney's a douchebag," Morales said with a grunt of disgust.

Chang turned back to Vic and Tony. "How do you want to play this?"

"What if we just grab the judge's signature and go in ourselves?" Tony asked Vic.

Vic shook his head. "No. I'm sure Sweeney will have units waiting for us outside the Tremont." He turned to Chang and Morales. "We need to get to Kelsey before tomorrow night."

Chang looked at Morales and glanced at the uniforms watching them. "We must have beat you here. You spotted us and took off. We never saw you."

"Thanks," Vic said.

"If I can do anything, call me. Do you want me to go to the chief and let him know what you said?" Chang said.

"No. Don't say anything. We don't know who's involved yet. But thanks. I owe you."

"No, you don't. Just watch your ass. Sweeney's probably gonna have everyone looking for you. Don't go home," Chang said.

They shook hands and walked back to their cars.

One of the uniforms approached Chang. "Sarge, I don't want to be an asshole, but are we going to get in trouble for this?"

Chang turned to the other uniforms. "Listen up. We've known that guy a long time, and he's one of the most honest cops alive. Whatever is going on, I can promise you he's not the bad guy in the situation. I'd put my life on it."

———•———

They parked on the roof of a parking garage downtown. Tony sat on the hood, looking at the lights of the Hancock Tower glowing against the night sky. Vic stood in what Kelsey always called his "deep-thought pose," the fingers of both hands clasped together on top of his head as he stared into the distance.

"Sorry I got you into this," Vic said.

"Don't be ridiculous. If you didn't slug him, I would've. He's a piece of shit."

Vic paced the roof until he stopped short. He dropped his hands from the top of his head and stared as if his eyes were focused on something in the distance, but he was visualizing something else, piecing a puzzle together in his mind.

He rushed over to Tony. "I have an idea, but it's a long shot."

"What?"

"The elevator at the coffee shop. Neary said it hides that people are going down to the basement because when they get on in the lobby, no one knows what floor they're really going to. Anyone who sees them get on doesn't know where they're getting off. They just assume they went up to a higher floor."

"Yeah, I get that," Tony said. "But that doesn't help us. Once they go down, they're already in. We can't follow them because of the thumb scanner. And even if we got on the elevator with every person who got on, they won't use the scanner in front of us. They'll wait for us to get off, and if we don't, they'll get off on another floor and leave."

Vic's face formed a slight smile. "Yeah. But what if we reversed it?"

"What do you mean?"

"Okay. So, when they're going in, we don't see where they go. But what if we watch the people getting off in the lobby?"

"I'm sorry. Maybe I'm tired. I don't get it." Tony's eyes narrowed.

"There are six floors above the lobby. If we watch all six elevator doors at the same time, we can monitor everyone who gets off in the lobby. But if someone gets off in the lobby we didn't see on any of the six floors above, that means they had to be coming from the basement, right?"

Tony's eyes widened, and he lifted his hands as if someone were handing him some invisible object. "That's brilliant. So we need five more guys."

"Yeah," Vic said, "but seeing someone staking out the elevators on every floor would get noticed."

"What about video?" Tony asked. "We could put small cameras on each floor and monitor them from the coffee shop. Do you think Eddie from surveillance would do it? He has all that stuff and knows how to set it up."

Vic shook his head. "I don't know. His wife just had a baby."

"Fuck," Tony said. "We could just buy the stuff, but I don't know how to work it all."

Vic considered their options until a thought occurred to him, but it was a thought he wasn't sure he should entertain.

He squeezed his eyes shut, shook his head from side to side, and let out a quiet grunt followed by a tight-lipped smirk. "The kid."

"Huh?"

"Kirby. He's a videographer. He'll know how to do this."

Tony laughed as they both got in the car. "That fucking kid. He's gonna love this."

24

ON ONE CONDITION

"YEAH, I CAN DO THAT," Kirby said as he walked to his equipment table. It was strewn with cameras, lenses and other videography items. He moved a few things around to get to what he was looking for.

Vic followed and looked at the equipment he was shuffling around as Tony dropped onto the sofa. "How long would it take to set up?"

Kirby opened a metal case. "Not long. Once I place the cameras, about ten to fifteen minutes to sync everything up."

"Great."

"If it works, you'll take me down with you guys, right?" Kirby said.

Vic shook his head. "We can't do that. I told you, it could get dangerous."

"So… you expect me to take my equipment, set it all up for you, work the cameras for you in the hopes of getting a lead, and if you do, at that point you guys go down and I just go home?"

"It's for your own good," Tony said.

"Come on! Find someone else then," Kirby said as he sat down in his chair and folded his arms.

Vic leaned over Kirby as menacingly as he could. He poked

his finger into the Bigfoot silhouette on Kirby's T-shirt. "Kid… I don't have time for this. You're going to do it."

"Or what?" Kirby said, his leg occasionally shaking.

Vic stared into Kirby's eyes. Vic was desperate, but he was also bluffing… and both of them knew it.

"Damn it!" Vic snapped. "Fine."

"Yessssss!" Kirby hissed.

Vic got into his face. "But you do exactly what we tell you to do. You stay behind us the whole time, and if we run into any trouble, you hit the floor and stay down until I tell you to get up. Understand?"

"Got it."

"I saw two people get killed over this. I won't have you being the third."

Kirby jumped out of his chair and started loading the cameras and equipment he'd need into a bag.

Tony looked at Vic with a raised eyebrow. "You sure about this?"

"What choice do we have?"

Tony got up.

"The coffee shop opens at six. We'll pick you up at five thirty," Vic said.

"Okay, good. Plenty of time to charge everything up. Are there electrical outlets near the elevators?"

"I have no clue," Vic replied.

"I'll bring extra batteries just in case."

The detectives headed for the door. They were drained, and the fact a plan was now in place somehow caused them to feel it. Their feet dragged slightly along with their growing aches and pains.

"Hey, wait," Kirby said.

They turned back to him, exhausted.

"When you pick me up, you'll bring a gun for me to use, right?"

"Not funny, kid." Vic shook his head.

25

SATURDAY MORNING STAKEOUT

F ROM THE TIME KIRBY GOT into the car, he bombarded
them about police work, their strangest cases, and all
kinds of other things. Tony answered most of them. Vic was
silent. His mind was on the day ahead—he was betting
everything on thin hopes at best.

When he drove down Tremont Street toward
Uncommon Grounds and passed by the Tremont, he saw
he was right. Sweeney had stationed several cops out in
front as well as in front of the Harvard Trucking Company
next door.

He wondered who was giving Sweeney his orders, how
high it went. Whoever it was, though, didn't know Neary
had told them about the entrance through the coffee shop.

———·———

It was a busy Saturday morning. Uncommon Grounds was
full of bearded hipsters, tourists, couples, singles, and the
occasional homeless person trying to use the restroom.

In one respect, they lucked out. On every floor above the
lobby, Kirby discovered there were two potted trees across
from the elevators, flanking a framed art print. The trees were
ideal for hiding cameras.

It took Kirby about thirty minutes to place them on each

floor and another twenty to get all of them synced to his laptop. He set up his screen to show all the floors simultaneously.

They set up base camp at a table with a clear view of the lobby elevator. Now it was a matter of watching and waiting. All three glued their eyes to the screen. Every time someone approached the elevators on the floors above, they waited for them to get off in the lobby. The plan was, if they saw someone get off they hadn't seen get on up above, they'd grab him and force him to take them back down below.

"Listen, kid," he said, "if we luck out and this works, we're going to have to move fast. Just stay behind us and try to keep up."

"I will," Kirby said.

As Vic drank his black coffee, he watched Kirby take a long sip through the straw in his peppermint mocha frozen coffee with extra whipped cream and felt a sudden wave of uncertainty.

———•———

By noon, Uncommon Grounds was packed. A table of five girls near them laughed loudly. Vic's eyes constantly went from Kirby's screen to the elevator. The smell of fresh coffee filled the air and triggered memories of his favorite weekend pastime with Kelsey.

Coffee. The Globe. *Sunday mornings.*

His stomach turned.

I'm coming, honey. Please, God, let me be in time.

Another customer came in. A man, late twenties, wearing a backward ball cap. He ordered, got his coffee, and headed toward the elevator.

Once he was on, Vic watched the split screen of the other floors.

On the third floor, the elevator opened, and Blue Cap got out.

Fuck, Vic thought.

26
SATURDAY EVENING

MICHAEL BARCLAY STOOD TALL AT the Tremont entrance as eighty-year-old billionaire Douglas Radcliffe arrived in his shiny black SUV. The chauffeur held open the door as Radcliffe and his stunning, twenty-two-year-old companion stepped out into the crisp evening air.

"Mr. Radcliffe!" Barclay said with genuine excitement, "Welcome back."

Radcliffe shook his hand. "Thank you, Michael. How have you been?"

"Very well, sir. Thank you."

Radcliffe turned to Becca. "This is my friend Becca."

"Nice to meet you, Becca," Barclay replied, taking her hand in his. "If there's anything I can do to make your stay more pleasurable, please don't hesitate to let me know." Barclay turned back to Radcliffe. "Mr. Radcliffe, Chef Randy has secured a three-pound lobster with your name on it."

———·———

Barclay escorted them inside and into the Tavern where James Winthrop and several other members chatted. Their smiles and laughs had an undeniable measure of arrogance. None more so than Winthrop.

Although several renovations had taken place, the room

retained the same classic look as when it first opened. There were several sitting areas, leather sofas, paneled oak walls, hand-carved fixtures, detailed woodwork on the ceiling. Framed black-and-white photos of past and present members lined the walls.

Above the fireplace was an oversized antique clock that once hung outside a building at Scollay Square at the turn of the century. Although over a hundred years old, the clock still worked. Several attractive waitresses served bacon-wrapped scallops, lamb with mint, and steak tips.

Displayed prominently in the center of the lobby, the handcrafted golden lid of the Egyptian coffin stood beside the pharaoh's open casket. Unlike in a museum, there were no glass barriers around the exhibit. Even the dozen or so golden artifacts discovered with the pharaoh sat on red velvet display mounts. If someone wanted to reach out and grab one of them, nothing would stop them. Barriers, glass partitions, and velvet ropes were for the lower classes, not these people. Special lights were installed above to make the gold sparkle as much as possible.

In his time, the pharaoh possessed supreme power and godlike worship. Three thousand years later, he stood in the center of the Tremont Club, reduced to being a piece of decor for the guests.

Tom Ackerman walked into the lobby and was immediately mesmerized by his surroundings. His eyes took it all in.

"Tom." James Winthrop smiled. "So happy you could come."

"Thanks for having me."

He guided Tom into the Tavern. Seeing all the formally dressed, mostly older men smoking cigars in this environment, Tom's mind flashed to the after-dinner scene in *Titanic*.

"George," Winthrop said to the first man they came upon. "I'd like you to meet Tom Ackerman. Tom, George Conrad."

"Hi, Tom. Good to meet you," Conrad said.

"You too, sir."

Pharmaceutical tycoon Franklin Dodd turned to join the conversation. "Hello," Dodd said, offering his hand. "Frank Dodd."

"Hi, sir. Tom Ackerman. Nice to meet you." Tom shook his hand and noticed how impossibly soft Dodd's skin was, as if the man had never handled anything rougher than a pillow.

One by one, he was introduced to the other current members. He was surprised at how many faces he recognized — several of them were often demonized in the press as the heads of evil corporations. Big tobacco, big pharma, big oil… all the billionaire boogeymen were here.

He also recognized a couple of well-known politicians. One was a current Republican congressman who had been Speaker of the House. The other was a retired senator. In any case, the members were quite an exclusive fraternity.

George Conrad, 74
CEO, Texas Oil Corporation
Net Worth $7 Billion

Franklin Dodd, 68
CEO, Quest Pharmaceuticals
Net Worth $12 Billion

Rick Jackson, 72
Owner, American Tobacco
Net Worth $9 Billion

Sherman Haynes, 77
President/CEO, Lexington Firearms
Net Worth $8 Billion

Rubin Mancuso, 76
Owner/CEO, RMM Media
Net Worth $28 Billion

Matthew Pond, 67
Lawyer, Congressman
Net Worth $900 Million

Jason Kirkland, 73
Lawyer, Senator
Net Worth $1 Billion

Keiji Fyujiyama, 61
CEO, Yama Manufacturing
Net Worth $11 Billion

Bryan Blackstone, 72
CEO, Bryan Blackstone Inc.
Net Worth $3 Billion

Elliot Cosinger, 70
CEO, Cosinger Holdings
Net Worth $5 Billion

Douglas Radcliffe, 80
CEO, Radcliffe Solutions
Net Worth $22 Billion

James Winthrop, 70
CEO, Winthrop Properties
Net Worth $30 Billion

Tom couldn't decide if he was being welcomed into the ultimate inner circle or tricked into the devil's den. He was surprised many of the men had young women with them. They were the most stunning girls he'd ever seen. Each one was dressed sexier than the last, wearing dresses that clung to them in all the right places. Tom was certain they had to be high-end escorts.

Winthrop had with him his two playmates from Vegas, Veronica and Joelle. They sat at the bar, drinking and chatting. They knew exactly when to give Winthrop space and when to stay close without being told.

Tom leaned closer to Winthrop and whispered, "I don't understand... if the club is a secret, why all the women? Aren't you worried they'll talk?"

Winthrop smiled. "Have you heard the expression three people can keep a secret if two of them are dead?"

"Yes."

"Well, the only one better at keeping secrets than a dead man is a beautiful whore who loves money."

"If you say so."

Winthrop went on. "In every smoky back room there have also been beautiful women. They don't talk. They never do."

One of the women walked toward them. She had pale blue eyes and a wild mane of chestnut hair. Tom couldn't take his eyes off her.

"Raquel," Winthrop said, "you look dazzling."

"Thanks, J.W."

"Tom, may I introduce you to Raquel? She'll be your date for the evening."

"Uh. My... Hi. Oh. Okay," Tom stammered. "Nice to meet you, Raquel."

"You too, Tom."

"Tom is the genius behind LittleBirdy," Winthrop said.

Raquel playfully poked Tom's arm. "I thought you looked familiar."

"Why don't you and Tom get yourselves a drink while I see to the other guests?"

Raquel turned to Tom, and when she looked directly into his eyes, he felt his knees buckle. "Great idea. Shall we?"

As they made their way through the room, Tom couldn't shake the feeling he was somewhere he shouldn't be.

"So," he said, "help me out. When he said you're my date for the evening, does that mean we sit together at dinner?"

Raquel smiled. "It means tonight it's my job to make sure you enjoy yourself," she said softly.

"Uh..."

She leaned closer. The scent of her perfume enveloped him, and her lips brushed against his ear as she whispered, "From now until tomorrow morning, I'm all yours. We can do anything you want to."

27

A BITE

THEY WATCHED THE ELEVATORS ALL day, with nothing out of the ordinary happening. It was dark outside now. Night had fallen, and with it, Vic's hopes. Through the coffee shop window, he saw the street come alive with people enjoying their Saturday night, laughing and walking among the traffic lights and colorful neon signs.

But then he saw a large, muscular guy in a leather jacket enter the lobby. He had something about him as he got a coffee from the counter and approached the elevator.

"Keep your eyes on this guy," Vic said.

When the doors opened, a woman got off and Leather Jacket got on.

Vic and Kirby had seen the woman get on the elevator on the second floor and expected her to get off. Now they kept their eyes glued to all the camera feeds to see if this guy got off as well.

He never did.

Vic felt a burst of adrenaline. "Where is he?"

"I don't know," Kirby said, just as excited. "We may have one."

A couple of women in yoga clothes carrying rolled mats walked their coffees to the elevator. When it opened, it was empty.

Vic slapped Tony on the arm. "We got one."

Twenty minutes later, a large man got off in the lobby, this one wearing jeans and a Celtics jacket.

Wait. Where did you come from? Vic thought.

"Hey," Vic said, "that guy didn't get on any of the upper floors."

"Where?" Tony asked.

"In the Celtics jacket," Vic said as he jumped up and pointed at the man. Vic turned to Kirby. "Stay here until I tell you."

"I got it. Go. Go."

Vic and Tony followed the man outside. He crossed Tremont Street and walked through the Common toward a busy underground parking garage. They followed along behind a group of loud college kids walking in the same direction. Their happy voices added to the chorus of noises surrounding them... impatient drivers honking, music from car windows, a loud motorcycle cutting through the traffic.

The parking garage was much quieter. They kept their distance as he approached a new-model Lexus. As soon as the car chirped unlocked, Vic pulled his gun.

"Don't move," Vic yelled.

The man jumped. "Jesus!"

Tony circled with his own gun drawn. "Hands on your head."

"Hey, take it. You can have it," he said.

Tony searched him for a weapon while Vic kept his gun on him.

"Nothing," Tony said and took the car keys from his hand.

"We're cops. We just want to talk," Vic replied.

"Got some ID?" Tony asked.

"It's in my pocket," Celtics Guy answered but didn't lower his hands.

"Go ahead. Take it out slowly." Tony motioned with his gun.

The man reached for his wallet and handed it to Tony.

"What's going on?" he asked. "I think there might be a mistake."

Vic holstered his gun and got closer to him.

"Evan Farris," Tony said, reading the driver's license. "Somerville."

"Did I do something wrong?"

"Where are you coming from right now?" Vic asked.

"Work."

"Where's that?" Tony asked.

"I'm a maintenance supervisor at the Westbrook. The apartment building above the coffee shop."

"Cut the shit. I know where you really came from," Vic said.

Farris stayed silent. His eyes searched the garage around them as if he knew someone else was watching. The detectives scoped out their surroundings. Satisfied the coast was clear, they turned their full focus back to Farris.

"What's down there?" Vic asked.

"I don't know what you're talking about," Farris said.

Vic punched Farris in the gut, causing him to bend over and dry heave. "Don't make me ask again."

"Wait," Tony said, "all we need is his thumb for the scanner."

Vic knew he was bluffing but went along. He pulled out his knife.

"Give me your hand." He ordered.

Without putting his gun away, Tony pushed Farris' face onto the hood of his car and held his arm out. Vic grabbed the helpless man's wrist and brought the blade to his thumb.

"I'm just security. I work the metal detector. I have nothing to do with anything else!" Farris said, wheezing as he spoke.

"Why is there a metal detector?" Tony asked.

"To make sure no one brings in any phones or cameras. I only see one area. I don't go inside."

"You're going to take us down there. Right now."

"If I do that, I'm a dead man. They'll kill me."

Vic put his gun to Farris's head. "If you don't, I'll kill you."

Farris pushed his temple back against the gun. "Bullshit. Just take me in so I can call my lawyer."

Vic snapped. He pulled the gun back and smashed it into Farris's face. It cut a deep slice just under his eye. "Asshole. I'm not a cop right now. There are no lawyers. There's just you paying for your shitty life choices." Vic's gaze bore down on him as he spoke through clenched teeth. "You're taking us down, or I swear to Christ I will kill you. If you try to run, I'll shoot you in the ass and drag you the rest of the way. Got it?"

Farris gulped. "Yeah."

As they walked back to Uncommon Grounds, Farris spoke up. "Look, if something illegal is going on down there, I swear I don't know about it."

"What did you think was going on with a secret elevator system?" Tony asked.

"I don't know," Farris said.

The three of them entered the lobby and headed for the elevator. Kirby ran over to join them. He'd loaded all his equipment into a backpack and slung it on his shoulder.

"Kid, look... I was wrong. You can't come with us," Vic said.

"You gave me your word," Kirby replied.

Vic grunted as Tony hit the elevator call button. "Fine. Remember, you do whatever we tell you."

"I will."

The doors opened, and the four of them got on. No one caught it when Farris snuck a glance at a portion of the control panel that hid a security camera.

Vic spotted the Crimson Elevators logo above the control buttons, just as Neary said. "Go ahead. Do it."

Farris stalled until Tony rammed his forearm beneath the man's chin and pinned him against the wall while Vic forced his thumb onto the spot Neary had described.

"Do it!" Vic repeated.

"Okay! Okay!" Farris pressed his thumb on the camouflaged scanner, and the elevator made a noticeable jerk before it began to descend.

Farris's mind was racing. He knew Jerry, the guy who relieved him every night, would be watching them on the elevator's security camera. Even so, the ride was nerve-racking. Jerry carried a Glock, and Farris didn't want to get caught in the cross fire if he or the cops panicked and started shooting.

He swallowed and said, "There's going to be an armed guard when the doors open. Just letting you know so nobody gets hurt."

Vic and Tony pulled out their guns.

"Get behind us," Tony told Kirby.

The elevator stopped with a light jolt. The doors opened, and Vic saw a man standing behind a metal detector with his gun aimed at them.

For several seconds, shouting filled the air.

"We're cops," Tony said. "Drop it!"

"Jerry, don't shoot," Farris yelled.

"Police, damn it! Put it the fuck down!"

"Drop it," Vic ordered.

"Do it, Jerry," Farris ordered.

Jerry stared at them over his gun sights. As Vic and Tony continued to yell at him, he slowly opened his fingers around the gun to show he was giving up. He relaxed his stance and aimed the weapon at the floor.

"Fucking drop it!" Tony barked.

Jerry slowly lowered it to the floor, his eyes never moving from them. Vic watched him over the sights of his own gun, still trained on him.

"What's going on here?" he asked Farris.

"Just do what they—" Farris started, but his sentence was cut off when Jerry aborted his surrender and fired several wild shots at them.

Vic fired back and put three bullets into him center mass. He was dead before he fell.

Tony grabbed Farris and bent him over the security desk. "Don't move. Don't breathe," Tony yelled.

"I'm not resisting," he said. "I'm not doing shit, believe me."

Vic picked up the handgun from the floor as he looked at the still man. No need to feel for a pulse. His pupils were fixed and a puddle of blood beneath him grew wider.

"Guys...," Kirby said.

They turned and saw Kirby clutching his stomach. Blood was leaking between his fingers, and his face was ghost white with an expression that would haunt Vic for the rest of his life.

———•———

When the man gave up and lifted his hands, Kirby stood up from the position he had been in behind Vic. He watched with a surreal feeling as if he had somehow entered a movie. He'd seen this play out a thousand times on TV, and a sense of relief filled him when the man lowered his gun.

As the man reversed and opened fire, Kirby ducked down fast. This was the first time he'd seen a gun go off in real life, and it was the loudest thing he'd ever heard. He covered his ears as he dropped to the floor. He didn't feel the bullet go into his abdomen. He didn't even know he'd been shot until after the deafening noise had stopped.

When he straightened up, he felt a sting in his stomach and side, like a burning sensation. His first thought was maybe he pulled a muscle from ducking so fast. It felt as if he'd just done a few hundred sit-ups and gotten a cramp. He put his hand on the sore area to rub it and felt warm liquid.

Oh God.

He looked down and saw a patch of blood behind a small hole in his shirt. Almost immediately his head felt heavy and his vision blurred.

———•———

Vic was leaning over him within half a second. "Easy, kid."

He ripped open Kirby's shirt and saw a dark hole in his abdomen, leaking blood. He applied pressure and pulled out his phone.

"Looks like you were right and I'm an idiot," Kirby said in short gasps, on the verge of crying.

The phone had no signal. Without lessening the pressure on Kirby, he turned to Farris. "Is there a phone down here that works?"

"No."

"Where is he hit?" Tony asked.

"Right over the kidney."

"I don't want to die. I don't want to die," Kirby said.

"You're not going to die," Vic said, staring into his eyes. "We've just got to get you back up top."

Without discussing it, Tony pulled Farris to the elevator and hit the button. Vic grabbed Kirby beneath the armpits and dragged him onto the elevator. He stood up and grabbed Farris by the neck.

"Do the scanner! Now!"

"You don't need to do it going up, only going down," Farris said.

"If you're lying, I swear to Christ..."

"I'm not."

Vic reached for the up button.

"Wait," Tony said. "I'll bring him up, you go after Kelsey."

Vic considered it but looked down at Kirby bleeding on the elevator floor and felt a thousand tons of responsibility crush down on him. His mind bolted through the questions in his head. If he went up, he might not be able to come back down.

Kelsey's down here somewhere. I can feel it, he thought. "Okay."

Vic pulled Farris away from Tony. He shoved him to the floor by the desk, handcuffed him to it, and then jumped back to Kirby.

"You're going to be okay, kid. I've seen guys hit in the same place, and they're all fine."

Kirby looked at him, sweating so much his pale face shone. "Promise me one thing, if I die..."

"You're not gonna die."

"Just listen! Promise me if I do, you guys will check in on my mom every now and then. She'll be all alone now. Promise me..."

Vic felt his heart melt and add to the guilt, mixing into a thick nausea that filled his gut.

"We promise," Tony said, "but you're gonna be fine."

Vic got off the elevator. Tony pushed the up button, and the doors started to close. The detectives looked at each other as the space between the doors grew smaller.

At the last second, Tony stuck his hand between the doors, and they opened.

"What are you doing?" Vic asked.

"I can't help him from here on up, and I won't be able to come back down unless I bring that asshole with me. Once we're up there though, anything can happen. The other guy was already drawing down on us when we came in. Someone might be watching us right now. You need me. There may be more checkpoints, other assholes. If we send the kid up by himself, soon as the doors open in the lobby, people will call 911 just as fast as I can. I can't help him, but I can help you."

Vic shook his head. It made sense, but the guilt he felt looking at Kirby was too great.

"He's right," Kirby said.

Tony got off the elevator, leaned in, and hit the up button again.

"Kid...," Vic said.

"It's not your fault. I forced you. Remember?" Kirby wheezed.

The doors closed.

Vic grabbed his head with both hands. "If he doesn't make it..."

Tony took the guard's pistol from Vic and ejected the magazine. "He doesn't have hollow-points in here. As long Kirby gets into an ambulance fast, he should be fine."

Vic knew that was most likely true, and time was running short on finding Kelsey.

He hunched down beside the handcuffed Farris as he scanned the area. There was a locker room off the room they were in. On the nearest wall, there were a handful of headshots of people with their names printed below.

"Who are they?" Vic asked.

"They're the only ones that we're supposed to let by," Farris said, pointing toward a door on the far wall.

"What's in there?" Tony asked.

"I don't know."

"How can you not know?" Vic asked. "You've never looked?"

"No."

"You think we're stupid?" Vic replied.

"It's true. We get paid a shitload of money to not want to look."

They approached the door, which had a keypad mounted to the wall.

"What's the code?" Vic asked.

"Six six, two five, six six, pound sign."

Vic punched it in, and the door gave a loud click. He pushed it open and looked back to Tony, who made sure Farris's wrist was cuffed securely to the desk.

"Don't try to get free. Just wait for us to come back."

Vic and Tony went through the door and let it shut behind them. There was no keypad on the other side, just a push bar. They were now in a long corridor with enough of a gradual curve that they couldn't see where it ended. The walls were closer together than a standard walkway, as if it were designed for single-file walking. Despite being well lit by an overhead light every ten feet or so, walking through it gave Vic a feeling of the unknown he hadn't felt in years.

"This is weird," Tony said.

"Yeah," Vic replied. "I'm trying to figure this out. From where the elevator was, we'd be walking up Tremont toward the club, right?"

"Maybe. In that direction, definitely."

It took several minutes of walking before they finally saw where the corridor ended. The passage came to a sharp turn, then continued and opened into a wider service hallway. Before the turn, there was another door. They exchanged a look and, without discussing it, decided to go through.

With guns in hand, they took their standard positions for entering what might be a hostile area. Vic aimed his gun at the closed door as Tony prepared to push it open. They gave each other a nod and burst through. Both were ready for anything except what they found on the other side.

28
COCKTAILS

JAPANESE MANUFACTURING GIANT KEIJI FUJIYAMA strolled into the Tavern. The only non-American member of the club, Keiji had been allowed to join because of the deep respect the other members had for his brilliant business decisions. He had a gift for recognizing upcoming trends in the market and moving quickly to take maximum advantage. Other habits he kept secret, such as his preference for eating sushi off nude women.

His date tonight, an American escort whose services he retained whenever in the United States, knew the habit well.

"Stacey," Keiji said in perfect English, "can you please get us a drink?"

"Sure thing," she replied with a smile. She kissed him and walked her perfect legs to the bar.

Keiji stared at Radcliffe's companion, Becca. Her tight dress accentuated her curves, and she had the fullest lips he'd ever seen. Her light green eyes exuded both desire and innocence at the same time. It was a rare combination and one that had Keiji completely entranced. He didn't know the extent of her relationship with Radcliffe, but he was very well accustomed to getting what he wanted. He decided he had to have her, no matter the cost or consequences.

Winthrop mingled with Blackstone and Radcliffe, each holding a glass filled with 1940 Macallan "M" scotch. He'd purchased the bottle at auction for $630,000. For the moment, their assorted lady friends spoke among themselves at the bar.

Radcliffe leaned into Winthrop and lowered his voice. "I'm looking forward to seeing the new acquisition. Is it as big as you thought?"

Blackstone listened raptly.

"Oh yes," Winthrop replied. "Even larger than we anticipated. Barely got it inside."

"Any idea how old it is?" Blackstone asked.

Winthrop smiled. "About a thousand years."

"Incredible," Radcliffe whispered.

"Guess what was embedded in one of its claws?" Winthrop grinned.

Both Radcliffe and Blackstone leaned closer.

"A British cannonball."

A waitress stepped up and offered a tray of shrimp. "Gentlemen?"

Only Blackstone took one. "Thank you."

As soon as she walked away, Radcliffe nodded toward Tom at the bar. "What are the projections for our young friend?"

Winthrop smiled, then looked across the room at Tom, who was standing awkwardly beside Raquel. "I'd say upward of five to six hundred million over the next two years."

"Christ," Blackstone said. "And how old is he?"

"Twenty-eight."

"Unbelievable," replied Radcliffe.

Winthrop put a hand on Blackstone's shoulder. "He's dying to meet you."

Blackstone swallowed the rest of his scotch and headed over to Tom, who was losing the battle to keep his gaze on Raquel's face and not her cleavage.

When Tom saw Blackstone approaching, he almost fell off his stool.

"Oh my god," he said to Raquel. "Bryan Blackstone's coming over."

Raquel giggled. "You haven't met him yet?"

"You have?" Tom asked.

Blackstone walked up with open arms. "Tom!" he said as he hugged the younger man.

"Mr. Blackstone…"

"Bryan please," the Hollywood mogul said.

"Bryan," Tom repeated. "I-I don't have the words. I mean, your films have given me more joy than I can ever tell you."

Blackstone smiled and placed his hand on Tom's shoulder. "Thank you. I appreciate that." The words came out of his mouth with a tone of sincerity Blackstone rarely used anymore. He'd received this kind of adulation for decades. Although he never intended to be condescending, his responses to the adoration had come to sound bored from sheer repetition. With Tom, however, he seemed to appreciate the praise.

"Hi, Raquel. How are you doing?" Blackstone asked.

"I'm very well, Bryan. Thank you."

Winthrop joined them. "Oh good, you two have met." Winthrop turned to Blackstone. "Bryan, when the time comes, can you guide Tom along?"

"It would be my pleasure," Blackstone replied.

"Very good," Winthrop said. "Excuse me then. I'm going to make sure everything is ready."

Winthrop walked away.

Raquel spoke up. "I'm going to freshen up so you two can chat," she said and gave Tom a peck on the cheek.

As she walked away, Blackstone watched her. He turned back to Tom with a raised eyebrow in an attempt at some male bonding. It didn't work because Tom's eyes didn't follow Raquel's body moving away. They were glued to his hero Bryan Blackstone, and he wore an ear-to-ear grin.

"I have so many questions for you," Tom said.

"Let's get a drink and you can ask me anything you want."

29

BENEATH THE COMMON

V IC AND TONY BURST THROUGH the door with fingers on their triggers, ready for anything. Seconds later, their guns dangled by their sides as they stared wide-eyed at their surroundings.

The room they stepped into was enormous, a cavernous space. The circular room was the size and style of a major museum lobby. The ceiling had sculpted woodwork flowing up into a rotunda at least fifty feet high. Certain portions of the walls were made up of large rocks, giving it the look of being underground and raw but in a controlled style.

The walls were lined with a series of oil paintings and skeletal statues. These were large canvases, each at least six by eight feet, complete in heavy, traditional gold frames. The paintings all seemed to be by the same artist, similar in style to Winslow Homer. While each one featured a different subject, they shared a common theme.

Each painting included a strange creature, from hairy, Sasquatch-type things in the woods to sea monsters attacking tall ships. What got Vic's attention, however, were the statues. Positioned between each painting were large, skeletal statues of the various monsters featured in them.

They were all roughly the same size, about ten or fifteen

feet tall, and spread evenly apart. They shared the same shiny charcoal color, but similarities ended there. One looked like it could be a bear but seemed too large. Another had what looked like batwing bones. One had humanlike bones from the waist up and those of a fish tail from the waist down.

"Holy shit...," Tony said. "It *is* a monster museum."

The kid was right. I'll be damned, Vic thought.

Waves of guilt and concern immediately followed the thought as he hoped Kirby made it to the hospital in time. He envisioned the elevator doors opening and people holding coffee screaming upon seeing him bleeding on the floor.

"How could they keep something like this up and running without anyone knowing?" Vic asked.

"Ask Jacob Neary."

"This doesn't make sense. It's incredible but not a reason to kill anyone." Vic looked around.

Across the lobby from where they came in, they could see the main elevator that led down from the Tremont Club, although this elevator was much larger than the elevator they'd seen there. The doors were highly polished wood interlaid with panels of etched gold. Gleaming gold columns flanked the doors. A bright red carpet led from the elevator and stretched around the edge of the circular room, giving a seven-foot-wide red outline to the polished black tiled floor.

Beside the elevator was an unmanned bar with several ice buckets of chilled champagne and a meat-and-cheese station so elaborate it could be featured on the cover of a cuisine magazine.

Vic felt nauseated. Whatever the hell this was, it wasn't any sex trafficking ring.

"Why would those guys not be allowed to see a bunch of paintings and some statues?" Tony asked.

Vic didn't have the answer, only questions. Suddenly, in the distance, they heard what sounded like a distorted version of a tiger's growl. They raised their guns and scanned the area.

"What the fuck?" Vic asked.

Another growl, and this time they could tell it came from one of the large openings on the other end of the lobby, opposite the elevator.

The square opening looked like a typical museum entrance but without any ticket counters or information booths. They entered and found an area comparable to an exhibit room at the Smithsonian Museum of Natural History.

It was a darker space. Most of the light came from a diorama that ran almost the entire length of the far wall. It had a glass window roughly the size of a highway billboard.

Behind the glass was a forest scene. The ground was uneven, covered with dirt, grass, and weeds. There were faux trees appearing to grow naturally from the ground. The walls within the room were painted with a realistic mural of a green mountain range with a three-dimensional tree line in front of it to give the illusion of depth. It looked completely authentic. A Hollywood set designer could do no better. The one thing not visible within the window was any sign of life.

"Doesn't it seem like there should be something in there? Like a statue of a gorilla or—"

Vic spotted something.

Movement behind the trees. Not quite behind the trees, but almost part of them. Something began to separate from them slowly. It was a strange feeling, like when you see a heavily camouflaged sniper slowly reveal himself from bushes. That was the feeling both Vic and Tony experienced as an eight-foot-tall Sasquatch slowly stepped into view.

Its hair was mostly dark brown with various shades of gray on its head and chest. Its shape was of a large human, except for the arms, which appeared longer. On its face and hands were areas of mocha-colored skin with deep wrinkles around its eyes and mouth. The eyes had dark pupils within a ring of yellow. The nose was wide with nostrils that opened more than a man's, almost apelike. It stepped to another tree and stared at its visitors.

The detectives' minds raced to make sense of it.

"Whoa," Tony said, "they're really going all out."

"You mean the mask?"

"Not just the mask. The suit. His hands are moving but there's no way his real hands could reach so low. He must have some way of controlling the fingers farther up the sleeve."

The creature slowly approached them.

"Okay," Vic said through the glass, "I've got some questions for you."

As it got closer, their belief it was a man in a suit became uncertain. It moved unlike any animal, yet at the same time looked natural.

Vic's smile dropped completely. "Wait. Is it..."

"No," Tony said.

Vic smirked and his shoulders relaxed. "It's animatronic."

"Ah. Yeah. Gotta be."

The creature was less than two feet from them now, close enough to see it was obviously not animatronic. It wasn't only the way it moved. The thing had an unquestionable genuineness. Vic locked eyes with it and saw it exuded feeling, like a dog, but more knowing. When it looked at him, he felt the connection of another living thing. It was something that could not be faked. The creature was real.

"Oh my god," Tony said to himself.

"This isn't a museum," Vic said. "It's a zoo."

Vic felt physically lighter on his feet as his cynicism was chipped away by the undeniable proof before his eyes. While Tony stared at the Sasquatch behind the glass, Vic took out his phone and recorded video of it looking back at him. He noticed beside the diorama window was an illuminated panel of information, similar to a regular zoo or museum.

AMERICAN SASQUATCH—
Bipedal primate/hominid found in Arkansas. The Bigfoot before you is a Male named Charlie. Charlie is estimated to be about 60 years old, stands 8'2," and weighs close to 900 pounds.

Vic put his phone away and stepped back from the glass

with Tony. Each of them now unsure of how many other things in life they had been wrong about. Until a few minutes ago, they were certain Bigfoot was a joke. How many of those other crazy stories they'd blown off were true? How many of those blurry, out-of-focus Bigfoot videos online were the real thing after all?

To their right was an adjoining room. The whole area was relatively dark but with some floor-guide lights and sporadic lighting above. Most of the light came from other dioramas. The next one was the same size as the first, also featuring a forestlike interior. It was slightly comparable, even down to having a cave structure.

The growl they'd heard earlier now echoed from the darkness in the cave. Tony froze when he saw another Sasquatch creature emerge. Its hair was darker than the first, almost black. The facial features were alike yet different. Some of the hair around its face was gray, straggly, and matted.

This one was bigger than the other, and its whole demeanor was drastically different. Charlie had looked at them with eyes filled with curiosity. This one looked at them with pure hate. Its lips rose and fell over long, yellowed teeth and its nostrils flared. It growled and charged at the glass like a stampeding gorilla.

They instinctually reached for their guns. It savagely pounded against the window with its fists, flashing its teeth. It roared again and fogged up the glass as it tried to get to them.

"Okay." Vic shook his head.

They headed for the next area. They could see the floor up ahead was illuminated from something within. The dark tiles outside the exhibit glowed almost blue. They entered a room designed to give a distinct winter feel. The walls looked like they were made of large blocks of ice. They were thick clear plastic, but the illusion worked well. The speakers in the room played the sound of howling winter winds.

Vic wondered who set up the sound system. If they were

still alive and a part of this or victims of another mysterious car accident or freak electrocution. The diorama window matched the decor. Within was a winter scene. The ground, trees, and foliage were covered in thick snow. The room's rear wall was also created to give the illusion of depth, in this case, snow-covered mountains. Inside the diorama was a deep hole in the snow, and standing just beside it, staring back at them, was a yeti.

The thing's arms dropped down much farther than the Bigfoot's. Its face had a slightly pronounced snout. The skin was almost as gray as its fur. Its eyes were bright blue, almost white, the brightest irises either man had ever seen. They looked like the eyes on a Siberian husky.

Its demeanor wasn't as friendly as the first Bigfoot or as savage as the second, but it made them uneasy. It stared at them as if they were its prey, waiting for the right moment to attack. They found themselves spellbound by the creature for several minutes. Vic walked over to the information panel.

HIMALAYAN YETI—
*Bipedal primate/humanoid found in Himadri, the
northern range of the Himalayas. The Yeti is female,
named Miss December. She's about 60 years old,
stands 9'3," and weighs close to 1200 pounds.*

"Nine three. Jesus." Vic shook his head.

"It's the abominable snowman," Tony said. "We're looking at the actual fucking abominable snowman."

"Snow *woman*."

"Huh?"

"That's what it says." Vic turned his attention to the rest of the space within the diorama.

On the back wall in front of the snow-covered mountain mural was a protruding wall of snow. It was designed to look like a natural snowdrift, but something about it got Vic's interest. He moved to the far left of the diorama's window to try to see what was behind it. Only with his face close to where the glass met the wall could he make out the faint lines of a door on the rear wall. It was too small a door for this thing to get through.

Is that how they feed it? he wondered. *Does it shit in there? Who cleans that up? How many people are involved in this?*

As if reading his mind, Tony asked, "How much staff you think this place needs?"

Vic answered while still watching the yeti. "No idea. Gotta be a bunch though. You know these rich fucks aren't changing light bulbs down here."

Tony smirked. He wasn't even thinking about regular maintenance. He was thinking about how many people it would take to care for these things. Its white-blue eyes locked in on them.

Vic looked at its hands. They were huge, the fingers like hairy white bananas. The tips had long nails, razor-sharp at the points. What would it do to them if the glass weren't there? They watched it for another moment and moved on.

———·———

Ahead of them, the corridor opened to what looked like another large room. They approached, having no idea that, as much as their belief systems had been rocked so far, they were about to cross into a whole new reality.

The detectives could never prepare themselves for what they were about to discover... the answer to a question that had bewildered humanity since the beginning of time.

30

FORMAL DESCENT

D URING DINNER, THE FEMALE GUESTS were relegated to dining in the Tavern while the all-male membership of the Cobblestone Club sat at the round dinner table in the Tremont's dining room. The wood-paneled walls were polished to a shine. Deep red draperies matched several of the colors in the fine carpet.

Short lamps illuminated every place setting around the table and put a warm glow on each member's face. The well-aged men drank well-aged scotch and enjoyed course after course of delicacies. While conversing with his fellow members, Winthrop stole glances across the table at Tom, who was deep into conversation with Blackstone.

———•———

Tom asked dozens of questions. The movie mogul took his time with each one, not only answering but giving him extra little nuggets of info he knew he'd enjoy about his body of work.

While his main intention was to secure Tom's membership in the club, which would include five percent of all his future income, Blackstone had been surprised to find he enjoyed the young man's company. In the most objective terms, he could see Tom was an unattractive little nerd who never got a break.

He'd been dealt a tough hand to play, and he'd played it. Despite the world laughing at him, he beat all the odds and now had the world coming to him.

Blackstone smiled. He realized Tom was the epitome of his ideal audience. He possessed a unique blend of intelligence and sensitivity. Yet he was also a personification of the underdog characters in his films. He liked him, plain and simple.

Tom noticed one of the men across the table... a balding man with big owl eyes and a neck like a turtle's drooping over his collar. "That guy... he's a politician, right?" Tom whispered.

Blackstone grimaced. "Senator Kirkland. Not one of my favorite people. A self-righteous, right-wing asshole. Such a phony prick."

Tom smiled. There was something unnatural and naughty in hearing his hero speak this way. In the four decades since Blackstone had become a household name, he'd never suffered a single scandal. The entire world had come to ascribe to him the innocence within his films. Hearing Blackstone talk smack about the senator was like hearing Santa Claus say *fuck*.

Winthrop looked at his watch and turned to the table of billionaires. "Shall we?"

Blackstone leaned to Tom. "Time to go. I think I'm more excited to watch your face than I am to see the new stuff."

———•———

The group of billionaires rejoined the women outside the Tavern and proceeded toward the rear of the room. Together the group passed through a set of double doors that opened into a smaller lobby.

Winthrop looked over the faces. "I think we're all here."

He nodded to a security man inside the room, who locked the doors after them. The man then walked to the elevators and turned a key to open all four elevators simultaneously.

As the group filled them, the security man said, "Enjoy your evening."

Tom and Blackstone got into the first elevator with

Winthrop, Radcliffe, and the women they were escorting. Once the doors closed, Winthrop placed his thumb on the secret scanner and the car began to descend.

"Very excited for you all to see our latest acquisition," Winthrop said with a smile.

All four elevators came to a gentle stop simultaneously. The doors opened into another lobby area. This one had a fully stocked bar and a tuxedoed bartender as well as several waitresses holding trays of chilled glasses of champagne.

Once Winthrop saw everyone had a glass, he looked to yet another tall security man who reached for an ornately framed impressionist painting on the wall.

He touched a corner of the frame, and the painting slid up within the frame to reveal another keypad beside a glass hand scanner. The man placed his hand on the scanner, and red lasers slowly scanned down from top to bottom and back up. Once the scan finished, a green light lit up, signaling the keypad was now unlocked.

The man punched in several keys. Suddenly the entire adjoining wall began to rise and disappear behind what had previously looked like an indentation in the ceiling to provide offset lighting around the width of the room.

Crazy! Tom thought. *I'd never have known that was there at all.*

Once the wall had risen completely, Tom could see another elevator behind it. This one was huge, easily twenty feet wide. Winthrop smiled at Tom's reaction.

"If you think this one is big, you should see the freight elevator," Blackstone said.

Once everyone got on, Winthrop placed his thumb on the control panel scanner. As the elevator door slowly lowered, it reminded Tom of the scenes in action movies where the hero had to run and slide under a lowering door just like this one.

The full group was on the oversized elevator, many of them joined by a beautiful guest for the evening. Part of the fun for the members was showing off these secrets. It was further proof of their dominance and superiority. Only they could provide them this experience… to show them things no other men outside this group, no matter how young or handsome, ever could. Letting the young beauties know this was the pinnacle, where true power lay. The billionaires believed it made the women more attracted to them, or at the very least more likely to try harder to pleasure them.

As the elevator descended, the men looked over each other's dates, silently comparing and rating them like items in a catalog. Even though each of the members was at least seventy and had enjoyed countless beautiful women over decades, the instinctual urge to pick out the girl in the room they'd most like to bed was very much intact.

The women were aware of the behavior but acted as if they were not. A couple of them were amused by the sight of Tom not taking part in the ritual but instead stealing starstruck glances at Blackstone. The girls shared a smile.

———•———

Tom whispered to Blackstone. "I don't understand how this can be kept so quiet with all the staff. Waitresses, bartenders. Don't they say anything?"

Blackstone shook his head. "None of the staff you saw up top knows there's anything below the building. They assume we took the elevators upstairs. The ones you just saw in the lower lobby don't know anything. They don't go past the point where you saw them. None of them have been where we're going. Even the security people you've seen have no idea what's down here."

"Amazing," Tom replied.

"There are only a few dozen or so people who do work down here, and they're paid very well to keep quiet. They get a generous annual income, their homes, cars, health, and children's educations are paid for."

"Oh."

"They also understand the ramifications of talking. Even their spouses don't know what they really do."

"How can you possibly know that for sure?"

"The club has multiple private investigation firms on retainer for the sole purpose of following and monitoring the conversations of every single employee who sees the inside. Wiretaps, video surveillance, twenty-four seven. It's part of where the dues go."

———·———

The elevator came to a stop, and the doors opened directly into the main lobby Vic and Tony entered earlier. Blackstone saw the expression on Tom's face and smiled.

"Whoa," Tom said, more to himself than to Blackstone.

Several women were wide-eyed at the enormous space around them, staring up at the large rotunda.

Radcliffe placed his hand on Becca's back. "What do you think?"

Becca answered while still scanning the room. "It's unbelievable… And no one knows this is down here?"

Radcliffe smiled. "Only the people involved. The public has no idea. Less than fifty people in the world know about it."

"Thank you so much for bringing me."

"You haven't seen anything yet. This is just the lobby." He grinned.

———·———

Keiji Fujiyama had a similar conversation with his date, Stacey. Yet even while he whispered to her, he stared at Becca a few feet away. He was determined to possess her. To have her for himself.

It will have to be done with extreme care, he thought. *Men like Radcliffe don't easily accept having their things stolen from them.*

———·———

An attractive man in his early thirties entered the room wearing a white tuxedo and a friendly smile. He also wore a headset microphone and carried an iPad. Roland, the man who served as the master of ceremonies for these events, had performed this service for Winthrop for five years running now.

"Good evening, everyone," Roland said. "So great to see you all again."

Roland mingled with the group and did his best to make eye contact with each of the men as he made his way through, shaking hands with all.

He switched on the microphone he was wearing. "Okay," he said, his voice now amplified through speakers. "Welcome! As you may have heard, we have a few new attractions to show you tonight. For those of you here for the first time, my name is Roland and I'll be leading you through the tour to answer any questions you may have and point out some interesting facts. Of course, if you'd rather break off from the group and explore on your own, that's fine too. Whatever you like."

With that, they started toward the main entrance.

31

WE ARE NOT ALONE

V IC AND TONY TURNED THE corner toward the second large
exhibit room. There was a short hallway before the entrance.
The corridor was dark except for track lighting that illuminated
rows of framed posters of 1950s and 60s science fiction movies.

*Invasion of the Saucer Men, War of the Worlds, Invaders from
Mars, The Day the Earth Stood Still, Forbidden Planet.*

At the end of the corridor were double doors. As they
approached them, the doors slid open, and both he and Tony
were momentarily blinded by the amount of light in the room.

The entire room was stark white with a futuristic feel. It was
circular, with several alcoves around the edges. Oval-shaped
faux windows played video of a star-filled galaxy to give the
illusion of being out in deep space. Even the lighting above was
impressive. Round, overlapping light rings lined the length of
the room, each one at a different level from the ceiling.

An oversized TV screen played clips of secret UFO footage
filmed by government aircraft and satellites over the years. Vic
and Tony walked through the room, looking over what
appeared to be chunks of metal wreckage and other
unidentifiable objects placed onto rectangular display stands
like modern sculptures. Beneath each were plaques listing
information.

PIECE OF UFO HULL
Found in Yellowstone National Park, 1964
Believed to have crashed in late 17th Century

ALIEN SKULL
Found in Swiss Alps, 1982
Dating of the surrounding rocks suggests
to be 4000 years old.

UNKNOWN ALIEN TECHNOLOGY
Found in an underwater cave during
construction of the Panama Canal, 1905
Estimated to be 20,000 years old.

Another area featured three cylinder-shaped containers that looked like cryogenic sleeping chambers. Inside each was the body of a gray, lifeless alien.

Despite having just seen live Sasquatches and a Yeti, the detectives didn't immediately consider the aliens within the tubes to be anything more than well-made fakes.

"So realistic," Tony said, getting a nod from Vic.

They entered another large circular room adjoining it. Inside was a fully intact alien craft. It was round, like the classic image of a flying saucer, equal in size to a military transport helicopter.

Its texture shone like metal, but upon touching it, Vic found it pliable. There were symmetrical lines all over it, so hair-thin they could only be seen from inches away.

Tony stared into another adjoining room.

"What?" Vic asked.

"Look."

Another diorama. It featured a partial interior of an alien ship, but this one, obviously man-made, was created more in line with Hollywood's version of an alien starship. It had a flight deck and what looked like a lounge area in front of a wide window overlooking a red Martian landscape. Above the red terrain was a star-filled sky, complete with a view of Saturn so close its colorful rings dipped below the horizon.

The detectives barely noticed any of that. They stared at the live alien looking back at them from behind the glass. It stood five feet tall with oval-shaped eyes the size of table coasters. Blue irises took up ninety percent of them with small black pupils. It had thin, almost translucent skin. Although its head was as wide as a beach ball, its mouth was tiny, no bigger than a coin slot. Its facial features moved slightly as it looked back at them.

The arms and legs were incredibly thin, no wider than a couple of inches at their thickest point. It raised a hand that only had three digits—two fingers and a long, opposable thumb.

Instinctually, both men raced through the possible ways it could be an illusion or trick. They came up with reason after reason to explain this, to get back to the safety of their cynicism. The alien placed its hand on the window. Its fingertips spread out and flattened against the glass. Vic leaned closer and saw the tips had lines and grooves in circular patterns. He looked at the alien's face, which gazed back at him with a few rapid, vertical eye blinks.

The detectives understood with sudden clarity that humankind was not alone in the universe, and another of their lifelong beliefs fell by the wayside.

Vic took out his phone and videoed the alien for a few seconds.

Tony spoke without turning from the glass. "Do you think it understands where it is?"

"I don't know. I mean… it's gotta be smarter than us. Right?" Vic turned, looking at all the other alien artifacts surrounding them.

They took a few steps back and saw a portion of another diorama in the next area.

"Let's keep moving," Vic said.

32

TOM'S FIRST TOUR

"THIS IS THE MOST AMAZING thing I've ever seen," Tom said.

He walked between Blackstone and Raquel, with her holding his hand. All his life he'd felt like an outsider. For the first time, he began to feel like this might be something he could be a part of.

Winthrop kept his eye on him. He knew he'd made the right choice in delegating Blackstone to secure his membership. He was pleased with himself, as he often was. Tom Ackerman's dues would bring them a much larger annual amount than Hamilton Towne's ever had.

Roland stopped the group just before the entrance to the first Sasquatch room. "For those of you here for the first time, prepare to have your minds opened to a much bigger reality."

Roland led them to a diorama Vic and Tony missed. As the group walked in, several of the elderly billionaires felt their escorts squeeze their hands tighter and heard them let out gasps.

———•———

Tom didn't see the Sasquatch right away and wondered what the women were whispering about. Once he did, he had the same amount of skepticism the detectives had. He stared into the face of the Sasquatch.

Do they think I'm a fool? Obviously, this thing is fake. I mean, look at the fur and the face. It looks like… like…

The creature looked back at him with glassy, knowing eyes, slightly squinting. Its nose flared a bit as it took a deep breath. Its skin was covered with various-sized pores and wrinkles.

Oh my god.

Tom looked to Blackstone, who smiled back.

———•———

Becca couldn't believe her eyes. She'd never given Bigfoot much thought. She'd seen a few fake videos pop up on Instagram now and then… and there were a bunch of Bigfoot-type horror movies she'd always scrolled right by. But this, this was crazy.

The creature behind the glass looked as real and natural as an animal at the zoo.

She turned to Radcliffe. "I don't believe it."

Radcliffe smiled. A rush of pride filled him. "I know. The world is suddenly different than it was a few moments ago, isn't it?"

As she looked at the Sasquatch again, she wrapped her arm around Radcliffe and leaned her head on his shoulder.

———•———

Several feet away, Keiji Fujiyama watched her like a bird of prey.

Roland stepped to the side and clicked on his microphone. "This Sasquatch was found in the wilds of Oregon."

The group listened intently, sipping their champagne.

"Shall we watch him eat?" Roland asked.

A polite murmur, more question than answer.

Roland pressed his iPad screen. Unseen to the guests, a door behind the diorama's rear wall opened and a majestic, six-point deer walked in. The door shut behind it, causing the deer to move deeper into the diorama and into view of the audience.

So beautiful, Becca thought.

The Sasquatch's eyes locked onto the deer. Once it got

within reach, the beast grabbed it by its antlers. It quickly turned the animal's head until its neck snapped, killing it instantly. It released the antlers, and the deer dropped to the ground. The Sasquatch sat down beside its kill and broke off one of the deer's back legs with a sickening crunch.

The entire group watched spellbound except for Winthrop, who appeared slightly bored. The Sasquatch lifted the dismembered limb like a Thanksgiving turkey leg and bit into it. Becca turned away. Tom also got no enjoyment from the sight but did his best to hide his emotions. None of the members showed any sign of compassion for the deer.

Roland guided them to the next window, where the second Sasquatch stood inside his own forest-filled diorama.

"Now, this guy is a little different," Roland said. "We call him Charlie, and he's a vegetarian." Roland pointed to a garden area inside the diorama. "He lives on plants, fruit, and vegetables. But the amazing thing is he knows how to grow his food himself. We had to install UV lights to help make it possible, but Charlie does everything else."

Tom stepped closer to the glass. "That's incredible."

Charlie approached the window and made eye contact with Tom. The skin below his eyes hung low, almost like a basset hound's. Tom was drawn to the creature.

"Can I touch the glass?" Tom whispered to Blackstone.

"Of course. Go ahead."

Tom slowly put his hand to the window and stretched out his fingers. Becca gasped as Charlie copied the action. He placed his hand against Tom's on the other side. Tom smiled. His whole hand almost fit in the space of Charlie's palm, which was the same mocha color as his face.

"Charlie is one of the only creatures down here who responds this way," Roland said. "He's over eight feet tall and weighs more than eight hundred pounds, but he's a pussycat."

Tom could see the intelligence, the soul behind his eyes, and was overcome with sympathy for the confined creature.

He lowered his hand and felt his pity grow deeper as Charlie kept his hand where it was.

This is wrong, Tom thought.

Roland clapped his hands together politely. "If you would follow me, I'd like to introduce you to someone else."

The group followed Roland into the adjoining area.

"This is our Yeti room," Roland said.

———•———

The wireless sound system Roland was using became audible to Vic and Tony.

"What do you want to do?" Tony asked in a low voice.

"Let's just keep out of sight for now."

They heard people approaching. Luckily, there were plenty of displays and other things in the room to help them stay hidden.

"Over there." Vic pointed to a large piece of UFO wreckage the size of a minivan. They quickly got behind it and watched Roland enter the area, followed by a group of older men in black tuxedos. Many of them were hand in hand with gorgeous young women dressed like they were going to an Oscar party.

"What the fuck?" Tony whispered.

———•———

Roland stood to the side as everyone walked past him. "I call this the Science Fiction room. Although there's absolutely nothing fictional about what you see in here."

The group explored the room as Roland pointed out items of interest. He introduced them all to the live alien, whom he called Mr. Gray. Even the members looked at him with wonder, and a few of them with a little fear. Not of physical harm. They each felt such a false sense of security from years of being protected by bodyguards and underlings, none of them ever considered bodily harm in the slightest.

The tinge of fear was based on what would happen if the world ever found out they were not alone in the universe.

Tom looked at Mr. Gray. At first he assumed it to be a puppet or mechanical toy. Unlike the Sasquatch, the alien didn't have eyes comparable to a human or an animal. They projected no feeling or emotion.

His brain did backflips, coming up with possible explanations for what he was seeing. As much as he wanted to believe it was real, his mind automatically tried to deny what he saw.

Maybe the whole window is a new type of ultra-high-resolution screen… like a 20K or something. Yes. That had to be it.

He felt he had the answer. The image was impressive. Crystal clear clarity he'd never seen on a screen. He smiled at his cleverness. It faded when he noticed something that blew his theory. Behind the alien was a metal wall. The metal wasn't shined to a mirror finish but was reflective enough to show distorted shapes and colors of anything in front of it. Within the reflections, Tom could see his own image and those of Raquel and Blackstone. Just to be sure, he slowly raised his hand and moved it from side to side. As he feared, he saw the matching reflection of his actions in the metal behind the alien.

It's not a screen. It's real.

With all doubt removed, he felt complete joy. His mind had played tricks on him over the years. Despite knowing he was wide-awake when he had his close encounter years earlier at camp, there were still doubts in him. Maybe he had fallen asleep. Maybe out of fear, he imagined the whole thing. Maybe he created it to distract himself from the fact he was a nerd left in the woods like a loser. There was no way to be sure.

Now he finally could be. He felt a huge rush of vindication from his own doubts. He looked at the alien and smiled.

The group explored the room and examined all the alien artifacts. After giving them sufficient time to see it all, Roland spoke up.

"Mr. Gray is just one of the aliens here," Roland said. "Please follow me."

Roland guided them around a corner to a room bigger than the last. It had three walls, each one with its own diorama window. Each contained a live alien being. The three extraterrestrials bore no resemblance to each other. They were clearly different species, none of them comparable to Mr. Gray.

The one in the nearest diorama looked like a six-foot-tall praying mantis on two legs. Its triangular head turned to them. The dark pupils within its huge eye spheres darted from side to side. The double joints of its long arms were also mantis-like, folded upward, leading into sharp points.

The next alien was even more menacing. Its size alone was intimidating, standing seven feet tall. It was humanoid in shape, with skin that seemed to be made up of thousands of various-sized wet leaves. Upon a closer look, not only did the leaves appear to be slowly moving and shifting in place but the thin veins within each leaf were also in constant movement. The alien had no facial features, no eyes or mouth, but there was no denying it could somehow see them. Its hands only had two elongated fingers, longer than human forearms. The way the leaflike texture wrapped around them and down to their tips reminded Tom of long, sloppily rolled-up tubes of paper with many of the underlying layers visible.

The third alien was the closest to appearing human. If it were silhouetted, you'd never know it wasn't a man. However, the smallest amount of light would expose the difference. It was covered in reptilian skin with shiny scales ranging in size on different parts of it. Its head featured two large eyes with vertical pupils, like certain snakes and lizards. Its mouth was closed, forming a long, thin slit from beneath one eye to the other. The scales on its face were various shades of yellow that faded to shades of green throughout the rest of its body. It had no nose, but like Earth's vipers, it had pit organs just above its mouth that served as a heat-sensing system.

In the control room within the facility, Lance was looking at a console with dozens of monitor screens. One of the screens was zoomed in on Becca. Lance worked the camera toggle, following her as she moved.

He shook his head from side to side in awe of her. "Good God. Look at you," he whispered to himself.

Lance zoomed in on her breasts as well as the body parts of Raquel and the other women. He went back and forth between his favorites. He zoomed out a bit and followed Becca as Roland led the group out of the room until they got to a point where they left the range of the camera.

"No, no, no," Lance whispered. "Wait for me. Wait for me…"

Lance switched camera toggles to the room the group was entering. He panned the camera to find Becca from the new angle, but before he could locate her, he spotted something else, and his heart dropped.

"Oh shit," he said. "Shit. Shit. Shit." He grabbed his radio. "Mason. Come in, Mason."

No answer.

"Mason! Come in! It's an emergency!"

———•———

Mason walked toward the holding room where Kelsey, Annika, and Gia were being kept. Lance's voice called out from Mason's radio repeatedly until he answered it.

"What?"

Lance answered immediately. "There are two guys in the UFO area, following the guests."

"That's impossible."

"I'm telling you I'm watching them right now."

Mason shook his head. "And how did they manage to get down here?"

"I have no idea. But they look like cops. One's tall and the other one's chubby."

Mason stopped in his tracks. "Stand by." He switched channels. "Jerry? Farris?" Mason called into the radio. "Come in."

———·———

Back at the security gate where Vic and Tony had come in, Farris was still cuffed to the metal detector, unable to reach his radio.

"Jerry, Farris! Answer me, goddamn it!" Mason's voice boomed from his radio.

"Fuck!" Farris blurted.

———·———

Getting no response, Mason switched the channel back to Lance.

"Okay. Something's up," he said. "Keep an eye on them. Don't let them out of your sight."

Mason considered his options, then picked up the radio again. "Let me know when they get close to the aquarium."

"Want me to tell Cobb to meet you there?" Lance asked while watching Vic and Tony on the monitors.

"No. I'll bring Red with me. Just tell me when they get there."

"You got it."

33

THE JERSEY DEVIL

ROLAND LED THE GROUP THROUGH the wide corridor toward the next exhibit.

"If I didn't know any better, I'd swear I was in a regular museum," Tom said to Raquel.

"I know, right?" she whispered back.

"This creature is the only one of its kind in the world," Roland announced as they arrived at the next window.

The inside of the display featured a forest clearing. Faux trees and brush lined the three back walls. The night sky had fiber-optic stars twinkling above. As Roland spoke, the group watched a dark shape slowly emerge from the trees. It stood to its full height, roughly seven feet tall.

The grotesque creature had a head shaped like a combination of man and horse. It growled at them, displaying several rows of jagged teeth. Its small eyes were jet-black. Its long neck stretched down to a body resembling a human torso but covered in dark, leathery skin. Its arms were much longer than a man's and had huge claws with razor-sharp talons. The thing's two legs had the shape and joints of a horse with twisted hooves for feet. It walked a few feet forward to the glass as it studied the group.

"Our extraction team caught this creature deep within the

New Jersey Pine Barrens where sightings of it had been reported for hundreds of years," Roland continued.

Without warning, the creature snapped open a pair of wide bat wings, shocking the group. The wings spanned over a dozen feet. The creature let out an unearthly growl that sent chills through everyone.

"How many different creatures are in here?" Tom asked Roland.

"With the addition of our latest find," Roland answered, "fifty-six."

As Roland continued, the monster he called the Jersey Devil eyed them all with a mix of hate and hunger. As Tom looked at it, he felt a sourness fill him. There was something ominous about this creature. Something evil.

Vic now accepted the things down here as real. He'd always had a solid understanding of the way the world worked and had come to believe it held no more surprises for him. He'd seen life at its sunny best with a second chance at love and happiness with Kelsey, and at its worst in the unspeakable crimes of the human monsters he'd encountered.

Now his beliefs were shattered. Knowing he'd been so wrong numbed his brain. Along with the realization, however, also came the overwhelming feeling that Kelsey was down here somewhere. He knew it. It was as if being within a certain radius of her set off an alarm in his soul.

From behind a row of faux trees, he and Tony watched Roland take questions. So far they'd been lucky. There were enough things in each area that they could stay out of sight. When Roland led the group out of the room, they waited a few seconds. They were about to move, but they heard footsteps behind them. A fortysomething man in a white doctor's coat passed by. The detectives read each other's expressions and burst from their hiding spot.

Tony put his hand over the man's mouth with a finger to

his own lips. "You yell or make a sound and you're dead. Understand?" Tony whispered.

The trembling man nodded, and Tony let go of his mouth.

"Where are the women?" Vic asked.

"Women? I just work here. I don't...," the man stuttered.

"Don't," Vic whispered and pressed his gun to the man's face so hard he could feel it against his cheekbone.

"Oh. Okay. I thought... Okay."

"Take us to them. Right now."

"I'll do whatever you want."

Tony grabbed his shoulder and pushed him.

"Go," Vic ordered.

———•———

Mason arrived at the holding area. He took one of the cattle prods mounted on the wall beside the door, then looked through the window and pressed the code to enter.

Kelsey, Annika, and Gia looked at each other, not knowing what to expect. Kelsey was ready to take another shot once he got close enough.

Mason entered the room with the prod and a pair of handcuffs. "Hands behind your back."

Gia was closest, so he moved to clamp the cuffs on her. Kelsey ran at him, and he gave her a poke of the prod. The jolt of electricity sent her down, clutching her side. Annika turned, more out of curiosity than in an attempt to fight back, and Mason yelled at her.

"Face the wall!"

She did, letting out an angry whimper.

Mason put the cuffs on Gia and she burst into tears, kicking and screaming. She went limp and tried to crawl away from the door. Kelsey, clutching her side, tried to ignore the pain and reached for her. Mason grabbed Gia's ankle and dragged her out. The door slammed shut, and Annika helped Kelsey get to her mattress. Annika, usually stoic, fought back tears.

Once Mason had Gia outside the room, he walked her

through a long, winding hallway. Her fear was so thick her head felt heavy and her legs rubbery.

They walked until she felt him pull back on her cuffed wrists.

He leaned her up against the wall beside a door.

"Wait, wait," she said. "Where are we...?"

He kept his eye on a control panel on the wall with an unlit bulb on it.

"Don't move," Mason said as he removed her cuffs.

Gia turned to face him. "Are you letting me go?"

"Yes." Mason shushed her with a finger to his lips.

34

VAMPIRE

"OUR NEXT ATTRACTION CAN EMPLOY an incredible hypnotic power," Roland said as he led the group to the next window.

It had a partition completely covering the glass. Beside the partition were a few shelves holding dozens of special sunglasses. They were thick with yellow lenses.

"If everyone could please take a pair of these glasses and put them on," Roland requested. "These are special lenses with a coating to block the hypnotic suggestions given off by the gentleman on the other side of this wall."

Roland looked around to make sure everyone had the glasses on, then pressed a button beside the partition. The wall slowly rose, revealing a window into another diorama.

This one was designed to look like the interior of Dracula's castle. A coffin lay on the floor against the far wall. Standing near it was a figure.

"I'd like you to meet our resident vampire, Bram," Roland said.

He was unnaturally thin, with skin so pale it looked like the sun had never touched him. It resembled how skin looks after removing a tight Band-Aid after a few days — white, wrinkled, and loose. He was mostly bald with long strands of gray hair in patches. His eyes were human-shaped, but the pupils were yellow with a thick black line circling them. The whites of his eyes were so bloodshot they appeared solid red.

When the group moved closer to the window, the thing bared its teeth with a silent snarl. It put a shudder into several of the newer guests. Most film vampires had near-perfect teeth with the addition of two longer incisors like those of an animal. This foul thing had two long yellow teeth in the front of his mouth, like a rodent.

The dirty clothes he wore were black and nondescript. They could have been made in the 1800s or last week.

Tom was no longer automatically questioning what he was seeing. By this point, he was a full-fledged true believer. A newfound sense of wonder and mystery excited and thrilled him. If becoming a billionaire had given him the belief anything was possible, seeing this place opened an entirely new universe.

He looked over at Winthrop, who glanced back with a warm smile. Tom smiled back and nodded. Whatever the cost was, it was worth it. The Cobblestone Club had its newest member.

Roland continued. "Bram's been with us for about twenty years. We first heard about him during a rash of killings in Europe. A dozen young girls were found drained of all their blood, their throats and breasts slashed open. Naturally, the police believed they had a serial killer on their hands."

Tom turned to look back at the thing behind the glass. It was impossible not to think about all the vampires he'd seen on TV and in movies. The pretty-boy vampires were laughable now. This thing was right out of a nightmare... and the way it looked at them even though it was the one in captivity... as if they were the helpless ones... like a snake staring at a mouse. It stayed perfectly still as it glared at them.

A vampire, Tom thought. *A real vampire.*

He broke the silence. "Roland. What would happen if we removed the glasses?"

"Honestly, Mr. Ackerman, you wouldn't be in any real danger. But you might just break your nose walking into that glass."

"You're saying he would hypnotize me into giving myself to him?" Tom asked.

"Exactly," Roland said. "Our scientists have discovered that to put his prey into a trancelike state, Bram is able to trigger extremely realistic hallucinations, somehow based on the memories of his prey."

Raquel, Becca, and the other women looked at Bram with a combination of fear and disgust. The way he stared at them, so perfectly still, was chilling.

"Let me demonstrate," Roland said and pressed a button on his iPad.

———————

In the service corridor behind the vampire diorama, Mason kept his eyes on the control panel beside the door. Once he saw the bulb light green, he opened the door and guided Gia inside, into a small space. Once she was all the way in, Mason shut the door behind her, then pressed another button on the keypad that opened the second door into Bram's diorama.

———————

Gia felt a flash of hope as a small amount of light flowed in. She walked forward, her hands feeling her way. Once she was completely through, the second door slid shut behind her.

She couldn't tell where she was. There was a structure in front of her resembling something she'd seen in a documentary about Hollywood. Like what the back of the buildings in an old Western town set looked like. She turned the corner and found she was in another room, but it was strange. The first thing she saw was a glass wall with a bunch of people watching her.

"What?" she muttered.

She'd been turning tricks on the street for years, yet, standing in front of all these people in her bra and panties, she felt the urge to cover herself up. Some watched her, some were looking at something behind her, and she realized she wasn't alone in the room. She turned to see Bram's bright yellow pupils trained down on her.

Tom looked at Blackstone, who was mesmerized by what was happening before them. He stared, and his special glasses made him look like he was enjoying a solar eclipse.

When Gia first saw the vampire's face, she screamed. She didn't know what he was or what he was supposed to be. All she knew was he was hideous. But then she saw his eyes and could not turn away.

The longer she looked, the more infatuated she became. They were strangely beautiful. The eyes stared back at her, wide and still. Suddenly her demeanor changed. All her fear fell away. She looked at Bram with intense curiosity.

Everyone watched as she stepped closer to him. She didn't see the people behind the glass anymore. Within a few seconds, it was as if she were in a fog that not only surrounded her but also numbed her senses. It felt good. Suddenly the eyes that mesmerized her were gone.

They'd faded into the fog and blocked everything else out.

Something was in front of her, in the mist. She couldn't see it, but she could somehow sense it. A figure came into focus several feet in front of her. A good-looking, college-aged, blond man.

How could this be? Nicky? she thought to herself.

She realized she was no longer where she thought she was. The fog dissipated. She was now standing in her college dorm room, boy band posters on the wall. The red light bulb her roommate had on her nightstand illuminated the room with a pink hue. Her mind raced, trying to figure out how she had somehow gone back in time like this, but then it didn't matter anymore. Nothing mattered. Nicky was right in front of her, just like he'd been that night.

Although Nicky was her first college hookup, he wasn't her first sexual partner. That was Pete, her high school sweetheart. The gentle, sweet guy who waited two years for her to finally give in to her feelings (as well as his pleadings) and go all the way.

She and Pete stayed together for another couple of years, even while she was away at college. But then she met Nicky. She was at a frat party with her friends when Nicky, with his beautiful, tanned face and blond wavy hair, started flirting with her. The drinks were flowing, and she ended up back in her dorm room with him, where they were now.

She and Nicky were about to have sex... and that's what this was. Sex. There was no romance like with Pete. No deep feeling. No history. No guilt. Gia understood what was about to happen was a one-night stand, something she swore to her mother and God she would never do. But she'd been studying for finals and working her ass off. She deserved some fun, didn't she? Yes. She decided she did.

Gia stuck her thumbs under the elastic band of her panties and slowly pulled them down, a part of her feeling a sudden pity for Pete.

Poor Pete. If he knew about this, he'd be so hurt. I made him wait so long... more than a year just to touch me above the underwear, let alone take them off.

All thoughts of Pete disappeared as her panties fell to the floor and she stepped out of them. For a few seconds, she and Nicky just stood there, several feet apart, looking at each other in the pink glow of the room. She had never been this turned on before, and for the first time in her life, she thought of herself not as a girl but as a woman. Tonight, with a handsome, well-endowed stranger standing naked before her, she felt completely uninhibited. She could feel how ready she was for him and moaned without realizing it.

———•———

Tom and the rest of the group watched Gia as she stared seductively at the undead, foul thing in front of her. Her eyes never shifted, and her lips trembled.

Jesus Christ, Tom thought, *she's looking at that thing like she wants to fuck its brains out.*

———•———

Radcliffe and Fujiyama looked on in wonder. They'd seen this display before, but the sex oozing off her was something new even to them. They were almost as entranced by Gia as they watched her step closer to Bram. As she moved, her fingertips lightly caressed her neck and chest. Tom's eyes were transfixed.

She reached her hand out to touch Nicky's face. He held it as he pulled her closer, close enough to feel his nakedness poke against her navel.

Shivers ran through her whole body, and she shook with excitement. The group was spellbound. Even the women in the room, most of them beyond jaded from working in the sex trade themselves, found the sight immensely erotic.

Gia let out a louder moan as Nicky kissed his way down her breasts. She looked like she was lost in complete bliss. She leaned her head back as far as she could and ran her fingers through her hair, unable to contain her pleasure.

She had no idea she was bleeding to death. She didn't feel it when Bram sank his teeth into her throat. He had already drained more than four pints of blood from her. It got all over his white face, giving him the appearance of a sloppy clown.

He lapped it up like a coyote chewing on a fresh kill. His long, ghastly fingers squeezed her flesh around the area he was sucking on as if to push out as much blood out as he could, his nails digging into her. Through it all, Gia continued to moan with pleasure. She didn't stop smiling, even after she was dead.

In shock, Tom looked at Raquel, who watched the scene with the hint of a sadistic smile. He scanned the room and saw several of the old men with the same expression. Others just watched with looks of indifference. The only people who seemed shocked were Becca and a few of the other escorts.

<hr />

Watching a woman get murdered wasn't Tom's idea of fun. The part of him that wasn't in absolute shock was horrified and disgusted. He wanted to get out of there immediately.

Raquel saw how upset he was and placed her hand on his chest, causing him to jump. "Hey. Are you okay?"

Blackstone could also see he had a greenish look about him.

"That girl. Who was she?" Tom asked.

"Shhh," Blackstone said. "It's all right."

Realizing his hero was fine with the situation increased his disgust. "What? No. It's not."

Winthrop approached, put a hand on Tom's shoulder, and guided him away from the group.

"Easy, Tom," he said. "Let me explain."

"Please do."

"I should have mentioned this earlier. That woman... she wasn't forced to take part in this. She chose to," Winthrop said.

"Why? Why would she want that?"

"The club makes a deal with less fortunate people with terminal diseases. When they know they have little time left, they grant us their bodies, and in exchange, we give ten million dollars to their families."

Blackstone listened along with Tom. It was the first time he could remember Winthrop lying to a new member, but if that's what it took to secure Tom's membership, so be it.

None of the regular members had any qualms about killing hookers and junkies for their own amusement. No one would really miss them. If anything, they were helping to clean up the streets.

Tom listened but couldn't get past the fact the group just watched a life end for entertainment.

Oh my god.

He whispered to Winthrop, "Do you know where the nearest men's room is?"

"Sure. Go back into the corridor and there's one on the right."

"Thanks."

Once Tom walked away, Blackstone and Winthrop exchanged a concerned look.

When he got to the main corridor and was out of sight, he broke into a run. He got inside the men's room and immediately threw up in the wastebasket. He washed his face and exhaled as he stared at his reflection.

This is bad. This is bad. I don't want any part of this.

He closed his eyes until his breathing slowed to a normal pace.

Just finish out the evening, then let Winthrop know I changed my mind.

After deciding he'd made the right choice, Tom walked over to the urinals and unzipped his pants. There were four urinals, deeper than normal. Inside each one, just above the drain, was a human skull mounted to the porcelain.

Uh, okay, Tom thought.

He started to piss, aiming his stream at the skull, which he suspected was the point of having it there. The stream hit the skull's head, went into its empty eye sockets and open mouth. It had a dime-sized hole in its side. Tom aimed for that too.

Tom finished and flushed. As he washed his hands, he heard a flush behind him in one of the stalls.

Out walked Franklin Dodd.

"Hi," Tom said.

"Hello." Dodd joined him at the next sink, washing his hands.

"Are you okay?" Dodd asked.

Tom forced a smile. "It's a lot to take in."

"Yes. It is." Dodd looked at the urinals, saw the one Tom used was still running.

"Do you really want to be thrown for a loop?" Dodd asked.

"I think I already have been."

"Are you Jewish?" Dodd asked.

Tom's antennae perked up. *Where was this going?*

"Yes."

Dodd smiled. "Congratulations then. You've done something millions of Jews have wanted to do."

"What do you mean?" Tom asked, beginning to feel more

uncomfortable. Was he intimating Jews shouldn't be allowed in the club?

Dodd pointed to the urinal.

"You just pissed on Hitler's face."

Tom's face flashed confusion. He turned to the skull in the urinal. Then he understood.

"Seriously?" Tom blurted. "That's Hitler's skull?"

"Yes."

"Come on. That's impossible."

"It wasn't easy to get, but we did. You should have learned by now that nothing's impossible down here."

Dodd clearly enjoyed Tom's realization of the situation.

Tom pointed to the other two skulls. "Who are they then?"

Dodd pointed to each as he spoke. "Osama Bin Laden and Charles Manson."

"Amazing." Tom looked at the last urinal, which was skull free. "Why is that one empty?"

"That space is reserved." Dodd smiled. "Come. Let's get back. I wouldn't want you to miss anything."

———•———

In the holding room, Kelsey and Annika sat on the same mattress. They didn't speak.

Why are they taking us one at a time? Kelsey wondered.

"Listen," she said to Annika, "Whether they try to take just one of us or both of us, we have to do whatever we can to stop them."

Annika nodded.

"I mean it," she said. "We've got to go crazy on them no matter what kind of weapons they have. Understand?"

The younger woman nodded again, but this time Kelsey put her hands on her cheeks to force her to look into her eyes.

"We're not going to just give up."

Tell her the truth. It may be the only way to get her to fight back.

"They're going to try to kill us anyway. We have nothing to lose. It might be our only chance to stay alive. We have to make it as hard for them as possible. We're gonna fuck them up."

Annika nodded, but her eyes were full of fear.

Vic and Tony made their way through the museum, never letting go of the man in the white coat. He directed them which way to go, stopping from time to time when they thought they might be spotted.

"How much farther?" Vic asked.

"A couple of minutes."

"If you're leading us to a trap, the first thing I'm doing is blowing your head off. Understand?" Tony jabbed him with the gun.

"Yes."

Roland led the group into another area. It was an equal-size room to the one they'd just left but circular with several smaller, vertical dioramas lining the wall. Each one had a zombie within, with different surroundings.

"This… is our Hall of the Undead."

When the group moved into the adjoining room, they dispersed a little, everyone choosing a window to check out. Roland pointed to the first one.

The zombie inside was almost a skeleton. He wore a gray suit close to the color of the long-dead skin on his face and hands, one of which held an old rifle. The barrel dragged on the floor beside him.

"This man's name is Santino Farrante. He was a mob hit man who worked for crime boss Carlos Marcello. This man you see before you… is who actually killed John F. Kennedy."

Tom's eyes widened.

Blackstone saw his expression and nodded. "Santino was the shooter stationed behind the grassy knoll fence. It was his bullet that blew Kennedy's head open in frame 313 of the famous Zapruder film."

The moving cadaver shambled about in the small space.

Another voice from the group asked a question. "How did he become a zombie?"

"The same way these others did," Roland replied. "It took our scientists more than ten years to create a modern, pharmaceutical version of a three-hundred-year-old potion created by witch doctors in Haiti. It's a mixture of powders that can reanimate human remains, even in cases with no brain tissue left. Once our genius team mastered the process, it was just a matter of acquiring the corpses of interesting people."

Roland strolled to the next window. "Of course, some corpses are so old, like this next one, there's not much to work with. In this gentleman's case, he was little more than skull and bones when we retrieved him. Before he was reanimated, he had to be literally put back together. Once his skeleton was rewired, the team developed a procedure using a combination of synthetic muscle, tissue, and human skin grafts to make him look more presentable."

The face of the man in the window had a taxidermy look about it. His eyes were like black glass marbles. His skin had an unnatural color to it, more orange than true flesh. He had an old-fashioned mustache and long sideburns that connected on his cheeks.

Roland went on. "Using his skull and the same computer programs the FBI and CIA use to develop facial features for unidentified, decomposed murder victims, they were able to give him a face ninety-five percent accurate of how he looked one hundred and thirty years ago."

The result was like a nightmare version of a wax figure at Madame Tussauds. Because the synthetic muscle and skin grafts on his face were only attached to his skull, his expression never changed. His mouth still opened and closed, but it had almost no effect on the rest of his face, which was almost puppetlike. His teeth were his original ones, and they were ghastly.

"This gentleman's identity was unknown until just a year ago, when newly uncovered evidence and advanced postmortem, mitochondrial DNA testing proved conclusively who he was. His name is Aaron Kosminski. You would know him as Jack the Ripper."

"Jesus," Tom muttered.

Blackstone smiled.

"This is insane," Tom added. "Jack the Ripper. *The* Jack the Ripper."

Tom's head was spinning. He still felt nauseated from watching what happened earlier, and now Jack the Ripper and Kennedy's assassin, just down the hall from live aliens?

So what? he asked himself. *You really want to be associated with a place that feeds people to vampires? But, as Winthrop said, they did it for their families. It was a deal. Vampires and zombies… aliens and Jack the Ripper. Just thinking about it is insane.*

As his conscience battled his curiosity, he gazed at the Ripper. A large knife was permanently attached to his hand. The Ripper stood in a night scene facade of the Whitechapel area in London, complete with an authentic 1888 streetlight. Even a layer of fog pumped into the space and floated around the Ripper like death itself…

Tom couldn't turn his eyes away.

That is absolutely the creepiest thing I've ever seen.

As if it heard his thoughts, the Ripper turned his black glass eyes toward him.

Holy Christ. He sees me. I can tell he sees me!

The knife in the Ripper's hand swung in front of him, puppetlike.

Tom felt a chill up his spine.

Roland saw others in the group looking toward the next window. "Once they developed the process of rebuilding and reanimating, we considered who would be the most interesting to have with us."

He stopped at the next window. "This man is still considered the most famous gangster of all time… Al Capone."

The waxy figure, once the ruler of the Chicago underworld, moved around the area he was in. The wall behind him flickered with various black-and-white film clips being projected onto it—flashes of Chicago circa 1920s, archival footage of Capone himself, mixed in with shots of newspaper headlines about Capone's latest news.

As for the undead Capone standing in front of it, he showed no emotion. His face was blank except for an occasional flashing of his teeth. The engineers who reconstructed him had done an amazing job. His face looked remarkably like the newsreel footage playing behind him.

Tom looked down the row of infamous zombies and could tell exactly who they were. Beside Capone was Pablo Escobar. Next to him was a guy in Old West gear.

Must be either Jesse James or Billy the Kid, he figured.

After introducing Escobar, Roland confirmed the gunslinger to be Billy the Kid.

Tom understood why such infamous killers were on display.

It's all ego. Each of these men was feared. Capone, Escobar… They were all-powerful in their day. They ruled empires that controlled thousands of people and killed whoever got in their way. Now they're nothing more than some weird artwork hung on the wall for amusement.

35

THE WENDIGO

THE DISPLAY WINDOW IN THE next room was thirty feet high. Inside was a series of thick pine trees and a strange structure made of long sticks and branches, like a giant badger nest.

Roland pressed his iPad, and although none of the guests heard it, a subsonic tone caused the inhabitant to walk out of the stick structure. Of everything seen so far, this ten-foot creature was by far the most hideous. Its humanoid torso connected to a pair of legs like those of a large elk or moose. Its arms stretched all the way to its feet.

Its enormous claws dragged on the ground, each finger easily a foot long. They appeared to be made of wood or bare bone, topped off with nails longer than steak knives, which looked like they were somehow carved into razor-sharp points.

Despite having broad shoulders, its body had little mass. The thing had hair that was thick in some areas but sparse in most. It was beyond skinny, more like emaciated, to the point of looking decomposed. Ribs jutted out through its sides. It resembled giant, walking roadkill.

It had a long snout, which along with part of its face also appeared to be bare skull. Double rows of uneven, jagged teeth filled its mouth. The eyes were small and glowed bright red, giving it a demonic aura. The hair stemming from the skull just below the eyes got thicker as it reached the top of its head, from which grew its most legendary feature, two racks of deerlike antlers, six points each.

Roland turned to his audience. "Ladies, gentlemen, this beast is the legendary wendigo."

The thing looked at the group as if it was counting them. It stood to its full height, the antlers bringing it to almost fifteen feet, and let out a scratchy growl that sent chills through them.

Roland pressed his iPad, and a moment later a man, shirtless in hospital pants, stumbled into the area. He had an unkempt beard and long gray hair. His skin was dark and covered with rashes. He appeared drugged and walked in, oblivious of the wendigo.

The members watched as the creature drew closer to him. Tom had no intention of watching another person, terminally ill or not, get murdered or eaten before his eyes.

What is with these people? Why do they get off on this? They're the most powerful men in the world, and they're feeding these monsters for enjoyment like they're seventh graders giving mice to a pet boa constrictor.

"Excuse me," he said to Blackstone and Raquel.

Winthrop watched him walk away, a look of concern on his face as he turned to Blackstone in the distance. Blackstone shrugged.

He may not work out after all. Oh well, Winthrop thought.

As Tom walked back into the main corridor, the screams of the man echoed behind him.

Vic and Tony followed the man in the white coat through a maze of corridors. The detectives could see he was trying to remember the right way but wasn't sure if he was confused because he didn't know the route well or if he was just terrified. Vic had no way of knowing it, but even as they got closer to where Kelsey was being held, just minutes away, she was about to be taken to her death.

———•———

Cobb entered the holding room with cuffs and the cattle prod. Kelsey instinctively stood up and got in front of Annika.

"Where's Gia?" Kelsey asked. "What did you do with her?"

Cobb came closer. Kelsey and Annika backed farther away.

"Make this easy, okay?" Cobb said. "Just let me put these on you."

"Go fuck yourself," Kelsey said.

"You sick motherfucker!" Annika added.

Kelsey and Annika both let out primal screams and ran at Cobb. He jabbed the cattle prod toward them, but this time Kelsey dodged it and tried to disarm him. Annika flailed away at him, screaming the whole time. He tagged Kelsey with the prod. Her body contorted in pain when the voltage hit her. Annika continued her attack and received her own jab of the prod.

Cobb realized Kelsey would fight him every step of the way, so he injected her with a small dose of propofol, and it took effect quickly. He got her to her feet and guided her out of the room. Annika crawled after them, whimpering.

"No!" she cried. "No…"

"I'll be back for you in about thirty minutes," he said.

The door slammed shut, and she burst into tears.

———•———

Vic and Tony got to the holding room just minutes later. Tony pinned the man in the white coat to the wall beside the door as Vic looked in. He saw Annika but no Kelsey.

"Open it," he ordered the man.

"I don't have the code. I swear to God I don't."

"Don't fuck with me!"

"I swear! I don't have anything to do with this part."

Annika heard the commotion and ran to the door. Vic slid open the food slot and dropped down to it.

"Please help me! Please get me out of here!" she begged.

"I'm trying. Have you seen other women here?" Vic asked.

"Yeah! There was three of us!"

"Do you know their names?"

"Gia and Kelsey."

Vic's hands formed into tight fists and trembled. Energy exploded inside him. He leaned on the door as he struggled to maintain eye contact with her. "What happened to Kelsey? Do you know where she is?"

"They just took her."

"Did you see which way?"

"No!"

"Okay look, we'll find a way to get this door open and get you out, but first I've got to get to Kelsey."

"No! Don't leave me!" she cried.

"I promise! We'll be back!"

Vic turned to the man in the white coat and slugged him, knocking him out cold before he and Tony took off running.

36

MERMAIDS & SEA MONSTERS

O N EACH SIDE OF THE entrance stood a ten-foot-tall marble statue. One was of the Greek god Poseidon, looking fierce and holding a trident. The other was a mermaid, captured in midswim. Both statues had impressive detail work, from the hair in Poseidon's beard to the scales on the mermaid's tail.

Roland led the assemblage inside the exhibit area, which was the largest yet, almost the same size as the enormous lobby. The room had two open levels, one lower than the rest of the facility. The group walked down a double ramp to get to the main floor.

The area was quite darker than the others, most likely to better display the many large aquariums throughout. A half dozen individual tanks lined the walls. Each one had some type of sea creature within. The wall tanks were of various sizes, ranging from the width of a garage door to a movie screen. There were also several freestanding round tanks.

The tanks were illuminated from within, casting light blue ripple reflections onto the floor, walls, and ceiling. The largest tank in the room took up the entire far wall. It was colossal, a hundred feet across and eighty feet high, covered with curtains.

———·———

"Ladies and gentlemen," Roland announced, "this is our Sea Monsters section."

Radcliffe brought Becca closer to one of the wall tanks. She was reluctant. Like Tom, she was horrified by the gruesome displays seen so far. It caused her to doubt if she knew Radcliffe as well as she thought she did. But he took her hand lovingly, and she let herself be guided. The old man pointed at a small mountain of rocks and seaweed in the center of the tank. The rocks varied in size from pebbles to stones to as large as queen-size beds. His eyes followed the fish within as they glided by. A large shark swam past.

He recognized it as a blacktip. Sea life was one of the few things that interested him as much as making money. Suddenly, within an eye-blink, the smaller stones at the base of the mountain at the tank's center instantly broke apart from the mound in a large clump, sending up a small cloud of sand.

Becca saw the clump was not a bunch of small stones at all. It was a large, living creature whose skin perfectly matched the side of the rocky mound. As it revealed itself, she could see the thing was shaped like a man from the waist up with a head, shoulders, and arms. Below the waist, its stomach and legs formed long octopus-like tentacles. It resembled a male mermaid but with a lower cephalopod body and tentacles instead of a tail.

There was a significant amount of webbing between each tentacle and the torso. Each tentacle had dozens of suckers. Its head was large and bulbous with big, round eyes. The skin texture was also octopus-like, a dark maroon color covered in various degrees of spots.

The creature attacked the blacktip. It ripped the shark apart with its claws as its tentacles gripped it. It happened so fast it was hard to see. Clouds of blood billowed from the frantic shark. The creature feasted on it, spinning around like a crocodile making a kill.

Scraps of the shark slowly drifted to the bottom, and the blood clouds floated away. Now the creature could be seen more clearly.

Roland stepped forward. "We call this one Benchley, in honor of Peter Benchley's novel *Beast* about a giant squid." As he spoke, Roland turned toward the glass tank. "Technically, it's not accurate. Benchley here is closer in relation to an octopus than a squid, but we like the name anyway. Benchley can also breathe air. At least once a day, he sits on the rocks above the waterline and dries himself beneath the solar simulator over the tank."

Roland walked to the movie-screen-sized tank. It contained quite a bit of small fish and other sea life. The group gathered around the tank and gazed at the crabs and lobsters crawling over the rock formations covering the bottom.

"This is my favorite of all the things down here," Roland stated. "You can't see them yet, because they're extremely cautious and as soon as we entered this room, they hid."

The group listened and looked at the tank, trying to spot whatever Roland was talking about.

"They have a special ability, much like Benchley. Their skin can mimic anything they choose to, a rocky ocean floor or other species."

Roland pushed a button on his iPad. Within a few seconds, several large striped bass swam into the tank from an opening at the top. Each one was about three feet long.

Becca thought she saw something move behind the coral. She tugged at Radcliffe's arm and whispered to him. "Did you see that? Something is right there."

He smiled down at her, enjoying the wonder in her eyes.

Suddenly a mermaid swam into full view.

"Oh my god..." Becca gasped.

The mermaid looked back at all of them, her gaze moving to various members. She didn't look like the traditional mermaid they'd all seen in movies. This was not Disney's *Little Mermaid*.

Her face was more fishlike than human. Her head was human-shaped, but her eyes were large and round, no different from any other fish. Her nose barely protruded, almost flat. Her mouth was shaped like a fish as well, with thick lips. Flowing from the top of her head were long skinny fins similar to the strings below a jellyfish. They had a pattern to them, and from a distance could be confused for dreadlocks.

The skin on her face and body was greenish blue with spots varying in shade. Below the navel, her torso formed into a tail, very much like the shape of a mermaid from popular culture. The fin at the bottom was wide and constantly flowed back and forth in a graceful, almost mesmerizing motion.

Her hands were completely webbed from the fingertips down with sharp, pointy nails at the tip of each. Two more mermaids appeared from the rocks. They were similar in shape and design but with slightly different colors. All three of them began to swim through the tank. Their movements were completely inhuman. They swam with a natural, almost slow-motion glide, beautiful to behold.

"We've found them to be easier to train than dolphins. Watch this." Roland pushed a button on the iPad, and a tone echoed inside the tank.

All three mermaids swam to a spot in the center of the tank. They looked at him through the glass, waiting for a command. He pushed another button and a different tone played. The mermaids separated and swam together in a circular pattern, following each other from tail to head.

The old members smiled at the sight, and the women let out gasps and laughs.

Roland spoke up. "Also like an octopus, they know what other species to mimic to either escape a predator as well as to lure something closer to them to get the drop on them."

Roland hit a cue, and another tone played.

This time all three mermaids seemed to morph into a different type of sea creature. The first one's skin turned dark gray, and she contorted her body until she was the same shape as a shark. She didn't change shape, but her skin took on all the markings, color, and shadows of how a shark would look from a distance, as if she were a blank screen with a shark projected onto it.

The next one contorted into a ball. All her hair fins pulled in tightly and she took on the appearance of a large sea turtle. All the patterns of a turtle's shell appeared.

"Amazing," Tom said.

The last mermaid still drifted with her tail slowly gliding, awaiting her instructions.

Roland put his fingers on the iPad. "For years, marine biologists and scientists have stated all the sightings of beautiful mermaids by fishermen and sea captains over the past hundred years were nothing more than mistaken cases of sea lions and manatees. But…"

Roland played the tone.

All three mermaids used their chameleonlike skin to take on the appearance of human women. Their skin kept its rough texture, but the color changed to a warm pink. Their flowing fins divided to make them even finer, like hair. Their faces became human as well. If you looked close enough, you could see their facial structure hadn't changed, but parts of the skin altered to resemble a woman's eyes, lips, and contours.

Even the look of their tails changed. Amazingly, a strip of scales going down the center of the tail grew dark, creating the illusion of two legs held tight together.

"More than one fisherman, after months at sea, would jump overboard to save what he thought was a woman somehow lost out on the waves," Roland said.

With that, he hit a button, and a seal swam gracefully into the tank as a treat for their tricks. In lightning-fast movement, the mermaids reverted to their natural forms and attacked it like hungry piranhas.

As they ate, their mouths opened much wider than would be expected, exactly like a largemouth bass. They opened to a hole more than half the size of their face and extended, accordion-like. However, much different from a bass, these mouths were filled with short, sharp, serrated teeth in double rows like a shark. They devoured the entire seal in just a second or two, a cloud of blood and chum drifting away in its place.

------·------

It was time to see the largest tank, the one that took up the entire far wall of the room. Winthrop had a flair for the dramatic, so he'd had the tank covered with curtains so no one could see the latest acquisition until after Roland properly set it up.

Roland had his back to the group and his mic muted for the moment as he radioed Lance in the monitor-filled control room. Lance was stressed, watching Vic and Tony rush through the facility with Mason trying to catch up to them.

"You all set with the projector?" Roland asked with a finger on his other ear.

Lance jumped back, startled by Roland's voice. "Uh, yeah, but..."

"But what? Is it ready or isn't it?" Roland snapped.

"All good to go."

On that, Roland switched his mic back on and spun around to the group. "Now, something none of you have seen before."

The crowd was attentive, none more than Radcliffe.

"In 1868, a cargo ship named the *Charlotte Mary* was attacked by a creature so big it destroyed the ship within a matter of minutes. Miraculously, a single crewmember survived. He was rescued while floating on a piece of debris five days later. The man described what he saw to an artist friend of his, and the likeness was then printed in newspapers all over the country."

In the control room, Lance flicked a button that turned on a projector in the aquarium area. The illustration Roland spoke of appeared on the curtains in front of the colossal tank, clear and crisp. In the flat drawing style of the late 1800s, the enormous creature attacked a tall ship. Its tail wrapped around the vessel's entire width as it snarled.

Most illustrations of turn-of-the-century sea monsters

resembled large octopuses or giant squid. This one looked like a giant sea serpent with crab claws, mixed into one unnatural-looking monstrosity.

"And here is our newest acquisition," Roland said, throwing his arm up theatrically.

The projected image turned off and the curtains opened as they would at a movie theater, revealing a tank eighty feet tall and just as wide. The inside of the tank had a floor of rocks and an actual sunken fishing boat. Other sea life within the tank swam around... stingrays, sharks, and turtles.

No one saw any of them. They didn't pay any attention to the sunken boat either. Moving slowly through the water was the biggest living creature any of them had ever seen. It looked exactly like the creature depicted in the illustration come to life, a gargantuan sea serpent with two crab arms. Its long body twisted and flowed as it moved, dwarfing several whale sharks beside it.

The skin of the monster had scales made of crustacean shells. Its mammoth body was sixty feet long, if not more. It had a hideous, piranha-like head the size of a garbage truck. Its body got thinner as it flowed back until it formed into an eel-type tail. Its claws were big enough to pick up and crush a speedboat. So enthralled by the size of the monster were they, none of the members or their guests even noticed the two detectives enter the room behind them.

Vic and Tony followed Roland's voice until they made it into the aquarium. They stopped in their tracks when they saw the massive creature.

"Jesus," Tony said.

"Holy shit."

"Don't move," Mason whispered.

They turned to see Mason and Red approaching between them and the guests. Mason had a pistol, and Red held an AR-15.

"Put the guns down," Mason ordered.

"Fuck you. We're cops. You put yours down," Vic replied.

"I don't give a shit. Drop them." Mason motioned with his pistol.

A few of the members became aware of the situation. Blackstone signaled Winthrop something was going on. Winthrop saw the standoff and turned to approach them.

———•———

Out of view above the largest tank, Kelsey winced as her vision cleared up slowly. She realized she was walking. Cobb pushed a set of double doors open and helped her through. She was able to focus more, and although the drug made everything seem to be moving at the wrong speed, she could see he was guiding her along a metal catwalk. When she looked down, it looked like they were above a large swimming pool at night.

"Where are we going?" she slurred.

"It's okay," Cobb replied.

They got to the end of the catwalk, and he took her handcuffs off. Kelsey leaned on the railing and looked down at the water, not yet seeing the creature within. From her position, she could see the group of people in evening gowns and tuxedoes through the tank, appearing skewed and disproportionate through the water between them.

Cobb leaned down and attached one of the cuffs to her ankle and the other to a steel loop welded onto an anchor.

"Wait... Where...," Kelsey mumbled.

Cobb said, "Shhhhh."

Kelsey looked straight down through the metal grates of the catwalk. She saw the creature moving below. The sheer size of it shocked her.

What is that?

She couldn't take her eyes off it.

A loud voice filled her head, godlike. They were standing close to a speaker from which Roland's microphone was booming.

"Now... let's watch the big guy have his dinner."

Cobb guided her closer to the edge. He unlatched the

railing and swung it open. The catwalk was about ten feet above the waterline. The effects of the propofol had worn off enough for her to realize what was about to happen.

"Oh my god."

———•———

"Gentlemen," Winthrop said, "what's going on here?"

"Boston police. Tell them to put their guns down," Vic said.

By now, many of the members were watching in the distance, as if no matter what happened, it would have absolutely no effect on them.

"Please. Let's all just take a breath and bring it down a notch, shall we?" Winthrop said.

"Tell them to put them down or I'm shooting you first," Vic ordered.

Winthrop saw he meant it. "Put them down. Go ahead."

"Mr. W—" Mason started.

"Do it. And then we'll all have a drink and chat," Winthrop said.

Tony kept his gun on them as Mason and Red handed their guns to Vic.

"Why the AR-15?" Tony asked.

"I assure you these weapons are completely legal, and these men are properly permitted," Winthrop said. "Now please tell me what this is all about."

Vic stepped closer to Winthrop, but Tony kept his gun on them.

"We're looking for someone."

———•———

Winthrop turned to Roland across the room and subtly shook his head.

The younger man got the message and immediately put his finger to his ear to radio Cobb. "Cobb. It's Roland. Don't throw her in."

———•———

Cobb didn't hear the message because Kelsey was fighting

back with all she had and had knocked his ear radio off in the struggle. She did her best, but her leg was cuffed to the anchor.

"Don't make it so…," Cobb uttered.

Kelsey smashed him in the face and pressed to overpower him, but she was still too sluggish.

He locked her into a tight hold, his mouth roughly against her ear. "You fucking bitch. I'm going to enjoy this."

His breathing was heavy from the struggle, and the feel of it on her face disgusted her. He released her and pushed the anchor over the edge. The weight of it cuffed to her ankle dragged her down behind it. At the last second, she gripped his shirt tightly enough to pull him over the edge with her.

For the half second they were in free fall, Kelsey saw the blur of the water zooming at her and had the presence of mind to take the deepest breath she could. She hit the surface hard, and the anchor dragged her straight to the bottom. Cobb splashed down on top of her.

———•———

The sight got everyone's attention, including Vic, Tony, Winthrop, and his men. Vic realized who was connected to the anchor. Overwhelming terror consumed him.

"Kelsey!" he yelled.

He grabbed the AR-15 from Tony and bolted toward the tank, barreling through the tuxedoed billionaires and their guests.

Tony followed behind yelling, "Out of the way!"

Not getting the response he wanted, he fired his gun in the air. Only then did everyone scatter.

Without slowing down, Vic blasted the AR-15 at the tank as he ran. The sound was deafening. The members scrambled to take cover as fast as they could, which at their age was clumsy and awkward. Vic screamed as the muzzle flash lit up his face, and bullets smashed through the thick glass of the tank. He emptied the full magazine, which put thirty holes into an area the size of a beach blanket. Water sprayed out from the holes, but the glass didn't shatter as he'd hoped.

He dropped the rifle and pulled out his handgun. He blasted seven more holes into the same area. Mason and Red ran to stop him. Tony saw them coming and shot at them, giving cover to Vic to keep up his attack on the glass.

———•———

In the tank, Cobb tried to swim to safety, but the creature's giant claw crushed both his legs and pulled him under the surface. Water rushed by his ears and filled his mouth, which was wide open in a silent scream. The giant creature brought him toward its head and opened its jaws.

Cobb flailed helplessly as the creature slammed its jagged teeth down on him, and he was killed instantly. The lower half of his body sank like a broken mannequin, leaking red clouds the whole way down and chased after by hundreds of smaller, normal-sized fish.

———•———

Vic saw the glass around the bullet holes splintering as water sprayed out, but nothing was happening fast enough to help Kelsey. Vic could see the look of helpless horror on her face. Nausea mixed with his panic. The thing's serpentlike body glided through the tank, and it circled back and turned its attention to Kelsey.

Vic ran to the nearest piece of furniture, a nightclub table with a heavy metal base. He picked it up and slammed the base against the damaged area of the glass. Water sprayed all over him from the holes as he smashed the glass over and over.

Tony shot at Mason and Red until he ran out of ammo. As soon as he did, the two men rushed in and tackled him.

"I got him—stop the other one!" Mason ordered Red.

Red started to go, but Tony grabbed his ankle. Mason slugged him in the face and Red kicked at him, but Tony didn't let go.

———•———

Kelsey's lungs were about to burst. Her mouth gasped open

desperately to get air, and water poured into her throat. The intensity of her panic exploded.

The tank glass thudded and crunched as Vic kept up his attack, putting all his strength into it. He did his best to focus on the task at hand but couldn't help looking at Kelsey. Her mouth was wide open, and her body shook and convulsed as she gasped for breath.

NO!

His biceps were on fire, but he swung harder and faster and screamed from his soul. The damaged area of the glass buckled and gave way. A jagged hole the size of a car burst outward in a torrent of glass and water. Hundreds of thousands of gallons erupted into the room. The hole remained for a few seconds, then doubled in size for another second or two before the entire front of the giant tank shattered open. Time stood still for an instant, and then twenty million gallons of seawater burst out and hit the room with the power of a tsunami.

37

CHAOS

WITHIN AN INSTANT, THE ROOM was submerged as the rush of water smashed through. People were swept away as if they weighed nothing. It was equivalent to a rogue wave, and when it blasted through the room, it destroyed walls, support beams, and portions of ceiling.

The room was on a lower level than the rest of the facility. Even though the overflow of water sent waves spreading throughout the corridors and surrounding exhibit rooms, much of it flooded the entire lower level, creating a dark pool.

While several people were swept completely out of the room, the ones remaining frantically tried to get to safety. The giant sea monster was loose and thrashing among them. The flooded area wasn't deep enough to submerge, and it slithered around the vast space like a clumsy, angry snake. Screams filled the room. People hid wherever they could or tried to escape without taking their eyes off the beast as it prowled beside and above them.

Vic burst to the surface. His face stung from the rush of seawater that filled his nose when he bounced beneath the crush of water. No sign of Tony. He saw Kelsey, unconscious on a portion of the raised tank floor barely above the waterline. Fish flopped around beside her. He struggled through the chest-high water and climbed up onto the base of the destroyed tank to get to her. She had no pulse.

"No. No. No, you don't."

Vic started CPR, and so intense was his focus he paid no attention to the humongous creature. He was putting every ounce of energy into trying to bring his soul mate back.

"Come on, baby. Come on," he blurted out between blowing air into her mouth and doing chest compressions.

When Tony finally managed to control his body after being bounced beneath the crashing current, he found himself across the room. He coughed the saltwater from his throat and saw everything had erupted into chaos. The head of the huge sea thing was towering above, and people were screaming in the water.

He spotted Vic giving Kelsey mouth-to-mouth on the raised floor of the destroyed tank and moved as fast as he could to get to them.

Over and over, Vic breathed air into her mouth as screams of horror echoed in the background. Tony climbed out of the water and crawled to them. He said nothing, squeezed his eyes shut tight, and prayed as Vic fought to save her.

Vic registered his presence beside him but didn't slow down for a second. His ears were filled with a constant static sound, and nausea coursed through him. The stubborn cynic who ruled his brain whispered, as if it to another unseen onlooker, that it was all over.

Fuck you.

He refused to quit, and after he'd pushed more air into her, she snapped awake, coughing out water. Tony was overjoyed and watched the toughest guy he'd ever known burst into happy tears.

"Kel! Honey!" he cried. "Thank God. Thank God."

Kelsey tried to speak but couldn't stop coughing.

"Easy, baby. Take it slow."

Tony collapsed onto his back in relief.

Once she caught her breath, she reached for him. He took her in his arms and squeezed her tight. Both shook as they embraced, crying into each other.

He took her face in his hands, and his wet eyes stared into the ones he feared he'd never see again.

"If you say I told you so...," she started.

"Shut up."

"Where are we?" she asked.

"Long story. First, we get you out of here."

"Who's with you?" she asked.

"Nobody," he said, "we're on our own. But that's..."

His words were drowned out by an ear-piercing noise from the sea monster. It was a sound no human had ever heard, a bizarre mix of growl and whale cry.

All three of them watched spellbound as the creature shot its giant head down onto a lifeless woman floating facedown. It picked her high out of the water and, in one awkward move, snapped its head back to flip her completely into its mouth. Its jaws opened and closed a few times and swallowed what was left of her. It turned in their direction.

Tony was the first to react. "Quick. Get behind the boat."

Vic helped Kelsey up and saw her ankle was cuffed to the anchor. He desperately searched his pockets for his keys with no luck.

"Damn it! You have yours?" he asked Tony.

The giant sea monster rampaged toward them.

"We can't stay here," Vic said.

"You carry Kel, I'll carry the anchor," Tony said.

Vic lifted her as Tony picked up the fifty-pound anchor with an unintentional grunt.

They stumbled their way behind the boat. The rocky tank bottom was not only uneven and jagged but slippery as hell. Kelsey whimpered as Vic lowered her to the floor as gently as he could. Tony was unable to put the anchor down as gracefully. It thudded down hard.

They huddled together against the side of the boat as the creature searched for them. After long seconds, something else got its attention, and it moved on.

Tony dug through his pocket for his keys. "Got 'em."

She groaned in relief as Tony took the cuff off her ankle, leaving a deep line in her skin. "Thank God."

The creature was learning how to move out of the water, using its enormous crab claws to steady itself even as it attacked anything in its sight. As they watched, it picked up a large whale shark and devoured it.

"Where are we?" Kelsey asked. "What aquarium is this?"

Vic and Tony looked at each other, unsure where to start.

"We're underground. This is all under the Common," Vic answered.

"Underground? What?" she asked.

"I know. It's crazy. But it's true."

Kelsey scanned the area.

"It's a fucking monster zoo," Tony added.

She stared at Tony, trying to decide if she was still drugged. Between almost drowning, seeing that… whatever the hell it was, she didn't know what was real and what wasn't. As she tried to figure it out, she saw Benchley, the half-man, half-octopus thing, rise out of the water in the distance.

───·───

When the room first erupted in gunfire, pharmaceutical tycoon Franklin Dodd went for the exit. Before he could reach it, the tank exploded and Dodd felt a wall of water hit his back like a speeding truck. With his asthma, Dodd's breath-holding ability wasn't enough to sustain him for more than a few seconds, and he took in a mouthful of seawater as he was tossed in the current. When he finally managed to stand, he pulled his inhaler from his pocket and took a frantic spray. The freezing water was up to his chest; people were screaming. The giant sea monster was slithering out of the broken tank, its head swooping high above.

Dodd looked around to get his bearings and spotted the double ramp out of the room. He moved toward it as quickly as a man his age could. His pulse was racing; his legs hurt like hell.

Suddenly his body jerked back a bit, and he thought his tuxedo jacket was caught on something. He turned to try to free himself and felt a sharp ache in his shoulder and lower back. He grunted in pain, figuring it was muscle cramps from the awkward twisting and turning.

But then Dodd saw something that didn't make sense. The water level was going down, but it was going down much too fast… as if someone had opened a giant drain nearby. Within two seconds, it was below his ankles. His feet rose out of the water completely, and he realized the water wasn't going down at all. He was going up.

He craned his wrinkled neck as far as he could and saw the monster was holding him in its claw. He screamed and kicked as the creature brought him closer to its mouth. He struggled wildly to free himself and fell twenty feet with a splash into five feet of water.

Dodd stood up, his back in a wild spasm, and tried to move again, using his hands to try to push the water past him. The sea monster's claw grabbed him again, this time squeezing him around his torso so tight he could feel, and hear, his ribs break.

It was the most painful thing he'd ever experienced. Until that second anyway. It was quickly surpassed when the creature used its other claw to pluck one of his legs off. The claw squeezed his thigh area and pulled it to its mouth. It tore off the leg as easily as a normal crab would tear apart a sea worm. The last thing Dodd saw before he died was his leg grinding up and down in the creature's mouth.

———•———

The force of the water shattered all the freestanding tanks, shooting glass and debris in every direction. Large chunks of wall crashed down into the rising water like meteors. One of the pieces came down on Winthrop and Veronica.

He was knocked aside, but it pinned her. As soon as he regained his footing, he heard her voice among the screams. She was half-submerged with a large portion of wall on her legs.

She was hysterical, shaking, and screaming. "Jimmy! Help! Please help me!"

Winthrop realized something was behind him. He turned and saw the new acquisition he'd been so excited to show off just minutes earlier now above him. Its twisting body sent waves of water crashing all around it. Winthrop turned back to Veronica.

She was crying, her eyes wide and desperate. "Hurry, Jimmy! Hurry!"

He quickly moved away from her, grabbing at the water around him as if he could somehow pull himself away faster.

"JIMMY!" Veronica screamed. "JIMMY! *JIMMY!*"

Her screams abruptly cut short when the monster's head shot down and it snapped its jaws onto her. It devoured her and moved on.

It had been out of the water for several minutes now. Feeling itself beginning to suffocate, the seventy-ton beast panicked. It let out another thunderous, stuttering whale cry and erupted into a frantic rampage through the facility. Searching desperately for water deep enough to submerge in, it smashed its way through everything in its path.

The entire facility shook with the force of an earthquake. The monster blindly swung its claws through walls, corridors, and ceilings. The aftershock of reverberations shattered all the glass in the entire facility, including all the windows of the dioramas.

After blasting a path of destruction throughout the entire facility, the old monster fell dead. Screams, both near and distant, filled the air. Adding to them were dozens of nonhuman screams, growls, and other unearthly noises.

Amid the chaos of the flood and the collapsing structure, all the creatures were now set free.

———·———

In the control room, Lance watched the monitors in shock. Several of his screens went black when the giant sea beast crashed through power lines in the walls, causing many of the lights to flicker or go off completely. The guests scrambled through the bedlam, trying to find their way back to the elevator.

Despite their affluent and entitled status, all the elegance and etiquette previously on display were gone. The world's wealthiest one percent pushed and shoved each other out of the way like refugees. Some tripped and fell, and the others stepped on and over them.

Lance moved the toggle on the security cameras that still worked. The realization of what was happening put a twitch in his eye. On every screen, creatures and monsters roved free. He jumped up, locked his door, and feared he'd be trapped alone in the room forever.

———·———

Mason got to his feet. He was in three feet of water, the air around him thick with clouds of dust and dirt. The way people were running by gave him an eerie sense of déjà vu. The stench of the tank water overpowered the smell of the broken construction. Clouds of dust floated down into the water. He looked around for Red or Winthrop but didn't see them.

What he saw was complete madness. He made it back to the flooded aquarium area where people were yelling and trying to get out of the water. To his right, Mason saw a Sasquatch playing in the water. The sight stunned him so much he didn't turn away until he realized the creature wasn't playing. It was holding a woman under the water as her feet splashed up.

His survival training kicked in, and he moved on.

Winthrop managed to crawl onto one of the ramps in his soaking-wet tuxedo. Even knowing the layout as well as he did, in the loud pandemonium he needed time to figure out his bearings. He remembered where the main corridor was and knew it to be the fastest way to the elevator. He moved as swiftly as his body would allow.

The lights ahead were flickering, and what Winthrop saw through the strobe-like atmosphere sent a chill through him. Coming toward him were several large things casting shadows through the flickering light. The way they were silhouetted, he was unsure which creatures they were and didn't want to find out. Unaware if they saw him or not, he turned and rushed the other way. He nearly tripped multiple times over fallen pieces of debris.

He realized the things were following him. He could hear their uneven footsteps crunching on the broken glass covering the floor. His nerves were on fire. As they got closer, he thought of all the people torn apart and killed by his creatures over the years. The pulsing in his ears grew so loud it drowned out the screams of the victims in his memories and turned the sizzle reel of death scenes into a horrifying silent movie. He was about to die. He could feel it, and somewhere deep in whatever was left of the soul he was born with, a quiet voice told him he deserved it.

But then he saw the door to a supply room.

Oh God, please. Please. Please, he begged of the god he didn't believe in. *Be unlocked. Be unlocked.*

It was. Winthrop rushed inside and slammed the door behind him. It had no lock. He moved backward away from it through the small room, tripping over boxes until his back hit the rear wall. He slid down and stared at the door, hoping with every bone in his body the creatures hadn't seen where he went. He had no clear plan. He knew he had to get to the elevator, but the dangers in doing so were too many to count.

A noise grew louder behind the door. Something was just

outside. He hoped he was wrong, but whatever it was banged against the door. He looked around the room for something to use as a weapon and found nothing.

The doorknob shook.

Dear God, no. Please. No.

The door swung open. Winthrop's heart stopped, then filled with joy when Mason rushed in and shut the door behind him.

———•———

When the tank burst, the current forced Tom Ackerman into sideways somersaults beneath the surface. His knee smashed against the hard tile floor and triggered the instinct to put his hands over his head to protect it from also smashing into something as he spun.

As he pulled himself onto some debris, he coughed out saltwater and tried to catch his breath. When he finally got the stars to stop flickering, he spit out the last drops and looked around.

It was turmoil. People were screaming as they scurried through the high water. He saw Rick Jackson, the tobacco giant, trying to escape from some sea monstrosity gaining on him. Another sea creature was ripping apart one of the female escorts.

Tom saw a dry spot a few yards away where a collapsed cement wall had folded down upon itself, creating a small, triangular space in the middle. He ran to it and climbed into the tight gap. On his stomach, Tom buried his face between the wet fabric of his forearm and bicep and squeezed his eyes shut like a child under the covers, hiding from the monster in the closet.

———•———

Winthrop and Mason compared notes on what had transpired. Mason had done his bidding for years without question. Winthrop was smart enough to know that under the current circumstances, he couldn't count on Mason to put his safety above his own need to survive.

He also knew it was a long way back to the elevator and the place was swarming with things that would eat him alive.

"Tell you what," he said. "You get me out of this, and I'll give you a bonus."

Mason stifled the urge to laugh. He knew he was as helpless as Winthrop in this situation. "How much of a bonus?"

"You tell me. A million? Ten million?"

Mason knew he had all the cards in his favor. It was just a silly gamble anyway. He might be able to guide the old man, but if one of these things caught them, there would be nothing he could do. But he might as well play along.

He smiled at Winthrop. "Make it an even billion."

Winthrop raised an eyebrow but more out of surprise than anger. It didn't take a genius to realize that without Mason's help, odds were good he'd never live to spend another dime. As if the powers that be were trying to help Mason's negotiation, a piercing Sasquatch scream echoed outside the room.

The older man turned to Mason. He knew there were ways out of a deal like this once they were back safely on the surface.

"Done," Winthrop said and extended his hand.

Mason shook it tightly.

Before letting go, Mason gave him a stare that never failed to scare the hell out of anyone on the receiving end. "Just so you know… If I do manage to get you out of here, and you try to renege…"

He didn't need to finish the sentence. His point was taken. It was the first time Mason had ever spoken to his boss that way. The balance of power had most definitely shifted.

Winthrop nodded. Even arrogance as abundant as his buckled beneath such a clear and honest threat. He knew what Mason was capable of. If he had to kill a dozen people to get to him and keep his word, he would do it without hesitation.

Mason cracked open the door and scoped the area. "Come on," he said to Winthrop, and the two of them headed out.

Winthrop felt a boost of hope he would see the sun again.

Tobacco CEO Rick Jackson couldn't escape the sea creature chasing him. The thing was in one of the tanks Roland had not introduced yet. It was humanoid, with thick turtle-like skin and layered shells on its back and sharp nails at the end of its webbed claws.

At one point, Jackson made it far enough up the ramp that the water was just above his ankles. Before he could get to the exit, he fell. He was sure he broke his nose. Pain stung his face and his eyes filled up. He looked back to see the creature closing in. Jackson got to his feet, slipping and sliding, and tried to run. The creature swung at his back, and its claw sliced so deep it grazed his spine.

Jackson again fell face-first. He was panting so hard his breath caused ripples in the inches of water beneath him. The monster savagely flipped him onto his back. His ears were now submerged. All the screams he heard, including his own, took on a distorted, dreamlike quality.

He watched helplessly as the creature lowered its head closer to his shaking face. The thing opened its mouth, and Jackson went into shock, unable to do anything but shake and tremble beneath the monstrosity. Instead of using its mouth to bite him, the creature used its razor-sharp claws to pull pieces from his body, bringing bite-sized chunks of flesh to his mouth.

Jackson yelled and flailed and punched at it. The billionaire screamed as the thing repeatedly ripped away small chunks of chest, arms, and torso. His body rose and fell with each rip until he went into cardiac arrest. A whistle came out of his mouth as he fought for breath, and fear contorted his face into a final death stare.

Vic took off his wet jacket and put it on Kelsey as Tony peered from behind the boat to scan the area.

Tony looked to the right. "I'm pretty sure it was back that way."

"What was?" Kelsey asked.

"The elevator," Vic said.

Kelsey's head raced until Annika's face filled her mind. "Wait. We can't leave."

"Why not?" Vic asked.

"There are others here. I have to get them."

Vic remembered the girl in the holding room. "Honey, look...," Vic said. "I know who you're talking about. We saw her. She's in a locked room we can't open. Let us get you out of here first. Get you to safety. Then I'll come back down with a whole SWAT team to get her."

"No," she said. "We have to try."

"It's too dangerous. We'll come back with help. I promise."

"I'm not just leaving her here."

Vic felt his blood boil. He knew he was right and she wasn't thinking clearly. "Kel. The odds of us even finding our way back to that girl in the middle of all this are a million to one."

Before he could continue, she looked into his eyes and repeated the words she'd heard him say to the uniform cracking jokes over the dead carjacking victim the first night they met. "Hey, asshole. This is someone's daughter."

The words hit home, as she knew they would.

"Damn it," Vic said.

"Which way was it?" Tony asked.

"Somewhere that way." Vic pointed, then helped Kelsey to her feet.

She winced when she stood up.

"Are you okay?"

She nodded. "Yeah. I can do it."

Vic took a deep breath. "What's this girl's name?"

"Annika."

38

CREATURES ON THE LOOSE

L ANCE HEARD THE COPS ON the monitor and knew he had to join them to get out of there alive. He also knew getting to them was impossible. The monitors showed several obstacles between him and the cops. All the creatures were taking out their anger at being held captive on any and every human they could find.

Seventy-six-year-old Senator Kirkland only managed to run a few yards before his hip pain kicked in, and when he stopped to lean against a wall for support, the largest of the Sasquatches approached him, making the most horrific sound Kirkland had ever heard.

The beast towered over him, and the senator, one of the most powerful politicians in the country, covered his ears and slid down the wall. The beast reached down. Its palm covered the top of Kirkland's head, and the fingers stretched all the way to his neck.

His legs kicked against the floor as the beast dragged him closer to one of the shattered dioramas. All that remained was a jagged line of three-inch-thick glass at the base of the window about two feet high in some places. In other areas, it was lower, giving it the look of a child's drawing of a pointy mountain horizon made of glass.

Kirkland sniveled as the beast dropped him. His face crunched against the broken glass, and his hip exploded in pain. He rolled over onto his back, and his mind went numb. Pieces of glass were stuck to, and into, his face.

From his position on the floor, the thing above him looked twenty feet tall, although nine was more accurate. It let out another deafening growl, bent down, and wrapped its hands around each of Kirkland's ankles. In one motion, it lifted Kirkland from the floor, upside down, and swung him up and over its head until his face bounced against the monster's hairy back.

He stayed like that for an instant before the beast used all its strength to flip Kirkland forward over his head so fast that for a split second, Kirkland's body was stretched out to his full height in midair directly above it. Kirkland's arms flailed as the beast brought him down hard and slammed his back onto one of the larger points of the jagged glass.

The senator came to a sickening stop as the glass impaled him. Blood filled his throat and burst from his mouth. For the past twenty years, he had been the leading force in the senate, able to summon presidents and destroy the lives of his political enemies with a phone call.

His fellow congressmen and a large portion of intelligent Americans saw him for what he was—a lying, hypocritical piece of shit who cared only for his own needs. Now he lay impaled, broken and sobbing like a child. His legs dangled limply out of the diorama; his hands twitched and shook as blood poured out of him. His breathing was rapid, as if he were giving birth.

"No... please, God...," he cried in his Southern drawl.

Kirkland's mind raced, more out of conceit than hope, trying to imagine a scenario where he survived this. The beast lumbered over him and stepped up into the diorama. The senator's eyes widened as he watched the beast lift its enormous foot in the air over him.

He let out a final whimper as the beast stomped its foot down on his chest, pushing his body deep enough against the jagged glass to cut him completely in half. Only strips of skin and tuxedo fabric kept him from falling apart in two pieces.

The beast picked up Kirkland's lifeless upper body by the arm, ripping it clear from his mangled waist. It lifted him high enough to see his dead eyes. Satisfied, the creature threw half of the seven-term senator to the floor like the trash he was.

———·———

Tom stayed hidden until the area looked clear of any creatures. He climbed out and headed back to the elevators, out of shape and his chest on fire. Closing his eyes for a few seconds, he tried to catch his breath but opened them quickly when a loud growl echoed through the area.

Shit.

He looked in every direction for someplace to run. Something heavy was getting closer.

Please God. Please God. Please God.

A reddish-brown Sasquatch approached. It stopped several yards from him. The thing was partially illuminated by a fallen light that separated it from the fog-like dust filling the air behind it. There was no question the beast saw him. It stood and stared in a way that caused Tom's knees to shake.

Another sound filled the air, this one much different. It had more of a wet screech.

Coming out of the dark to his left was Benchley, the half-man, half-octopus. Tom stood between the two monsters. The creatures faced each other, sizing the other up. The Sasquatch snarled and attacked. Tom fell to the ground on his back and crawled away as fast as he could. In a lightning-fast move, Benchley shot a tentacle around the Sasquatch's neck. It growled and tried to pull the tentacle off even as another one wrapped around one of his arms. The Sasquatch went crazy, twisting and turning to free itself, pulling Benchley along with it. The sea creature supported itself with only three of its tentacles, leaving the other five free to fight.

Tom knew he should use this time to run, but the sight of the battling monsters had him spellbound.

This can't be happening, Tom thought.

The sea creature soon had tentacles wrapped tight around the Sasquatch, rendering him helpless as he dropped to the floor. It enfolded a tentacle around the Sasquatch's head and pulled it back until the giant beast's neck gave an ugly crunch.

The sound broke Tom from his spell. He ran into the main corridor, which was littered with debris and rubble. Moving cautiously along the wall, he tried to find his way to the lobby. A disturbing scream from an unlucky human echoed in the distance. Tom's mind raced through the horrors he knew were now running free.

He leaned around the next corner before moving forward and jumped back as he came face-to-face with Vic. "Shit!"

Vic put his hand over Tom's mouth to shut him up.

"Keep your voice down," Tony said, his own voice a forceful whisper.

"Please. I just want to get out of here," he said.

Vic pulled him closer. "Oh, so it's not so fun being the one that gets eaten, huh?"

"Listen," Tom said. "I swear. This is my first time here. I had no idea what was going on."

Tony let out a grunt of doubt.

"It's true. I was disgusted and puked when I saw what they were doing."

Kelsey stepped closer to Tom.

"Wait. Are you Tom Ackerman?"

"Yes."

"Who's Tom Ackerman?" Tony asked.

Kelsey said, "The LittleBirdy guy."

"Lucky him," Tony said.

"How did you get involved with this?" Vic asked.

"James Winthrop," Tom said. "But I swear I didn't know about…"

Vic took a step closer. "Okay, Rich Boy. This is what's gonna happen. You want to get out of here alive?"

"Yes please."

"You're going to stay close to us. Don't do anything we don't tell you to do. There's someone else down here we have to get, then we're heading up and out."

"Yes. Whatever you say. Thank you."

"But," Vic added, "once we're out of here, you're going to tell us everything you know."

"Done."

"And," Vic continued, "you're going to testify on all of it."

"Get me out of here and I'll do anything you want. I swear. I'm a good guy. If I'd known ahead of time what was going on, I never would have come."

Vic, Kelsey, and Tony, cops who were lied to regularly, knew instinctively he was telling the truth.

The rush of water carried Keiji Fujiyama almost two rooms away. He felt a piercing pain in his head, and when he touched it, his fingers were covered in blood. As he looked around, the pain eased with his left eye closed. He got to his feet and found himself in the main corridor, just outside the entrance to the Jersey Devil room.

He walked closer to the aquarium entrance and saw the damage. Several lifeless bodies were on the ground. The sunken room was flooded, and the surface of the murky water was completely still. Dark areas were all around him. Broken power cables dangling above dripped sparks that reflected on the water.

Something moved to his right.

It was George Conrad. He and Conrad were not the best of friends. They'd worked a deal together years before in which both thought the other had taken advantage. In the time since, they were cordial but mainly kept away from each other. Old grudges didn't seem to matter now.

"George," Keiji said.

Conrad limped to him. There was a huge rip in the pant leg of his tuxedo with a deep, bloody gash from his thigh to his knee.

"Who was that guy?" Keiji asked.

"I don't know," Conrad answered.

Keiji felt a tightness in his chest. "How could someone get in? Why didn't anyone stop him? I thought Winthrop had security down here at all times."

In the distance, they heard a loud crash and a man screaming for help.

"Fuck," Conrad whispered.

Keiji turned back to him, still closing his left eye. "Do you know the fastest way back to the elevator from here?"

Conrad looked in both directions. "I think it's that way."

"Can you walk?"

"Yes." Conrad nodded.

Keiji peeked around the corner into the main corridor and saw no movement.

He nodded to Conrad, and they walked on.

———·———

Bryan Blackstone regained consciousness at the far end of the aquarium. He found himself lying on a fallen wall just above the surface of the water, half buried in Sheetrock between this room and the next.

He pushed pieces of debris off, sat up, and surveyed the area. "Jesus."

A woman screamed. He turned to see a humanoid creature about twenty feet away on top of Stacey, the woman who had come with Keiji Fujiyama. It had thick, dark blue, scaleless skin. Its head was sharklike with small, solid black eyes. A row of spikes protruded from its back and led from its neck down to its lower back before separating and continuing down the backs of its human-shaped legs. The thing's claws held her down, one of them pushing down on her head. The webbing between its two long fingers covered half Stacey's face, allowing only one mascara-smeared eye to search for someone to save her.

She flailed helplessly, screaming and crying as the thing took bites out of her body. Its mouth was the size of a bear trap, and its jaws slammed down on her flesh with the same force as one. Her screams came to a sudden and sickening stop as if someone had turned them off with a flick of a switch.

Blackstone puked. He wiped his mouth and looked for a way out. The only way past the man-fish thing was the ramp on the other side of the flooded room. He lowered himself into the dark water. It was up to his chest and ice-cold. He felt submerged objects under his feet, most likely pieces of wall and tank. His knee hit against something hard.

Ow. Fuck.

The water was too dark to see beneath the surface. He moved to the right to go around the obstacle and could feel the top of it with his hands.

He tried to push himself around it, felt it give way beneath the water and fall over. It caused him to slip a little, and as he corrected himself, the dead face of one of the escorts bobbed up to the surface. Her eyes were gone, along with the skin from half her face.

"Jesus! Fuck!" Blackstone blurted.

He rushed past it as a burst of sparks fell from the hanging power line above. The heavy cable was lying across another, thinner wire that stopped the power line from falling completely into the water. Blackstone could see that the thinner wire was straining against the weight of the electrical line. If it broke before he made it out of the water, he'd be electrocuted.

He picked up his pace and again tripped on something. This time he fell below the surface awkwardly and felt the sting of saltwater up his nose. He sprang back up and kept going.

When Blackstone was halfway through the flooded room, he saw something move in front of him. He was sure of it. He froze in place. His eyes scanned the surface. Aside from the ripples radiating from him, nothing else moved. Another burst of sparks shot from the power line.

Fuck! Hurry.

Something breached ahead of him, rising out of the water just enough for him to see a dark shape before it submerged again. His eyes searched the room as he took a slow step forward. Then another breach to his right.

Damn it. What…

He realized the mermaid tank was smashed and empty. His heartbeat started to drum. A sound cut through the silence. It was a voice. Roland's voice.

"Mr. Blackstone!"

Blackstone immediately turned. "Roland?"

The younger man was standing on the ramp, motioning to him. "Get out of there!"

Blackstone moved toward Roland, who extended his hand to pull him out of the water.

The famed director was almost to him when one of the mermaids rose from the water in front of him. Her big round eyes stared at him as she tilted her head slightly. The movie mogul froze in place, his eyes full of fear.

He started to speak, but not a syllable was formed before the mermaid swung her webbed hand across his head. The claws moved so fast Blackstone and Roland only saw a blur but heard the sound of it slice through the air.

Whatever words Blackstone tried to say came out in a gurgle. The right side of his face was gone. From his ear to where his nose once was, only thin bits of dark-pink-and-red flesh remained. One eye was gone, leaving an empty socket.

It happened so quickly Blackstone wasn't sure what had occurred other than his eye had something in it and wouldn't work. He instinctually took a few steps back until he bumped against another mermaid that had risen out of the water behind him.

Blackstone felt his face start to sting.

"Something's wrong," he whimpered to Roland, who stared at him with a look of horror. Blackstone watched him run away. "Roland!"

The mermaid behind him put her webbed hand over his

ruined face. It was as wide as a catcher's mitt, and she jerked his head back as far as it would go. The other mermaid opened her jaws wide, showing rows of teeth. In an instant, she turned her head sideways and lunged down on him, tearing away most of his throat.

Blackstone's mouth opened wide, but no sound came out. They savagely pulled the legendary director under the surface and shredded him. There were no emotional farewells, no moody orchestral score, and no moving cinematography... just bubbles of blood in the dark water.

———•———

Roland found the corridor ahead filled with zombies and stopped in his tracks. There were too many to get by. They blocked the entire hall. One slip and they'd be on him.

A low growl came from behind the horde of zombies. Roland saw a couple of the zombies in the back suddenly fly up in the air. The walking dead continued to be cast aside as something pushed through them.

It looked like the scene in the movie when something mysterious is heading toward you through the jungle and treetops are pushed out of the way on both sides until whatever it is comes into view. More zombies flew up and out of the herd in both directions until Roland saw that it was the yeti storming toward him.

Roland took off in the opposite direction. He ran into the next entranceway where Raquel, the ten-thousand-a-night escort provided for Tom, was crouching behind a fallen metal display.

When she spotted Roland, she stood enough for him to see her. She put her index finger to her lips and pointed to the other side of the room where the Jersey Devil was dragging a lifeless body behind it.

He ducked down and rushed to Raquel. The hair that was so perfectly coiffed earlier was now a mess, and her smoky eye makeup formed war paint down her cheeks. Her Jimmy Choo heels were gone, and her dress was all torn up.

"Please help me," she whispered. "Please."

Roland looked at her. His instinct was to calm her, but he had no idea how. Watching the mermaids tear Blackstone to pieces had turned his mind into a hurricane of thoughts and fears.

"Do you know how to get back to the elevator?" she asked.

"Yes," Roland whispered back. "But I have no idea what's between here and there."

"What do you think we should do?" she asked. "Is there any kind of emergency rescue on the way?"

"No," Roland said, "I wouldn't count on that."

He went over the route to the elevator in his head. It was a series of twists and turns that any of the creatures could be in.

"Okay," he said. "We'll just have to go slow and make sure any space we're about to go through is clear."

"Don't leave me, okay?" Raquel asked.

———•———

"Over here. I found a way up," Vic said.

He stood by a zigzagging metal staircase attached to the outside of the tank. It was ten flights to the top, where it connected to the catwalk Kelsey had walked on earlier.

"Yeah. That looks familiar," she said.

They climbed the stairs as quickly as possible. The metal steps creaked as Kelsey, Tony, and Tom made it to the top and waited for Vic, who was coming up last. Tony leaned his head over the edge to see how far behind them Vic was and saw what Vic didn't. The Jersey Devil was behind him, silently latching onto the metal staircase and climbing up like a giant gargoyle.

"Vic!" Tony shouted.

Vic was about to shush him when he saw Tony point. He turned and looked back.

"Shit!" he yelled and climbed faster.

The creature reached for Vic with its claws, banging against the staircase and causing it to shake. Vic tried to stay close to the side as he moved, kicking back at the creature as it grabbed at him.

The Devil flapped its huge bat wings and jerked the metal staircase so hard the top of it became detached from the upper catwalk. Vic struggled not to bounce off as he climbed.

The creature pulled on the railings, and its wings flapped faster. Vic made it to the top of the shaking stairway, which now dangled and swung free several feet from where it had been attached, leaving a large space between Vic and the others on the catwalk.

Tony leaned as far over as he could with his hand outstretched to Vic. "Jump!"

Tom got beside Tony and outstretched his hand as well.

Vic looked down. It was a ninety-foot drop. The bottom of the staircase was breaking away from its base, and the Devil was still pulling. In a few seconds, the whole thing would crash down like a steel tree into the flooded area. If the fall didn't kill him, the many things prowling below certainly would.

"Now!" Tony yelled.

"Hurry!" Kelsey screamed.

Vic jumped, barely making it to the catwalk. If Tony and Tom hadn't grabbed his arms, he would have easily fallen backward. Seconds later, the Devil gave enough of a jerk on the staircase to break the base loose. The entire thing fell and crashed below with thunderous clangs and splashes.

The Devil let out another angry scream. Its wings flapped harder and faster until it took flight, rising to where the group was on the catwalk.

"Hurry!" Vic yelled to the group. "There! Go!"

They ran for the doorway at the end of the catwalk as the creature bobbed in the air above. It swiped at them furiously, each flap of its wings echoing like claps of thunder.

The group made it through the door and fell to the floor on the other side. The Devil tried to follow, but its large frame didn't fit into the corridor. It fought and screamed and struggled to get in as the group backed away and ran through the strange tunnel they found themselves in.

Lance watched the whole situation on his monitors and saw that the cops were just down the service corridor from him. He ran to his door, opened it, and took a step out. He could hear them coming from around the corner.

"Hey!" he yelled. "Over here! Hurry!"

Just as they turned the corner to see him, the Devil managed to rip through enough of the Sheetrock and doorframe to make it into the corridor. It was still too tight for him to spread his wings, but he thrashed after them as they ran toward Lance.

"Quick!" Lance yelled.

Tony got to Lance's control room first, then turned back to help Kelsey and Tom inside. Vic was farther behind, the Devil just yards behind him.

"Vic! Don't look back! Just move your ass!" Tony yelled.

When Vic was a few feet from the door, Tony reached for him and yanked him into the room.

"Go! Go! Go!" Tony said as he rushed in behind Vic, slammed the door shut, and fumbled with the lock. A second after the heavy dead bolt clicked, the door shook as the Devil banged against it.

"That's not going to stop him," Tom said. "He'll go right through that."

Lance looked at his console. One of the monitors showed the area outside the door with the Devil fighting to get in. The others saw what he was looking at and approached the console.

They were all panting from the chase. Vic bent over with his hands on his knees and watched the monitor. The Devil seemed to be searching for a weak spot.

Lance had an idea. At the other end of the corridor was a set of double doors that he could open and close from his console. He pushed the button, and the doors swung open with a click.

It worked. The Devil turned its grotesque head and stalked toward the other doors. The group listened close as the sound of the screeching creature got farther away.

Tony exhaled and lay down on his back with his knees up. Kelsey sat against the wall, her head leaning back. Vic dropped into Lance's chair.

One by one, they turned their attention to Lance.

"Who are you?" Vic asked.

"I work here."

"Doing what?" Vic asked.

"All kinds of things. Whatever they ask me to."

"So you knew what was going on," Kelsey said.

Lance started to pace. "No. I mean, not at first." He stammered. "I never hurt anyone. I had nothing to do with any of that stuff."

"But you saw what they were doing and didn't try to stop them or tell anybody," Vic said.

"I wanted to. But if I had, they would have killed me."

Kelsey recognized the ring on Lance's hand from when he'd delivered meals through the slot. "You! You knew they were going to kill us and you didn't do anything," Kelsey said. "You brought me food, the whole time knowing they were going to feed me to a fucking sea monster."

She stood up and approached him.

"I'm sorry," he said. "There was nothing I could do."

Kelsey punched him in the mouth with such force it split his lip open.

She grabbed his collar. "You're going to show us where Annika and Gia are, and then you're going to show us the way out of here."

"Gia's dead," he said. "I'm sorry. But Annika is still alive."

"Damn it!" Kelsey cried.

She shoved him against the wall and proceeded to punch him in the face repeatedly. After several blows, Tony looked at Vic, his eyes asking if he should stop her.

"I'm fine with it," Vic said, as if agreeing to a restaurant suggestion.

"Once we get out of here, you're going to prison," Kelsey yelled into his face.

Tony grunted. "I think we should leave him down here. It's worse."

Lance pleaded. "No! Please!"

Vic pushed him to the console. "Show us the way out."

———·———

It might as well be hell to cross through. For the first moments after the tank burst, it was mayhem. Creatures were all over the place, attacking every human they could catch. Screams filled the air. Now the chaos had subsided.

Little over an hour earlier, these people were billionaire CEOs and political leaders used to being pampered and obeyed. They now found themselves at the very bottom of the food chain with no more power and influence than a worm on a hook.

They hid wherever they could, trembling behind whatever they could find, as monsters from their childhood nightmares stalked around them.

———·———

Keiji Fujiyama crouched behind the rubble of a fallen wall. Sweat stung his eyes as he searched the darkness. George Conrad was no longer with him. They'd been making their way through one of the darkened corridors when they stopped at the sight of an alien in front of them.

It was a tall green one. The texture of its skin resembled worn leather. Its long, ultra-thin limbs made it appear nonthreatening.

"Oh shit," Conrad said.

"It may not mean us harm," Keiji said.

"I don't want to find out."

Keiji looked back where they came from. "I don't think we can get to the elevator any other way."

"Damn," Conrad said.

Keiji took a breath and stepped forward.

Almost mimicking him, the green alien did the same.

Conrad smiled. "I'll be damned."

Keiji and Conrad took another step. Again, the alien copied them.

Within the next few steps, they were within feet of each other. The alien looked at them. His large eyes blinked every few seconds.

"Do you understand us?" Conrad asked the alien.

The alien gave a slight nod of his head.

Keiji found himself intrigued. He'd seen the alien before through the glass, but this was much different.

Conrad took a step closer and reached out his hand. The alien's head loomed closer to it, as if to study it, then it leaned back and lifted its own hand slowly until it grasped Conrad's.

He let out a small laugh. "It feels so strange. Not like skin. It vibrates like solid energy."

Keiji watched, fascinated.

Conrad started to speak again. "I think…"

Keiji turned to see what he was about to say, but Conrad stopped talking.

His smile faded, and he let out a couple of odd noises. Something was wrong. As the alien held his hand, Conrad's whole body trembled. His face changed as if he'd aged twenty years in a second. Bags formed beneath his eyes; his skin became wrinkled and spotty.

Keiji took a step back.

As he watched, Conrad aged so rapidly that within a few seconds, he shriveled into a dried-up corpse that barely resembled a man anymore. The alien absorbed the life energy from him until the man looked like a pale, dried-up raisin.

The alien let go, and the crumpled substance that was left of Conrad fell to the ground within the tux. Keiji backed away and ran.

That had been a while ago. Now Keiji stayed as quiet as possible, hiding in two feet of water behind some rubble. In the time since he'd found this spot, he'd watched several creatures move past. He had no plan or desire to risk moving.

Keiji heard something to his right, coming from the dark, adjoining room.

It sounded like someone whimpering.

He looked around to make sure it was safe and lifted his head just high enough over the rubble to see. In the low light, he could make out blond hair.

"Is anyone there?" a soft voice whispered.

Keiji stood up and saw Becca, the stunning beauty who'd accompanied Radcliffe and had so captivated him. She was alone. He scanned the room, and seeing it was clear, made his way over to her.

When she saw him, she said, "Thank God!"

"Shhhh," Keiji said. "We must be very quiet."

He took her by the hand and led her back to his hiding spot, gently guiding her down behind the rubble.

Even in this low light, he was awestruck by her beauty. Her bright eyes, full lips—everything about her projected sensuality.

"Please," she whispered. "Please help me get out of here."

Keiji saw her torn dress exposed even more cleavage. He nodded. "We will get out. We will."

"If you promise you'll get me out of here… I'll do anything you want."

Keiji couldn't speak. Her eyes bore into his with an intensity he'd never experienced in any of the hundreds of beautiful women he'd been with.

There was a splashing sound approaching them.

No, he thought, *not now.*

"I'm so cold," Becca said and leaned closer into him, nuzzling her head against his. He put his arm around her, his hand on the soft skin of her back. Her lips brushed against his skin and he realized he had his fullest erection since puberty, with or without any blue pill.

His brain was rapidly creating scenarios in which he would spend the rest of his life with her. He envisioned her moving into his home, swimming in his pool, dining with him, making love to him daily.

"This way," a voice whispered. "I think it's this way." More splashing.

Keiji peeked over the rubble to see Douglas Radcliffe moving through the shallow water with... Becca.

"Wait. What...," Keiji whispered. He assumed his eyes were playing tricks on him and it was another blond woman.

He focused more clearly and saw it was, in fact, Becca with Radcliffe. Confused, he turned back to the Becca beside him and instead saw Bram, the vampire. Its ghastly mouth was covered with blood from the large open gash on Keiji's neck. He finally realized what was happening to him. He tried to pull away, but his effort felt small and weak and the vampire's grip was strong as a vise. He could feel the cold bones of its fingers squeezing through its white flesh.

Keiji struggled but only seemed capable of moving in slow motion. By this time he'd lost several pints of blood, and his eyes were losing focus.

"Iie..." he uttered in his native Japanese as he fell into thick, cold darkness.

———•———

Neither the real Becca nor Radcliffe heard Keiji's final whimper over the sound of their legs moving through the flooded room. Even as Bram's fangs dug deeper into his prey, his yellow pupils followed them as they moved past.

39

GAME PLAN

V IC GRABBED A SHEET OF paper and a Sharpie from the
console and thrust them into Lance's hand. "Draw a map."
Lance sketched out the route they would have to take.

"Do you have any water in here?" Tom asked.

He pointed to a small fridge on the far wall.

Tom took out a few bottles. He handed the first one to
Kelsey.

"Thanks," she said and started gulping her water. "Part of
me still doesn't believe this is real."

"Yeah," Tony agreed. "It's nuts."

"Do you have any guns?" she asked Lance.

"Not in here. But security room B does. It's between here
and the holding area."

"Okay," Vic said, "that's our first stop. How far is it?"

"Down the hall. Maybe twenty yards."

"Maybe everyone else should wait here while we go get the
guns," Tony said, "Then once we have them, it'll be safer to
go from there."

"Yeah," Vic replied.

"No," Kelsey said. "We all go together."

"Kel…," Vic started.

"No."

"You'll be safer in here," Vic said.

"But you won't," Kel replied. "If someone or something attacks you on the way to get the guns, we'll have better odds of fighting off whatever it is if we're all together."

Lance shook his head and let out a weird noise. Everyone turned to him.

"What?" Vic asked.

"You can't fight off anything that would attack you down here. Even if there were twenty of you," Lance said.

Vic's eyes caught something on one of the monitors. It was Radcliffe and Becca making their way through a collapsed area.

"Hey." Vic pushed Lance. "Is there some kind of intercom or loudspeaker?"

Lance saw what Vic was looking at. "Yeah." He fumbled for the intercom button. "Hey. You down there... Sir."

They could see Radcliffe and Becca stop moving and look upward.

"Tell them how to get here," Vic ordered.

Lance held down the button again. "I'm going to guide you to us."

———•———

Radcliffe and Becca listened to Lance's voice filling the air. She was now half carrying the older man, his arm draped over her shoulders.

"Thank God!" Becca said as she wiped the sweat from her eyes.

They moved on, following the voice's directions.

———•———

Elsewhere, Winthrop and Mason also heard the intercom.

Winthrop looked at Mason. "They're in the control room."

"That's a long way from here," Mason said. "The elevator is a lot closer."

Winthrop leaned against the wall. Up until this moment, his primary concern had been survival. Now he was able to think more clearly. He'd put too much of his life into this to just let it go. He didn't know how many members were dead or if the damage could even be repaired.

Would it be possible to bring a team down to recapture the creatures, fix all the damage, and get back to normal? Possibly. But it would require a lot of new exposure.

Winthrop considered the two cops. He didn't know if they were on their own or part of a larger operation. He'd installed the new captain to contain them, but he didn't know if the cops might have told any loyal friends.

If they were part of an official investigation, there would have been a lot more than just two of them. I can't risk them getting out. They'd have all the evidence necessary to bring charges. I'd have to go into hiding and live like a fugitive.

Winthrop considered his options and made his decision.

They can't leave here alive.

"Listen," Winthrop said to Mason. "If those cops get out, it won't matter if we make it or not."

"That wasn't part of the deal. I said I'd get you out. That's it."

Winthrop looked miffed. "I'm giving you a billion dollars. Don't get greedy."

"You're not *giving* me anything. I'm earning it by putting myself between you and anything that tries to kill you. There's a big difference between trying to get you to the elevator in one piece and hunting down cops while all these creatures are hunting us at the same time."

In the distance, a loud growl echoed through the air.

"You don't get it," Winthrop said. "If the cops get out, both of us will be on the run for the rest of our lives. We'd have to become invisible."

"All I've got is an ankle gun with half a magazine left. Maybe you should try to make it to the elevators by yourself, or you go kill the cops in the control room. Personally, I'll just head to the elevators."

Winthrop's blood boiled. He wasn't accustomed to being on the weaker side of a negotiation. He was even less accustomed to being denied. In fact, it had been three decades since he'd heard the word no.

He hated the word, despised it, and the few times he'd heard it in his youth still burned deep in the blurry ocean of his memories.

"How much?" Winthrop asked through clenched teeth.

"Another billion."

Winthrop decided he was going to screw Mason out of paying him anything despite the danger of his retaliation. He'd figure out a way to eliminate him once they were in the clear. His pride demanded that Mason pay for exploiting his helplessness.

"Fine."

"Good," Mason said. "First, we've got to get to security B and get some bigger guns."

Winthrop nodded.

"Fastest way will be cutting through to the service corridor."

Roland and Raquel were crossing through the UFO room when they heard Lance's voice on the intercom.

"Somebody else is alive," Raquel said. "We should get to them."

Roland knew where the control room was. "I don't know. The elevators are closer than that."

"But won't we be safer with other people?"

"I don't want to scare you, but no," he said. "Our best bet is making it to the elevator."

"Okay," she replied. "Elevator."

Becca supported Radcliffe as they followed Lance's instructions until they made it to the control room. Vic opened the door but offered Radcliffe no help. Once the door was shut and locked, everyone turned to the new arrivals.

"Thank you. Thank you so much," Becca said as she helped Radcliffe into a chair.

Vic turned to Tom. "Who is this?"

"Douglas Radcliffe," Tom said.

Tony asked, "One of the regulars?"

"Yes," Tom answered.

Vic knelt next to Radcliffe, who was having trouble breathing. "Hey, asshole."

Becca spoke up. "Can't you see he's—?"

"I don't give a shit." Vic focused back on Radcliffe.

"If you don't die of a heart attack, I'm going to feed *you* to one of these things and see how much fun you think that is, you prick."

"Please…," Becca said.

Tony turned to her. "Hey, dummy. Don't you realize your grandpa here was killing hookers just like you for shits and giggles?"

"I'm not a hooker," Becca said.

"Oh, forgive me," Tony replied. "I didn't realize you two crazy kids were in love. What is he, eighty?"

Vic hit his open palm against Radcliffe's forehead. "Listen, you billionaire fuck… not only are you just another snack for these things, but you're also the weakest one of us. We're getting out of here. You can try to keep up, but we will not risk shit for you. If you fall behind because you're old as hell, we're not gonna wait for you. Got it?"

"I'll pay you to get us out," Radcliffe said as he held Becca's hand.

"Excuse me?" Vic asked.

"I'll give anyone who helps us get out of here a million dollars."

"You don't get it," Vic said. "Your money means nothing now. You're the absolute lowest link on the food chain, and you can't buy your way up."

Radcliffe's face drained of the little color it had as he realized Vic's words were accurate. All the money, all the power… were useless.

He turned to Becca. She was looking at him with an expression he didn't recognize. Pity. He was pathetically helpless now. And he could see that she knew it.

———•———

Vic turned to Lance. "Is the room with the guns locked?"

"No. It shouldn't be. But there's a code just in case. Two, eight, four, five, seven, eight, pound sign."

Vic repeated it and turned to Tony. "Ready?"

"Not really."

"Lock this once we're out," Vic told Kelsey.

"Wait." Tom pointed to the monitors. "There's something outside the door you're going to."

They all turned to the monitors to see a hazy, ghostly woman hovering by the door to the gun room.

"It's Dee-Dee," Lance said, using his nickname for the ghost. "She's one of the ghosts."

The visage faded in and out between the control room and security room B.

"You have ghosts down here?" Tony asked.

Kelsey squinted at the screen.

"Yes," Lance replied.

"Jesus," Kelsey said under her breath.

Tony looked at Lance. "Can it hurt us?"

"No. I don't think so," Lance replied. "They just appear and disappear."

"So… we can just go past it and it won't do anything?"

"I've never seen them attack, but normally they're confined."

"All right," Vic said to Tony. "We'll just ignore it."

Lance spoke up. "Wait."

Everyone turned to him.

"It's Mason and Mr. Winthrop," Lance said without turning away from the monitors.

Everyone else got closer to see.

"That's the main guy behind all this," Vic told Kelsey.

"The asshole with him," she said with a glare. "He used a cattle prod on us."

"A cattle prod?" Vic asked.

The thought of Kelsey being tortured that way sent waves of anger through him.

Tony asked, "If the elevators are the other way, where are they going?"

"They must be going after the guns too," Lance said.

Vic turned to Tony. "Come on. We've got to beat them there."

Tony handed his pistol to Kelsey while darting his eyes at Radcliffe and Lance. "Just in case." He leaned in and whispered, "It's empty."

"Thanks."

Vic looked at the monitor again to make sure it was clear other than the ghost in the corridor. He opened the door and scanned the hallway. He could see the other door but not the ghost.

"Why is the ghost on the monitor but not in the corridor?" he asked Lance.

"I don't know. Stuff like that happens sometimes."

"Great," Vic said.

He and Tony stepped into the corridor, and Kelsey watched from the slightly opened door behind them. They jogged quickly but cautiously toward the door to security B.

A loud screech blared through the hall.

"What the fuck is that?" Tony whispered.

"I don't want to know. C'mon."

The corridor ahead split two ways, and a long shadow moved across the wall between. Whatever the sound was, it was just around the corner.

"Shit," Tony said.

"Fuck this. Let's go," Vic said as they broke into a run for the door.

When the door was just feet away, the ghost appeared right in front of them, inches from their faces as they ran into her.

She wore a ghastly expression and let out a silent scream. Vic raised his forearms as he ran through her. Tony fell backward on his ass. Vic helped him up, and they made it to the door.

It was locked.

"Son of a bitch!" Vic yelled.

Whatever was around the corner let out another blaring screech as its shadow showed it was getting closer. Vic punched in the code.

The ghost appeared again, slowly hovering toward them on the other side of the corridor.

The code didn't work. The panel beeped and flashed a red light.

"What?" Vic said.

Ahead of them, the shadow on the wall finally grew sharp as the towering yeti came into view. Its bright blue eyes focused on them. It made a low, guttural growl as it lumbered completely into the corridor.

Vic tried the code again.

"Just hurry!" Tony said.

The yeti stepped closer. The huge gray-and-white beast hunched down a little as it approached, almost like a dog that was about to pounce. Its teeth became visible as it snarled.

Vic added the pound sign this time, and the light flashed green.

He swung the door open and pushed Tony inside just as the yeti lunged. They slammed the door and locked it.

The yeti swung a fist at it, and the whole wall vibrated.

Vic scanned the room. Beside the door was a tall gun safe.

"The safe!" he said.

They got to it as fast as they could.

"You push! I'll pull!" Vic yelled as the yeti bashed his fists against the door and the wall around it.

Tony got one side of the safe and pushed as Vic grabbed the top from the other side and pulled it toward him.

"Fuck!" Tony yelled.

The heavy safe started to budge. The wall it was against joined another wall about four feet away.

"Use your feet against the wall. Push off!" Vic said.

Tony maneuvered around so he could get some leverage right as the yeti punched a large hole through the door and started reaching inside wildly. It clawed at Vic's back, ripping through his shirt and into his skin. He screamed in pain but kept pulling on the safe until it slowly rose onto its edge.

Tony grunted as he pushed off with everything he had and the safe finally fell. Vic jumped back and barely rolled away in time. The room shook when it hit the floor. Tony came down with it and bounced off.

It didn't cover the door completely, but the space it left was too small for the yeti to get through. It kept trying, growling and clawing against the safe and doorframe.

There were wall-to-wall guns. Handguns, assault rifles, shotguns, submachine guns, Tasers, and cattle prods. Vic's attention went back to the yeti as it smashed another large portion of the doorframe and wall away, spraying splinters of wood and plaster toward them.

"Fuck!" Tony said, seeing what the yeti had done to Vic. "Your back!"

"I'm fine. Grab a shotgun!" Vic said.

Tony grabbed one, made sure it was loaded, and pumped it. He rushed closer to the yeti to get a clear shot at its head. Before he could fire, the yeti grabbed the barrel. It pulled Tony toward it, smashing him against the wall.

Vic pulled another shotgun from the wall and aimed at the yeti as it continued to destroy the door and wall. Vic fired, hitting the yeti in the upper torso. A blast of red flesh popped open in the beast's light gray fur. It let out a roar so loud that it vibrated through them. Vic pumped the shotgun and fired again. This time the yeti backed quickly out of the damaged doorway.

Tony was on the ground, his face contorted in pain. There were a few seconds of silence. They couldn't tell if yeti was gone or just out of view.

Vic rushed to Tony. "You okay?"

"I think my shoulder is fucked." Tony huffed.

Vic's eyes went back to the doorway. "Stay down for a sec."

He walked to the doorway. With pulse-pounding caution, he leaned out just enough to see if the creature was still around.

"Looks clear for now," he told Tony. "Can you walk?"

"Hell yeah, I can walk," Tony said. "But I may not be able to carry as many guns as you."

Vic helped him to his feet while scanning the room. He spotted some backpacks on the floor. Once he got Tony steady, he grabbed one and emptied its contents. Then he rushed to the wall of handguns.

Vic picked a few of them, making sure they were all the same caliber. He found a drawer of ammo and stuffed as much as he could into the backpack.

"Think you can carry this?" he asked Tony.

"Yeah. Just help me put it on."

Tony clenched his teeth and let out a groan as Vic pulled the backpack over his good shoulder. Vic turned back to the weapons.

He reached for an AR-15 and ejected the magazine out to see what caliber it was.

".223," he said to himself as he looked for more of that caliber ammo to take with them. He stuffed boxes of it into his jacket pockets and the backpack.

He took down three more AR-15s.

"You're gonna have to help me over the safe," Tony said.

Vic nodded. "You ready?"

"No. But let's do it."

Vic stuck his head out of the ruined doorway. It looked clear.

"All right. C'mon," he said.

He helped Tony get up onto the safe so he could spin around to get on his feet on the other side.

Tony did his best to ignore the pain, but it was so excruciating he couldn't help but let out some grunts.

Once they were both into the corridor, they hurried back to the control room.

As they moved, Vic feared he'd made a mistake and once inside, he'd find that the guys he'd left Kelsey with had not been as harmless as he thought. He tried to shut down the thought, but all the years he'd spent being unpleasantly surprised by human behavior only made him move faster.

Approaching the door, he was relieved to see it swing open.

———— · ————

Kelsey stepped out to help them inside. "Thank God you're okay. When I saw that thing... Oh my god! Your back!"

Vic dropped his bag of guns onto the floor. "I'm fine. We'll deal with it later. But Tony might have dislocated his shoulder."

Kelsey turned to Lance. "You have any pain medication in here? Advil? Anything?"

"Yes." He reached into a desk drawer.

Kelsey handed the bottle of pills to Tony as he sat down, keeping his right side stiff.

Lance approached the guns Vic was spreading out.

"Whoa," Vic said, "back away. You don't touch those."

Lance looked shocked. "But you can't expect—"

Vic cut him off. "If I see you reach for a gun, I'm gonna shoot you in the head. You understand?"

"Yes."

Vic turned to Tom. "You know how to use one of these?"

"I went to the shooting range a few times. I know how to use the handguns, but if you could show me how to work one of those things..." He pointed at the AR-15s.

Vic gave him a quick lesson. "Think you got it?"

Tom nodded. "Yes. I think so."

"Most important thing," Vic said, "never aim it toward anything you don't want to shoot. Whether we're just walking, or if we're hiding behind something, never point it at anyone. Always be aware of where your barrel is aimed."

"Understood. Thank you," Tom replied.

"Good," Vic said. "How about loading all these magazines for us?"

"You got it."

Despite his mind being filled with more important concerns, Vic realized he was treating a multibillionaire like a rookie assistant.

He picked up the map that Lance had drawn. He pointed to part of it as he held it toward Lance. "This is where the other girl is being held?"

"Yes," Lance said, "but I don't know what condition the room is in or if she's still alive."

Vic looked at the monitors. "Can you see it from here?"

"No. It looks like that camera is out."

"Damn," Vic whispered.

As if reading his thoughts, Kelsey walked to him. "We have to try."

"I know."

Vic took a couple of handguns from the backpack and made sure they were loaded. He stuck one in his holster and another in the waist of his jeans.

Kelsey took the backpack with the rest of the guns and the ammo and picked up one of the ARs.

After Tom finished loading all the extra magazines with Kelsey's help, he followed Vic's example and stuck a handgun in his waistline.

Lance watched all of them prepping, and fear filled him. "This is crazy," he exclaimed. "You're going to need me to have a gun too."

Vic looked to him. "Here's the thing. Do you want to go to prison for the rest of your life if and when you get out of here?"

"Of course not. But I didn't..."

"Shut up. It can go two different ways for you. You knew what was going on down here and did nothing. We could arrest you right now for conspiracy to commit murder and obstruction of justice."

"But...," Lance yelped.

"Shut up," Vic said. "Or you could testify about everything you know, and we could report that you were brought into this not knowing what was happening and were forced to go along to protect your own life."

"Yes! Please!"

"For us to do that, you're going to have to prove you deserve it."

"How? What do you want me to do? Whatever you..."

"You're going to stay here," Vic said.

"What? Why?"

"You're going to watch these monitors for us as we head back to the elevators. You're going to let us know with the intercom if we take a wrong turn or if anything is sneaking up on us or if anything is up ahead of us. You're going to guide us out and tell us everything we need to know."

"But then..." Lance went pale.

"Once we're back up top, I'm coming back down with a SWAT team, and we're going to take you, your boss, and anyone else who's still alive into custody."

Lance sagged. "Fine."

"Good choice." Vic stood up and turned back to Lance.

"Listen closely though. If you try to fuck us in any way... If you start thinking you'll let us get killed and try to make it out on your own, or if you endanger us in any way... If I think you're doing that for a second, I'll head right back here, cut your nuts off, and make you choke on them. Do you believe me?"

Lance nodded.

———•———

Vic took a deep breath and turned to the group. "Everyone ready?"

They all nodded.

Vic hugged Kelsey again and kissed her. "Stay close to me."

She smiled at him.

Vic looked at Tony. The two men had been partners for so

many years they could read each other's thoughts. Tony nodded. Vic could see how much pain he was in, trying to find a position for his arm that didn't make his shoulder throb.

"You need to rest, you say something," Vic said.

"I will," Tony replied.

Vic looked at the map again and pointed to part of it in front of Lance. "Tell me again. We're right here, and the holding area is here?"

"That's right."

"How does that area look on the monitors now?" Kelsey asked. "Anything dangerous near it?"

Lance looked at his screens. "This one's broken, so I don't know about that area. But the others look okay."

They all looked at the monitors. Several screens showed creatures either eating their victims or prowling for more. Sasquatches, aliens, something that looked like a werewolf— all moved through the facility on various monitors.

Vic looked at Kelsey. The two of them exchanged a glance that was part concern, part "Can you believe this shit?"

He gripped the AR-15 and unlocked the door.

"All right," he said. "Let's do it."

40

DARK MAZE

ROLAND AND RAQUEL WERE ALMOST to the lobby. The ancient sea monster was lying dead just ahead of them. The massive carcass was strewn across the ruins of what were once several rooms.

It had carved a path of destruction that turned the once beautiful facility into a cavernous maze of wreckage and debris. As they passed by the mountainous corpse, Raquel couldn't resist the urge to touch it. Her fingers ran along the side of one of the crablike claws that was now imbedded in the floor. Up close, she could see that the shelled surface was covered with barnacles.

A noise to their left startled them. Roland pulled her down low and hunched behind some debris. He looked around but saw nothing. There were several lights still working in this area, a few others only flickering. From where they were, Roland could see the lobby ahead of them. He also saw three dead members on the floor.

Damn. They were almost to the elevator.

The sound got louder. It was a flapping noise. He and Raquel saw the Jersey Devil fly into the lobby. Its large bat wings came to a stop as it landed beside one of the dead bodies. The creature pushed at it with its hooved foot.

No. Don't, Roland thought.

It ripped away what remained of the tuxedo and tore off a large piece of flesh with its teeth. It lifted its head as it swallowed it down in a couple of gulps.

It had the mannerisms of a crow eating a dead possum by the side of the road. Roland could now see the man was Rubin Mancuso. The media mogul looked like a stuffed doll dangling from the creature's claws. His face had an expression of shock frozen onto it.

Roland sensed something behind him and turned to see the reptilian alien looming over them. Within a millisecond, it wrapped its long, scaly fingers around his neck and head like boa constrictors. Raquel screamed, causing the Jersey Devil to drop the body from its mouth and take flight toward them. She stood to run, but the alien grabbed her before she could get clear. Roland gasped for air as he tried to pry loose the alien's fingers. He panicked and punched blindly to free himself.

The Devil swooped in with flapping wings and sank its teeth into Roland's leg, just below the knee. It used its arms and claws to get a better grip on him as he thrashed. The Devil's claws dug into Roland's leg on each side of where its long snout was biting. The alien hissed at it, not wanting to give up its prize.

The two creatures fought over Roland, each one pulling savagely against the other.

The alien dropped Raquel to be able to use both its arms in the battle over Roland. She fell to the ground and shuffled backward on her ass, away from the fighting monsters. She got to her feet and ran with no idea where to go. She circled the giant sea monster's body and climbed down into an open hole in the floor beneath its tail. She peeked out and saw the dreadful sight of the alien and the Devil clashing over Roland, pulling him apart in the process. The worst part was that he was fully aware of what was happening to him.

He sagged helplessly, gripped by his head and his leg, pulled viciously back and forth like a dog's chew toy. Roland felt his muscles tear and his bones break. He let out a scream that was muffled against the scales of the alien's fingers.

Roland was dead seconds before his body came apart in the struggle. Both creatures took their portions and backed away.

Raquel watched in horror with her hands over her mouth. Tears mixed with sweat as she prayed that neither creature would spot her.

Winthrop and Mason were almost to the service corridor when Mason realized they were being stalked. He put a finger to his lips and motioned for Winthrop to get behind him.

They did their best to blend into the wall adjoining the aquarium. It was partially dark, full of ominous corners and patches of blackness from which something could strike at any moment. The tanks were destroyed, but the lights used to illuminate them from within were still working. Their glow bounced off the flooded room and sent reflections across the walls and ceiling. It would have been beautiful in any other situation.

Mason was too smart to try to cross through the water. He knew the mermaids and other sea creatures were in there somewhere. He also spotted the hanging power line that could fall into the water at any moment. Not everyone was as clever. A couple of half-eaten bodies floated on the surface.

Billion-dollar chum, he thought.

Mason heard something and motioned for Winthrop to get down. He stared in the direction the sound was coming from, and both men's hearts stopped for a second when they saw the wendigo lumber forward.

Shit.

It was the one creature that terrified Mason. All of the other so-called monsters down here didn't intimidate him. He considered them simply rare animals that were smart enough to hide from the world. They didn't scare him any more than a gorilla or grizzly would. They were dangerous, but he knew he was far deadlier than any of them.

The wendigo was different. It didn't just look like a monster, it looked like a diseased, rabid zombie version of one, and it chilled Mason to his core. For the first time, Winthrop saw fear on Mason's face.

———•———

Vic and Tony guided the group into the corridor. Kelsey and Tom followed with Becca trailing behind, helping Radcliffe.

Lance's voice echoed through the loudspeaker. "The holding room is just ahead on your left. The code is three, three, one, six, seven, eight, pound sign."

They got to the door, and Vic punched in the code. The lock clicked open, and everyone rushed in.

Annika sat back against the wall on her mattress. She didn't know what was going on and braced herself for anything until she saw Kelsey.

"Kelsey!" she yelled and ran to her.

They hugged and sobbed into each other.

"It's okay. It's okay," Kelsey said. "We're getting out of here."

Annika released her and looked at the other people in the room.

Kelsey said, "This is Vic."

Annika looked at him in awe. "She said you'd find her."

———•———

The wendigo stalked through the area where Winthrop and Mason were hiding. It barely made any noise even as it entered the flooded space.

Mason watched and remembered something his father had told him on a childhood hunting trip. In the woods, small animals make a lot of noise and big things make none. It was true, young Mason learned. Hearing a lot of brush move was more likely to be a squirrel than anything else. Deer or moose made almost no noise at all. The same rule seemed to apply to the wendigo.

It stalked closer and its head turned in various directions, searching for food. From where they were hiding, they could see through a hole in the rubble without having to stand.

As it crossed through the room, it went in and out of the darkness, at times fully visible, sometimes just a silhouette. Its large rack of antlers brought it to fifteen feet. The creature turned toward them. Its red eyes glowed in the low light.

It sees us, Mason thought. *It either sees us or smells us, but it definitely knows we're here.*

The wendigo turned its head downward. It stood in three feet of water that hardly rippled as he moved through it. With one fast motion, the wendigo pulled up a mermaid by the throat. The mermaid went into a storm of movement, swinging its webbed hands savagely to get free. Its tail flapped like salmon in the mouth of a bear.

The wendigo took a bite out of her, leaving a gaping wound on her shoulder. She let out an unnatural, ear-shattering scream. It was a sound Winthrop and Mason had never heard before, and it echoed through their minds as if coming from within. The wendigo dropped her.

It splashed its elongated arms through the water, trying to catch her again. The frustrated creature reached toward a pile of debris protruding from the water and pulled loose a six-foot pole with a sharp point. It lifted it and aimed the point down as its eyes scanned the water.

After a few seconds, it stabbed the pole down and pulled up the flailing mermaid. She was impaled through the stomach and flapping frantically. As she screamed, the creature plucked her head from her body as easily as pulling a grape off a stem. The scream stopped instantly. The wendigo lifted the mermaid's head to his mouth and bit into it with a crunch.

The sound of the bite sickened Winthrop. His body shook as if he had caught himself midfall. Mason saw him shaking and put his hand on his shoulder to stop him from giving away their position.

Finding insufficient meat on the mermaid's head, the

wendigo tossed it aside. Just a foot from where the head splashed into the water, another creature rose slowly from the surface. It was Benchley, the half-man, half-octopus. It stood silently in the water behind the wendigo, two of its tentacles pushing its humanoid frame higher until it was almost equal in height to the hairy beast. The rest of its tentacles rose from the water without any sound.

The wendigo was too busy feasting on the torso of the dead mermaid to notice. With uncanny speed, Benchley attacked. His tentacles wrapped around it and squeezed with incredible force. The hairy creature fought back as best it could. Its elk antlers swung from side to side as the beast tried to pull off the constricting tentacles.

Benchley used its humanlike arms to grab onto the antlers to both subdue the wendigo and protect itself. The tentacles had one of the wendigo's arms trapped by its side while the beast ferociously struggled to free itself.

"Now. Let's go," Mason whispered.

He led Winthrop out of the flooded area and into the darkened corridor, unaware that something else was following along as well.

———————•———————

Kelsey finished bringing Annika up to date on everything.

"I know it sounds crazy," Kelsey said. "I wouldn't have believed it either if I hadn't seen it myself."

Tony looked at Annika. "Hey… whether you believe or not, you have to trust us and do whatever we say to get out of here."

Vic looked at the map and put it back in his pocket. "All right. We're going to go left, then right at the end of the corridor. Stay close." He looked directly at Tom. "Remember to keep it aimed down, and don't shoot at anything unless we say so."

Tom nodded. Tony punched in the code, opened the door, and glanced out. "Clear," he said to Vic.

Vic went first, the rest of the group close behind him.

41

A HIGHER POWER

L ANCE'S VOICE ECHOED ABOVE. "ALL good. Keep going."
As they turned the corner, they entered the UFO area. Although it was half-destroyed, several lights still worked. All the alien containments were demolished and empty, and artifacts were smashed on the floor. The flying saucer was in one piece but knocked onto its side with part of the ceiling collapsed on top of it.

Kelsey and Annika exchanged a look, both seeing this for the first time.

Lance's voice came through the intercom. "Wait. Don't move. Something is up ahead of you."

Vic, Tony, Kelsey, and Tom gripped their guns as they looked around them.

Becca squeezed Radcliffe's arm until her knuckles were white.

"The opening straight ahead of you, it looks like…," Lance started.

The gray alien appeared in the doorway. Its feet didn't touch the ground. It just glided slowly toward them. The group took a few steps back as it drew closer. The alien stopped a few feet away from them, its eyes blinking as it looked them over.

As the group braced itself, Tom stepped forward. The alien looked at him, showing no expression whatsoever. He lifted his hand to the being to touch it.

Vic stepped closer. "I wouldn't do that."

Tom heard him but paid no attention. He brought his hand to the alien's shoulder and lightly ran his fingers over it.

It was a sensation he would never forget. Its skin was solid but felt like it was made of pure energy. As his hand brushed over it, he could feel a pulsating softness that flowed into his own fingers as they went across the skin. The alien didn't attempt, subtly or otherwise, to protect itself from him. Its higher senses detected no ill intent on Tom's part. The alien blinked again, and Tom smiled.

The alien turned its head toward the group and raised a hand. Its two long fingers were pointed up, together at first, but then separated a little, looking almost like the alien made a peace sign. The fingers continued separating, and as they did, a thin layer of skin between the two fingers rose from the base of the fingers, then higher until it reached the fingertips. The fingers continued separating until they completed clockwise and counterclockwise turns, eventually touching again with the two fingers aimed down but also with the extra skin stretched out into a full circle. It looked as if the alien now had a disk for a hand.

Everyone watched, frozen in place, clueless as to what would happen next. The center of the circular shape began to glow. It grew brighter until it lit up all their faces, which wore masks of wonder and fear.

From the glowing light came a silent flash. They had no idea the alien was scanning them. Not scanning their physical forms but what they would refer to as their souls. The being had the ability to read the character and intentions of living things. It could see the group before him was scared but had no intention of bringing harm... except for Radcliffe. The alien sensed he was different from the rest. In the others, he understood they cared mostly about staying alive. They were here against their will. Radcliffe was here because he wanted to be. He had been here many times before and was one of the beings responsible for the alien's long imprisonment. A hole opened in the glowing light of the alien's hand plate.

The hole widened and glowed, turning into what looked like a portal. It grew until it was equal in size to a car tire.

From the opening came a bright beam of light, like a wide flashlight in a smoky room. It lit up Radcliffe, who slowly rose several feet in the air. He tried to fight against it but was unable to move. Even his face was petrified in place, turning the scream he was trying to make into a low gurgle.

Becca reached for him as he floated closer to the alien, but Tom and Kelsey held her back. The light beam intensified and began to pulse around the old man. His head was drawn into the portal, and as his body followed, it twisted and turned with each pulse of light, contorting unnaturally to the shapes of the pulse until his entire body squeezed into the hole.

"No!" Becca cried. "Somebody do something!"

Once Radcliffe was all the way through, the light dimmed and the portal to the other world dissolved back into the plate hand of the alien. The webbing on its hand retracted as the two fingers began rotating back to their normal position. Becca dropped to her knees, crying.

The alien looked at Tom again, and as Tom returned its gaze, the alien was able to communicate with him. The alien filled his head with silent messages based solely on emotion. It was a strange sensation, but within a few seconds, Tom understood what the alien wanted him to know.

"He doesn't want us to be afraid," Tom said. "He wants to help us."

"How do you know that?" Vic asked.

"Is he talking to you?" Tony added.

Tom turned to Tony but answering wasn't easy. "It's like he's making me feel it."

Becca stood up, visibly upset and angry.

"He wants to help us," Tom repeated.

"Help us?" Becca screamed. "He just killed my friend!"

Kelsey stepped forward. "Wait a second."

She approached the alien and reached out to touch it.

"Kel, don't!" Vic said as he moved to stop her.

The alien looked at Kelsey as she placed a hand on him. The alien wasn't unaware of the effect its touch had on them. In fact, it was quite intentional. The alien purposely exuded positive energy to let them know he was a friend, and the effect was all-consuming.

Kelsey felt her soul radiate within herself as if it were being washed and rinsed with clean, bright love. Everything she'd ever dreamed of was instantly possible. She saw her perfect future, sitting with Vic at the beach, watching their children and grandchildren splash in the waves and play in the sand. It was more than a vision. It was so real she could truly feel the immeasurable love for her kids only a mother would know. She heard the surf, smelled the salt water, and felt the breeze through her hair. A tear of joy ran down her cheek.

Upon seeing Kelsey's reaction, Tony approached the alien. When his hand rested on it, it was with a certain amount of trepidation. He flinched as positive emotion pulsed through him. It also brought with it a familiarity he remembered from his youth. The feeling of anything being possible, of the future holding only goodness and exhilaration, filled his brain. His eyes swelled up, and he felt a faint sigh leave his open lips.

Annika stepped up as well. Her life had always been filled with sadness and despair. Her circumstances had beaten her spirit down so low, years had passed since she smiled without being high. When her fingers touched the alien, an ocean wave of optimism crashed through her mind, washing away all the negativity and filling her with hope and light. She felt as if she'd been standing in a cold, dark room for longer than she could remember, and it suddenly opened to a warm day so bright she had to blink against it. Her mind lit up like the sun, and its rays of love cleansed her soul with the force of a waterfall. She could feel it pounding through her skin. She didn't just smile… she let out a happy laugh.

Vic saw everyone's reactions and realized he wanted to touch the alien but resisted the urge.

Kelsey, who knew his face better than anyone, smiled. "You have to."

He stepped closer.

For as long as Vic could remember, he'd always felt he was, if not the smartest one in the room, at least the most logical. He'd never been the guy who had to be talked out of doing something silly or inappropriate. His was the voice of reason. He was proud of it, although he secretly also feared his circle of friends found him annoying.

When his hand rested on the alien, a rush of emotion burst into him. Within a fraction of a second, his mind exploded with feelings of happiness and pure bliss. It occurred to him the feelings washing through him were not his own but those of his friends when thinking about him. The alien was giving him a high-energy shower of the feelings that Kelsey, Tony, and everyone who knew him felt toward him.

It was more than he could have hoped. It wiped his insecurity from existence and filled him with a sense of love that shone brighter than all else. Every regret and bad decision he'd ever made that had haunted him flashed by and was just as quickly transformed into positivity. Colorful waves of love dissolved each instance into a mirror of his good intentions that reflected the true virtue within himself.

The alien saw Becca back away from them. It registered her feelings and understood why she felt them. She looked at it with a combination of hate and fear. She backed up against the wall as it got close to her. It raised its two fingers toward her face, and she trembled.

"Someone help me," she cried.

The alien placed its fingers on her cheeks, and instantly she stopped shaking. She felt the same vibrating energy pour into her, followed by immense love and warmth. Within seconds, the alien flashed emotions into her mind that explained why he'd done what he had to Radcliffe. It didn't erase the love she felt for him, but it showed her aspects of him that she hadn't been able to see before, all through pure emotion. The alien projected visual thoughts into her that seemed to be memories of things she had never experienced but contained the feeling of pure truth.

Once the alien convinced her his removal of Radcliffe was for the greater good, it filled her with the same positive energy and love that flowed into the others. Becca had always been treated well by anyone who met her, largely due to her beauty. She was constantly greeted with smiles and happiness wherever she went. However, the overwhelming feeling of bliss that filled her now was far beyond anything she'd ever felt. A strong current of clear love in its most pure form blew through her.

As the alien pulled back its fingers, she was unable to speak. They all were. They just looked at each other, understanding that they had shared something extraordinary. It was as if together they'd all just seen and touched the face of God.

The moment was shattered by Lance's voice through the intercom. "What are you still doing in there?"

It'd been almost thirty minutes since Raquel saw the reptilian alien and the Jersey Devil rip Roland to pieces. She didn't move an inch and stayed hidden within the hole beside the carcass of the giant sea monster. She watched in revulsion as the creatures devoured Roland's remains. Even after the creatures moved on, she stayed glued to her spot.

Mason and Winthrop entered the same room. Mason knew the door to the service corridor was nearby. Once in the corridor, if empty, it was just a minute to the gun room.

As they passed by the vast sea creature, Raquel spotted them and crawled out into the open. "J.W., please. Help me. Please."

She ran to Winthrop and hugged him, trembling and crying.

"Shhhh. It's okay. Everything's going to be fine," he whispered.

"Do you know a way out?" she asked.

Mason stood silent, his eyes continually scanning the area.

"Don't worry. We'll get you out," Winthrop said.

Mason wasn't sure why the older man would risk slowing themselves down for some hooker, even a high-end one.

To use as a hostage with the cops? As bait to throw to one of the creatures? he wondered.

"Stay close and as quiet as you can," Winthrop said.

"Thank you. Thank you so much."

42

NOISES IN THE DARK

V IC'S GROUP CROSSED THROUGH AN area the two detectives hadn't yet seen. They were all silent in the lingering afterglow of their experience with the alien, who now glided along with them. Each of them spent as much time stealing glances at their new ally as they did their surroundings. As they entered the new area, the scent of dew filled the air.

Half the room was illuminated. Portions of the wall appeared to be an old decrepit porch from a river shack in Louisiana. It had peeling shingles, old-fashioned lanterns, even a couple of vintage rusty metal signs for soda and tobacco.

There was one long diorama window, most of which was broken and scattered across the floor. It had an interior that featured a realistic swamp. Cypress trees stood in a murky, moss-covered body of water.

At first Vic thought the sounds he heard were from a speaker. Then he realized the display was full of actual chirping crickets, frogs, and whatever else was making it sound filled with life.

While Vic, Tony, Tom, Annika, and Becca looked at the display, Kelsey noticed a shape on the floor. It was the partially mutilated body of a man. It was Congressman Pond. One of his arms was gone, and part of his stomach was slashed. Pond's eyes were shut tight and his mouth wide open, like he was frozen in midsneeze.

He whimpered, causing them to jump and curse. His eyes rolled around in his head as he coughed out blood.

"Help me," he gurgled.

Vic knelt beside him but could see there was nothing he could do, even if he wanted to.

"He looks familiar," Tony said.

"Yeah," Vic answered. "He's a congressman."

"Hel-help... me...," Pond stammered.

Suddenly the background of chirping stopped all at once, and an eerie silence spread. Vic raised his AR-15. Without warning, something burst from the murky water. It was humanoid and seven feet tall on two legs. Its arms were broad, wide-reaching, and led down to four-fingered hands with wide, sharp claws the size of cell phones. Its body was covered in dark green, almost black, skin that looked like alligator hide. Its eyes were large and yellow and looked at the group in a way that sent shudders through them.

Vic opened fire. The muzzle flash lit up the room like a lightning storm. Tony did the same, but neither rifle had any effect. They couldn't tell if the bullets were missing, bouncing off, or just embedding into its thick hide. It bolted toward them, covering several yards in an instant. Everyone scattered.

Vic pushed Kelsey behind him as they backed away but tripped over the congressman. They fell awkwardly to the ground. Pond let out a groan when they came down on him.

As the thing got closer, they stumbled back. Their feet pushed off the wounded man as they tried to put space between themselves and the creature. They crawled backward until they hit a wall.

It stepped forward, now standing over the defenseless congressman. The creature hunched down. Swamp water dripped from it onto Pond's face, which turned to Vic and Kelsey with a pitiful expression.

"Please. Please," he said, barely loud enough to hear.

The creature put one of its claws on Pond's leg as it leaned over and bit him hard in the shoulder. The congressman screamed, and a large blood bubble came from his mouth and popped as he cried for help. The beast lifted its head, taking the politician's upper body with it. The arm that Pond had left flailed as he dangled helplessly.

Vic saw Tony and the others across the room and contemplated making a run for it with Kelsey.

"Move away slowly," Vic whispered.

"No. Don't," Kelsey answered.

In a move that took less than a second, the creature opened its mouth, dropped the congressman, and slammed its mouth shut again on his face before he fell farther. Its jaws locked with a sickening crunch.

Pond's arm fell limp. The swamp creature's eyes focused on Vic and Kelsey as it gobbled.

The thing dropped what was left of the congressman and moved closer to them, stepping on the mutilated body.

"Fuck," Vic said.

The creature lurched forward again, just two yards away now. They could smell the algae of the swamp water on it.

"When I say run, you run," Vic said without turning away from the thing.

"No." Kelsey shook her head, knowing she had no better ideas.

Vic slowly stood up.

"Wait. No. Don't! Vic, Vic, Vic...," Kelsey said.

The creature took another step and began to hunch down as if it were preparing to lunge forward.

"Run!" Vic ordered.

Instead, she stood up beside him and readied herself for a fight.

The creature launched at them, and they instinctually raised their hands in front of their faces to protect themselves. As the creature was in midair, just a foot from reaching them, something came out of nowhere and intercepted the beast in a blur of motion. Whatever it was crashed to the floor, tangled up with it. Vic and Kelsey stood frozen for a second, then ran to the others, then turned back to see what it was that saved them.

It was the dark brown and gray spotted Sasquatch Roland had referred to as Charlie. The angry swamp creature stood up and lunged at the Sasquatch with its mouth open wide and its claws outstretched. Everyone watched in shock as the two beasts ferociously attacked each other.

Charlie let out a deafening growl when the swamp creature slammed its teeth into his bicep and shook its head savagely. The Sasquatch went crazy and twisted the swamp beast off, taking a chunk of his own arm with it.

The Sasquatch got a solid grip of its head and bent it back until there was a loud double crack and the swamp beast fell lifeless to the floor. As the group watched, Charlie grabbed his wounded arm and let out another cry. He turned toward the humans, and for several seconds they stood looking at each other.

This was Kelsey's first look at Bigfoot. Her eyes locked with the wounded creature as it stood to its full height. It turned and lumbered away, its massive hand nursing its wounded arm. They watched their hairy savior vanish into the darkness.

"That thing did that on purpose. It saved you guys," Becca said.

Tony let out a nervous laugh.

"What's funny?" Vic asked.

"Oh, I don't know," Tony said. "A vegetarian Bigfoot named Charlie just rescued you from a swamp monster. Totally normal stuff."

—————•—————

On the monitors, Lance saw that Winthrop, Mason, and a woman were approaching the control room. He didn't know if that was good or bad.

The cops didn't take my license or anything. If I get out with Winthrop and Mason, I can just move away. I can start a new life somewhere. This whole thing could be over for me. Though, if Winthrop heard me on the intercom helping the cops, he might be pissed. No. I can tell him they gave me no choice. What was I supposed to do?

Lance heard Mason punch in the door code. It opened, and he, Winthrop, and Raquel entered.

———·———

"Mr. Winthrop," Lance started. "I'm so glad you're okay."

"Same to you," Winthrop replied.

Mason got closer. Too close. His face was an inch away from Lance's. "Why did we hear you helping those cops?"

Lance felt his stomach turn. "What was I supposed to do? They're cops."

Winthrop put a hand on Mason's shoulder. "He's right. He had no choice."

Raquel had known this whole thing was morally murky, but she'd been told everything was legal… the same lie about terminally ill people signing agreements. It was a bit on the sick side, but not illegal. These guys were now acting like they were guilty of something, but she knew she needed them to get back to the surface.

Just keep your mouth shut, she told herself.

Winthrop eased Lance into one of the chairs by the console and sat beside him.

"Everything's fine," Winthrop said. "But I need to know what you told them."

Lance's lips went numb. "I didn't tell them anything I shouldn't have."

"Did you give them my name or anyone else's?" Winthrop asked.

"No. I said I never met any of the bosses, that I was hired online."

Mason watched Lance, thinking he was full of shit.

Winthrop leaned closer. "If you said anything, it's fine.

They're police officers and I'm sure that was intimidating. I'm not upset, but I do need to know so I can handle it. So what did you tell them exactly? Tell me every word."

"I told them I answered an ad online for a maintenance job. I told them... I acted like I didn't know that all this stuff was real. Like I thought it was just special effects and animatronics."

Winthrop nodded. "That was clever of you."

"Thanks."

Winthrop stood up and looked at the monitors. The security cameras had night vision, and the image on the screen was high resolution and clear as day.

"Is... is that Mr. Gray with them?" he asked.

"Yeah," Lance replied.

Mason looked over Winthrop's shoulder. "That's nuts."

Winthrop saw Vic and the group moving on-screen. His eyes scanned each monitor until something caught his attention.

"Okay," he said as he folded his arms. "Here's what you're going to do. Get on the intercom and tell them to go to the left."

Lance looked at the monitors and saw that if he directed them to do as Winthrop said, he'd be sending them dangerously close to the zombie room. Not only were there more than a dozen zombies walking free in the adjoining room, but there was also a smashed-open portion of wall the zombies would be able to cross through to get to them if they heard them.

Mason saw what Winthrop was doing and smiled.

"Go on," Winthrop said.

Lance turned to Winthrop and nodded. He switched the intercom on.

"Hey. Don't go that way."

On-screen, Vic and everyone with him stopped and looked at each other.

Lance continued. "That way won't work anymore. Go to the left, through that room instead."

———•———

Vic's inner alarm went off. *Something about his voice is wrong.*

Tony noticed it too. He and Vic exchanged a look.

Vic whispered to him. "We don't have much choice."

Tom spoke up, lowering his voice as Vic did. "Isn't he just doing what you told him to do? To warn us of stuff?"

"Not sure," Vic replied.

They looked at the map.

—— · ——

Winthrop leaned on the console. He watched them closely.

These two are smart.

"Tell them you didn't notice that there's a collapsed wall blocking the way," Winthrop said.

Lance did so.

—— · ——

That might be true, Vic thought. In any case, they had to keep moving.

"Let's go to the left," he whispered to the group. "Just keep your eyes open."

The group followed Lance's direction. They entered a room darker than the area they'd come from. Very little light came from around the corner ahead, hiding that the large hole in the wall they'd crossed by was filled with motionless zombies.

—— · ——

Winthrop looked at Lance. "Good. Now close the doors to that room."

Lance knew that if he did, he'd be essentially locking them all in with the zombies. He hesitated.

"Do it." Winthrop spoke with a kind tone, as if he were telling Lance to try a taste of something new.

Lance did as he was told, and the doors ahead and behind the group dropped from the ceiling.

—— · ——

Vic saw the doors sliding shut ahead of them.

"Run!" Vic yelled.

Vic, Kelsey, Tony, Tom, Annika, and Becca sprinted for the door ahead of them as the divider came down but didn't make it. They slammed into it.

"Shit!" Vic yelled.

"That son of a bitch. I'm gonna kill him," Tony added.

Mr. Gray looked on, emotionless.

——— · ———

Winthrop, Mason, and Lance watched the monitors. They could see the zombies were now aware of the people nearby and were moving toward the hole in the wall. The trapped group still had no clue they weren't alone.

"Let's make it fair," Mason said.

He leaned to the console and pushed a button.

Emergency lights flashed on in the area Vic's group was trapped in. The room lit up and Mason smiled as the zombies got closer to the hole in the wall.

Lance saw the look of glee on Mason's face and felt a chill. Raquel saw it too and realized she was in more danger than she'd thought. The hair on the back of her neck stood up, and dread filled her.

I'm with the bad guys, she realized. *Fuck.*

43

THE UNDEAD & THE CHUPACABRA

W HEN THE LIGHTS CAME ON, Vic and the group found they were in another creature exhibit. Other than a large portion of the wall smashed open into another area, the room wasn't badly damaged. The diorama window was long, almost twenty feet. The glass was still in place but had long spiderlike cracks stretching from the top where the window met the ceiling down to the base.

The diorama behind it featured a grassy scene with large rocks and trees lining the back wall. Through the cracked glass, Tom saw something moving behind the rocks. He looked at the plate at the base of the window. It read:

> *CHUPACABRA—*
> *Quadruped/canine/hominid found in Texas. In addition to being a strange hybrid of dog, coyote, and human, the chupacabra also shares features with bats and reptiles. This one weighs 200 pounds and can run faster than a cheetah.*

Before Tom finished reading, the chupacabra vaulted from behind the rocks and rammed itself against the glass. The whole window pushed forward from the impact. Everyone jumped back, but the glass was holding.

At first glance, it looked like a giant shaved dog. Its shiny black skin appeared to be leather, but a closer look revealed tiny scales. Its front legs looked like muscular human arms with the shoulders and biceps of a weightlifter and much longer forearms with equally pronounced muscles.

Its paws were tipped with claws. Unlike its front legs, its back legs looked like an odd combination of canine and human. The muscles were similar to a man's legs but with the joints of an animal. The head was grotesque. It had small eyes, deep-set behind a bat-like nose. Its ears were also bat-like, large and pointy. The thing's mouth was wide, and jagged, yellow teeth jutted from its dark gums.

"Fuck, that's ugly," Tony said.

"That glass isn't gonna hold," Vic replied.

It was damaged enough that a few more hard bangs and it would shatter. Everyone else also took notice. Even the alien was enthralled, its large eyes blinking as it stared at the chupacabra.

Tom touched around the area where the door had slid down, trying to find a way out. Kelsey felt the urge to say some reassuring words to Annika but saw that the younger woman was the only one not looking at the window. She was looking behind them, her face horrified. Kelsey spun around to see what she was looking at as two zombies stumbled into the room through the hole in the wall. The first one fell forward, and the next one crawled over him, followed by several more.

"Vic! Tony!" Kelsey yelled.

The detectives wheeled around and saw the zombies.

"Get behind us!" Kelsey yelled to Tom, Becca, and Annika. Mr. Gray glided to the side as well.

Once Vic saw they were safely behind him, he and Tony opened fire with the AR-15s. Bullets burst through their rotting flesh and out their backs along with tatters of skin and dried flesh, but the zombies didn't react at all to the bullets. It was as if they were shooting at lifeless scarecrows or dummies. Yet they kept approaching.

Tom yelled, "The heads! Like in the movies! Shoot them in the head!"

Vic took better aim and fired at their heads. There was no change. Pieces of head, skull, and flesh blew off them, but they kept coming.

Tom watched, feeling as stupid as he was terrified. The walking corpses made it into the room with dozens more following behind.

Kelsey searched the area for a way to escape. She saw a vent in the wall that was big enough for them to fit into, but it was at least seven feet from the floor.

"Look!" she yelled to them, pointing at it.

Vic saw it and looked around the room for a way to get up there. Kelsey fired her rifle at it, hoping the vent cover would come off.

Tony ran to the wall and stood under the vent. He put his rifle down and clasped his fingers together.

"Vic!" he yelled.

Vic ran to him and stepped onto his clasped hands. Tony's face contorted in pain as he strained to lift Vic high enough to get to the vent. The pain in his injured shoulder was excruciating. He had to lean against the wall to get through it.

The damage Kelsey did to the vent was enough for Vic to easily rip the cover off, but as soon as he did, a zombie got too close, and Tony had to drop Vic to protect himself.

Tony kicked the zombie in the stomach to push him back. Instead of knocking it backward, his foot went right through the zombie's rotted midsection. He fell with his foot stuck in the zombie's rib cage. The moving corpse looked at Tony with empty sockets, its rotted teeth opening wide as its skeletal hands grabbed at him.

As he struggled to free himself, another zombie closed in.

"Vic!" he yelled.

Vic grabbed his AR-15 and rammed the butt of it into the zombie's face. It gave him enough time to help Tony free his foot.

Annika heard Becca yell and turned to see three zombies

surrounding her. Annika picked up a jagged two-by-four from the wreckage of the wall and ran to the other woman. She shoved it into the chests of the zombies approaching Becca, backing them away.

"Get over there!" Kelsey told her.

Annika saw where she pointed, and Kelsey pushed her toward it. Tom also made his way to the spot under the vent.

All through that, the alien stood still and calm. None of the zombies had any interest in him. Once the rest were under the vent together, Vic and Tony faced each other to boost up the others. They didn't discuss, they just instantly went into action.

"Kel! Go!" Vic yelled.

"No. Them first!" she yelled back, pointing at Annika and Becca.

Kelsey supported Annika's back as she stepped up onto the men's hands and was lifted to the vent. She awkwardly pulled herself inside. It was dark and tight. There wasn't enough space to turn around once inside. She crawled forward to give the next person room to get in and waited, twisting her head as much as she could to see behind her.

They did the same thing for Becca, who was rambling her gratitude nonstop.

"Thank you! Thank you! Thank you! Thank you!"

Once Becca was inside the vent, Vic pulled Kelsey into position to go next.

Kelsey stepped back and pushed for Tom to go next.

"No. You," the billionaire replied.

The chupacabra gave out an earsplitting growl and threw itself against the damaged glass again, causing the long cracks to multiply.

"No time, goddamn it!" Vic yelled at Tom as the entire horde of zombies closed in.

Tom was determined to let Kelsey go next. "Go!" Tom yelled at her.

Kelsey stepped up, and the three men boosted her up to the vent.

For a split second, as Kelsey placed her bare foot into Vic's palm, he saw a flash of the two of them lying on the couch and watching a movie, him running his fingers over her feet as they lay crossed in his lap.

She squeezed herself into the vent and shuffled on her belly a few feet in and waited. Fear that Vic wouldn't make it in filled her head.

If he waits to go last, how will he get in? There's not enough room for Tony to turn around and help pull him up. Oh my god.

Her heart pounded so loud she could hear it as easily as the sounds of the metal vent creaking around her.

The zombies closed in on Vic and Tony. They were so close they had to let go of Tom, who was only a foot into the vent. The detectives turned to face the zombies, leaving Tom to pull himself the rest of the way into the vent himself. There was nothing for him to grab onto other than Kelsey's feet. Panicking and feeling himself slipping back, he grabbed her ankles.

When Kelsey felt Tom grab her, she instantly knew he was having trouble pulling himself in.

"It's okay!" she yelled back to him. "Go ahead! Use me!"

He did, and although it helped him maintain a grip, the bulk of his weight was still outside the vent, and he started to slip back, pulling Kelsey with him.

"Shit!" Kelsey blurted.

Becca's feet were too far ahead for her to reach.

"Becca! Quick! Crawl backward! Please!"

Hearing the urgency in her voice, Becca quickly slid herself back through the vent until Kelsey could reach her ankles. Becca yelled ahead to Annika to do the same.

"Hey! She needs us to back up! Hurry!"

Annika pushed herself back through the dark as fast as she could until Becca got hold of her ankles as well.

"Everybody pull each other forward!" Kelsey's voice echoed through the vent.

It worked. It gave Tom the help he needed to pull the rest

of his body up. Once inside completely, he let go of Kelsey's ankles and lowered his forehead to the vent's cold metal.

"Thank you. Thank you," he uttered.

"Everybody stay right where we are," Kelsey hollered. "We may have to do that again. Please stay close!"

"We ain't goin' nowhere," Annika said.

———•———

The hands of the foul-smelling corpses were all over Vic and Tony. They kicked back at them, knocking them away a yard or two but not giving them enough time or space to continue the escape.

"Vic! Vic! Tony!" Kelsey started screaming. She couldn't see what was happening, and it was driving her crazy.

"Don't worry!" he yelled, "We're coming!"

"Hey!" Tony said.

Vic turned to him.

"They're so slow. Let's duck under, run to the other side of the room, and after they follow us there, we'll have enough time to get in the vent."

Vic scoped it out and agreed. "Ready?"

"Let's do it."

Both men dropped and rolled themselves out from under the net of corpse limbs reaching for them. Once outside the throng, they bolted for the far side of the room. After they broke free, it took them three seconds to reach the far side of the room. Judging the zombies' speed, it would give them about a minute to get inside the vent.

As the detectives leaned against the wall and waited for the undead to get farther away from the vent, Vic noticed the gray alien standing where they had come in. The zombies still showed no interest in him. He stood motionless, his blinking eyes the only evidence he wasn't a statue.

"I guess they can't smell him," Vic said.

"Why can't he do to them what he did to that old bastard before?" Tony asked.

"I don't know," Vic answered. "Maybe he..."

Vic's sentence was drowned out by another scream from

the chupacabra just before it rammed itself against the glass again. This time the glass pushed forward a few inches as more cracks spread throughout it.

"Fuck!" Tony said. "That thing's gonna get loose."

Vic looked back at the vent. "I'm taller than you. Once we go, you go up first."

"How would you get up there without help?" Tony asked. "You can't."

The chupacabra smashed against the glass. The cracks reached the ceiling. Zombies were getting closer, opening space beneath the vent.

"I can jump and reach it," Vic said.

Tony looked at the vent again. It was seven feet up. Vic was six foot two. He might be able to do that. But just reaching it and being able to pull himself inside was a different story. Tony's stomach turned.

"No," Tony said. "You go before me."

"You're too fucking short," Vic replied. "You'll never make it."

"I'm not fucking around!"

"Listen! I swear! I can make it up there!"

Tony loved Vic and considered him a brother. As he listened to him promise he could climb up on his own, emotions battled within him. He didn't want to die down here, eaten by a bunch of zombies like some poor bastard in a horror movie. As he started to believe Vic could climb out of there, his mind raced, trying to figure out if he really believed it or if it was fear brainwashing him into believing it out of subconscious self-preservation.

He felt the urge to scream. The zombies were almost to them.

Vic yelled at Tony. "Now! Come on!"

Tony nodded.

They ran toward the wall of approaching zombies, and just before reaching them, they ducked under them and came up on the other side, then bolted for the vent wall.

Vic got there first and clasped his hands together for Tony, who hesitated. He looked at the zombies turning back toward them. The chupacabra was going to smash through the glass any second.

"Go!" Vic screamed.

Tony stepped onto Vic's clasped hands, and as he did, his eyes filled up. He grabbed the vent and struggled to ignore his burning shoulder as he pulled himself up and inside.

"Okay!" Tony yelled back. "Come on!"

The zombies got closer. Vic took a quick look at them and jumped up for the vent. His hands didn't come close enough, and he fell back down. He took a few steps back to get a running start. He ran and propelled himself up as high as he could. His fingers were only able to graze the vent.

He'd convinced himself he'd be able to do it. Now he had the sickening feeling that maybe he couldn't. He tried again, putting everything he had into the jump. He reached it, but his fingers couldn't hold him, and he dropped.

Oh my god, he thought.

The zombies were getting closer, and the chupacabra made enough of a hole in the glass to get its head through. It twisted it from side to side, trying to squeeze through, foaming at the mouth. It let out a loud screech that Vic barely heard. The sickening fear rushing into him caused all sound to form into a distant echo.

"Vic! Vic, hurry!" Kelsey begged.

"Kel! I love you!" he yelled back to her.

Kelsey instantly knew what it meant. He was about to die.

"*No!*" she screamed. She started to push her way backward, her feet kicking against Tom.

For his part, Tom felt completely helpless. He knew he could do nothing to save Vic, but at the same time, God forgive him, he was grateful to be safe for the moment, and it made him sick.

Tony went backward a few feet so that he could stick his feet out enough that maybe Vic could get a grip on his ankles.

"Vic!" he yelled. "Grab my ankles!"

Vic felt a flash of hope. He leaped up again. He grabbed Tony's ankles and managed to hold on. He swung his other hand up to get a better grip.

Sharp pain shot through Tony's shins as Vic's weight pulled them against the edge of the vent. He clenched his teeth together and grunted as Vic tried to climb up.

Gonna make it. Gonna make it, Vic thought.

Tony's shoe fell off, and Vic's hands with it. He crashed to the floor, and the shadows cast by the zombies standing over him darkened his face.

"No! Damn it!" Tony yelled.

Kelsey screamed Vic's name so loud it echoed through the vent.

Tony lowered his face against the vent as he heard Kelsey burst into tears.

Vic looked up at the faces of the dead as they descended on him. He'd always wondered what his last moments would be like. The treasured idea of dying in bed surrounded by family and loved ones, the kids and grandkids he and Kelsey would produce looking on solemnly. Dying alone in a hospital with doctors and hospital staff. Even bleeding out from a gunshot wound at some crime scene.

He'd never imagined being eaten alive by zombies in some secret, underground monster zoo.

"I love you, Kel!" he yelled as he felt the cold hands take hold of him.

He felt something else. A tingling in his stomach, like a thousand little needles poking around inside him. It spread to his midsection and chest. It was both warm and cold at the same time, and it felt somehow... right. As if it was good that it was happening.

The tingling turned to a familiar sensation, although one he hadn't felt in a long time. It was a hollowness in his gut, exactly like the two seconds after the rollercoaster crested and dropped straight down.

He realized the hands of the zombies grabbing at him were now somehow underneath him, reaching up.

What's happening?

Vic turned sideways and saw he was floating above the zombies, now safely out of reach. He also saw the chupacabra smash completely through its window in slow motion. Shards of glass flew sideways through the air below him like a beautiful shower of crystals. He watched the glittering glass sail across the room beneath him, and that's when he saw the alien. It was looking up at him with its two long fingers raised toward him.

It's him. He's saving me.

Vic looked at the alien, but its expression didn't change. Just cold eye blinks.

When Vic's body was at the same height as the vent, he felt the tingling inside him stop pulling him vertically and start pulling horizontally. He glided through the air toward the vent.

Just as his body entered the vent, Vic saw the chupacabra attack the alien. It seized him with its front claws and took a bite out of the alien's neck.

"*No!*" Vic said. He heard his own voice with a dull echo to it.

He floated into the vent, and his view of the alien got smaller and smaller as he got deeper in. Just before he lost sight of the alien, he could see that it was still standing despite the attack, spending its focus on getting him to safety.

The alien could have saved itself but instead saved him.

As the chupacabra attacked, the alien started to shake. The mortally wounded extraterrestrial let out a sound no human had ever heard. It vibrated through the heads of everyone. Although Vic was completely inside the vent now, he still floated a few inches above the metal bottom. Suddenly, as life left the alien, Vic dropped to the floor of the vent with a thud.

Unable to see behind her, Kelsey yelled, "Vic! Is that you? Tony! Did he make it in?"

"It's me, Kel. I'm in," Vic answered.

Both Kelsey and Tony burst into tears.

"Thank Christ," Tony said.

Kelsey had similar words. "Oh God… thank you. Thank you. Thank you. Thank you."

Thank God? Vic thought.

Vic might have uttered those words during times of crisis, but to him, they were only words. He had no more belief in God than he did the tooth fairy. He'd seen too much evil. In his opinion, religion was the predominant source of war and hatred in the world. He completely agreed with a quote he'd heard years before from some French philosopher. "Men will never be free until the last king is strangled with the entrails of the last priest."

Now, as he felt the warm glow of the alien's power fading from his body, he thought that maybe he'd been partially wrong about God. Maybe God was an alien. Or aliens.

He sacrificed himself for me.

You can't have a purer heart than that. All that ran through his mind, stopping suddenly when he heard Tony's voice.

"Come on, man. Let's move," Tony repeated.

"Right behind ya," Vic replied.

———•———

Winthrop and Mason watched the security screen, baffled.

"I don't get it," Mason said. "That alien has been down here for over ten years. If it had powers to do things like that, why wouldn't it have used them to escape?"

Winthrop heard him, but his eyes remained on the monitor. The chupacabra had partially devoured the alien and was now ripping apart the zombies.

"I don't know," Winthrop said.

Lance and Raquel sat on the floor against the wall, silent.

"Where does that vent lead to?" Winthrop asked. At one time, he'd known every pipe and drain through the entire facility, but he'd long since forgotten the mundane matters.

Lance ran through the facility's structure in his head. "I

think it comes out in the service corridor behind the lobby. If they make it to that point, the elevator's right there."

Damn, Winthrop thought.

He turned to Mason. "Go get some guns. We have to beat them to the lobby."

———•———

Vic, Tony, Tom, Kelsey, Becca, and Annika crawled through the darkness of the vent with no idea where they were heading or what they'd be facing when they got there. Now that they were, for the most part anyway, momentarily safe, each one of them felt remnants of the positivity and light the alien had flowed into them.

None felt it deeper than Annika. As she crawled, the optimism didn't just linger; it took root. When she got out of this, she was done hooking forever. Kelsey had come back for her when she didn't have to. She cared. She could definitely help her get some kind of real job.

A whole new life. A clean life with no shit. No drugs. No nothing.

A job, a new place to live. It won't be easy. But I'm doing it. Whatever it takes. It's going to happen this time. I can feel it. I can feel it like it already happened.

Annika smiled in the dark as she crawled toward her future.

———•———

Mason returned with several guns but didn't give one to Winthrop or Lance. If the time came when he needed their help with more firepower, he'd give them one then.

Always five steps ahead of everyone around him, Winthrop registered Mason's mistrust. Lance didn't.

"Which one is mine?" Lance asked.

Mason shook his head. "The only thing more dangerous than the things down here is the idea of you with a gun."

Lance frowned and shot an embarrassed look at Raquel.

Winthrop stared at Mason. "You realize I need you alive to get us out of here, right?"

Mason smirked.

Fuck, he's smooth. Us? As if he gives two shits about Lance or the hooker.

Mason calculated Winthrop wouldn't risk killing him until they got close enough to the elevator for him to make it the rest of the way on his own. Too much chance that any one of these things could pop out of nowhere and attack.

Mason handed him an AR-15. "You know how to use it?"

"Yes."

"Okay then," Mason replied. "As we're moving, barrel always down and finger off the trigger."

Winthrop nodded despite his revulsion at being told what to do even in this situation.

———•———

The air duct system had little light to guide Vic's group. There were sporadic areas where working lights from the rooms below illuminated short areas up through vent grates, but they were mostly crawling through the darkness.

It was a strange mix of terror and comfort. Moving deeper into the dark after discovering monsters were real and could be waiting ahead of them, ready to pounce, was enough to drive anyone crazy. The only saving grace was that the tight space also gave them a skewed sense of safety.

Vic didn't feel as much of that as the others. Having Kelsey back, even in the current circumstance, allowed his mind to drift to thoughts of Kirby. The worry that the kid was dead filled him with overwhelming guilt.

———•———

Annika leaned her head back to Becca as she crawled. "Can I ask you somethin'?"

"Sure," Becca answered as she crawled behind her.

"Why was you with that old man?"

"It wasn't like that," Becca answered. "He was more like a grandfather to me."

"For reals?"

"I was working for a catering company doing an event at

his house," Becca started. "He took an interest in me, and we became friends."

"Girl, you can't be that naive. Grandpa was trying to hit that pooty."

"No." Becca grunted, as much from the crawling as from the conversation. "He never made any kind of move on me. He knew I was engaged. He liked my fiancé as much as he liked me."

"You got a man? He lets you hang out with other guys in a dress like that?"

"He's... He died."

Annika stopped crawling. "Oh. I'm sorry. What happened?"

"He was in the wrong place at the wrong time. He got shot in a store robbery."

"That's terrible," Annika said. "I'm sorry."

She turned back and crawled on.

———•———

Tony felt no measure of safety in the vent. He'd always suffered from minor claustrophobia. The feeling of the metal walls tight against him on all sides was watering the seeds of a panic attack. He knew the signs and always kept a few Xanax in the inner flap of his wallet.

Most times, just knowing the pills were there prevented the thoughts from developing further. There had been years when he'd go six months without taking a pill. He knew when the initial feeling of panic showed itself, the opportunity to handle it with a pill had a small window. If he let it grow too much, it could turn into a full-fledged attack, and once that happened, it was too late. He'd still take the pill, of course, and it would eventually take effect and calm him down, but there would be no avoiding the heart-pounding panic that would make it hard to breathe and turn him into a sweaty ball of distress.

The worst was when it happened in front of other people. The urge to get away from everyone, to get outside as fast as possible, was all-powerful. His face would go numb and his skin would tingle until he could get free.

And now he could feel the metal walls of the air duct closing in around him. It was getting tighter, and his mind raced at the thought that he was trapped, that he had no idea how much farther the air duct went on.

It's fine. You're okay. Take a pill. Quick.

He couldn't get to his wallet. It was too tight. Once that sank in, his panic skyrocketed. It got hard to breathe. The pulse behind his eyes pounded.

"Hey," he said to Annika, up ahead of Kelsey.

What was her fucking name?

"Hey, uh, can you see how much farther it is? Can you see anything?"

Annika replied, "No. I can't see shit."

That's no help. I don't care. Just lie to me.

"Kel? Can you see the end of this thing?"

"No. Nothing."

Vic could hear the tone in Tony's voice and instantly knew the situation. "Tony," Vic said, "it can't be much longer. Hang in there."

"I'm okay." Tony kept his voice even. "All good."

Almost the second the last syllable left his lips, the panic overtook him.

"No!" he said. "Gotta get out. Please. Go faster."

Tony started to crawl faster, bumping into Tom's feet until he pushed the billionaire forward through the vent. It caused Tom to push Kelsey and Kelsey to run into Becca and Annika.

"I'm sorry," Tom said to Kelsey. "He's pushing me... I can't..."

Vic heard the movement and the metal vent bending around him. "Tony!" he said. "Can you reach your pills?"

"No!" Tony replied.

"Hold up," Vic said. "Maybe I can get to them."

"You won't be able to," Tony answered, his voice shaking. He went into full panic mode.

"Gotta get out! I'm sorry! I have to get out! Go! Just fucking go!"

He started shoving Tom harder in front of him.

"Tony! Stop!" Kelsey yelled back as Tom was being pushed into her.

Vic grabbed onto Tony's ankle to stop him from shoving and maybe calm him down.

Annika started to say something. "Wait! I think there's a—"

Her sentence turned into a scream that sounded like she was being pulled away from them at high speed.

Terror filled Becca. "Annika? *Annika?*"

"What's happening?" Vic yelled. "Is there something in here with us?"

Whatever had happened to Annika, Tony was still pushing Tom and Kelsey closer to where she had just been.

Confusion took over with each of them yelling as Tony pushed harder. Vic tried to grab Tony's ankle again, but he'd pushed so much farther ahead, he couldn't reach him.

"Hey! Wait!" Kelsey yelled.

Becca screamed, and her voice also trailed off as if she was quickly pulled away.

Vic heard Kelsey trying to get everyone's attention.

"Everybody shut up!" Vic yelled. "I think she sees something! Kel, what is it?"

"It seems like the vent is starting to... Wait... no! Vic! Viiiiic!"

Kelsey's voice zoomed farther away, as fast as Annika and Becca's had. Now it was Vic who was shoving forward. Tony was still ahead of him, pushing Tom closer to whatever fate Kelsey, Becca, and Annika had experienced. He begged for Tony to stop, but it was useless. Within a few seconds, Tom's voice also vanished, followed by Tony's.

———•———

Even in the dark, Vic knew he was now alone. He didn't care. He felt no urge to stop moving out of self-preservation. The past few seconds had been so chaotic all he could focus on was getting to Kelsey as fast as possible.

His sweaty hands reached for more metal vent ahead of

him until he understood what had happened to the rest of them. The bottom of the vent came to a point where it bent down in a sharp drop, like a slide. They hadn't been attacked by anything. Nothing had pulled them away. Tony had just pushed so much that they couldn't stop themselves from sliding down.

At this point, Vic hesitated. He had no idea how far this thing dropped. Was it built this way, or was it bent down because of the damage? What was at the bottom?

Kel is at the bottom, he told himself.

Vic pulled himself over the edge. He tried to use his hands to control his descent until the angle increased so much that gravity took over and he sped down into the dark.

44

THE HUNTERS

MASON LED WINTHROP, LANCE, AND Raquel through the maze of darkness. Winthrop saw the extent of the damage. Walls were demolished, exhibits destroyed, the structure itself was compromised.

Damn. It would take years to rebuild everything to the way it was, he figured.

"Get against the wall, quick," Mason whispered. "Stay flat against it."

Raquel saw it first — a large, gray shape. Mason silently put his finger on his trigger as he watched the yeti come into focus. It was holding its torso where it had a wound. A long strip of dark red blood streaked down its leg.

Fear filled Winthrop. He'd seen many times what the yeti could do to a human being. Lance and Raquel froze in place as they watched the beast rummage around. It stopped suddenly, looked toward them, and for a few seconds, they each thought it had seen them. It saw something else. The yeti turned and moved away until its gray color faded into the darkness.

———•———

Mason thought he heard something. It sounded close, but he couldn't detect where it had come from. He scanned the area and motioned to move on.

Raquel thought she heard something too, but if Mason thought it was safe to keep moving, that's what she would do. Before she started to move again though, she turned back to look at Lance. When she did, she saw that his head was gone.

What the…

For a few long seconds, Lance's body swayed with his hands moving around like he was trying to mime something. His head had been somehow ripped from his neck, which was bubbling dark blood upward like an old-fashioned water fountain, the kind where the water never went high enough from the spout.

Raquel stepped backward and let out a few syllables of something. Lance's body fell to the floor. Only then did she scream, and Winthrop quickly put his hand over her mouth. He managed to keep it there as his own eyes widened at the sight of Lance's headless body creating a pool of blood.

Mason realized what the sound had been. "Get down. Now."

He hunched down as well and raised his rifle. He scanned every direction.

Goddamn it, he thought.

He lifted his eye from the gun's sights but didn't take his finger from the trigger. Following Mason's lead, Winthrop removed his hand from Raquel's mouth.

"What did that?" Raquel stammered. Her whole body was trembling.

Mason and Winthrop exchanged a glance, curious to see if they both agreed on which creature it had been.

"Devil?" Mason said quietly.

Winthrop nodded. "Or the…"

Something moved in the dark corner of the room. Mason spun his rifle toward it, but the dim light from the adjacent room wasn't enough for them to see. Mason motioned for them to move to the nearest wall. There was a chunk of stone on its side a few feet from the wall. Winthrop recognized it as a two-million-year-old creature fossil. They squatted down between it and the wall.

Raquel kept her eyes on the dark corner where the noise had come from. Mason leaned over the fossil with his rifle, aiming at whatever was watching them in the dark. He considered firing into the shadows but didn't want to waste any ammo, or worse, attract anything else.

Two glowing slits of red appeared, each one the size of a butter knife.

Winthrop was too nearsighted to see them. Raquel buried her face in her hands and prayed. She was shaking like a leaf, and they were so close together, her trembling vibrated into Mason's leg.

He didn't feel it. All his focus was on those two glowing eyes. He put the rifle's front sight directly between them and slowly pulled the trigger. Just as he was about to fire, the eyes disappeared. Mason grunted.

Come on. Come back.

A loud whoosh sound sliced through the air as something flew at them from the darkness. Something thrown with such force, it embedded into the wall just above them.

Winthrop was closest to where it hit. He looked up at it and became so overcome with fear he suddenly went deaf. It was Lance's head. His one visible eye stared straight ahead. Sound returned to Winthrop as if he'd come up from being underwater. Raquel was screaming. Mason was trying to quiet her down and then saw her eyes widen. He wheeled around to see the Jersey Devil step out from the dark.

As it moved into the low light, the rest of its grotesque face filled in around its glowing red eyes.

Mason fired a burst from the AR-15. The muzzle flash lit up the creature as it flew at them. The bullets hit home, and its flight turned awkward as it flapped its enormous bat wings in distress. It dropped to its feet and growled as it kept coming at them.

Seeing the hollow-point bullets had an effect, Mason rushed from behind the fossil to get closer. He blasted a long burst into the Devil's head from just several feet away. It let out another scream as its wings jittered and stopped flapping. It toppled forward, dead.

Mason took no chances. He approached the still creature and put the barrel of his AR-15 an inch from its head and fired several more shots. He put his boot on the Devil's head and pushed it to the side.

———•———

Winthrop stood up from behind the fossil.

He did it. It's dead.

Memories flashed through Winthrop's mind. The Jersey Devil had been one of his earliest acquisitions, and he remembered how much time and money had gone into its capture, transfer, and containment. He had still been fine-tuning the operation back then, and seeing the creature now dead at their feet filled him with anger. Not out of any feeling for the beast but all the work that had been wasted.

Raquel hurried to join the two men as they stood over the lifeless monster. No one spoke. Mason surveyed the room as he reloaded his rifle, hoping the gunfire hadn't attracted more creatures. He took a last glance at Lance's head stuck in the wall and signaled Winthrop and Raquel to follow him.

45

WITHIN SIGHT

V IC SLID DOWN THE AIR duct at a ninety-degree angle, in complete darkness. Warm air rushed by his face as he stretched his hands out to protect himself from whatever he might slam into.

Suddenly the vent was gone. Nothing supported him, and instant panic filled him as he dropped through the air, not knowing how far he was falling. It could be a few feet or a minute-long death plunge. It turned out to be a seven-foot drop to a hard floor. Vic groaned as his hands bent back and his body folded like a car crashing into a wall. He flipped onto his back in an unintentional, sloppy somersault. Pain throbbed into his shoulder and mixed with the constant sting from the gashes in his back.

"Kel?" he grunted, hoping she wasn't hurt.

"I'm here." She hugged him as hard she could, her face buried in his neck.

He breathed her in, and for just a moment, he cared about nothing else. She was in his arms, and nothing else mattered.

His eyes adjusted to the low light. The room was barely lit, but compared to the blackness of the vent, it was a welcome change.

He saw Tony, Tom, Annika, and Becca.

"Sorry, man," Tony said. "If you'd come out three seconds later, we could have helped catch you."

The last few words hung in the air. Vic took a few steps toward Tom, Annika, and Becca.

"How about you guys?" he asked. "You all right?"

"I'm okay," Annika replied.

"I'm fine," Becca replied. "I think he might have a concussion," she added, turning toward Tom.

"He landed on his head," Tony said. "He's got a bump the size of a golf ball."

Vic made as much eye contact with Tom as he could in the little light they had. He gently put his hand on Tom's chin and turned his head to get a better view of his wound. Vic winced at the sight of the bump.

"Are you dizzy?" he asked.

"When I first stood up. But I'm okay now."

Vic didn't recognize the room from any of the ones they'd seen earlier. One wall was broken glass from floor to ceiling and was filled with various types of skulls. Some looked human, others were much larger, and several of them were elongated. Others were hybrids, appearing to be both human and animal with skeletal snouts and horns.

The passageway to the next area was demolished. A mountain of rubble blocked the exit. The pile rose almost to the ceiling and left only a space of two feet high that they'd have to get through if they could manage to climb up the rubble. Whatever was on the other side had working lights that glowed through the opening.

Kelsey began to climb the rubble.

"Wait," Vic said.

"Just gonna see what's on the other side."

It wasn't easy. The rubble was loose, and she could feel rough edges scrape against her bare feet. The mountain was made of bricks, cement pieces, metal poles, and other sharp wreckage. She bent over as she climbed, using her hands to find steady places to step.

The rest of the group watched as she made her way up to the opening below the ceiling. She pulled herself up to the edge and peeked over. Kelsey hadn't seen it before, but the huge room on the other side was the lobby.

The wall of the far side of the room had an enormous hole where the sea monster had smashed through. Its dead carcass lay halfway through the hole it had created. It was gigantic, and the smell of it reached her. It was a stench that put a grimace on her face as she scanned the rest of the lobby. Seeing the rotunda, the paintings, and red carpets was surreal.

How could all this be down here without anyone knowing? she wondered.

She spotted several dead bodies littering the floor. She hadn't noticed them at first because their black suits blended with the dark tile.

She turned back to Vic. "It's the lobby," she said. "Three dead on the floor."

Vic didn't give the bodies any thought. He just felt a rush of relief. "Can you see the elevator?" Vic asked. "It's much bigger than a normal one. Maybe twenty feet wide."

Kelsey looked around the room. On the far wall, she saw the large, art-deco-styled golden door. "Yeah."

"Great," Vic replied.

She took in as much of the area as she could, scanning for signs of danger.

Nothing moved.

"Come on up," she said, fully aware it was easier said than done. "Be careful. There are a lot of sharp things."

Tom's vision got blurry. There was a continuous stab of pain in his forehead, and his stomach rolled. Still, he was able to remember both Annika and Becca were barefoot.

"Ladies," he said, not knowing of a better way to address them, "would you like to take my shoes? Even if each of you takes one, it might be easier for you."

Becca was well used to being pampered and politely smiled

at Tom as she turned down his offer. Annika also refused, but the offer itself took her back a bit. Vic and Tony helped the women up the mountain of debris. It wasn't easy. Tom followed along, doing his best to ignore the throb in his head. It took several minutes, but they joined Kelsey at the top. Each one leaned down on their stomachs as they looked through the crack into the silent lobby.

Tom squinted through his headache, focusing on the gold elevator.

"There it is," he said through a pain-filled smile.

Becca felt her eyes fill up. The rest of them also felt a rush of hope. It mixed with fear and panic and created a fresh type of anxiety… the urge to bolt to the elevator.

"Let's go," Annika suggested. "Why we waitin'?"

The only one not feeling it was Vic.

Something's not right. Don't go anywhere.

"Wait," he whispered.

Tony knew his expression. "See something?"

Stepping from the entranceway into the museum came the wendigo. It lumbered into the light and turned its huge antlers from side to side to scope out its surroundings. It dragged a man behind it. Most of his clothes were torn off, and his body looked like it had been partially devoured.

The wendigo's arms were so long that its other claws scraped the floor as it walked. It stopped at one of the other dead bodies on the floor and poked at it. It was almost directly between the elevator and where the group hid.

Vic's mind raced for a solution. The wendigo picked up the body, its fingers so long they encircled around the corpse's torso. It lifted it as if it weighed nothing. The beast brought the body to its nose and smelled it. Not liking what it found, it dropped the dead billionaire to the floor with a cruel thud. Several of the group shuddered at the lifelessness of the sound. Then they heard something else.

The wendigo heard it too and turned. It was a human

moan. The body the beast dragged behind it was still alive. The man was unrecognizable. He had long, deep slashes all over him. Half his face was torn away. The sound coming from him was a combination of crying and gibberish.

The wendigo hunched down beside the once-powerful man. The man saw the thing leaning over him and began to sob. Terror filled the group as they watched from their hiding place, but none could turn away.

The wendigo brought its hand to the man's midsection. Each wood-like finger was a foot and a half long. The claws appeared as if they had been carved into sharp points.

The creature stabbed them into the man's torso. His whimpering turned into a scream followed by the sickening sound of his ribs breaking. He felt pain beyond anything he'd ever experienced. Blood spurt from his mouth as he screamed. The creature ripped a section of the man's ribs out, sank its yellow teeth into it, and bit flesh off the bones.

They all felt similar revulsion as the creature ate. The helplessness was the thing that bothered Vic the most. The elevator was just thirty yards away. He knew all they could do was wait. Eventually the thing would finish what it was doing and move on. Wouldn't it?

He felt something hit his leg, and he jumped. Upon turning around, he saw Becca tapping his ankle and turning her head back and forth from him to the bottom of the rubble mountain below. Vic felt pressure in his temples again.

Damn it. Now what?

He squinted as he tried to see. Then he heard the distinct sound of loose bricks scraping against each other. They all heard it. Each of them tried to spot whatever was moving in the darkness below them.

Kelsey stopped trying to see what it was and looked for a possible place to escape. There was nowhere to go. They were trapped. The only question that mattered was whether whatever was approaching them in the dark below was worse than the thing on the other side of the crack.

The sound of bricks rumbling got louder. Vic's panic turned to anger. He adjusted his body so that he was facing the sound. Out of bullets, the only weapons available were the pieces of rubble they were standing on. He picked up a brick with a portion of mortar stuck to it and lifted it to strike at whatever came out of the darkness.

Tony did the same. Kelsey braced herself. Becca and Annika also picked up something to throw. Tom seemed unaware of any danger. He didn't hear the strange noises over the ringing in his head.

The maker of the noise came enough into the light for them to see. It was the reanimated, wax-covered corpse of Jack the Ripper. It crawled up the hill of rubble toward them, staring at them with lifeless glass eyes. It moved awkwardly; its limbs stuttered as it climbed, giving it the effect of a stop-motion filming technique from an old black-and-white monster movie.

Although technically a zombie, it couldn't bite. For the safety of the artisan engineers who had rebuilt him, the long-rotted teeth that remained in his skull were wired shut. So while they were in no danger of being bitten, the butcher knife permanently fastened to his hand was another issue. The blade gleamed as it came into the light, and the Ripper swung it from side to side to slash whatever was in front of him.

Everyone backed away, but the loose rubble beneath them shifted, and none of them got more than a foot or two. The Ripper came within slicing distance. Becca kicked at it, but her balance was so off that it barely connected.

Vic threw his heavy piece of rubble at it. It hit the Ripper's shoulder and caused him to twist sideways and stumble for a few seconds. It didn't do much damage besides leaving a big white scuff of mortar dust on the Ripper's nineteenth-century overcoat.

Vic got his footing as fast he could and tried to get to the Ripper before it could swing the knife again. When the group first climbed up the hill of rubble, they each learned quickly how best to do it. They adapted their climbing into a practice of first lightly testing to see how secure the place they stepped or grabbed was. After a few minutes working their way up, it didn't get less awkward, but they fell less frequently.

Now, seeing the reanimated monstrosity with a butcher knife going toward Kelsey, Vic's urgency caused him to move too fast. His right foot came down hard in a spot loose enough for his leg to sink through the rubble to his knee, and pain erupted as he felt something sharp stab into his calf. Tony also moved too fast without caution. He fell forward onto his stomach and tumbled several feet down the hill.

Although her mind was filled with panic and confusion, Kelsey retained her care in negotiating the rubble. She wasn't just some damsel in distress who needed a strong man to save her. True, she was in a less than perfect situation. She was barefoot, in her underwear, weak from hunger, sleep-deprived, and standing on an unsteady pile of jagged rocks. She was also a strong-willed woman who never backed down from any kind of fight. She was, as many of her male cop associates lovingly referred to her, a tough bitch… and at the moment, she was pissed off.

Kelsey stood up. Her bleeding feet found enough purchase to prepare a defensive stance. She made a quick study of the Ripper's movements, and after his next swing, she grabbed the wrist of his knife hand, and with all the force she had, bashed her other fist into his face. For all the sparring and actual altercations Kelsey had been through over the years, she'd never expected to see such a result from a punch.

The reconstruction of the Ripper's face was designed to be seen, not hit. Her fist scraped off all the wax and synthetic flesh from its left cheek to just above the eye. The flesh-looking substance hung down from the head in almost one piece, dangling over the chin like a raw chicken breast. Except for a few ragged pieces of synthetic tissue, half of the Ripper's face was now just an exposed skull. The full glass eyeball was now visible, and Kelsey could even see the thin metal wiring that fastened it within the socket.

The ghastly sight threw her for a few seconds, and the Ripper jerked his hand back, slightly cutting the inside of her arm.

Vic struggled to pull up his leg, but whatever was stabbing into it kept him in place. He could only watch as the Ripper swung again at Kelsey.

She waited for the right moment to strike. It came fast, and she sprang her attack, grabbing the wrist again. Instead of punching, she twisted the wrist sideways. Normally the pain from the move would cause her opponent to involuntarily spin around so she could apply a chokehold. The Ripper-Thing felt no pain and did not spin. She used her weight and bent his knife hand backward far enough to break the arm.

Kelsey heard the bones crack and expected the arm to fall useless by its side. Instead, the Ripper's forearm broke at the elbow, and the hand still gripping the knife fell out of the dark jacket sleeve and hit the rubble below with a clang.

Time froze as she took in what had happened. She looked at the knife-wielding forearm below her and back at her attacker.

His eyeball stared at her, and what was left of his arm continued to swing at her. The empty portion of the sleeve below the elbow flapped in the air with each move. Realizing it was no longer a threat, Kelsey bent down and grabbed the Ripper's ankle. She pulled it up hard, causing him to sail back down the hill of rubble.

Even while he felt warm blood flow down his stinging calf, Vic looked at Kelsey with pride.

"That's my girl right there," Annika said.

Whatever small feeling of victory Kelsey felt vanished when she saw the mask of pain Vic was wearing. "What's wrong?"

"I'm caught on something."

Tony headed to Vic as well, half-falling with almost every step.

Becca crawled back up to the opening of the crack to look through. Kelsey and Tony started moving the loose pieces of debris from around Vic's leg until they got to the area where he was caught. He could tell by the way they looked at each other that it was bad.

A thin metal pole about a half inch in diameter was sticking upward into his leg, between his shin and his calf. The bottom of the pole stemmed from a large chunk of concrete. When his leg fell through the loose debris, it had impaled him. The entire leg beneath the wound was slick with blood.

"Christ," Tony said. "It looks like it's sticking in about five inches. We've got to pull his leg straight up."

Kelsey felt her stomach turn, thinking about how much pain Vic was about to feel. "I'll cup my hands behind his knee. Can you get yours under his foot?"

"Yeah."

As they got ready to pull the leg up, Kelsey looked at Vic. "This is gonna hurt."

"It's okay," he replied. "Just do it."

"Wait," Tony said as he looked at Becca. "Hey. Blondie. What's your name again?"

"Becca."

"Becca, do me a favor and rip some material off your dress. Once we free his leg, it's going to bleed like hell."

She reached down to tear off some material from the bottom of her gown but couldn't start a tear. Her shaking fingers fumbled. She even tried pulling it up high enough to use her teeth, but it wouldn't rip.

Becca jumped back a bit as Annika handed her the Ripper's dismembered forearm with the butcher knife in its hand.

"Shit!" she yelled as Annika passed it to her.

Becca let out a moan of disgust but knew there was no choice in the matter. She tried to take the knife from the hand. Only two of the Ripper's fingers were on the knife's handle. She didn't see the handle had been wired to the palm. When Becca tried to pull the knife out of the hand, the rest of the Ripper's fingers slammed shut around the handle.

"Jesus!" Becca yelled as she dropped it. "What the hell!"

Annika picked up the Ripper arm again, and with her own

fingers on top of the Ripper's on the handle, used the blade to cut off a strip of the dress.

Becca watched her do it, disgusted and amazed.

Once Annika finished, she threw the arm down to the bottom of the rubble and handed the strip of fabric to Tony.

"Thanks," Becca said to Annika.

After a quick countdown, Kelsey and Tony pulled the leg up, sending excruciating pain through Vic. He hoped he wouldn't pass out.

"Almost there, honey," Kelsey said.

Tony could feel the spiral ridges on the rebar fighting against the muscle and tendons in the leg as he pulled. Between that and the agony he felt from using his own wounded shoulder in this way, he was close to vomiting.

With a final pull, the leg slid off the pole, which Kelsey saw came to a sharp spike. Almost immediately, blood poured from the wound. She wrapped the strip of dress around as tightly as she could.

Tony dropped his head to the rubble. His shoulder was on fire. He winced as he felt the cold brick against his forehead.

"It's gone," Becca said.

She was looking through the crack into the lobby. Kelsey was shocked that she had somehow forgotten about the creature devouring a human being between them and the elevator.

Tony pulled himself together. Nursing his shoulder, he climbed the short distance back to the top of the rubble to look through the crack. The wendigo was gone. The man on the floor was now nothing more than chunks of flesh and bone in a puddle of blood.

"She's right. It's clear."

Kelsey helped Vic get up. Dizziness came fast, but he closed his eyes and fought it off.

"Wait," Vic said, "The punch code for the elevator. Memorize it before we go."

Even in his current state, he was concerned about them not

being able to escape if he was the only one who knew the code and something happened to him.

He took out the paper and handed it to Kelsey.

"You know I'm not going anywhere without you," she said.

"Just in case."

As they squeezed through the crack, Tom passed out and fell forward onto his face. His head hit a slab of concrete with a dull thud. Annika was closest to him, but she didn't know what to do.

She turned to Kelsey. "He out cold."

Kelsey leaned over Tom and felt for a pulse. She found one, but he was drenched in sweat. The bruise on his head looked like it had gotten bigger, and there was clear fluid dripping from his nose.

"He might be bleeding into his brain," Kelsey said.

Vic grunted in frustration. He looked down to the lobby.

Getting him through the crack will be hard enough, but down the other side of the rubble is gonna be a pain in the ass.

His eyes scanned the lobby again and turned to Tony. "Let's each grab an arm."

"Gotcha," Tony said.

"Honey," Vic said to Kelsey. "You stay close to me. Please."

She nodded, then turned to Annika and Becca. "And you two stay right with me."

Vic turned back to Tony. "All right, damn it. Help me get him through."

Once Vic made it all the way through, he quickly surveyed the lobby before turning back to help Tom.

Vic got to his feet, and his wounded leg buckled as soon as he put weight on it. The pain of the torn calf muscle burned like hell. He growled and took hold of Tom by the armpits. With the last pull, they got him completely to the other side.

"Okay, Kel. Come on," he said.

One by one, Kelsey, Becca, Annika, and Tony made it through.

Annika and Becca held each other for support as their bare

feet took each painful step. Tony stumbled more than once, shooting sharp pain through his hurt shoulder as he stepped down hard to regain footing.

Once they were all down the mountain of rubble and onto solid footing, it took them a few seconds to regain their balance, as if stepping onto a dock after a boat ride. The initial relief only lasted a second or two before the pain of their injuries returned along with new aches from using their muscles in such an awkward manner.

Vic tried to ease Tom to the floor as gently as possible, but the pain shooting through his leg forced him to drop him. From this position, they could see the colossal body of the sea monster stretching into the lobby, its carcass draped over portions of the crumbled wall. Debris and dirt spread out across the lobby floor from the gigantic mammal's final plunge.

The gold doors of the elevator shone with the promise of survival. Vic motioned for everyone to get closer to him.

"Be as quiet as you can," he whispered.

He bent down through the pain and took hold of one of Tom's wrists. Tony grabbed the other, and they pulled him toward the elevator.

After a few feet, Kelsey saw the severe limp Vic had and took his place with Tony dragging the billionaire. Vic put up no fight. He just nodded, exhausted.

Annika and Becca followed, equally fatigued. The group looked down at the mutilated bodies as they passed by, and although they all felt a strange mix of gratitude and sympathy, the amounts of each emotion varied among them.

Another thought occurred to several of them, almost as if it took the place of the worries and fear as their sense of danger faded with each step. What a story they would have. What *would* they tell people? Who would ever believe any of this?

For Vic, there was one certainty. He would definitely tell Kirby.

Please let the kid be okay. Please.

He pictured him recovering in the hospital, his face lighting up at hearing the details. He'd most likely bombard him with questions as well as a generous amount of "I told you sos."

It didn't matter. He owed it to him. He had Kel back, and there was no way to deny it wouldn't have happened without the kid's help.

Tom woke up and saw the blurry, high rotunda above him. He was puzzled why it was moving until he came to his senses enough to understand he was being dragged.

"What's going on?" Tom asked.

"Shhhhh," Kelsey whispered. "We're almost out of here."

"You didn't leave me behind."

"Yeah, well... we'll send you a bill, moneybags," Tony whispered.

"You got it," Tom replied. "Wait... I can walk."

They stopped and helped Tom to his feet.

"Take it slow," Kelsey whispered.

"Thanks," Tom replied.

Once he was on his feet, they continued the short distance to the elevator.

As soon as they made it, Tony leaned his back against the wall beside the keypad.

The others watched as Vic took out the paper and started to punch in the code.

Kelsey turned back to watch where they'd come from to make sure nothing was coming after them. Annika and Becca did the same.

Tony closed his eyes and took some deep breaths, focusing only on the sound of the beeps from the keypad as Vic entered the code.

A new sound broke the spell of the beeps. Something faint in the distance, coming from the smashed wall near the entrance. In his exhausted state, Tom thought there might be a chance it was just in his head, like an echo bouncing around in his tired mind. Then he saw Kelsey heard it too.

"Shit!" Vic said.

"What?" Tony asked.

"It's not working."

Kelsey walked to him. "Do it again slower. Maybe you hit a wrong button."

Another noise, louder than the first.

Whatever it was, was coming closer.

———·———

"Vic," Tony said.

"I'm trying. Something's not working."

"Let me try," Kelsey said. "Fresh eyes."

"It's not anything I'm doing wrong," he said, his voice filled with frustration.

"I know. Just let me try."

She stepped to the keypad and punched in the code. Nothing happened.

A growl in the distance.

"Damn it!" Tony said.

Becca looked in all directions, anticipating something would come charging at them. She and Annika backed up against the doors of the elevator.

"Should we hide?" she asked.

No one answered her.

Vic's exasperation was boiling over. The pain in his leg was throbbing. They'd made it all this way, and now this keypad was the only thing stopping them from getting out alive.

Kelsey punched in the code again despite hearing the professorial voice in her head quoting the old definition of insanity… doing the same thing over and over and expecting different results. It repeated in her head as she punched in the code again and again.

Suddenly the elevator door began to rise. The entire group instantly felt a huge rush of relief and glee.

When the door opened high enough for them to get in, they saw Winthrop standing inside with Mason, who aimed an AR-15 at them.

46

PREDATOR & PREY

RAQUEL STOOD BEHIND WINTHROP AND Mason, knowing she was on the wrong side but unable to do anything about it. Vic and Tony looked at them with hate.

Tom, despite his current state, understood they were in a standoff. He and Winthrop locked eyes for a moment but didn't speak to each other. Kelsey shot daggers at Mason.

Becca was confused.

Why are we just standing here and not getting on? Didn't they hear those growls?

"Who did you tell about this?" Winthrop asked the detectives.

"About what?" Vic replied.

Winthrop's lips formed a tight seal.

Mason barked, "Answer the question."

Becca had attracted so much attention from men over the years that almost all of her naivete judging a man's motives had been long chipped away. The tiny fraction that remained got the best of her as she remembered Winthrop's warm smile and friendly manner earlier in the evening.

"James," she said, "Doug's dead."

Winthrop repeated his question to Vic as if he hadn't heard her. "Who did you tell?"

Becca took a step forward. "Why are you doing this? Just let us on. Please."

As she pleaded, Winthrop's eyes unlocked from Vic's just long enough to glance at her as he spoke. "Shut up, you silly bitch."

It wasn't what he said that chilled her into silence. It was the expression on his face. As he spoke, he had the same warm smile and kind eyes that he'd had earlier when he greeted her with a glass of champagne.

"Doug would be furious if he knew you spoke to me like that."

Winthrop chuckled. "Really? You think you know my friend of forty years better than I do? You don't even know that he had your boyfriend killed."

The words themselves stole her breath. She understood instantly he was telling the truth. The words swirled through her, blending with the ugly emotions about Douglas Radcliffe that the alien had shown her. She realized she'd been tricked into caring for the man who'd had the love of her life murdered. She blinked and felt revulsion explode within her.

At that moment, that second, the tiny remaining glow of little girl that had managed to keep smiling within her, the fraction that fought to stay happy, carefree, and dancing in the part of her soul where the summer sun always shone, died, and the last of her innocence was gone.

Mason, true woman-hater that he was, enjoyed watching her face go pale and smirked. To him, nothing was better than seeing a spoiled bitch get her due. Becca saw the smirk and something snapped. She no longer saw the gun. She no longer saw anything but that ugly smirk. She ran screaming at him to scratch it off his face.

She stormed at him so suddenly he fired two quick shots. The first round went astray; the second hit Becca in the shoulder. Vic grabbed the rifle. Kelsey rushed to help him. Before Winthrop could react, Tony put all his weight behind a punch to the old man's face. The single blow popped his lip open and sent his front two teeth into the back of his throat. He didn't even feel himself hit the floor.

Mason wasn't so easily handled. Tony hurried to help Vic and Kelsey subdue him. Vic repeatedly punched his face as Kelsey and Tony tried to rip the gun away. Even with all three fighting him, Mason managed to hang on to it.

Kelsey leaped onto his back and dug her nails into his eyes. He screamed and jerked from side to side but couldn't get loose. Her fingers went knuckle deep into his sockets. Blind and desperate, he managed to get his finger on the trigger and fired a wild, rapid-fire continuous burst until the magazine was empty.

For a few seconds, all anyone could hear was a loud tone from the gun being fired in such a confined space. Smoke filled the air. Kelsey applied a tight choke hold. He dropped the gun and started to reach back for her. Vic and Tony each clutched one of his arms as she squeezed the breath from him. He finally went limp and fell to the elevator floor with Kelsey still on his back.

She felt a sting in her side as she hit the floor under him but didn't loosen her grip. If the choke she'd used was applied correctly, within six to eight seconds, the average person would lose consciousness. After thirty seconds, they would die of asphyxiation.

Kelsey squeezed for almost a full minute before releasing her grip. Vic pulled Mason's limp body off her and helped her to her feet.

Tony helped Tom and Annika with Becca as they tried to stop the bleeding.

"It's not that bad," Tony told her. "You're going to be okay."

Becca nodded, her face contorted in pain, and her body trembled.

As the tone in Tom's ears dissipated, he noticed Raquel's lifeless body on the elevator floor. He ran to her and saw two dark holes in her head and neck. Her eyes stared straight ahead.

Vic hobbled to help Annika get Becca to her feet.

"C'mon," he said. "Get on. Quick!"

He helped them in and got to the buttons as fast as he could. Vic's hands fumbled over the controls. There was no keypad, just a couple of old-fashioned buttons on a bronze plate… an arrow for up, an arrow for down. He pushed the up button, and it illuminated with an orange ring around it. Once he saw that, he turned to help Tom and Annika ease Becca into a sitting position against the elevator wall.

After a few seconds, when the elevator door didn't close, Vic went back to the buttons. He pressed the up button several more times. Each time it lit up, but nothing else happened.

"Come on!" he yelled.

"Why aren't we going?" Annika asked.

Vic saw why, and his heart froze. There were bullet holes in the upper part of the bronze panel.

"No," he said, so low no one heard him.

He turned to the others, his gaze landing on Kelsey.

"What?" Tony asked.

Kelsey rushed over. She started to ask what was going on but stopped when Vic pointed to the holes.

She pressed the buttons frantically, hoping for a miracle. Nothing happened.

"*No!*" she yelled.

Tom had been trying to convince himself they'd be back on the surface within a few minutes. Now realization set in. He dropped to his knees.

"The other elevator we came down in. You remember which way it was?" Vic asked Tony. He squinted as he spoke, as if it hurt to try to remember.

"I… yeah. I think we came from that way," Tony replied, pointing to the demolished area of the lobby. Dread filled both men as they realized the section they'd come down in was destroyed, flattened by the sea monster.

"Blackstone told me there was a big service elevator," Tom said.

"That's right," Vic said. "Up to the trucking company."

"Do you know where it is?" Kelsey asked.

"No."

Vic looked down at Winthrop, unconscious on the floor. "Is the prick alive?"

Tony walked over to Winthrop and kicked him in the ribs. Winthrop didn't wake up, but his body reacted slightly.

"Son of a bitch," Vic said.

He and Tony pulled him up, his lips bloody and swollen.

"Hey," Vic said as he slapped him.

Winthrop's left eye opened.

"Hey. Asshole," Vic said, slapping him harder.

Winthrop made a low noise. It sounded like the air was letting out from him against his will. Vic grabbed his chin and shook it but stopped when Winthrop began to choke on something. It was the teeth Tony had knocked out, now stuck in his throat. He coughed them up and spat them out.

"Can you hear me?" Vic asked.

Winthrop managed half a nod.

"Where is the service elevator?"

The words cut through the fog in Winthrop's head.

Vic felt his blood pressure increase when he saw Winthrop's swollen, bloody lips form a faint smile.

"You think this is funny?" Vic asked.

Despite the pain he was in, Winthrop understood they needed him to survive. Once again, he was back in the game and holding all the cards. He let out a chuckle. Vic understood the reaction but disagreed with his assessment.

"How about this?" Vic lifted Winthrop's hand and, without any hesitation, pulled back his index finger until it snapped with a loud crack.

Winthrop let out a wheeze that sounded like an old door creaking, and whatever feeling of power he'd felt seconds earlier vanished.

"Let's try again," Vic said.

Winthrop tried to pull his hand away. Vic pulled it back with such force the old man's whole body jerked forward.

"Tell me where it is or I'm breaking every fucking one."

The detective didn't give Winthrop time to think about it. Winthrop groaned as Vic broke another finger and immediately moved on to the next one and snapped it too.

Winthrop screamed. "Okay! Stop!"

"You're going to lead us to it. Right now," Vic said as he pulled him to his feet and shoved him against the wall.

"How far is it?"

It took Winthrop a few seconds to get his bearings. "A five-minute walk."

Vic turned to the rest of the group, who didn't look ready for another hike into monster-filled territory. They were all a mess. He doubted they could make it ten feet, let alone what they might have to go up against, but there was no other choice. He eased himself down to Mason's corpse and searched for weapons and ammo. There was no ammo for the rifle, but he found a Sig Sauer pistol and a few full magazines.

Vic pulled the slide back as he hobbled to Kelsey. "Ready?"

"Yeah," she replied. "What about you though?"

"Never better," he said.

Vic turned to Tony, who approached awkwardly, holding his shoulder.

"Don't give me any shit," Vic told him. "If I fall behind, or something happens, no matter what, you get Kelsey on that elevator."

Tony gave him a confused look. "I was kinda counting on you guys to get *me* on the elevator." Even exhausted and wounded, Tony could still manage a joke.

He moved to the others. "You guys ready?"

Tom and Annika each had one of Becca's arms over their shoulders.

Vic noticed that although Tom sounded a bit better than he had before, when he made eye contact with him, Tom's line of sight was slightly off. Becca's face was pale. The lines of dark makeup that ran from her eyes to her chin made her look like a character from some postapocalyptic sci-fi movie. She was shivering from loss of blood.

"You're going to be fine," Vic told her with as much false confidence as he could muster.

She nodded rapidly.

Vic stepped out of the elevator. The lobby was still. The smell of spent gunpowder mixed with the stench of the sea monster carcass.

He turned back into the elevator and put his face so close to Winthrop's the older man only saw blurry clenched teeth. "You do anything I don't like, anything at all, and you're dead a second later."

Winthrop nodded, his good hand cradling his ruined one.

"Which way?" Vic asked.

"Straight across the lobby, to the left of the entrance," Winthrop replied.

Vic shoved him out of the elevator to lead the way. Each one of them felt defenseless in the open cavernous space with nowhere to run if something attacked. Winthrop led them to the right of the sea monster carcass. They couldn't help but stare as they passed by. The mouth was wide open and looked like a realistic version of an entrance to a spook house at a carnival.

━━━━━•━━━━━

They made it to the set of double doors that led to the main service corridor.

Vic lifted the pistol and glanced at Tony to pull one of the doors open. It led into a wide corridor with a ceiling almost as high as the lobby itself. The corridor turned in both directions, and straight ahead of them, it branched into what looked like an airplane hangar. Several oversized forklifts and other moving equipment were parked against the wall to the right.

"Where now?" Vic asked Winthrop.

Winthrop pointed to an area a hundred yards away. "That's the elevator."

"That whole room?" Vic asked.

"Yes. It's just a platform. No doors."

Vic could see that the entire rear of the massive room was, in fact, a loading dock. It looked like a huge empty box. The space within was deep enough for several eighteen-wheeled trucks to park. The old man took a few steps toward a control panel on the wall.

"Hey. What are you doing?" Vic asked.

"We have to hurry. The elevator is powerful but takes a while to get going."

Vic believed him but followed close behind.

Winthrop hit a button, and a loud crack came from the loading area. The sounds of gears shifting and working machinery echoed through the room.

"What's the code for the inside?" he asked Winthrop.

"There isn't one. Just regular buttons."

Vic stared into his eyes. "So, we don't need you anymore?"

A growl echoed in the distance. It came from the corridor to the right and caused all of them to turn simultaneously. The sound of the working elevator had gotten attention.

Vic looked to Annika. "Can you run?"

"Yeah."

"Okay. Get onto that platform and be ready to hit the up button soon as I tell you."

Annika ran to the elevator, looking in every direction as she moved.

"Let's go, everybody. Come on," Vic said.

Tom helped Becca to her feet. Tony got on the other side of her to help.

"Thank you." She whimpered.

Another loud noise echoed from the lobby behind the double doors they'd just come through.

"Shit," Kelsey said.

They moved as fast as they could toward the elevator. As Vic shambled beside Kelsey, he kept one eye on Winthrop and his finger on the trigger as they crossed the big space.

Annika made it onto the elevator platform, huffing and puffing as she quickly found the buttons within. She put her hand beside them and stared at the group. When they were about halfway to the elevator, they heard more noise behind them. Not just growls but movement and destruction.

Annika felt sudden anxiety at the thought of not hitting the button fast enough when Vic told her to. She panicked not just that she would screw up it up somehow but also had the terrifying thought that she would hit the button and nothing would happen. The longer she stared at the button, the more certain she was it wouldn't work.

Something caught her eye... something coming from around the corner behind them. It looked like two men. One was in a tattered, bloody tuxedo.

Survivors? she thought. *If he's in a tuxedo, he's one of the asshole bad guys. Fuck them.*

The men got closer, and she could see that the guy in the tuxedo was Asian and the other guy was... not normal. His face was hideous.

His skin was almost white, and his eyes... Even from this far away, his eyes were... so interesting. She couldn't turn away from them. It was as if looking at them calmed her, making her feel much less anxious... even relaxed.

Kelsey helped Vic hobble toward the elevator platform. She could feel in her gut that something was going to attack before they could make it and had to force herself to stop turning around every few seconds. Instead, she tried to focus on getting to Annika. But when she saw her face, she knew something was wrong.

Annika was staring at something behind them with a strange smile. Kelsey turned to see what she was looking at.

"Two men behind us," Kelsey said to Vic.

Vic turned as he limped and spotted Bram the vampire.

Keiji Fujiyama walked alongside him as if in a trance. His neck had deep gashes in it, blood covering him.

"Those aren't men," he said. "Tony. On your four."

Tony saw them, grunted, and turned back to Tom. "Come on, moneybags!"

———•———

Something pounded on the double doors they had come through. The bangs echoed through the hangar, adding to the collective sounds of their hearts drumming and pulses hammering in their ears. All of which were drowned out by the sound of one of the metal doors breaking off its hinges.

Many things were trying to get through the door. Sasquatches, the wendigo, the yeti, aliens, Benchley, the chupacabra—all were trying to fit through the doorway at the same time and fighting each other to do it. They let out a horrific chorus of growls and screams.

"Faster!" Kelsey yelled to everyone. "Don't look, just run!"

When the group was five feet from the platform, Vic yelled to Annika. "Annika! Hit the button! Now!"

She didn't react. She stood motionless, smiling at the vampire.

"Annika!" Kelsey yelled.

Kelsey's voice broke Annika from her spell. She snapped awake, alert but confused.

"The button!" Kelsey yelled. "Hit the button!"

Annika did. Another loud gear shifted, and the large platform began to rise slowly.

It was only a foot high when the rest of the group finally made it. They shuffled on clumsily, helping each other roll onto the platform.

The creatures smashed their way through the other metal door as well as the wall surrounding the doorframe. Chunks of wood and Sheetrock exploded forward. The beasts all piled through the opening and formed a wild stampede of monsters headed toward the rising platform.

Only then did the group see how many creatures were coming at them. It wasn't only the ones they'd seen earlier.

There were also werewolves; the Mothman; something that looked like a half-man, half-dragon; a horrific red demon thing with horns and multiple arms; an enormous three-headed dog; and at least a dozen other terrifying creatures.

Vic aimed for the closest one, the stampeding werewolf, and fired the pistol until the magazine was empty. He loaded another magazine and fired away, this time more into the thick of them as they closed in. It looked like something went down, but the others rolled right over it. He fired until the hammer came down on an empty chamber.

He put his arm around Kelsey as the platform slowly rose. His jaw pressed against her head, and they both dreaded this would be the end. Tom and Tony laid Becca down. Annika dropped to her knees. They all braced themselves, helpless at this point to do anything but watch the monsters close in and hope the platform rose high enough in time.

Even Winthrop could do nothing but watch and wait. There was no place to run, no place to hide. They all started to yell for the platform to rise faster. They yelled at the platform itself like frantic gamblers at a racetrack, screaming their lungs out at a galloping horse they'd bet their lives on.

Vic realized they weren't high enough to be out of reach. *We're not going to make it.*

He turned to Kelsey, who, along with the rest of the group, stared wide-eyed at the approaching throng of death.

They all experienced the next few seconds differently, as if time itself had its own velocity for each of them. For some, time froze and the horror of what was happening was delivered to them in single pieces, each piece transfixing them as it played out. For others, it was chaotic with everything happening so fast there was no time to think.

The elevator platform was ten feet from the ground when the closest Sasquatch leaped up and grabbed the edge of the rising floor. The beast swung one of its arms onto the platform to pull itself on. It growled at them as it struggled. Vic rushed over and slammed his good foot onto the Bigfoot's hands, almost falling from the pain in his other leg.

Tony joined in, stomping on the mammoth hands. The creature howled in pain and struggled savagely to get inside. Vic saw the Sasquatch wasn't the only danger. To their left, the wendigo was also climbing inside, its antlers swinging as it pulled itself up. To the right, Benchley managed to attach itself to the bottom of the platform and three of its tentacles stretched into the space.

Vic got close enough to the Sasquatch to kick its face and it slid backward out of the elevator, flailing wildly but unable to stop itself.

He felt a rush of hope they were going to make it after all until he saw the tentacles slithering inside.

Vic looked up and saw the rising elevator was still about fifteen feet from the point where the bottom of the platform would pass the ceiling of the facility and be out of danger.

"Vic!" Tony yelled.

He was trying to stomp on the wendigo's hands, but the monster's swinging antlers made it impossible. Tony kept trying until one of the antler's side points stabbed into his thigh. He yelled in anguish as the creature cast him aside. Tony fell close to the edge, almost falling out.

The cutoff point was approaching. Without warning, a tentacle shot up and caught Tony's leg. It wrapped around his shin and calf. Tony wailed in pain as it jerked him onto his back and two more tentacles wrapped around his injured leg. Within a second, the tentacles pulled him to the edge. Tony realized he was being dragged off the platform and scrambled for something to grab onto.

Vic dove to the floor and caught Tony's wrist as the sea creature pulled him to the edge. The two men faced each other, both full of fear and frustration as they gripped each other as tightly as they could.

———————

Right before the tentacle grabbed Tony's leg, Kelsey, Tom and

Annika rushed to Becca, who'd passed out and had no pulse or heartbeat. None of them saw Vic trying to save Tony. Kelsey was applying CPR as best as she could, her own heart racing as she fought to revive Becca. Tom and Annika did their best to alternate with her as Kelsey instructed them how to do it.

Winthrop sat nearby, watching them trying to save the girl. He nursed his broken fingers and pressed his tongue against the part of his aching gums where his teeth had been knocked out. Everything was moving slowly for him. His vision was hazy, and the air around him was heavy.

But then he saw the situation the two cops were in. His vision, as well as his mind, cleared while he watched Vic struggle to save his friend.

They're helpless right now… and so close to the edge.

He got to his feet. His back throbbed, and his hip hurt like hell, but he limped closer to where the two cops were fighting to survive. Vic was on his stomach with both hands gripping Tony's arm as the tentacles pulled him off the platform, and he started to slide toward the edge himself. He didn't see Winthrop behind him.

The old man bent over and used his good hand and the wrist of his ruined one to grab one of Vic's ankles and lift it as high as he could.

Vic craned his head back and realized what the old prick was doing. If he let go of Tony to fight him off, Tony would completely slide off within seconds.

"You motherfucker!" he yelled.

Vic tried kicking Winthrop off, but it caused them to slide closer to the edge. Tony's body slid a full foot, and another tentacle shot up and wrapped around his forehead. Winthrop looked at them, delighted at how helpless and pathetic they were beneath him. He lifted Vic's leg higher. He looked like a little kid trying to bowl with the ball between his legs, but it was working. The cops slid closer to the edge. Tony's legs dangled off the platform.

He locked eyes with Vic. *Not like this. Please not like this.*

Vic twisted sideways to try to shake Winthrop off. He felt his biceps strain and saw the edge of the ceiling above close in. Even if he managed to hold on to Tony, he'd be cut in half by the platform in twenty or thirty seconds. They both screamed pure, primal rage.

Winthrop smiled for a few seconds until Tom came from behind him and kicked the old man between his open legs as hard as he could. Winthrop's balls exploded in pain, and he dropped Vic's ankles as a flood of sour nausea filled him.

The older man fell onto his back, coughing and dry heaving. Tom rushed to help Vic pull Tony back onto the platform. The tentacles were strong, and it took everything they had to pull Tony in.

Another tentacle shot around Winthrop's arm and dragged him closer to the edge as he wheezed. Vic looked up and saw the edge of the ceiling just feet away. He realized it would be the thing that saved them. It would cut the tentacles in half.

Winthrop also saw the ceiling edge getting closer, though for him it would be no salvation. He was on his back with his head hanging off the platform. His hands reached frantically for something to grab, anything to pull himself back on.

He looked at Vic, Tony, and Tom. "Please!" he begged. "Pull me in! Quick!"

Vic saw Winthrop was seconds away from being decapitated. His cold eyes locked with the old man's desperate ones. "No."

The small word that Winthrop despised more than anything, the word he had managed to all but erase from his existence, was the last sound he would ever hear. The edge of the ceiling came down and crushed his head before tearing it from his body. Winthrop's arms and legs shook for a few seconds and went still.

The tentacles holding Tony all severed and fell to the floor of the platform, twitching like a lizard's dismembered tail.

Once Tony was able to stop huffing, he pulled the limp tentacle from his head and looked at Tom. "Moneybags. I owe you."

Tom shook his head. "No, you don't."

They helped each other to their feet.

——————•——————

Becca gasped awake. Kelsey sat back and took deep breaths as sweat poured down her face.

"You did it!" Annika leaned over Becca and wiped her forehead. "You gonna be okay. We on our way out."

Becca didn't speak. Her lips formed a slight smile as tears filled her eyes and dripped down the side of her head.

Kelsey's breathing returned to normal, and the men collapsed beside them. They all looked at each other, no one knowing what to say.

"This is the slowest fucking elevator I've ever been on," Tony said.

The rest of them let out sounds that could be considered laughter.

47

AFTERMATH

ONCE THEY FIGURED OUT HOW to get out of the camouflaged elevator area inside the Harvard Trucking Company, they made their way out to Tremont Street. The cool night air felt as good as a fresh shower. Across the street, the tops of the trees in the Common were silhouetted against the rising cobalt blue of the early-morning sky.

With Kelsey and Annika in underwear and borrowed jackets, Becca in a ripped-up red sheath gown, Tom in a tattered tuxedo, and Vic and Tony limping beside them in their torn clothes, they looked like survivors at the end of a horror movie. In addition to their individual wounds, all were covered in thick layers of blood, dirt, and sweat.

A pair of headlights approached.

Vic limped into the street with his badge held high.

———◦———

Kelsey sat beside Vic in the ambulance. As the EMTs treated his leg and back, Vic yelled for them to turn off the siren. He was on the phone, his other hand tightly covering his ear.

"Hello?" a female voice said on the other end.

Vic recognized the voice as that of Kirby's mother. "Mrs. Cronin, this is Detective Mitchum. Please, is Kirby... tell me how Kirby is."

The silence was unbearable.

Please, please, please, please…

"He'll be fine, no thanks to you."

He closed his eyes in relief as she continued.

"What kind of police force do we have when people are getting mugged in elevators?" she asked.

Whether Kirby lied about his wound to cover for him and Tony or to protect him and his mom from being silenced by the Cobblestone Club, the kid's cleverness added even more shine to the news that he was okay, and Vic smiled.

"We're doing our best, Mrs. Cronin. We'll catch the person responsible, I assure you."

"I hope so."

"How is he doing? Are you with him now? Can I talk to him?"

"He's asleep. The doctors said he was very lucky. The bullet just missed his kidney. He'll be able to come home in a few days."

"That's fantastic. Please tell him I'll be by to see him."

A rush of joy filled him and Kelsey watched his shoulders relax.

Thank you, thank you, thank you, thank you, Vic thought.

As he listened to Kirby's mom rant on about crime, he only half heard her. He was more curious about who he had just thanked. Was it God? Or was it an alien being that humans considered a god a thousand years ago? Were they one and the same?

Over the next few hours, Vic, Kelsey, and Tony gave their own matching accounts of what transpired while getting medical attention. Tom and Annika were also questioned while being treated. Tom had a severe concussion. Becca required emergency surgery and wasn't questioned until the next day but eventually told a story that corroborated everyone else's.

They kept it simple and easier to believe than the complete truth. A group of wealthy men was responsible for having prostitutes and homeless people abducted and brought down to their secret club where the sick bastards fed them to wild, rabid animals for their own amusement.

When Vic and Tony rescued Kelsey, Becca, and Annika, several suspects were killed, including James Winthrop. They also declared Tom's innocence and his brave help in their rescue and escape.

Sweeney was fired, and to avoid being charged with conspiracy, he revealed the name of Winthrop's contact in the governor's office who had orchestrated him replacing Guidley. Guidley was immediately reinstated and ordered Chang and Morales to lead a squad down into the facility.

Vic realized that sending a handful of cops expecting to find simple lions and tigers would only get them killed. He arranged an emergency secret meeting with Guidley, Chief Adams, and Mayor Kent. Kelsey and Tony also attended. While staying within the frame of the wild-animal story, they gave further details of the Cobblestone Club's influence. Following Tom Ackerman's praise, suggestions, and five-million-dollar donation, several things happened quickly.

Chief Adams put Vic in charge of heading a special task force with carte blanche to use SWAT and all other departments and support however he deemed necessary to clear out the underground facility. The entire Harvard Trucking Company building was cordoned off and covered in a tent as if being treated for termites.

A command center was set up inside the trucking company. A special subterranean cellular communication system was installed so that constant communication would be maintained.

Only when briefing the sixty-man SWAT team did Vic and Tony finally tell the whole truth about what was truly down there to prepare them for the danger they'd be facing. Despite the detective's strong disclaimers about how insane it all sounded, many of the officers thought they were nuts. They joked among themselves about the silly creature talk until they saw with their own eyes.

They searched every dark corner of the facility, using thermal and other technology to locate and dispose of the creatures. It took less than three hours for their heavy firepower to take care of every threat, and although some of the monsters were more difficult than others to put down, the team managed to do it without losing a single man.

The SWAT leader announced the facility cleared, and the entire area was designated a crime scene. Electricity was restored and high-powered lights were brought in. The cavernous lobby was transformed into a combination base camp and lab. All the human remains were collected and laid evenly on metal gurneys. Some gurneys only had partial heads or dismembered limbs. The sight of almost twenty gurneys lined up reminded many people present of a scene after a plane crash.

The dead creatures were laid out as well, although most were too large to fit on gurneys. Conference tables were used instead. Even though the area was deemed safe, a dozen armed SWAT officers remained. Police coroners examined the bodies of the creatures, fascinated. Due to the growing stench from the massive sea monster carcass that stretched into the lobby, a dozen men were given the task of cutting it up with chainsaws.

When Mayor Kent learned the truth, he had to see for himself. After the disbelief, shock, and wonder subsided, he notified a close friend who headed the biomedical engineering department at MIT, whom he knew to be a cryptozoology enthusiast. On the condition of complete secrecy, the professor was permitted to bring a few of his prize students down to examine and run tests on the dead creatures.

A decision had to be made as to what to tell the public. Seeing all the official activity coming and going from the tented building had the press beside itself, trying to find out what was going on. A statement had to be given soon. Mayor Kent realized that if the truth got out, the entire world would be cramming into Boston.

For a moment, Kent considered that to be a good thing. The local economy would explode. But at heart, the mayor was a true believer in the celebrated magic of Boston. A big part of his popularity was that everyone knew the city had no bigger fan than he. He'd been raised to take pride in his town's history and never missed an opportunity to brag about where he was from.

To him, it was where the story of America began. It was the home of the Freedom Trail. Paul Revere. John Adams. The Kennedy brothers. (Whose framed photos hung in his office and he always referred to as Jack and Bobby.) The Patriots, the Red Sox, and the Celtics.

If he allowed the story to get out, for the rest of eternity, Boston would become known as the place where monsters became real. Not to mention the horrific human trafficking aspects of the story... hundreds of prostitutes and homeless people abducted and eaten alive. Just the thought of it made him shudder.

He decided he didn't want the rest of the world to shudder when they thought of Boston.

Every single person who had either seen the creatures firsthand or had been told of them was brought into his office one by one. They were instructed and politely threatened to never repeat what they'd seen or heard. To keep their jobs, they each signed nondisclosure agreements and were given a large bonus that came from Tom Ackerman's donation. Once that was all handled, Kent put out a statement.

> *In recent days, we learned that a large cavern below Boston Common had filled with methane gas. If the situation wasn't taken care of, the gas would have eventually leaked up to the surface and caused a major health concern to thousands of people in the area*

above. To prevent a panic that could bring further danger, we decided to handle the situation as quickly and quietly as we could. I can happily tell you now that the gas has been neutralized and any passage the gas would have taken to the surface has been sealed so that and there will be no further danger of a leak. For the time being, the area above will be restricted while scientists from MIT, in conjunction with city health officials, run tests and install further safety measures.

I want to thank MIT for their assistance with the process as well as the Boston Department of Health, and especially all of our brave police officers and first responders who put themselves at risk in order to keep the people of Boston safe. Thank you.

The statement worked. The press covered it but quickly put it to bed. Nothing was less exciting than a gas leak. That was the easy part. The trickier part was solving the mystery of what happened to the eleven Tremont Club Members in town to see the pharaoh exhibit. Each of the billionaires had dozens of family members and staff, not to mention every cable news outlet, investigating their sudden disappearance. It was as if they'd vanished into thin air. Multiple theories, both reasonable and fantastic, were thrown around.

It was discovered that James Winthrop's yacht was also missing, leading many to believe that the group of men went out for a late-night cruise and somehow ran into trouble. The harbor was searched, but nothing was found.

The crazier theories involved an Egyptian curse attached to the pharaoh exhibit that swallowed them all up. A few clever reporters tried to connect the men to the gas leak story but hit walls.

In the end, the world at large would never know what happened to the members of the Cobblestone Club. Their families and loved ones would have no more answers or closure than those of the many souls they'd silenced over the years for their own twisted entertainment.

48

CHARLIE

KIRBY LEFT THE HOSPITAL AND returned home. He devoured every news story about the gas leak and the mystery of the missing billionaires with a series of eye rolls and mocking grunts. He left a dozen voice mails for Vic, who sent back infuriatingly vague texts promising to tell him everything as soon as he got a chance.

———•———

Vic, Tony, and Kelsey went back down to the facility. The lab in the lobby was up and running with scientists, MIT professors, and students bouncing around in awe of what they were examining. A few of the trucks from above were parked in the lobby after the mayor authorized MIT's request that large refrigeration units be brought down to preserve the creatures' bodies for continued tests.

The detectives discovered they were something of celebrities to the scientists, who bombarded them with questions about how the creatures behaved when they were alive.

Tony was in the middle of describing how the octopus-man thing moved when Vic noticed one of the nearby SWAT officers flash a look of concern. He turned to see what he was looking at and saw a live Sasquatch slowly lumbering out from the entrance.

"Get down!" the SWAT officer yelled as he raised his rifle.

Kelsey saw the gray spots on its dark brown fur, its bloody arm, and knew immediately this was the same Bigfoot that had saved her and Vic from the swamp monster.

"No!" she yelled as she threw her hands up in front of the SWAT officer. "Don't shoot!"

Vic turned to her. "Honey…"

"That's the one that saved us," she said.

"It's Charlie," Tony said.

The SWAT officer didn't fire but kept his rifle aimed at the creature. Kelsey took a step toward it.

"Kel! Don't be crazy," Vic said. "Just 'cuz it looked like he saved us doesn't mean he's harmless!"

Kelsey took a few more steps to the creature.

Tony turned to the SWAT officer. "Brett, keep your sights on him but don't fire unless I say."

Vic hobbled on his crutches behind Kelsey as she walked right up to the Sasquatch.

The creature looked down at her, maintaining eye contact the whole time. Other than his size, nothing was threatening about him. His glassy eyes still expressed the warm soul of a human.

Kelsey smiled up at him. "Do you remember me?"

The Sasquatch did something that blew them away. He nodded.

"Holy shit. Did you see that?" Tony asked.

"Can you speak?" Kelsey asked, her voice warm.

The Sasquatch made a growl sounding like a large dog when it wants the treat you're holding.

Vic smiled. "I'll be damned."

By now all the scientists and security had gathered around to watch.

"Do you think I could get a blood sample?" one of the scientists asked.

Kelsey gazed down at the bloody gashes on his arm from the fight with the swamp creature. "No, but you can cut away some of his bloodstained hair as you dress his wound."

Kelsey took the hand of Charlie's good arm and led him to a place where he could sit down. The towering hominid appeared to trust her and walked beside her without fear.

The young scientist who'd asked the question was a different story. "Wait... Dress his wound? Um..."

Vic laughed. "Yeah. Get something to clean the gashes on his arm and bandage it."

———•———

The Sasquatch sat on a piece of equipment as the young MIT scientist cut the hair away from the gashes on his arm. When he turned on an electric razor to shave around the wound, Charlie's expression turned to curiosity. The Sasquatch flinched when the buzzing razor touched him, causing the scientist to jump back.

"What's your name?" Kelsey asked the nervous young man.

"Roger."

"Roger, you're doing great. He's not going to hurt you. I promise."

Kelsey ran a hand over the top of Charlie's head as Roger continued cleaning the wound.

Vic leaned over to Tony. "What are we supposed to do with him?"

"I was hoping you had an idea," Tony replied.

Roger picked up a bottle of rubbing alcohol with a shaking hand. "Um... This is going to... It might, uh..."

"Oh boy," Vic said.

Unsure of how the massive creature would respond to the painful sting, everyone except Kelsey and Roger took several steps back, causing Roger to grow even more terrified.

"Uh, I really don't want to do this. Please don't make me do this," Roger begged.

Kelsey took the alcohol from him and picked up a sterile towel as well. She got face-to-face with the creature, then pantomimed what she was about to do.

"This is going to hurt," she said, not knowing what her patient could understand.

"Kel, maybe he doesn't need that anyway," Vic said.

She thought about it for a second or two and then poured the rubbing alcohol onto Charlie's bloody wound. The Sasquatch's eyes flew open wide. He shot up to his full height and let out a scream that echoed through the entire area. Vic dropped his crutches and moved between Kelsey and the angry creature. Roger backed away so fast he bumped into everyone behind him. The SWAT officer raised his rifle again, but Tony gently eased it back down.

"Easy, big guy," Kelsey said as her hands reached out to Charlie. "Easy."

The low growl coming from Charlie grew softer as Kelsey guided him back down.

"Hand me the bandages," Kelsey said to Roger.

Charlie relaxed as Kelsey wrapped the bandage around his arm.

Vic put a hand on Kelsey's shoulder as she finished up. A nearby scientist picked up his crutches for him.

"What now? Any ideas?"

"We're going to set him free," Kelsey replied.

Tony's face dropped. "Really? You gonna let him loose into the Common?"

"I was thinking about the mountains. New Hampshire." She smiled.

Vic thought about it and knew she was right. He hobbled to the SWAT officer. "Brett."

"Yeah?"

"Can you have someone take your place for a few hours?"

"Yeah, sure."

"Great, thanks. Do me a favor and open up the back of that truck and make sure it's got gas."

Kelsey reached out to the creature. Charlie looked at her hand and slowly grasped it with his own, dwarfing hers. Each finger was almost ten inches long. Kelsey put her other hand on his and gave it a caress. She turned it to be able to see his palm. The brown skin was smoother than she expected it to be. It had deep creases and wrinkles.

Vic's curiosity got the best of him, and he ran a hand down Charlie's good arm. Within a moment, everyone nearby, the coroners, the scientists, the other SWAT officers, all touched him, ran fingers through his hair, and each felt a sense of youthful wonder fill them.

"Vic?" Brett said. "The truck's good to go."

Kelsey looked into Charlie's eyes. "How'd you like to go home?"

Charlie tilted his head.

Still holding his hand, Kelsey led him to the truck, which was idling by the elevator. The scientists and everyone else watching stepped apart so they could get to the truck.

One of the older MIT scientists stepped in front of Kelsey. "Wait. Please," he said. "Please don't do this. Think of what we can learn if we hang on to him."

"He's been locked up long enough," Vic said.

Kelsey started to walk again, her hand clasped with her giant friend's. She climbed into the back of the truck and motioned for Charlie to join her in there.

The back of the truck dropped several inches when he climbed in.

"I'm going to ride back here with him," she said.

"Are you sure?" Vic asked.

"Yeah," Kelsey said as she flipped on a light inside the truck.

Vic looked at Brett. "Can you ride in back with her, just in case?"

"No problem," he said and climbed in.

Vic looked at Kelsey, Brett, and the Sasquatch all sitting on the floor of the truck and thought for a split second that he might've lost his mind and was really lying in some hospital somewhere with his wrists strapped to the bed. He shook it off.

"You know it's going to take at least an hour and a half to get to the mountains," Vic said.

"We'll be fine," Kelsey said.

Vic pulled the back door down and closed the safety lock. He looked at Tony. "Can you drive with your arm, or should I?"

"I got it," Tony replied.

Vic grunted as he used his crutch to climb up onto the passenger seat.

As soon as Tony got behind the wheel, Vic turned to him. "We have to make one stop on the way first. Head for Kirby's house."

Tony laughed. "Oh, this is going to be great."

———•———

Kirby answered his front door and leaned against the doorframe. He moved slowly for fear of loosening the stitches in his side. He looked at Vic with a mix of disapproval and anger.

"Hey," Vic said.

"It's about time."

"Yeah. Sorry. It's been crazy."

"Methane gas?" the younger man said sarcastically. He looked down at Vic's crutch. "You okay?"

"Yeah. How about you?"

"I'll live."

Vic took a step back to the porch railing and leaned against it. "My girl is fine too. Thanks to you."

"Wait," Kirby blurted, "tell me what really happened. Tell me everything."

Vic smiled wide. It was weird for Kirby to see. Since meeting Vic, he couldn't remember a single time he'd ever seen the guy smile.

"I can tell you about it on the way. I need you to take a ride with me."

Kirby looked behind Vic to see a double-parked truck with Tony at the wheel. "Where to?"

"Just shut up and come with me."

Kirby stepped a foot back into the house and yelled, "Ma! I'm going out for a while! Love you!"

"What are you talking about? You're not going anywhere!" she yelled back.

"The doctor said it's fine as long as I'm careful."

She appeared beside Kirby and saw Vic. "Oh… Lieutenant. Do you have any leads?"

"We think so. We'd like Kirby to come look at some mug shots."

"Oh. Okay." She turned to Kirby. "Take your phone. And when I call, you answer."

"I will. I promise," he said and gave her a kiss on the cheek.

She watched the two of them hobble down the stairs like old men and shook her head in amusement as she closed the door.

"What's with the truck?" Kirby asked.

"Just temporary."

"Where are we really going?" Kirby asked as they crossed the sidewalk.

"I want to introduce you to my girl."

"Oh. Cool."

Vic smiled again. "And she has a friend I want you to meet."

—END—

ACKNOWLEDGMENTS

First and foremost, I'm indebted to my wife Dana for always believing in me. From our first date to our twentieth wedding anniversary, her endless love, support, and assistance can't be put into words. I love you with all my heart and can't imagine life without you.

My kids Ivy and Toby, who fill me with pride every day, deserve complete credit for the initial story idea. It came during one of our countless neighborhood strolls when they were still young enough to hold my hand. A magical time I'd give anything to go back to, if even for a day. With complete sincerity, they asked why the LA Zoo didn't have any werewolves in it. The thought stuck with me for years until finally evolving into the novel you now hold.

My dad Jack, my mom Sheila, sister Amy, and brother Hal, have always been there for me with unconditional love and support, even though I'm the black sheep of the family and can't name a single current New England Patriot. I love you.

Ma, I miss you so much. No one believed in me more than you.

I owe a tremendous amount of gratitude to the friends who offered guidance and kind words through my early drafts. Diana Burke, Julie Schlosberg, Kristen Thomas Easley, and Erica Ferencik. If I'm forgetting anyone, I'm deeply sorry.

A special thanks is due to my best friend and comedy brother, Robbie Printz. Over the past thirty years, whether we were collaborating on a screenplay, a sitcom pilot, or an incalculable number of jokes for each other's stand-up act, he always brought the goods. When it came time for my first novel, his advice was just as invaluable. As usual, it was offered between hilarious insults and late-night laughs.

A huge thanks to my editor, Anne Victory at Victory Editing. Her talents and skills are immeasurable, and I was lucky to have her.

Many thanks also to the following friends who shared their professional expertise to help in my attempt to make the unbelievable a bit less so:

My good buddy Forensic Pathologist Jonathan Eisenstat, for his staggering knowledge of the human body and the effects of violence upon it.

Long time Pewter Pot pal, Retired Police Chief James Guido, for educating me on proper law enforcement practices.

My friend, superstar attorney E. Jay Abt, for taking the time to assist with the Cobblestone Club's threatening legalese. Thanks for not billing me.

A heartfelt thanks to all the wonderful baristas at Tanner's in West L.A., and Starbucks in Sandy Springs, for letting me take up a table for more hours than I can count.

Last and most important, I thank you the reader. I hope you had a good time.

ABOUT THE AUTHOR

Growing up in Revere, Massachusetts, TODD PARKER spent his youth reading comic books, watching Creature Double Feature, and being picked last before every neighborhood sports game.

He majored in graphic arts and illustration but somehow transitioned into becoming a professional stand-up comedian. He toured the country from coast to coast and in his mid-twenties moved to the bright lights of Hollywood to become a star. He didn't.

Todd married a southern belle named Dana, and soon after they welcomed two kids, Ivy and Toby, into the world.

Besides writing television pilots and film screenplays Todd also enjoys oil painting. His paintings and prints have been exhibited and sold in galleries in Boston, San Diego, Florida, as well as The Los Angeles County Museum of Art.

He still loves doing stand-up, but his true happy place is hanging out at home with his family while working the grill with hairband power ballads playing in the background.

Billionaire Boogeymen is his first novel. He hopes you like it.

Made in the USA
Middletown, DE
19 September 2023